P9-DCY-255

THE GIRL BEFORE YOU

Nicola Rayner was born in Abergavenny, South Wales, and works as a freelance journalist, specialising in dance and travel. *The Girl Before You*, her debut novel, was runner-up in the Cheltenham First Novel Competition in 2018. She lives in London with her husband and Jack Russell.

WATERLOO PUBLIC LIBRARY
33420014009329

THE GIRL BEFORE YOU

NICOLA RAYNER

avon.

Published by AVON
A division of HarperCollins*Publishers* Ltd
1 London Bridge Street
London SE1 9GF

www.harpercollins.co.uk

A Paperback Original 2019

First published in Great Britain by HarperCollins*Publishers* 2019

Copyright © Nicola Rayner 2019

Nicola Rayner asserts the moral right to be identified
as the author of this work.

A catalogue copy of this book is available from the British Library.

ISBN: 978-0-00-833273-0

This novel is entirely a work of fiction. The names, characters and incidents
portrayed in it are the work of the author's imagination. Any resemblance
to actual persons, living or dead, events or localities is entirely coincidental.

Typeset in Sabon Lt Std by Palimpsest Book Production Limited,
Falkirk, Stirlingshire
Printed and bound in UK by CPI Group (UK) Ltd, Croydon CR0 4YY

All rights reserved. No part of this text may be reproduced, transmitted,
down-loaded, decompiled, reverse engineered, or stored in or introduced
into any information storage and retrieval system, in any form or by any
means, whether electronic or mechanical, without the express written
permission of the publishers.

MIX
Paper from
responsible sources
FSC™ C007454

This book is produced from independently certified FSC™ paper to ensure
responsible forest management.

For more information visit: www.harpercollins.co.uk/green

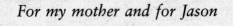

For my mother and for Jason

For there is no friend like a sister
In calm or stormy weather;
To cheer one on the tedious way,
To fetch one if one goes astray.

Christina Rossetti

Everything in the world is about sex except sex.
Sex is about power.

Oscar Wilde

Author's Note

Anyone looking at a map will struggle to find the university town of St Anthony's. In truth, the inspiration for this fictional setting comes from an amalgam of places: it is halfway between Durham and St Andrews, and the town's history also draws on that of Alnmouth in Northumberland – a place shaped by what it lost.

Prologue

The last time I saw my sister she was getting ready for a party. She took particular care that night and we were quiet as we prepared, unaware of all those years of silence to come. Ruth used coconut oil, as she always did, to smooth down her unruly red hair. As she closed the hot tongs, the steam from the oil smelled like summer – suntan lotion and Malibu. It should be a happy scent, but every time I come across it now, it takes me back to that night. We had talked our way through her problem and come up with a plan. And I had confided what had been gnawing at me, too. We both knew what we had to do.

I can see her as she pats her pale face with foundation, flicks mascara on her lashes and adds a slash of red lipstick. She pins up her hair and puts on an emerald dress. When she is ready, she grabs her handbag. It holds her cigarettes, a lighter, of course, her wallet, her lipstick and condoms. These were the last things she carried.

Her eyes looked so bright and full of hope. I wish

1

I had said something else, something different, but I just said: 'Don't forget your Dorothy slippers.' And she grinned and slid her feet into the red sequinned shoes.

At the top of the stairs I hugged her and was surprised once again by how little there was of her, as if she'd started disappearing already. I said, 'Good luck.' Then, as she left, I called down the stairs, 'Love you.' It was an afterthought, a superstition. The words got lost, pinging down the steep wooden staircase, and I couldn't be sure she'd heard me as she pushed the door open and slipped through.

Alice

January 2016

The rattle and hum of trains always make Alice sleepy. She had been up at five to get the six fifteen to Edinburgh from King's Cross. At the shrill bleep of the alarm, George had groaned and rolled over, burying his face in his pillow as she pulled her clothes on in the dark. His hangovers had got particularly bad since he'd made the move from politics to TV. She'd felt half glad she was out of London for the day.

Edinburgh had made her nostalgic. She and George had visited the city for a couple of days early in their courtship. There had been something special about that weekend: away from the influence of his friends, George was tender and attentive – plus, of course, Edinburgh on the run-up to Christmas was magical.

They'd ice-skated hand-in-hand in the shadow of the castle, warmed up with hot chocolate and even taken a trip on the big wheel. As it was caught at the top of its cycle, hovering between travelling up and coming down, George had looked at her for a long time as if he were going to say something, but didn't.

Later, in the Vietnamese restaurant where they'd had supper, he listened to Alice's career plans with particular attentiveness – though family law was hardly the most romantic of subjects – and surprised her by chatting to the waiter in Vietnamese. She'd looked at him so proudly then, with an ache that had long since faded.

Coming out of the restaurant, walking downhill to their B & B, George stopped Alice mid-path with a kiss. The wind was wild that night and, as he stood in front of her, his red scarf flapped in front of his face and her hair blew into her mouth. He almost had to shout it when he said: 'I love you, Alice Reynolds.' It was the most romantic thing that had ever happened to her.

'I meant what I said,' he told her that night at the B & B between squeaks of the bed. 'You have saved me.' She didn't ask: from what?

Alice exhales. Her breath mists up the window and she wipes her hand across the cold glass. Taking the newspaper from her bag, she settles in for the journey home. Behind her she hears the refreshments trolley rattling its way through the carriage and decides to have a gin and tonic. There's no lemon, of course; the surly girl serving looks at her as if she's mad when she asks, but there's ice, at least.

As the sting of alcohol hits the back of her throat, she sighs. It has been a good day, work-wise; the conference went well. But she can't shake the fluttering sense of disquiet, of something coming back for her. She has started waking in the middle of the night, frightened for some reason, unable to remember why. Her doctor has prescribed sleeping tablets. Opening her handbag, Alice touches the small packet with a fingertip. She thinks, for just a second, of having one, so she can sleep all the way back to London, and then pushes the thought away, taking another slug of gin. That will do. She doesn't need them often.

The train judders to a halt at Durham and as the doors hiss open they let in an icy gust of January air. A large, suited man, carrying a briefcase, folds himself into the seat opposite Alice. She crosses her legs, irritated, tidies the miniature bottle of gin into the brown paper bag the girl had provided and unfolds her paper.

She glances for a moment at a photo of George in the television pages. His first show is airing tonight. She still can't get her head around George's new career – he had been in politics as long as she'd known him, president of St Anthony's student union the year they met. She hadn't been sure how he would fare as a presenter, but in the previews she had seen he'd done well. His sense of humour came across. The show, the first in a series exploring the lives of famous British politicians, allowed him to make a few self-deprecating jokes and a few at the expense of other people, too. George would just say what he thought and in television today that seemed to be a key requirement. Alice has always envied him that quality. He's looking jowly, though, she notices – something she never sees when he's right in front of her.

She skims through the piece but finds she wants a break

from work – hers and George's – and instead gets out a pen to do the crossword. Even then it isn't long before the letters begin to swim before her eyes. Scrunching up her scarf, she tucks it under her head, insulating herself from the freezing glass of the window. She feels her shoulders unclench and closes her eyes.

As she drifts in and out of sleep, Alice feels as though she is being watched. She opens her eyes once or twice, glances at the man opposite her, but he is hiding behind his paper – reading the story about George. It makes her feel peculiar. A part of her is taken over by a childlike desire to say, 'That's my husband – you're reading about my husband.' She swallows hard and closes her eyes again. There is a faint smell of something tropical in the air. It's an unlikely scent at this time of year but pleasant, like sun cream or rum.

The carriage fills up as she dozes. She hears a group of boys get on at York. They sit in a huddle not far behind her, and the hiss and click of their cans of lager permeate her sleep. At one stage, one of them comes over and tries to talk to someone across the aisle from her. 'All right, darling. Haven't I seen you somewhere before?' Alice strains to catch the reply and, though the girl speaks too softly for Alice to hear her words, their meaning is clear in the young man's hasty retreat.

Nosiness gets the better of Alice and she takes a quick look at where she imagines the girl is sitting, but she can't see much – just a pair of slim legs crossed towards her. She closes her eyes again and drifts off.

When, at last, she wakes up properly, Alice feels sticky and hot. The sun has gone down and the lights on the train have been switched on. She squints out of the window into the darkness, trying to work out how far they've got, but there's now too little light for her to tell – just dark, indecipherable shapes whistling by. She looks for a second at her own face – pale, almost haggard in the dark glass. It's not a flattering light; she runs a tired hand through her hair.

She scans other faces in the reflection. The man opposite her is looking at photographs on his smartphone, running his fingers over the screen. Alice thinks she spies the flesh tones of naked skin and holds her gaze a little too long, trying to make out what the shapes are – porn? Glancing up, the man catches her looking at him in the window. The faintest of smiles flickers on his lips, but Alice frowns and looks away.

On the other side of the aisle, a mother and her small daughter reading together cause her a twinge of pain. She still has them: phantom visceral experiences. Nothing dramatic like giving birth or breast-feeding – maybe because she doesn't know what they would feel like – but other sensations. She'd bought a friend's child a cardigan recently, a dear hand-knitted thing, and she'd had the sense, as she held it, of dressing an infant: pushing its arms into the sleeves, the wriggly feeling of resistance in the child's limbs; it had been so strong, so clear, that she felt the weight of the baby in her arms for a moment.

Alice's gaze falls upon the girl who'd been chatted up, two seats behind the mother and child; she is sitting by the window, facing Alice. Her face is obscured by a curtain of hair and the angle at which she's sitting. Her hair is an almost shockingly bright red and the sight of it – the feeling of envy Alice experiences as she looks at it – stirs a sense of déjà vu. Alice shivers, pulls her scarf tighter around her shoulders. She feels spooked. Just for a second she has pictured the girl's hair under water – spread out like seaweed. Why would she think of that?

The cadence of the train changes as they enter a tunnel. The world outside – smudged grey before – becomes reflective black. Alice glances at herself again. Her reflection now is sharper, harder-edged. She can see more detail on her face. She runs a finger along the rings beneath her eyes and thinks about an old university friend she'd bumped into at the family law conference. He had aged well. He was so thin at college but he'd grown into his face now; he still carried himself in the same way, though: calmly, lightly, as if he knew his place in the world.

They had been close during Alice's early days at university. He would fetch her for lectures and listen to her chat on the way there. In the morning light, St Anthony's looked like a film set. There was no one else around to worry about or impress and he had a soothing presence.

One morning, he had asked her to his room for a smoke and Alice, unused to marijuana, had giggled and giggled. They ended up lying on his narrow bed listening to reggae, their slender arms round each other, feeling almost weightless. Alice had never felt so relaxed. She had longed for him to kiss her, but he hadn't.

When she'd told Christie about him, her best friend had simply said, 'Dopehead,' screwing up her nose. And, not long after, Alice had got together with George. They passed the dopehead once after a black-tie do. Alice had had a couple of glasses of wine and was teetering on her heels. She had shrieked his name as he slunk past. 'This is George,' she said, proudly pushing her new boyfriend forwards. The boy never really talked to her after that and at the conference, though he had been friendly, that wariness had remained.

Alice brushes a hand over her eyes. Later, she will wonder why her gaze returned to the girl with red hair. She looks back in the dark glass to where the girl had been sitting and sees she has moved into the aisle seat. She is reading and her hair is pushed back.

She looks up from the book and towards Alice. Hers is a memorable face – not one Alice would forget. Her skin looks pale against the black backdrop of the glass. Her eyes are like black holes but, for a fraction of a second, there is a telling tension around them as she squints in recognition and then looks quickly away. Alice stares. She can't move. For seconds she is frozen. As she stands and turns to look at the girl straight on, she notices the edges of her field of vision are starting to turn black, like looking down a tunnel. She takes a step and starts to speak, but her own voice sounds strange, as if she's listening to it through water. Her ears feel like they need to pop. She says abruptly: 'I think I'm going to faint,' and feels her knees buckle.

She slumps back in the seat, staring up at the luggage rack. The man sitting opposite her pops into her line of vision. 'Are you OK? Can I get you some water?'

Alice sits up slowly and looks over to where the girl had been. There is no one there. She feels washed out, diluted. She asks: 'Did you see a girl with red hair, just opposite?'

'No, I don't think so.' He smiles sheepishly. 'But I was just looking at my baby.' He waggles his mobile at her and Alice glances at a photo of a naked infant. 'You look terribly pale.'

Alice tries to control her breath. The man is looking at her closely.

'I had a shock,' she says quickly. 'She looked so like someone I was at university with. But she . . .' Alice lowers her voice so the little girl across the aisle won't be able to hear. 'She drowned – the girl – so it couldn't have been her.' She realises she sounds a bit mad.

He smiles kindly. 'Did you know her well?'

Alice looks down at her lap. 'Not particularly,' she says eventually. She tries to recall the girl's name. She used to know it. Christie would remember. She adds: 'I'm not usually like this. I'm a lawyer.' As if that makes a difference.

On the tube home, it comes back to her: Ruth Walker. Alice murmurs the words to herself in the noisy carriage. It was a name she'd heard a lot the summer that Ruth drowned. She hadn't really known her, but stories and superstitions about Ruth's death had rippled through the student community at that time and somehow things had never been quite the same afterwards. Her name became a way of chiding a friend for staggering home alone drunk or turning down the suggestion of an impromptu night swim. It was as if a shadow had been cast over them – though, of course, her disappearance hadn't been the only loss that summer.

Perhaps for this reason, she promises herself she won't say anything that night. But then a few glasses of wine loosen her resolve. It's simply too good a story. It's just a kitchen supper with Christie and Teddy to celebrate George's first show, which they guffaw their way through after too much Sauvignon Blanc. Alice's feeling rather giddy and emotional, and it suddenly feels important – imperative – to tell the story out loud, to someone other than George, who had merely held a hand to her forehead and asked how she was getting on with those tablets. She wishes she hadn't told him about those either.

So when she finally says it, her voice sounds strange – a touch too high – as she stands up to clear the plates. 'You remember that girl Ruth?' She talks over her husband's shaking head and addresses the table beyond. Christie's the only one really paying attention, as usual. George is looking rather pale and Teddy is holding an empty champagne bottle up to the light to see if there's anything left. 'The one who drowned,' Alice adds.

And that seems to get their attention: Teddy puts down the bottle, George murmurs, 'Not now, darling.'

Christie frowns. 'What about her?'

Alice leans her hip against the dresser, still holding the plates. 'I had the weirdest experience,' she says. Pronouncing the word 'experience' is a struggle: she is drunker than she thought. 'I was coming back from Edinburgh today and there's this girl in the aisle opposite . . . woman, really – well, our age. In her thirties. And she looks the spit, the absolute spit of Ruth – or how she would look now. Extraordinary. And she died – what? – fifteen years ago.'

'Spooky,' breathes Christie, 'a doppelgänger – do you think we all have one? I remember hearing, actually . . .'

'No,' says Alice firmly, not about to surrender the conch so easily. 'It wasn't just a resemblance; it was more than that. I couldn't help myself: I got up to say something. Now here's the thing . . .'

'Now here's the thing,' mimics George, stabbing the air with a fork.

'Shut up, George,' says Alice. She considers leaving the anecdote unfinished. Tonight, after all, is a celebration.

But Christie, scraping her pudding plate with a teaspoon, is waiting for the end of the story.

'What happened?'

Alice pauses. 'She disappeared,' she says eventually. 'I felt very odd – had a sort of turn – and when I looked again she had completely vanished.'

Before taking a tablet, Alice tries to send herself to sleep by making lists in her head: clients she needs to email, thank-you letters to be written, ingredients for the week's suppers or, on happier days, things she would like to do – perfect her Italian, learn how to knit. But today she can't focus on the lists. Her attention keeps getting tugged back to the woman on the train and the look that flickered across her face.

And just as she is sinking into sleep, half-dreaming, half-awake, Alice's drifting mind alights on a memory of a party. She was on the periphery, uncertain of herself: a first year at this third-year gathering. She remembers spotting George. She had started to notice him at parties. On the other side of the room, his arm propped him up in the doorway as he surveyed the scene – with the care-less arrogance, she had thought then, that only the obscenely good-looking or wealthy could afford. George, with his squat looks, hadn't been particularly blessed in the former department, though he made up for it in self-belief; but he'd had Dan with him – tall and chiselled. Yes, it may well have been to him, next to George, that her eye was first drawn, before she noticed the approach of the girl with red hair, who charged towards George, holding her face inches away from his, and shouted something with such vehemence that Alice had flinched.

Was that detail added by her drifting mind, in the process of a memory becoming a dream? Alice wonders, suddenly awake. Had George laughed in her face and had she, the girl, spat some invective at him before storming off? Had it been at this same party that George later appeared by Alice's side with a warm glass of wine in his hand and said, 'I saw you looking,' in such a way that had made her laugh?

'I think you knew her,' Alice says aloud to her gently snoring husband.

'What, darling?' His arm, heavy with sleep, slumps over her body.

'That girl,' says Alice. 'Ruth. I think you knew her.'

Naomi

It hasn't happened for years. I'm in the Co-op staring at the fish, deciding between mackerel and cod, and the woman next to me in the cold section begins to fidget, interrupting my train of thought. She keeps glancing towards me as if she recognises me.

'We've met before,' she says at last.

She has a Geordie accent, is small and birdlike, with a nest of wiry hair and steel-rimmed glasses perched on the end of her nose.

'I don't think so,' I say politely. I reach for the mackerel, put it in my basket and begin to walk away.

That is it for a moment. And then she remembers where she's seen me.

'I was there,' she calls after me. 'In St Anthony's. The whole town . . . the whole town was looking for her.'

I turn back. I should have known from her accent.

'One of my friends found the dress. Red, wasn't it?'

I stand very still. 'Green,' I say.

'I always thought it was red.'

'No,' I say. 'That was her shoes.'

'I worked that night at the ball.' She takes a step towards me. 'She kept coming to refill her glass. I felt dreadful when I heard she'd gone swimming afterwards. She never should, in that state.'

Everyone with even the slightest connection to Ruth's death loves to tell their story. She takes another step. Her hair is in a dreadful state close up: coarse and dry. Her teeth are yellowing. Her breath smells faintly of fish. Such small things, matters of hygiene, make my stomach turn at the moment.

She says: 'I'm so sorry. That's all I wanted to say: I'm sorry. It must have been terrible.'

'It was,' I say.

'I have a feeling,' she continues in a low voice, 'that in some way she'll be back in your life before the year is out.'

'Thank you.' My voice sounds flat and strange. 'But she's gone.'

'Well, maybe it's just her spirit living on in you.' She looks down at my belly, though I'm not showing yet. I'm only eight weeks in.

'What do you mean?'

'Like I said,' she nods, 'I have feelings about these things.' She looks pleased with herself. 'It's a boy,' she adds. 'I know you and your partner would prefer a girl, but it's a boy.'

I look at the door.

'It's not over,' she says.

'It'll never be over,' I hear myself reply. 'She was my

sister.' The hiss of the first syllable, the rap of the second. Not a soft, gentle word, really, in the way it's not a soft, gentle thing – which you would think it might be, if you didn't have a sister. Before, in my other life, it was a noun I had used and heard thousands of times. 'Is Ruth Walker your sister?' 'Your sister is in trouble again.' 'You must be clever, like your sister.' Words, questions, phrases that made me irritated or proud but can never be used lightly or unthinkingly now. I've got to get out of here.

Walking away I'm careful not to look around, but I can feel her eyes on my back. My breath is trapped in my chest: a tense little pocket of air. I can't always see panic approaching before it's there, breathing down my neck. I place my basket on the floor as carefully as I can, and walk swiftly through the whirring cold section of the store and out through the sliding doors. As I glance back, I think she's still there, standing like Lot's wife, watching me go.

The frosty air hits my face like a slap, but it staves off the panic. I grasp a bike railing for a second to steady myself and tell myself firmly: Naomi, calm the fuck down. I cling on as the dizziness subsides. The cars slosh past on South Ealing Road, their headlights piercing the drizzle. The moment passes. I pull my hood up, tuck my chin into my chest and pace home. It's not far, but the fresh air clears my head. And I think of Ruth.

She was fearless. I can never silence the small voice in me that reminds me something can go wrong – a flash, a premonition of an accident before it happens. My mother is the same – she would watch Ruth on her pony

16

through splayed fingers and only I, standing next to her, would hear the sharp intake of breath as the animal approached a jump, see the quick smile on her face when they landed safely on the other side.

But Ruth loved jumping: the euphoria of leaving the ground, the purpose of it, the way the pony's muscles would tense before taking off then stretch out as it soared. The knack was to lean forwards, not to try to contain it but to move with it, embrace the leap. I think she got that kind of thrill-seeking from our father; my mother and I have a different kind of courage.

She left her shoes behind. I gave them to her, her Dorothy slippers, red and sparkling. She was wearing them for luck that night. She placed them on the beach so neatly – which was rare for Ruth – with her handbag next to them. The police told us that often happens when people go missing.

A stinging wind picks up and, as I turn into our road, it really begins to pour. I run the last stretch, slapping my feet against the wet concrete. I think of the tiny being inside me and wonder if he or she can feel the impact as we run.

Carla has started cooking as I get home. The sweet, woody smell of cumin seeds fills the kitchen. It needs a good clean, I notice as I come in, but there'll be time enough for that once I'm off work. I bury my face between Carla's shoulder blades and she curls an arm behind her to hug me.

'Did you get those bits?'

'No. Sorry.' I reach for Carla's glass of red wine on the counter, breathe in its oaky fumes. 'Something happened.' I hesitate. 'A self-styled psychic. One of those. She wanted to talk about Ruth.'

'It's been ages since you've had that sort of thing.' Carla frowns as she stirs the popping seeds. 'Did she know her?'

I take a small sip of wine. 'No, not really. She was from St Anthony's.' I put the glass down, and try not to think of Ruth's dress lying sodden and torn on the beach. 'She could tell I was pregnant. We're having a boy, apparently.' I try to smile.

Carla looks down at my belly, puts a possessive hand over it. 'That *is* weird. You really can't tell yet.'

You would think, what with Carla being a therapist, that she would be familiar with the more esoteric aspects of human nature, but the fact is she's the most down-to-earth person I know. We met in a group therapy session she was leading. It was instantaneous.

At the end of the first session, I waited to talk to her. She was shuffling our questionnaires into a blue folder. I hadn't planned what I would say and, as I approached her, she didn't look up at me at first, just said: 'I think you ought to join another group.'

'Really? I like your group,' I said petulantly.

'I think you know why.'

She looked up at me then. And she was right, I did. It was frightening falling for someone like that, after the last time.

'I don't know what to do about it,' I whispered.

She laughed at me: 'Well, after you've quit my group, we'll go for a drink and take it from there.'

And, really, it was remarkably straightforward. I joined

18

another group and we dated the British way, at the pub. I went back to her flat one afternoon, a few weeks after that first meeting, and never left.

That night, the dream returns. The one I always have. We are running through St Anthony's, up one of the roads that winds from the sea. Ruth is calling: 'Come on, slow-coach. Last one there's a rotten egg.' But she is always ahead of me, pushing further on until, eventually, she moves almost out of sight. I see a flash of her red shoes, her red hair disappearing around the corner. I hear her feet ringing out on the pavement just in front of me. And then I realise I can't hear them any more. It is silent. And I start to shout: 'Ruth? Ruth?' There is just the sound of my own voice returning to me.

The panic begins then. And even though it is a dream, I can tell I have felt that particular sensation before. Because there's more I need to ask her. There's so much more to say.

The way I'm moving is less like running now, more like drifting, floating above the ground like a helium balloon. And as I turn the final corner, right at the top of town, I come across her red shoes on the pavement. They have been left there placed parallel, as if on purpose, as if they were a sign.

I wake gasping for air. The jolt of my waking stirs Carla. She murmurs something in her sleep, curves her body in a question mark around mine. It takes my eyes a few moments to adjust to the shadowed room. I lie in the dark, listening to Carla's steady breathing, left with the sensation of the dream: that Ruth was just here; that she has only just gone. And, as always, at times like this – in the cold hours of night when I've woken with a jolt – the same old questions come flooding back. It's as if they have been waiting for me.

What was on her mind as she got into the water? And did she think of me as she fought for her life? How it might feel to carry on living in the world without her? But there's always one question that's louder than the others, more insistent: was my sister in the water on her own? Or was there someone with her? Someone who placed her shoes and bag on the ground so neatly. Someone who wanted her gone.

Alice

Alice puts the last of the previous evening's plates in the dishwasher. After a broken night, she finally drifted to sleep at dawn, missing George as he scrambled out of bed to get to a morning radio interview. He hasn't really paused since his career change in the way she hoped he might. He's on his phone the whole time, only half there in the evenings or the weekends, always in another place while he's in the room with her.

She's not much better. Often, the pair of them will sit together at the kitchen table at their laptops or side by side on the sofa tapping away on their own devices, which reminds her: she needs to email her newest client – the wife of one of George's former colleagues. Alice frowns: George hadn't been happy that she'd agreed to take on the case – a high-profile divorce between the Tory MP and his wife, a couple in their sixties who are separating after almost four decades of marriage. But she's always got on well with the other woman, who, with her iron-straight bob and an unfussy, businesslike way of dressing, reminds Alice a little of herself.

As she fetches a cloth and wipes down the kitchen table, she notices that the uneasy feeling from yesterday has persisted. The episode on the train has a dreamlike quality as she reflects back. She thinks again of Ruth shouting in George's face. Was that the party where they'd first got together? He's always quite foggy about it – all the booze, no doubt – but Alice had thought she could recall it pretty clearly. And yet she hadn't remembered the girl before – perhaps that had been a different party . . .

She'd wanted to impress George that night, for him to notice her. She'd dressed with him in mind. By that stage, of course, Christie had already snared Teddy – Alice smiles at the choice of the word 'snared' – but it's one Christie, with her eye on Teddy's castle in Scotland, might have used herself. Back then, the third-year boys had seemed like prizes to the freshers. She smirks at the thought now. Of course, George's family has never had the sort of money that Teddy's did – but certain doors would always be open to the Bells. George's grandfather and his father were barristers. Perhaps that was why he'd ended up marrying a lawyer himself. They're a family who make things happen – even his mother serves on the parish council in the Oxfordshire village where they live, where she held sway in her usual terrifying manner, no doubt. No wonder George became a politician.

His parents had backed him all the way, down to helping him to find a cottage when he was MP for Witney. The papers had mocked him as a mummy's boy, but

George hadn't been bothered – 'Everyone accepts help from their family,' he'd say to her in private. There had even been a photo or two of his mother picking fluff off his collar in public, straightening his tie, that sort of thing, but George shook it off in the way a less charismatic man might not.

It's not that George is cool – more that he genuinely doesn't give two hoots about what people say. He could laugh off almost everything. Alice has the opposite problem, she thinks as she switches the kettle on: she cares too much about almost everything – her work, her clients, what people think. She's learned over the years to care less, or hide it better, but the old worries that somehow she's faked her way to success, that people might see through her, needle away at her. Her parents, both teachers, are very different from George's. Her father, as the head of the Warwickshire state school she'd gone to, had an inner confidence, but he is a quiet person, self-contained. Alice catches him sometimes watching George as if trying to figure him out, while her mother, even after all these years, is jumpy around George's family. She knocks things over, laughs too shrilly. Although she hates that she's embarrassed by such things, Alice notices herself working extra-hard to smooth everything over when they're all together – trying to overexplain or soften George's quips, or to encourage her parents to relax more. Needless to say, George never sees any of this silent work going on, she thinks, with a flicker of anger.

The whistle of the kettle breaks this line of thought. Alice makes a cup of tea and takes it to the kitchen table. She opens her laptop and checks her email. There's one from Elizabeth Gregory, the politician's wife, saying how pleased she is that Alice is representing her. Her husband is having an affair with a young researcher on his team. The pair of them shared an eye-roll at that at their last meeting. 'It's not just the cliché of it,' her client had confided. She'd closed her eyes – 'It makes me sad for something I've lost, too. Something the pair of us have lost that he's trying to get back without me.'

It was her sense of fairness that had drawn Alice to divorce law, that the quiet work of women should be recognised. Even in her own parents' marriage there were inequalities. Her father could forge ahead with his career because her mother had looked after Alice and her sister. Often, her father had been home in time for bedtime stories, it's true, but then that was the fun part of child-care – not the endless rounds of washing clothes, preparing meals, packing gym kits, remembering which child had which hobby on which days, driving around the country-side, and keeping their timetables and friendships and teachers in her head.

'What makes me mad when I think of it now,' Elizabeth had said, pausing to blow on her cup of coffee, 'is the way he used to talk about me. If someone asked me a question about the children, he'd say, 'Oh, I don't deal with any of that. Ask my wife.' The way he said it promoted me to the most important person in his life, but also made me, somehow, not important at all. How could I be absolutely crucial and yet as irrelevant to him as hired help? It's hard to explain.'

She hadn't had to: Alice had seen it enough in other marriages; though, in truth, it had always been different in her own. In his favour, George never demands too much of her in the way of housework or ironing. Their cleaner, Mrs T, looks after all that. Alice organises the Ocado deliveries, remembers birthdays, writes thank-you notes. What does George do? 'I bring the fun,' he would say. Not to mention their house in Notting Hill, which his parents had helped with. Distasteful as it is to think about it, there are advantages to being married to George, there's no doubt about it.

Alice tries to remember more about the party where she'd seen Ruth, but not much more comes to her. She closes her eyes and tries again, recalls, on a separate occasion, walking into the college bar with her hand in George's, and seeing Ruth and a friend of hers, Kat, exchange a glance, not a happy one, at the sight of them. They said a few words to each other and got up to go. As they passed George and Alice, Ruth looked as if she was about to say something, but Kat tugged at her sleeve: 'Don't.'

'Do you know those girls?' Alice had asked after they'd gone.

'What girls?' George asked, but then he'd seen Dan and bellowed a greeting at him. And that was that.

He and Dan were inseparable. They'd come up to St Anthony's from Eton together with Teddy and a couple of others – a gang with a point to prove, perhaps, having not made it into Oxbridge. Alice had always been quite envious of the way George had started with a ready-made group. But of all his friends, Dan had been George's closest. They made a funny pair – Dan was tall, slim and silent, George stout and loquacious. Dan's looks would draw the girls to them but George's charm would make them stay.

Alice had always liked George the most. A little shy herself, she'd found it hard to know what to say to Dan and he never gave much back. Whenever George popped to the bar and left them alone, Alice would find herself tongue-tied, unsure how to interact with Dan on her own. The thing was, she thinks now, it seemed that a part of him enjoyed how uneasy she was, as if it were a game.

When George came back from the bar, he'd say, 'How are you chaps getting along?'

And once, Dan had said, 'Oh, we're getting along *famously*.' It was a little piece of nastiness that only Alice could appreciate.

Another time, they'd gone out dancing and Alice, after a tipple too many, started mucking around with a pole, swinging around it sexily and giggling at George as she did.

George had grinned and blown her a kiss, but he'd been distracted by the time she returned to the table.

'Great dancing,' Dan had said in a tone that implied he meant quite the opposite. 'Really sexy.'

Once or twice, when George was in one of his tender moods, in bed perhaps or after a few glasses of wine, Alice might ask: 'Does Dan like me?'

And George would look completely puzzled and say: 'Of course, you silly thing. Why would you ask a question like that?'

But it didn't matter what he said, because Alice always knew, deep down, that Dan didn't – that he'd never thought Alice was good enough for George. Maybe it was that she'd gone to a state school, or that her family didn't have as much money as George's; maybe it was that she didn't have George's natural wit, or the confidence of the people who'd grown up in the same social circles as the Etonians. Maybe, she thought on some days, it was because Dan had been in love with George.

She blinks at the laptop screen. No, that was ridiculous. Dan had liked girls. Of course, he had.

But there had been such a strong connection between them, as if they shared some kind of secret. Maybe even a secret related to Ruth Walker – to why she might have hated George enough to shout at him, to leave a room when he entered. Alice sighs. She's not going to be able to concentrate on anything else unless she does some digging. She picks up her laptop and heads to George's study.

Kat

October 1999

Dressed in black, Kat smudges her lipstick on her third cigarette. The rush of nicotine makes her feel light-headed, insubstantial. She had been so full of hope for university – had had a rather precise idea about the kind of life she was going to lead. That was why she had picked this wild town on the edge of Britain over a civilised place like London. She had packed a couple of bottles of champagne, nicked from her father's wine cellar, and cigarettes and the *Collected Works of Dorothy Parker* – but she had been greeted at the gates by the freshers' rep, a pale, gangly boy with wispy hair that stuck out in different directions. Not fanciable at all.

She could tell he wasn't used to girls like Kat – not used to girls full stop – and it hadn't taken much to make him blush into his tea, make his excuses and scuttle off back to his dusty textbooks. Kat had never been one for making an effort with people she couldn't see the point of. It was something she had inherited from her father. Not a nice trait, she realised, but then her father wasn't a very nice man.

But if she liked someone, it was another matter entirely, as if a light bulb had been switched on. It had been like that the other night in what passed for this town's only nightclub. She'd met him a few drinks in, so she couldn't remember exactly how things had started. There she had been, waiting by the bar, and he seemed to have appeared beside her. Messy hair, dark eyes, low voice. Soothing to be around, a measured way of speaking and holding himself. And she had felt a kind of certainty, a kind of excitement.

And admittedly, she'd had five, or maybe six, vodka cranberries at that stage, so the certainty could have just been an epiphany created by booze and a handsome face. But then she had woken up the next day early and surprisingly clear-headed, sure that something important had begun, and a couple of days later the feeling had barely shifted.

No one she'd asked knew who he was. It didn't help that she couldn't remember his name. He was a second year – she recalled that much – and he played the guitar in a band and could quote Dorothy Parker.

And now, at this party, there he is again and Kat, who is never nervous, is experiencing a fluttering feeling in her limbs. Strange how liking someone can distil into a single detail: the smell of his cologne, the feeling of his arm under your hand, the sound of his laugh. With this guy it's his voice – low and calming – she can catch the cadence of it from where she is standing. He's talking to a small bloke next to him, with a keen, ratty face. Kat looks at him steadily, waiting for him to glance at her in return so she can smile, or look away, and let it all begin.

But he doesn't look at her, because he's looking at someone else.

Kat has seen the girl before at other freshers' events. She is wearing a long white dress – a bold choice for a redhead and a touch virginal for Kat's tastes. There's something knowingly Pre-Raphaelite about the combination. It calls to mind paintings of tragic heroines, tresses weighed heavy with water and flowers. Still, she has a lively, likeable face, but then, thinks Kat, putting out her cigarette and straightening her dress, before making her way to the messy-haired guy, so does she.

'Hello again,' she says.

'Kat, isn't it?' he smiles. 'This is Jerry.' He jerks a thumb at the boy he's standing next to.

'Richard's in love,' says Jerry.

Richard. That was it. Kat tries to smile again and looks over at the redhead.

'Shut up, Jerry.' Richard stops looking at the girl and turns to Kat.

'You can't take your eyes off her.' Jerry's mouth twitches. 'You know what they say about redheads?'

Kat doesn't believe for a second that this boy knows anything about redheads – or girls, for that matter. The three of them watch as the girl lights her cigarette in a knowing way and makes her way to the drinks table.

'Go and talk to her,' Kat says quickly to Richard.

She doesn't want him to – of course, she doesn't want

him to – but she will never be one of those women. A memory of her mother hovering around her father pops into her head – who holds onto a man's sleeve, who begs him to stay.

Richard bites his lip. 'Maybe later,' he says quietly. 'How are you?'

'When you like someone, you should just try,' says Kat, ignoring the question, aware of the irony. 'Just say hello.'

He smiles. 'Perhaps you're right.' He touches her arm to excuse himself. 'Wish me luck.'

Kat watches Richard as he picks his way across the room. At one point, stuck behind a tight cluster of maths students who won't make way for him, he glances back at Kat with what looks like a question in his eyes. She smiles brightly and gives him a thumbs-up. As he reaches the drinks table, the redhead is standing with her back to him, which is awkward – so difficult to approach someone like that: do you tap them on the back? Start a conversation with their shoulders? But Kat will never know how that conversation might have started, because there's a sudden movement in the cluster around the drinks table, a gasp and, as if in slow motion, a glass of red wine slices through the air towards the girl's white dress. There's a shriek and the guy who has spilt the drink is moving towards her, all apologies and hands, trying to dab at the jagged stain with his handkerchief.

'Oldest trick in the book,' Jerry breathes next to her, looking towards the student with the handkerchief: a sturdy-looking chap with aquiline features and an air of unshakable confidence.

'What?'

'George Bell,' says Jerry. As if that explained something in itself. 'He'll be saying, "Let's get you out of those wet clothes." Something like that.'

'Right.' Kat makes out the back of Richard's head in the shifting crowd.

'Classic George.' Jerry smirks. 'He'll always pick the most beautiful girl in the room and do that sort of thing.'

Kat blinks, pushes a strand of hair behind her ear.

What is Richard doing in all this kerfuffle, as George passes the redhead a cloth, as he pours her another drink, as he lifts his hand, briefly, to wipe away a few drops, real or imagined, from the girl's hair? There he is. Kat catches a glimpse of Richard's face, pale and grimacing, as he turns back towards them.

'What happened there?' she asks.

'George happened,' he says in a low voice so Jerry won't be able to hear. He looks into his drink.

Kat can catch the odd word of George's plummy voice across the room. 'Who's he?'

'He is'—Richard pauses for a moment as if to find the correct phrase—'an unspeakable cunt.'

Kat, usually unshockable, blinks at the word. 'Why?' she wants to say.

She looks at the girl again, who glances over at them. She narrows her eyes slightly as if in recognition of something. Kat smiles tightly and wonders if Richard has noticed.

The moment passes. The girl seems to be getting ready to go somewhere with George. She picks up her bag and turns her face towards him to say something as they leave.

Kat can't hear what she says, but George laughs heartily and presses a casual hand into the small of her back.

Then, Kat would think later, if things had gone otherwise that night, that moment, everything might have been different. But, instead, she takes another sip of warm white wine and sees, from the corner of her eye, George's group sashay out of the party, the outline of a white dress as they move away.

And though it should be a relief, though things should brighten, shift, now her rival has gone, that is not the case. She just can't win Richard's attention back, nor recapture the magic of the other night and all her usual tricks – a way of telling an anecdote, her hand on his arm, a certain sideways smile – fail to pique a reaction. Or maybe it's her. It seems to Kat there's a heaviness to everything she does tonight – the stories aren't coming out right. The rhythm of how she tells them is wrong. Or the intonation. She can't tell. But Richard and Jerry's smiles are polite more than anything. Jerry's glance darts around the room, while Richard keeps looking at the door. And even Kat's thoughts drift to the girl in the white dress, the way she walked across the room like a dancer, the way she had caught Kat's eye before she left.

Some girls had things easy, but Kat had always had to try. To be entertaining: that was the most important thing; that was something she'd learned from Dorothy Parker. And if nights like this made you feel sad and defeated, then you went to bed and woke up the next day and, generally, in Kat's experience, the darkness would have shifted.

Eventually, Richard finishes his drink and slips away saying something about the library.

When it's just the two of them, Jerry perks up. He moves closer to her when she speaks. His polite smiles become forced laughter. Occasionally he touches her, on the shoulder, her waist, as if testing something.

'Where did Richard go again?' Kat asks, anticipating another touch, stepping away, leaving his hand hanging for a moment in the space between them.

Jerry rolls his eyes. 'I wouldn't bother with Richard, if I were you,' he says. 'When he likes someone, that's it.'

Kat looks down at the art deco cigarette case in her hand, her remaining cigarettes lined up like soldiers. It was a present from her father for her eighteenth birthday last year, but she suspects his latest wife, his third now, only seven years older than Kat, might have had something to do with it. Should she bother with another cigarette or not? The feeling of light-headedness is back.

'That's it,' says Jerry again. 'Richard won't be swayed from his course.'

The engraving inside, though, that must have been her father: 'Faute De Mieux' by Dorothy Parker. He was a huge fan, too – sometimes it was the only thing that Kat could be really sure they shared.

'It's funny,' she says, snapping the case shut. 'I'm just the same.'

Alice

Standing in George's study, Alice enjoys the quiet order of the room for a moment. She has no idea if he guesses that she comes in here when she's alone in the house. It's one of the things they never talk about. She's always careful to leave it as she found it. She pops in sometimes as if she's looking for something, though she is not sure what. She'll wander around, picking up the odd book or trinket – a fountain pen, an ornament – and wonder where they came from. When they moved into the house, so much just arrived from George's parents and if she ever asks, George just shrugs and says, 'That old thing? My ma would know.' It's a source of irritation to Alice, who would have liked to fill her home with cleaner contemporary pieces, rather than so much creaking dark wood that he seems to care for so little himself.

His study is one of the tidiest rooms in the house. It's at the front of the building overlooking the street, though the shutters keep out the light. Political biographies and history books line the floor-to-ceiling bookshelves, as well as the odd spy thriller. Alice runs her finger along the spines. Quite a few of them are from his days in St Anthony's. For such an unsentimental person, George doesn't like to throw much away.

She settles in the dark leather armchair by the fireplace and switches on her laptop. First, she does an image search for 'Ruth Walker' but, though her screen is filled with lines and lines of Ruth Walkers, of all ages and sizes, in gym kits and business suits, grinning in Facebook photos or pouting on Instagram, Alice's Ruth Walker isn't there. Nor are there photos of her in any of the articles Alice can find. The first story to come up is an old one from a local paper in the Free Library under the headline 'Tragedy strikes in St Anthony's'.

The dress of St Anthony's student Ruth Walker has been found on South Beach this morning after a three-day police search. Ruth was last seen swimming on 23 June in the early morning after the university's memorial ball. Walker's family fear the worst . . .

Alice blinks. She remembers the day after the ball. Waking up to a terrible hangover and the pouring rain, all the bunting and balloons of the night before mashed up into the mud, to say nothing of empty bottles, plastic glasses, cigarette butts strewn throughout college. Cleaners scowling through cagoules, grim-faced porters trying to organise the students while their parents arrived in four-by-fours to pick up their children. And by afternoon, murmurs about the news – had anyone heard? Did anyone know any more?

The pulsing blue light of the police cars outside. A different world from the night before with its clowns and fairy lights and the treacly wall of heat in the quad as she had wandered through it hand in hand with George. Sitting on his lap as they watched some stand-up comedy, tutting as he and Dan heckled. And later dancing with her friends, spinning so her dress flew out around her, thinking in that moment she would never feel so carefree.

Alice gives herself a shake. She returns to her search. Most of the articles that the internet throws up are written by Richard Wiseman, Ruth's boyfriend at college, now a writer for a leftie national George wouldn't allow in the house. ('They've never got anything nice to say about me, darling.')

They'd gone everywhere together, Ruth and Richard. She could see them traipsing around college, lighting each other's cigarettes, sitting next to each other in the library. Richard had been good-looking in a ruffled sort of way: scruffy dark hair, faded jeans. He'd fronted a college band. Alice remembers seeing Ruth dancing at one of his gigs, leaping up and down with an abandon Alice had envied. These days he looked older, more tired, in his byline photograph, and his face had hardened in a way that Alice couldn't recall from college.

Ruth Walker and the subjects of mental health and missing people seemed to have shaped a lot of Richard's journalism. He'd even written a book called *The Disappeared* about unsolved cases with a chapter about Ruth, who appears in his writing as 'my ex-girlfriend Ruth Walker' or 'my student girlfriend Ruth Walker' or occasionally 'my girlfriend Ruth Walker'. Alice wonders how Richard's current girlfriends, or wife, feel about this. She notices most of the articles are from a few years back. Perhaps the obsession petered out.

Alice copies and pastes the most interesting of the links and emails them to herself. Then, almost out of habit, she has another wander before leaving the room. She goes to George's desk and tries the drawers. They are locked, as always. The feeling she has as she tries them is always the same: a sort of shame. It's a similar feeling she gets when she goes to an acquaintance's Facebook page and their privacy settings mean she can't see what they've been up to. It's not something you could ever talk about – only a snooper knows when they've been locked out. She never used to think of herself as a snooper, but she's got worse over the years. And it's become easier, too, with social media to find people, to peek at the way their lives are now. It's this period in particular, the university years, she can't leave alone. She scratches away at it like a scab.

Alice perches on the desk. There's a framed collage of photos on it, which Christie and Teddy had put together for George's thirtieth with Alice's help. There's a photograph of his parents at Ascot, standing to attention for the camera, with his father ruddy-cheeked, his mother in a monstrous hat. Another of George and her with Christie and Teddy on holiday in Greece, all looking a bit sunburned and worse for wear. There's a photo of Alice on their wedding day. She remembers it being taken, one of the last in a long, long session of photographs, and how, by that stage, her head was beginning to ache with the strain of the tight hairdo, the hairspray, the clips, the constant smiling.

There's another of George and Dan in black tie at the

memorial ball. They look so young – like children. It doesn't fit with her memory of George and his gang as impossibly sophisticated and cool.

The brrr of the landline makes her jump. It's an old-fashioned, heavy thing on George's desk. Alice looks at it guiltily for a second before picking it up.

'Hello?'

'Hi, darling, it's me.'

'Hello you.' Alice stands up as if caught out.

'What are you up to?'

'Oh, you know, pottering.' She glances down at the photo in her hand.

He pauses. 'Are you all right?'

'Yes, of course. Just enjoying my Saturday. How was the interview?'

'Not bad. Are you OK? You seemed a bit strange last night.'

'Well, I'd had a strange day. That's all.'

Alice's attention returns to the photograph. She picks it up to examine it more closely. George, rosy-cheeked from drinking, is clutching a bottle of champagne in his right hand with his left thrown around Dan's shoulder. A little out of focus, there's a cluster of people in the background.

'Yes, I know,' George says, more sympathetic than he might usually be.

'Well . . .'

Alice wants to wind things up, to be left to her snooping alone. She's never paid much attention to it before but there's someone standing next to George, just out of the photo. There's a sliver of a white shoulder, the strap of a dress and a thin slice of long hair.

39

Where had Alice been by this stage of the night? She must have been in bed; she'd still been recovering from glandular fever in her first year. She certainly hadn't made the survivors' photo. They had never bought one of their own but she'd seen them in the staircases or loos of other people's houses when they'd all initially made the exodus to London. You didn't see so many of them now – tasteful black-and-white photos of weddings and children had replaced student snaps.

'I sometimes think we're all stuck,' George says quietly at the other end of the phone.

Alice sits down; this is unusually reflective for George. 'What do you mean?' she asks.

'That what happened to Dan stopped us in our tracks somehow. That we're all still there – stuck at that time at the end of uni.' He laughs suddenly. 'Or maybe I'm just talking bollocks. It's probably the hangover.'

'No,' says Alice. 'I feel the same.'

She wants him to say more, for this version of her husband to stay on the phone, but then he's making his excuses, signing off, leaving her with the dialling tone ringing in her ears, the framed photograph still in her hand.

The thing is, she thinks, looking down at the photo, the thing she'd been thinking during the call, the thought she couldn't fight, is that the hair in the photograph is red, bright red. Maybe she *is* stuck, but maybe it's to do with this feeling – which she had even back then but was too ashamed to admit – of being left out; of knowing there was something she wasn't being told.

Kat

The next time Kat sees Ruth, she is wearing the same ridiculous Pre-Raphaelite dress again, though – Kat can't help noticing – it is wringing wet. Ruth's hair is wet too, plastered to her shoulders. She is not wearing a coat, so she might as well be standing in her underwear for all Kat can see, which is black under her white dress. She is standing outside the porters' lodge looking at Kat as if waiting for her.

'Haven't got my fucking keys, have I?' she says.

Her voice is soft. There is a Welsh lilt to it. She speaks as if she and Kat already know each other, as if they are in the middle of a conversation. You could see why boys might find it seductive.

'George suggested we go swimming,' the girl continues, though Kat hadn't asked. 'I think he meant skinny-dipping – thought he might see me with my kit off, but I went in fully dressed.' She barks a short laugh. 'And when I came out he'd disappeared.'

'Right.' Kat raises an eyebrow but says, in a voice that sounds like her mother's, 'That's actually quite dangerous.'

'It's OK.' The girl smiles quickly. 'I'm a strong swimmer. I love being in the water – it always clears my head.'

'Still . . .' Kat lets the word hang.

'Haven't I seen you before?'

'I don't know,' says Kat. 'Are you a fresher?'

'Yeah, Spanish. You?'

'English.' Buzzing the front door open and stepping in first, Kat holds its weight for the other girl. 'What's your name?'

'Ruth.' The girl steps after her. 'Yours?'

'Kat,' says Kat. 'How are you finding it all?'

'It's OK.' Ruth pauses. 'A bit disappointing.'

'I know what you mean.' Kat smiles. 'No one ever says that, do they?'

Ruth glances at the college clock tower. 'Do you fancy a drink? I've got some Tia Maria.' She starts to head towards a staircase in the far corner of the quad without waiting for a reply.

Kat finds herself following. 'I thought first years didn't get rooms in front quad?'

'Wait till you see it. It's tiny.'

Ruth hitches up her dress and starts to climb, her DMs clopping against the wooden stairs, a dripping train in her wake. They climb one flight then another. Kat starts to sweat.

'Nearly there,' Ruth gasps as they climb the fifth flight. 'I start to feel the cigarettes right about now.'

They reach a cramped landing, which can barely fit both of them on it at the same time. The door to the

42

room is small, too. Kat feels like Alice in Wonderland as she stoops. The room is, indeed, tiny with the bed high above on a raised platform, with a wooden ladder cut into it. Ruth has hung red drapes on all the walls and lit the room with fairy lights so that it feels like an enchanted cavern. There are piles of books in every corner and ashtrays balancing on the piles.

'Come into my lair,' grins Ruth. 'Now, I've got Tia Maria or . . . no, actually, just Tia Maria. Will that do?' She starts sloshing the dark liquid into mugs before Kat has a chance to reply, then flops on a beanbag on the floor, gesturing opposite her for Kat. 'So,' she says. 'Who do you fancy?'

'Just come out and ask,' laughs Kat. 'Don't hold back.' But she likes Ruth's frankness. She takes a sip of Tia Maria and feels the heat of it spread across her chest.

'I fancy George,' declares Ruth.

Kat nods, lights a cigarette. 'He's got quite the reputation.'

'Doesn't he just!' says Ruth gleefully. 'How about you?'

Kat thinks of Richard, she thinks of the way he looked at Ruth, and she finds she doesn't want to draw Ruth's attention to him.

'I'm not sure yet.' She flicks the ash off the end of her cigarette. 'I got burned by a guy on my gap year,' she says instead. She glances down at her chipped nail polish. 'There was this married man. He shagged me, of course, but he wouldn't leave his wife.' She laughs. 'I'm told they never do.'

She's found that anecdote usually shuts up other freshers. It's a sort of test. But Ruth looks captivated.

'Have you slept with many people?'

'A few.' Kat takes another sip of Tia Maria. 'How about you?'

Ruth takes a deep breath. 'Not one.' She leans forwards. 'Do you think it matters? Do you think they mind?'

Kat picks at a bit of grime on her mug. Ruth doesn't seem to have any sort of filter. 'God, no,' she smiles, though in truth the confession was not quite what she was expecting from someone so theatrical. 'They love it. Being able to show off.'

Ruth adds: 'I was waiting . . .'

'You're Christian?' Kat gives her a withering look and then tries to hide it.

'No, oh God, no.' Ruth hesitates. 'I was waiting for my Big Love.'

'Oh,' says Kat. It's not what she was expecting. 'Your Big Love?' she repeats. 'I like that. Me too – I mean, it's too late to save myself, but I'm waiting for a Big Love, too.' Maybe she's found that in Richard. She smiles. 'You look like Ophelia.'

'I'm not as mad,' Ruth grins. 'Not yet. But if I stay in this bloody freezing dress for much longer, I will be.'

She gets to her feet and starts to pull the dress over her head. Kat, who grew up as an only child in a non-naked house, isn't used to this sort of stripping. In front of guys, sure, but not like this: staggering around the room with your DMs on. She gets up to help.

'Are you stuck?'

The dress is made of heavy cheesecloth and it takes an effort to get it off. When it finally gives, Ruth pops out from it like a cork. She flings the offending item down on the floor. Without the armour of clothes, she looks thin and very pale in her black bra and pants.

'Sorry about that.' She starts to hunt for her dressing gown, which she finds in a crumpled heap in the corner by her sink. 'Where are you from?'

'London,' says Kat. 'How about you?'

'Haverfordwest.' Ruth's mouth shapes itself around the consonants.

'I know that place.'

Ruth laughs. 'Everyone says that.'

'I went there when I was eight and it rained.'

'Yes,' says Ruth, lighting a cigarette. 'Everyone says that, too.'

'What were you like as a kid?' asks Kat. 'I bet you looked like Anne of Green Gables.'

'Ha! I did,' says Ruth. 'With the same temper.'

'I don't believe that,' says Kat politely.

'I guess you haven't known me very long,' says Ruth, trying to blow smoke rings. 'I broke my sister's arm once when we were little.'

'What for?'

'I thought she was cheating. At Grandmother's Footsteps.'

'Well, it sounds as though she deserved it,' Kat laughs.

'No,' says Ruth, suddenly serious. She grinds her cigarette out, gets up to deal with her dress in the sink. 'It was the most terrible thing I've done. She screamed and screamed. It was awful; I couldn't make her stop. My mother said: "What have you done to your sister?" She shook me so hard, and all the time Naomi's face was scrunched up and muddy from where I'd pushed her over.

And I was still angry with her for screaming so loud. For bringing my mum over. I didn't know whether to comfort her or push her over again.' She pauses to hang the dress up on a coat hanger. 'So I ran away and hid for hours in our treehouse.'

'Ah.' Kat isn't sure how to respond to this story. 'You were just a little girl.'

'Sure,' says Ruth dismissively. 'But, you know, the worst thing is: I actually meant to hurt her. And then it was so dreadful when I did.' She sighs. 'She was such a good little girl, as if she felt she had to make up for all my naughtiness.' She is quiet for a moment. 'I don't feel about anyone in the universe like I do my sister. Have you got siblings?'

'No.' Kat thinks of her mum's quiet flat with just the cats for company. 'But I have a couple of younger cousins.'

'So you know what it's like then?' says Ruth, not unkindly.

Kat nods, but she isn't sure that she does. Not really. 'Why did you choose St Anthony's?' she asks.

'I like places on the edge of the world,' says Ruth, gesturing theatrically. 'All the universities I applied to – St Andrews, Edinburgh, Exeter – were near the sea. I grew up on the coast. Being by water always makes things better.' She takes a breath. 'How about you?'

Kat takes a gulp of Tia Maria. 'Mainly to get away from my mother.'

Ruth looks at her for a moment and then roars with laughter, leaning over to clink her mug to Kat's. 'Amen to that. I mean, I love my mum, but . . .'

'I know,' says Kat darkly.

'My mum gets sad,' says Ruth, getting up to put on some music. 'We grew up in a hotel and there were days when she wouldn't want to serve the customers. Not that I blame her for that. Or days when she wouldn't leave her bedroom, where she would sit at the window for hours and look at the sea.'

'Yes, my mum's depressive too,' says Kat. She hates thinking about her mother, especially these days: the way the antidepressants had bloated her, taken off her edges.

'My mum's father – my grandfather – walked into the sea one day and never came back,' Ruth says matter-of-factly as Kate Bush begins to sing. 'My sister and I nearly got lost at sea once, too,' she adds, swaying slowly to the music. 'But that was just an accident. A riptide pulled us out. It was really frightening: one minute we were standing to our waists in water. Then it was to our shoulders,' she gestures, making a performance of it. 'And then the sand seemed to slip away completely. Waves kept coming so hard that we could barely catch our breath between them.'

Kat frowns. 'It sounds pretty hairy.'

'I thought, "This is it,"' says Ruth. 'That we were going to die together like in *Mill on the Floss*.' She leaves a dramatic pause. 'But thanks to a couple of dog walkers, we didn't, in the end,' she concludes cheerfully. 'After that, our father made sure we had swimming lessons. Really good ones, with one of the lifeboat guys who . . .' She is interrupted by a dull gonglike clang of metal hitting metal outside.

'What the hell was that?' Kat asks.

'Someone out in Cathedral Square,' says Ruth, gesturing with her cigarette towards a tiny window above her bed.

'Some people find it *hilarious* to fuck about with the anchor out there.' She climbs up on her bed and looks out of the window. 'Hey, Kat, look at this.'

Kat climbs up the ladder and sits next to Ruth with her nose pressed up against the cold glass. 'What is it?'

'Down there.' Ruth taps her finger against the pane, and Kat sees George and Dan lumbering back to college, each with an arm slung around a girl.

'Hmm,' Kat says and pulls away from the window. She sits cross-legged on the bed. 'Maybe not your Big Love . . .'

'No,' Ruth smiles but her voice sounds flat. 'Maybe not him.' She glances to where her dress is dripping by the sink.

'I can't believe you went swimming in October,' says Kat sternly. 'It's actually really dangerous.' Everyone knew how the town had almost been wiped out by the sea in the great storm of eighteen-something. 'It's actually called St Anthony's because of all the fishermen who were lost here,' she adds.

'I know that,' says Ruth chirpily. 'There's a rhyme: St Anthony, St Anthony, bring what I've lost back to me.'

'I'm just saying,' says Kat. 'Be careful. It's dangerous.'

'Don't worry,' grins Ruth. 'It won't happen again.'

Naomi

Where we were from, people disappeared into the water from time to time. Once it was someone we knew – a man who used to drink at the hotel bar. I was around thirteen, Ruth fifteen. The wind was particularly wild that afternoon, filling our raincoats and puffing them up like balloons. As we headed back home along the clifftops, the hum of the search helicopter began to follow us and eventually we caught sight of it, hovering like a fly, skating the gorse bushes as it moved. When it passed we could see the face of a man squatting by the open door.

'Maybe they've come for us,' one of us joked weakly. But we both knew that the world felt slightly different from how it had that morning.

Later, men in fluorescent jackets appeared at the hotel with their walkie-talkies crackling. Our mother was asked to interrupt service to find out if anyone had seen anything. She had taken off her apron and washed her hands to make the announcement.

Speaking carefully, slowly, she said: 'A man has gone missing. He left home this morning with his wife's dogs: two collies. He told his wife that he'd be gone for an hour. The three of them haven't been seen since.'

'The dogs wouldn't have left him, if he'd fallen.' That was the general conclusion. He might have left his wife, but the dogs wouldn't have left him. People knew about such things where we grew up.

'It's the first thing all the diners said,' Ruth told me later, back in the kitchen. 'And, you know, they wouldn't.' She started picking the dough out of a bread roll, but lost enthusiasm for it and put it back in the basket. 'A man on his own – I mean, he's not exactly a target.'

'What do you mean: a target?' I asked, but Ruth ignored my question.

'Maybe he had an argument with his missus,' Damien, the chef, shouted from behind the hotplate. 'Or maybe he was still pissed from the night before . . .'

'But if you were going to disappear, why would you take your dogs? Wouldn't you leave them?' Ruth asked.

'And you couldn't travel on a bus or a train with two dogs without people noticing,' I pointed out, feeling very grown up.

'Exactly!' Ruth said with relish.

She loved a mystery. Our father got us into Agatha Christie and we would watch Joan Hickson in classics like *4.50 from Paddington* or *They Do It With Mirrors* on Sunday nights. It's about imposing order on disorder, they say – the love of a murder mystery, of a Sherlock Holmes story. I don't know about that but I do know that the memories of piecing those puzzles together as a

50

family are some of my happiest. My father pacing up and down the room, listing the clues off on his fingers as Ruth and I shouted things out.

The day after meeting the supermarket psychic, as I think of her, I wake with Jacques, our Jack Russell, curled into a comforting knot next to me. Carla is up, singing cheerfully. She has a lovely voice, low and tuneful. Before living with a therapist, I might have imagined them to be rather serious people, but Carla lives life lightly.

In the kitchen, she is cracking eggs into a frying pan. Recently, she has started cooking breakfast, insisting the three of us are properly fed before work. 'Rough night?'

'Yeah, I think it must have been that nutter yesterday.'

'The same dream?'

'Yes.' I put the kettle on. 'I can't believe it's been fifteen years.'

She touches my belly. 'You're bound to be thinking of her at the moment.'

When we were scrolling through donors at the Danish sperm bank where we found the father, we had talked about choosing a redhead, someone who might keep the memory of Ruth alive in some small way. We decided against it, though – it felt too strange and I'd be carrying those genes myself anyway, as my mother pointed out. In the end, we opted for a dark-haired, dark-eyed father to match Carla's colouring. Not your stereotypical Scandinavian. I wonder, though, if the child might end up looking like Ruth in any case. All sorts of unexpected things can happen in families.

'I don't want to forget her,' I say now.

'No one is asking for that.' She puts a warm hand on my cheek. 'Ruth will always be with you.'

It's a gorgeous morning. The sky is a singing blue and a cobwebby frost thaws out in the garden. The cold air stings my lungs. It's not a long trip to the tube and I've timed it right, I notice, as I grab a paper and glance down the platform – there are fewer people around, I'll probably get a seat.

The train comes in to South Ealing from Heathrow, scooping up travellers. One, tall and pale as a ghost, sits with a bulging rucksack at her knees. A couple of other women, who are small, perhaps Spanish, are deep in conversation. I listen for a moment. No, not Spanish, Italian. One of them, with an owlish though not unattractive face, wears a hat perched on the back of her head. The other has dyed hair and a strange bald patch behind one ear. The women, I think – it was always the women for me. But I know there is another reason why I watch travellers so intently.

I don't look at the paper until a few stops into the journey, after my hands have warmed up a little. And there he is on page four. He has put on weight, is greying at the temples, but there's still a smirk playing on his lips, as if he's enjoying a private joke with himself. I stare at his photograph for a long time and think of his hands on my sister all those years ago. Then I turn the page, so I don't have to look at him any more.

Alice

Today Alice has been feeling, not bad exactly, but a bit strange, as though her body chemistry has shifted, realigned. How much did she drink last night? She'd shared half a bottle of Merlot with George, which wasn't much by their standards, even these days. And they'd had a fairly early night. So what could it be?

Her colleague on the next desk slathers her arms with moisturiser as she trills on the phone. The smell, rich and musky, seems stronger than usual – Alice finds it oddly repellent. Bile rises from her stomach and she swallows hard.

She looks back at the screen. She had been thinking of Naomi, Ruth Walker's sister, who had been in her year at St Anthony's. She had been – still was – exceedingly pretty, with her huge dark eyes and olive skin. A history of art undergrad, she was gentler than her sister, less intimidating. Alice had liked her. They would bump into each other in the college bar and say, 'We must have that coffee.'

But Alice had become busy with the full-time job of being George's girlfriend and Naomi had fallen in with a different group, so the moment had passed. And later their gossipy exchanges became greetings and then nods, a raised hand across the quad. Alice suddenly felt sad. Had she been right to put all her eggs in one basket from the beginning, not to strike out on her own, to make George's life hers?

A thought occurs to her. She logs into Facebook and types 'Naomi Walker' into the search engine. The right Naomi Walker appears straight away. She hasn't changed her name. Alice can't really remember Naomi with boyfriends at college. Maybe she'd just been picky. Facebook asks Alice if she wants to befriend Naomi and, before she has time to think about it, she puts the cursor over 'Add Friend' and clicks the mouse.

'It's the man of the moment.' Alice is jolted back to the room.

'I'm sorry?' Alice definitely feels odd today.

'Your hubby,' says her colleague breathlessly.

George sometimes had this effect. And there he is, pacing towards her, with a wide smile and brandishing a bunch of sunflowers.

'George?' says Alice sharply. 'What on earth are you doing here?'

'I thought we could go out for lunch,' says George, striding over and giving her shoulder a squeeze and her colleague a conspiratorial wink. 'Can't a chap surprise his wife from time to time?'

'Well, yes, he can. But I think this is the first time

you've been here since the Christmas party. In 2010.' She adds mentally: where you drank too much and flirted outrageously with one of the interns.

'What's this?' George gestures at her computer screen with the sunflowers.

'Oh, nothing.' Alice hastily minimises Naomi's beaming face. 'Did you say you were going to take me out to lunch?' Her voice sounds unnaturally bright. 'What a treat! Where are we going?'

The restaurant is packed. City workers flushed with lunchtime wine – sleeves pulled up, ties loosened – lean towards each other in privately bellowed conversations. It is too hot, too loud. By the time they're seated, Alice has lost all enthusiasm for lunch; she doesn't really want to be here at all.

'Do you want wine, darling?' George asks, reaching for the list.

'Better not.' Alice glances down at the menu. 'I'm feeling a bit off today.'

Behind George, she notices a mother trying to nurse her baby. Even with a discreet napkin over her shoulder it's an incongruous place to breast-feed. The woman's face has the distracted, half-there expression of new motherhood.

'Maybe you're right.' George drops the wine list as quickly as he picked it up. 'Are you OK, darling?' He is being peculiar. Oddly attentive and fidgety.

Alice frowns. 'George, what's going on?'

He sighs, brushes a hand across his face. 'Look, I've got something to tell you.'

'Oh.'

'That girl you mentioned the other night?'

Before he says it, Alice has a sense of déjà vu: she knows, has always known, that this is the thing coming back for them.

'I have a confession to make: I did know her. We had a sort of thing in my second year. Way before I met you.'

'A thing?' says Alice sharply.

'Well, a fling thing. Yes.'

'So you lied.'

He shakes his head, adamant. 'No, not a lie. It wasn't a lie.'

'Yes,' she says. 'You said you didn't really know her.' She looks at his face, right at him.

George drops his gaze to the table. He picks up a knife and puts it down again.

'It wasn't important,' he says quietly. 'And I *didn't* really know her.'

He had made her look stupid again. And in front of their friends. Teddy would have known. Teddy and George knew all of each other's secrets from college.

'How long were you together?' She sounds shrill. The woman breast-feeding looks up. Alice lowers her voice. 'Were you in love with her?'

George frowns. 'A matter of weeks, really. No, it wasn't serious. And it was a long time ago.'

Alice closes her eyes. He's right, in a way. Why is she so worked up? But she imagines the looks exchanged between George and Teddy, the undercurrent of understanding. The feeling is like running her finger along an old scar – sensitive but not painful exactly.

'Why didn't you tell me before?'

'I was embarrassed. I didn't treat her very well and we fell out. And then, of course, when what happened happened . . .' He trails off.

'And what, George? You didn't want to be associated with a missing person? A possible suicide. Because what? It might reflect badly on you?'

George looks at her. He is pulling his honest face, one he does particularly well for the television cameras.

'Look – our fling was ancient history by then. It wasn't relevant. It's not relevant now. But I know you've got a bee in your bonnet about this girl. And once you'd done some digging, you might have found out.'

'So you're telling me because I might have found out.' Alice's fingers curl around the paper napkin on her lap, scrunching it into a tight ball. 'Nice one, George. That's brilliant.' She is angry now. 'Was she there?' she demands. 'On the night of the memorial ball? With you, I mean.'

George looks completely baffled. 'Darling, what on earth are you talking about?'

'There's red hair in the photograph.' She hadn't meant it to come out like this.

'What?' George rubs his forehead.

'In that photo of you and Dan, on your desk, there's a redhead on the edge of the photo. Was she there?'

'No,' says George adamantly. 'No. God knows where she was that night. Not with us. She couldn't stand me.'

'Why couldn't she stand you?' Alice can feel the bile rising again. 'Why?' she demands again.

There is no stopping it this time. Alice grabs her bag and coat and heads for the door. She makes it outside just in time to throw up in a window box.

She is still holding the napkin as she walks away from the restaurant. Alice wipes her mouth and fishes around in her handbag for her mobile and a mint. She'd known, somehow, from the moment she'd seen the girl on the train that George had been involved with her. She pushes the mint to the side of her cheek with her tongue. What else had she missed? She tries to call Christie, but the answerphone picks up.

'It's me,' Alice says. 'Call me back. There's something I need to talk to you about.'

She thinks next of Teddy, whose hand occasionally strays to her thigh under the dinner table, giving it a 'friendly' squeeze. He owes her a favour.

'Al!' He picks up immediately, sounding, as he always did, pleased with himself. 'What's up?'

Her voice comes out thin and formal: 'Teddy, hi. I've got a bit of a weird question for you, I'm afraid.'

'OK.' She hears the whine of his office door being closed. 'What is it? Everything OK? George all right?'

'George is fine.' She pauses, unsure how to begin. It starts to drizzle. She raises a hand above her head to protect her hair. 'I don't know if you remember my mentioning a girl we were at uni with the other night.' There's a silence. 'Who died?'

'Yes.'

She can hear him typing, imagines his fat fingers on the keyboard, his attention drifting already.

'I didn't know her very well.'

Alice takes a breath. 'George had a fling with her, didn't he?'

The typing stops. Teddy breathes rather heavily down the phone, not saying anything.

'I know he did,' Alice snaps after a moment. 'He's just told me.'

'Well, then why are you asking me?'

'What was she like?' Alice begins to trot to the tube station.

Teddy sighs. 'I honestly didn't really know her,' he says. 'And they were barely together any time at all.'

'You must know something?' Alice persists.

She can hear the tapping of his fingers again.

'She was a bit unstable,' he says eventually. 'I seem to remember her throwing George's things out of the window.'

Alice shelters for a moment under a shop canopy at Chancery Lane, watching people dash through the rain. Dropped newspapers melt into the pavement.

'Did he love her?'

'No,' Teddy laughs. 'Not at all. She was way too much.'

Alice imagines Teddy checking himself out in his monitor, running a hand through his thinning hair.

'Can I take you out for a drink, old girl? You sound as if you might need cheering up.'

'No, you're all right, Teddy.' Alice rolls her eyes. 'I'm not feeling very well. Thanks,' she says before she hangs up, though she's not sure what she's grateful for.

She was way too much, she thinks. It was a strange way to describe someone. And if Ruth was too much, what was Alice? Just enough. She sighs, feeling overwhelmingly nauseous again. Hesitating for a moment, she calls the office to tell them she'll be taking the rest of the day off. She makes an emergency afternoon appointment with her GP.

As she climbs down the steps to the tube, Alice hangs onto the banister like an old woman. She simply must have a seat on the train.

Finding her favourite place next to the door between carriages, she tilts her face towards the breeze coming through the window. The train snakes its way under London. So George had had a fling – as she suspected – with this girl. So what? Why did it matter? Because he'd lied? Again.

She'd given him an ultimatum when they had started trying for a baby. But perhaps the damage had already been done. It was like a nettle growing in her, stinging her insides. During their quieter, happier phases you could lop off the top, but never pull out the roots. The worst thing was the eternal sense of disappointment. And the slipperiness of it all: the never-knowing, the always-guessing, reading between the lines – sniffing the air, checking the sheets, watching the way he looked around a room. Constantly rubbing the clues between her fingers to see if it felt like another affair.

There had been a few dalliances, as he'd put it, when he first moved to London and she was in St Anthony's. Alice had got her head around those – just about – and retaliated with an unsatisfactory dalliance or two of her own. Much more painful had been the affair he'd had with a family friend in Witney when he was spending a lot of time there as an MP. After visiting one weekend, Alice had found a scrunchie in the bed of their cottage.

There had been a terrible scene. His mother had got involved, leaping to George's defence, of course. 'What do you expect him to do if you're in London working all the time?' she'd said accusingly. 'And it's not as if you have children.'

Her words stayed with Alice. It was as close as his mother had got to direct hostility, but there had been an undercurrent of disapproval as long as she could remember. When the affair ended around four years ago, she and George started trying for a baby, but she couldn't conceive. There was some talk of IVF after a couple of years, but then there had been a new case for her, a new project for him. There had always seemed to be something more pressing to focus on first and now her body was changing, her cycles were becoming longer. Her mother had had an early menopause, too. It seemed that their chance had passed.

The train fills up fairly quickly as it travels west. By Oxford Street, Alice is boxed in by bodies. It's stuffy in the packed carriage. Even the air whistling in through the carriage-door window smells stale. The acidity of the vomit burns her throat. Alice swallows, leans her head against the glass partition and looks through the door at the people clustered in the next carriage. One of them is wearing a green dress Alice recognises – she has the same one. It's made of wool with a high neck: she must be sweltering. Alice's gaze ascends the woman's body, up to her hairline. Her hair is swept up in a wide cream scarf, but the strands escaping it are, Alice can see, bright red.

She swallows again, closes her eyes and opens them. Her eyeballs are dry and tired. She pushes herself up a little from her seat, straining to see just a fraction of the woman's face, but it is turned into the crowd. You're being ridiculous, she tells herself. Are you going to do this every time you see a woman with red hair?

As the tube begins to slow as it reaches Bond Street, Alice sees the redhead push towards the door. If she could just check, just see her face, then she would know. She gets up from her seat, stepping over bags, nudging past people. 'Excuse me,' she mutters, swinging her arms out to steady herself. A woman in a too-tight navy skirt sighs at her loudly.

The blurred faces waiting on the platform come into focus. There's a wall of them outside. Alice fights through in the direction of the next carriage, but there is no sign of the woman she saw. She pushes faster through the crowd, but it is difficult against the tide of passengers getting on the train. Can she see red hair falling from a cream scarf? Is that a green dress vanishing into the distance?

Kat

Everybody knows what goes on in the first-floor loos during college parties. Still, Kat's heart sinks as she hears the unmistakable sound of two bodies shuffling into the cubicle next to her. In the right kind of mood, she might get a kick out of it, but she's feeling flat tonight. The twinges of pain in her abdomen had returned just as she and Ruth had arrived at the party and bumped into Richard. And even though Kat was wearing what she thought of as her Jessica Rabbit dress, with a slit in the fabric so high it almost reached her knickers – a poor choice, in hindsight – he had barely registered her.

'Who was he?' Ruth asked afterwards. 'He seemed nice.'

'Richard Wiseman,' Kat said shortly. 'And he is.' She'd thought of adding, *He likes you*, but then George, who had wheedled his way back into Ruth's favour, had bounded over and grabbed Ruth by the waist, and the evening had gone in a different direction. Kat wondered briefly if Richard's lack of interest had anything to do with the couple of one-night stands she'd had since she'd last seen him. Her most recent conquest, a skinny guitarist she'd met at the union, had been insatiable.

'You're really something,' he said, but a week later all that remained of him was a touch of this cystitis, making her dash for the loo and then just sit there in agony while nothing came out.

They're making a hell of a racket next door. It sounds as if he's carrying her into the cubicle like some chivalric knight, then drops her so she loses her balance, crashing against the flimsy partition.

'For fuck's sake, George,' giggles a girl's voice that sounds like Ruth's. 'Do be careful with me.'

'That wasn't my intention,' George chuckles.

The partition creaks as they push up against it, kissing. Kat shifts her legs away so that Ruth won't be able to recognise her shoes.

Very close to Kat's head, George grunts. There's the sound of a zip.

Ruth giggles again. 'We're all wrong on paper, aren't we?' she says.

'All wrong.' George's voice gets muffled in her hair.

More shuffling. The ceramic clunk of the toilet seat closing, the creak of George sitting down.

The noise of the music reverberates through the floor. There's the sound of another zip being undone, more kissing. Kat doesn't want to hear her friend have sex. She gets to her feet as quietly as she can. Somewhere on the landing a door slams, and the gust of air makes the bathroom door fan open and close again.

'George,' Ruth says and her meaning is unmistakable.
'George.'

His voice is thick. 'Are you OK?'

'Could we take it more slowly?'

'More slowly . . .' He says the words ponderously.

'Yeah.' Ruth's voice sounds small.

Kat feels a stab of empathy for her friend.

'I thought you were different.' The twinkle has gone from his voice. 'More adventurous.'

'I am.'

He sighs. 'OK. Do you want to go back down? Because I left the party for you.'

'How generous of you.' Ruth is trying to make light of it.

A zip coming up.

'George.'

'Look, Ruth, I know where this is going.' There's a rearrangement in the cubicle's choreography: Ruth moving off his lap, George getting to his feet. 'First time, you want it to be special . . . blah blah, candlelight and music. That's OK, that's fine. Go and do that with someone else and then come back to me when you want a proper fuck.'

'George.' Ruth sounds as if she has a knot in her throat. 'Why are you being such a prick?'

George chuckles, back to his cheeky self again. 'That's just who I am. You must have heard.'

The bolt of the door slides open and George is gone. Kat hears Ruth lock the door and there is a moment, as they both sit there, breathing, when she thinks she will say, 'Ruth, it's me. I'm sorry.' When she thinks she will repeat Richard's words: 'He is an unspeakable cunt.' But then there are footsteps and the sound of laughter, and Ruth is up and out of the cubicle and a girl's voice is saying, 'All right, Ruth?' And Ruth is saying, 'Yes, yes, just a bit too much wine,' and the other girl laughs and then there's the sound of the tap, the hand-dryer, footsteps.

Kat waits until the girl has gone into a cubicle herself before she returns to the party. She sees George before she sees Ruth. He is near the drinks table with Dan and after a couple of moments there's a burst of laughter from their direction.

Ruth is on her own, hiding in the far corner of the room, drinking in a determined fashion. Her glance keeps flitting back to George. He has his back to her. As Kat makes her way over to Ruth, picking her path delicately through the crowded room, she notices one of Ruth's hairs is streaked across the shoulder of his dinner jacket.

'You've got to stop looking at him,' Kat says quietly when she gets to Ruth. 'What happened?'

'It went wrong.' Ruth stares into her wine glass.

'How do you mean, it went wrong?'

'I lost my nerve.' Ruth looks down at her feet. There's a red line where her shoes have dug into her skin.

'He didn't want to wait.'

Ruth shakes her head. 'I don't think he . . .' she begins, then corrects herself: 'I think it's now or never.'

She glances over again. George's group has been joined by a couple of girls. One, in a particularly arse-skimming dress, has started to talk to him.

'Do you want it to be special?' Kat asks. 'Because it probably won't be. With him.' She takes out her cigarettes and offers Ruth one.

66

'I know it's not a grand romance, but I do like his spirit.' Ruth's voice sounds plaintive. 'I like making him laugh.' She takes a gulp of wine.

'For me, I just wanted to get it over with,' Kat says. 'I mean, it's uncomfortable however you do it, so why not do it quickly?'

Ruth nods. 'I shouldn't say this, but I can say it to you . . .' She lowers her voice. 'I feel like when I'm with George, people notice me.'

'You're daft.' Kat shakes her head, catches Richard's eye from the other side of the room. 'People notice you all the time anyway.'

Ruth takes another slug from her glass. 'I guess I hate to lose.'

One of the girls talking to George keeps touching her hair, gathering it up and dropping it down one shoulder, exposing her bare neck to him like a willing vampiric victim.

'I want another shot at it,' Ruth says. 'It was just a false start.'

'OK,' Kat says.

Richard's hair is messy, as usual. He's carrying a book in his hand.

'I don't want to be needy and clingy and *girlish*,' says Ruth, emphasising the last word. 'I want to be equal. I want to be powerful. I want to be free.'

'OK,' says Kat again, wondering if Ruth should ease up on the wine.

'I want,' says Ruth definitively, 'not to be a virgin any more.'

'Go and tell him.' Kat gives her a push. 'Not all of it – maybe just that last bit.'

George is still talking to the other girl. Their heads are close together as Ruth approaches; his hand is on the girl's forearm, as if to keep her attention. Ruth makes her way across the room towards them and stands for a few seconds, her face flushing while George ignores her. Kat wonders for a moment if she will give up on her mission – wonders, too, if Richard is watching as Ruth says, 'Excuse me,' to the girl, takes George's hand and leads him off, as Kat will hear later, not to the bathroom but a more private store room, where things go better the second time round.

Naomi

In the mornings our father smelled of aftershave and soap. When we woke, he'd be up already, starting his paperwork downstairs, but his scent lingered in the corridors of the hotel behind him. Our father was tall, with silvering auburn hair. He wore bow ties with his suits so as not to be like other people. It was embarrassing. He also wore leather shoes that clicked on the pavement as he walked.

'That's the sound of a real man walking,' our mother would say. 'I do like a man with proper leather shoes.'

'And a bow tie?' we would ask.

'Hmm,' replied our mother.

She always sounded less sure about that.

Our father's car was an Aston Martin with a personalised number plate, which was the most embarrassing thing of all. The Aston smelled of clean leather seats, as if it were still new. It purred along so close to the ground that we couldn't see over the hedges. The world looked different through the windows of the Aston. It didn't win our father many friends.

'You win some, you lose some,' our mum said of the car.

She drove a battered but sturdy Volvo without a personalised number plate. In her car, we would sit in the back, pushing our fingers through the guard to touch the dogs' wet noses. They weren't allowed near the Aston Martin.

But in the evening, the leather shoes and suit were gone, replaced with corduroys and old jumpers with patches on the elbows. He would do odd jobs in the hotel garden when he could – mow the lawn, build bonfires – and he smelled of wood smoke and beer when he came to kiss us goodnight. The rough texture of his jumper tickled us as we sat up in bed to hug him. He wasn't the best at bedtime stories – it wasn't really his thing. Our mother was better, revealing tantalising snippets from *Gone with the Wind* or acting out the narrative of operas with doll's house dolls – though not *Madama Butterfly* ('it's too sad'). Our mother had to be careful about things that were sad.

Our dad was good at sums and puzzles. Horses and riding. Dogs. Swinging us high in the air. Long walks on the windy clifftops. Our mother was for tummy aches and baking cakes and singing. She'd sing in the hotel bar on open-mike nights – never for long, just a couple of songs, which she'd murmur into the microphone with her eyes closed, her hair messy from a night's waiting in the restaurant.

The men in the bar would look at her face carefully then, as if they were looking at the sun. 'A rare beaut,' our father used to call her. 'You're my rare beaut,' he would say as he stood behind her in the kitchen and wrapped his arms around her, and she would smile and say, 'You're silly. Isn't your dad silly?' But she would look flustered, as though she liked it really.

The men who drank in the hotel never really forgave our father for stealing our mother – I think that's the way they saw it. They called him a spiv. Ruth dared me to ask our mum what it meant and I knew, even as I asked, that it was an ugly word – something we should have looked up in a dictionary rather than saying out loud. Our mother's fingers touched the corner of her apron, squeezing the material in a ball for a second.

'Where did you hear that?'

We had heard the word in the bar, from the mouth of Dai the Poet, a camp, overweight man in his fifties, with drama school enunciation and a nasty turn of phrase when he was drunk.

'What does it mean?' Ruth asked.

'It means people are jealous.' Our mother let go of the apron, brushed it down and looked away.

Of the many things our father was good at, making money was the one that attracted the most attention. It was his gift. He could see opportunities where other people couldn't; he could crack through the sums; he could glance at the restaurant or the bar and know, more or less, how much they would take that night or what they could do to make more. He had turned our grandmother's Pembrokeshire hotel from a bohemian labour of love into something profitable in just eighteen months.

'He came from nothing,' the posh men would whisper

in the bar. Like that was a bad thing: to create something from nothing.

'He's not even from here,' the locals would say. As if that were the final insult: that he had whisked away their most beautiful girl, made heaps of money and, worst of all, he didn't even have the decency to be Welsh.

The bar was full of tribes – the rich men who'd made their money early in life or inherited and come out to live on the coast; the locals who'd cram the bar on Fridays and Saturdays; or the holidaymakers whose drinking tended not to be bound by which day of the week it was – but our dad didn't belong to any of them.

Instead, we made a tribe of our own: Ruth and our father with their red hair, my mother and me, with our dark eyes. Neither parent had much tolerance for tales, though we never gave up trying to embroil them both in the ongoing battle of the halfway line, mainly in the car, where it existed as an imaginary border that separated Ruth's messy side from my neat one.

There were just eighteen months between us. We witnessed the very first moment we met on cine film, a silent movie in muted colours. Ruth, clutching Nunny, her pink toy rabbit, in our grandmother's arms at the front door, had stretched out to greet our mother as she came back from hospital carrying me in a large white blanket.

'Baby,' mouths our mother in the film, tilting my face, peeking through the blanket, towards Ruth.

'Baby,' repeats my sister, climbing out of our grandmother's arms to join me, heedless of the halfway line even then.

Alice

February 2016

It has been three weeks since Alice had approached Naomi on Facebook and had no response – three weeks, too, since the doctor had told her unequivocally that she was pregnant. The news had come as a shock to both of them: Alice wonders now if perhaps they had started getting used to the idea that they couldn't – or wouldn't. George had leaned heavily against the kitchen counter when she'd told him. He was quiet for what seemed like a long time. Eventually, he had said, 'Oh! darling, that's wonderful,' and come over to where she was sitting at the kitchen table to embrace her, pressing her face against his stomach.

A baby. A person made up from George and her. Alice tries hard to think of what such a person might look like and finds she can't picture it, can't imagine how George's strong features might be combined with her more delicate face. Lying in bed, she puts a hand on her stomach. Since her sixth week when she found out she was pregnant, she has been feeling extremely unwell indeed. She's had to take weeks off work and finds herself staggering around the house from the bedroom to the loo. It is not quite the euphoria she imagined. The sickness makes her feel light-headed, depleted. She has fitful dreams often set in St Anthony's, with Dan there too, and other people she hasn't seen for years. But the dreams are so vivid, so clear, it feels as if no time has passed at all.

When she feels well enough to get up, she wanders down to George's study. She trawls the internet looking up people on Facebook, searching for Ruth's face. In a weak moment, she decides to order Richard Wiseman's book but she clicks through too quickly and finds she has sent it to her work address. On a well-worn trail, she tends to return to George's desk, to try the drawers in case. Just in case.

Yesterday, a particularly bad day, she picked up the photo collage on his desk and looked at it again. It took her a moment to realise, but the photos seemed to be in a different order from when she last saw them. She rubbed her eyes and looked again. Yes, they'd been changed around. Her eyes returned to the photo of George and Dan, and it seemed smaller, as if it had been cropped. Alice traced her finger around the edge. The red hair had disappeared. It had been cut away.

She had called Christie to talk about it but found she couldn't quite bring herself to say it out loud. Perhaps she'd wait to see her in person. Instead, she said, 'Did you know Naomi Walker is pregnant, too? I noticed on Facebook.' It had been something a mutual friend had written, tagging both Naomi and Alice in the post.

Christie paused. 'No, I hadn't heard.'

'It just made me think,' said Alice, playing with the cord of the house phone. 'It just made me think that if Ruth were still alive, it might give her a reason to come back.'

Christie had been silent for a long time. She has been quite short with Alice recently. Maybe she just thinks Alice is being a wet blanket. Christie efficiently pushed out three bouncing boys without any fuss and was back to work within six weeks of the last one's arrival.

'Don't you think, darling,' she said, 'that you're being weird about this?'

What had she been like before she met Christie? Alice tries to focus. She had always thought of herself as, if not mousy exactly, someone who had to try rather hard. She had started college a term late because of glandular fever, which had lingered for months after her A levels. By the time she arrived, other freshers had separated into clusters. She'd had to make up for the lost months. So she was grateful to have happened upon Christie, who had the bedroom above her and invited her up one morning for coffee. Sitting there, as Christie fussed over a compact Italian coffee machine, Alice noticed the Post-it notes on the wall above her desk: 'Fit not fat' and 'You can always do better'. And while part of her shrank from the blatant ambition, another part admired it. Was this what it took to improve oneself?

Alice and Christie weren't alone in striving in that way. Alice recognised the signs in other girls: grey smudges under their eyes, the way they pushed their food around their plates in formal hall, watching the men, watching the other girls, measuring up the competition. Alice spent her days measuring, too: measuring her waistline, measuring time, calculating hours left in the library or minutes on the rowing machine in the college gym.

There was always so much to be done. There were cocktail parties and yoga classes, ballroom dancing, rowing, the library – always the library, armed with lists of books so long that she would feel a lump in her throat when they were handed to her in tutorials.

Alice observed how Christie took care of herself: her manicures, her glossy hair. Christie, she noticed, never drank too much. She sipped her drinks, put them down for long stretches of time, and seemed to listen intently to other people without saying a huge amount herself. Despite not having the obvious charisma of other, more show-offy girls, Christie's cool self-possession and dry wit meant friends flocked to her, but for some reason she chose Alice, of all people, to be her closest confidante. 'I can tell we're both alike,' she said that morning over a cappuccino. 'I think we know the value of things.'

One afternoon, after Alice had fallen into bed with a handsome rugby player and was feeling rather dreadful following his retreat, Christie had popped down to see her. Surveying the dark room, Christie had pulled the curtains open, drenching it with light. She'd perched on the end of Alice's bed and said crisply: 'I don't want to lecture you, but they don't stay with the ones who sleep with them straight away.'

'It doesn't sound very modern,' huffed Alice.

'It isn't,' Christie agreed. 'But it works. Especially with the rugby boys – they're the worst. Or you can just muck around, have fun.' She made it sound like a bad thing. 'It's up to you, of course, but did you have fun? Really?'

Alice thought of the previous evening – the flush of flirtation over cocktails, the initial rush of excitement, yes, but with sweatiness, disappointment, the prickling of embarrassment hot on its heels.

'My mother says these are the years,' said Christie.

'The years for what?'

'Finding the right person. We'll never have it as good as this – never again be surrounded by so many bright young men.' She looked hard at Alice. 'Do you know Magnus? The only decent hairdresser in town. He's *da bomb*.' Christie had the unfortunate habit of trying to pep up her rather conservative way of speaking with occasional street lingo. It didn't really work.

Alice put a hand to her hair. 'No, I don't.'

'I'm going to take you to see him. He'll sort you out. My treat.'

As she sat in Magnus's chair, her hair falling from her in drifts, Alice suddenly felt unspeakably sad, as if she were being shorn of her old self; as if pieces of her childhood were falling away from her. She closed her eyes.

'It's going to be *so* worth it,' said Christie from behind her, reading her mind. And, strangely enough, she was right. Alice emerged from the salon as if from a chrysalis. Her brown hair became a short blonde bob, framing her eyes and making her look neat, in charge and altogether less mousy.

'We need to get you some clothes to match,' Christie said. 'Let's start with a dress.'

That night, in her new Karen Millen dress, George, in

his final year, noticed Alice for the first time. It was not a style Alice would have normally gone for, with a bodice in turquoise and a hot pink skirt, but it attracted the eye, as Christie put it, and emphasised her tiny waist. It cost her a serious chunk of her student loan, but it was worth it for the reaction it got. In between making eyes at George, she calculated how she was going to live for the rest of the term. She'd certainly have to work through the holidays.

At the end of the night, George walked her back to her room, but she allowed him only to the bottom of the staircase.

'So, which one's yours?' He smiled, looking up the stairs.

'You'll see.' She smiled back. 'Maybe.'

His mouth looked sulky for a moment; he took a step closer to her.

'But it would be fun to see it now.'

Keep it light, Christie had said.

'Yes, but it'll be something for you to look forward to.'

Alice stepped closer too, glanced up through her eyelashes at George.

He reached for her hand, his eyes glassy, unfocused. It wasn't quite how she'd imagined it. Standing on tiptoes, she kissed his cheek for a second, inhaling the whisky and aftershave smell of him, then turned quickly and trotted up the stairs.

'Anna, come back!' George had called after her petulantly. 'Anna!'

'No,' she shouted back. 'And it's Alice.'

Naomi

She always had a temper. She broke my arm as a child – an accident, of course: I'd been cheating at Grandmother's Footsteps and she pushed me too hard, misjudged her own strength.

Then there was my first boyfriend, Jamie Havers. A boy with brown hair and freckles. He used to follow me around Pony Club Camp when I was eleven. I liked him, but I didn't want to kiss him, so he stopped talking to me and told the other boys I was frigid. It made me cry.

The day after he dumped me, Ruth asked the boys if she could join in with their game of touch rugby. I remember it was a hot August day and being outside all week had tanned the boys' noses. Mrs Jenkins, who was in charge of looking after the children at camp, was wedged into a deckchair outside her caravan, keeping an eye on everyone and watching the game.

Ruth considered the scene for a bit and then approached the biggest of the boys. 'Can I play?'

He squinted down at her. 'There aren't any other girls playing.'

'So?'

'Let her play,' said a cheery dark-haired boy who was friends with Ruth.

She hung back at first, running for the ball but not trying too hard. She was biding her time for when Jamie got hold of it, which he did before too long. He was a good player, tenacious and nippy. But Ruth was faster. As he ran for the try-line, she began to give chase and just before he reached it, she caught the edge of his T-shirt in her hand and gave it a yank so that he fell, stumbling, to the floor. Then the pair of them were wrestling for the ball, rolling over and over each other. It got so vicious that the other boys started jeering and even Mrs Jenkins sounded panicked as she heaved herself up from her deckchair to disentangle them.

Ruth came out of the tussle wild-haired, with a scratch down her face, but she laughed off any fuss from me. 'It's just rugby,' she said. 'Just a fight for the ball.'

Where we were from rugby was a religion. The bar didn't have a telly – Grandma wouldn't hear of it – but the locals would gather afterwards to discuss the game. Everyone had an opinion on it.

We knew our father was different, though: he didn't care as much for rugby as other men did, but he had to pretend. He was proud of the differences he'd chosen – the bow tie and flashy car – but there were ways in which he wanted to be the same, wanted to fit in with the posh crowd. Loo not toilet, lunch not dinner, long-sleeved shirts not short. There was so much to remember and apart from the voice, the slight flatness of his vowels, you'd almost never have known.

'What do you think about these changes to the scrum rules?' he asked one day in the bar after a game, cribbing from a newspaper article he'd just read.

'It'll make it harder on the pitch. Not that *you'd* know.'

It went quiet, the hum of conversation dying down for a moment the way it does in films. Dai the Poet had been drinking in The Swan all day. His hands looked swollen on his glass as he handed it to our mother for a refill. No please or thank you.

'What do you mean?'

Our father wasn't as drunk as Dai – he didn't drink like that – but he'd had a couple of beers and you could tell, if you knew him well, when he was about to lose his temper: a quick tightening of the mouth, which Ruth inherited, a change in the focus of his eyes.

Dai's laughter came out like a breath. 'Not a game *you* played at school, I imagine.'

Our mum, with Dai's glass in her hand, paused for a moment before filling it.

'Where was that again?' Dai said. 'Your school?'

Our father ignored the question. 'I played rugby at school,' he said shortly, looking away from Dai as the lie came out.

He never talked about his childhood. And you could see that Dai – I never knew why they called him Dai; he sounded as English as they came – guessed, too, and that it was a test.

When the glass she had been holding shattered on the tiles, our mother didn't do anything to clear it up, just

81

looked at Dai steadily: 'I remember coming to see you play rugby.' She glanced at our dad. 'He wasn't very good.'

Later, chopping avocados in the kitchen, she said to us: 'Public school boys. They are soft on the outside and hard on the inside.' She held up the stone of an avocado. 'Be careful of them, girls. They seem so polite, so courteous . . .' She paused, looking for the words. 'I don't know what those schools do to them.' She didn't usually speak to us like that. As if we were already grown up. 'And the worst thing is,' she added, looking sadder than I'd ever seen her, 'he wants to be one of them.'

Kat

The first time sets a precedent. George likes doing it in dangerous places, Ruth tells Kat. In places where they might get caught. Their relationship – if that's what it can be called, for there is no wining or dining or snuggling or watching films – involves doing it in risky places. They do it in George's car a lot at night and sometimes in wild places during the day. When they are particularly bored or drunk they do it in the toilets of clubs, once after hours on the pool table in the college bar. They do it on golf courses and on the beach, though Ruth draws the line at George's suggestion of the Shack – a tiny stone changing room on North Beach, with dripping tiles and the stench of urine.

Kat doesn't see Ruth much in these early weeks and when she does catch her there are subtle changes – her eyes glassy, a high colour to her cheeks. Some girls, once they discovered sex, well, that was it. There had been a girl at school – quiet, bookish – and then she'd got into men and completely flunked her exams. Kat knew as well as anyone how unhinged it could make you. But she'd found, though she was still getting to know Ruth, that she missed her when she wasn't around, missed her loopiness, her irreverence.

When Kat asks, over lunch, how things are going, Ruth goes quiet for a bit. She says eventually: 'It's the most exciting sex I've ever had.'

Kat smiles and says, before she can stop herself: 'Well, it's the only sex you've ever had, really. Still . . .' She clinks her glass against Ruth's. 'Well done.'

'Thanks.' Ruth looks irritated.

'At least one of us is getting some,' says Kat, trying to make up for it.

They're at the Two Pheasants on the outskirts of town. Kat had wanted to go somewhere new and she'd heard about the four-legged stuffed pheasant mounted on the bar. The two pheasants, which had been sewn together by a taxidermist with a dark sense of humour, were encased in glass sharing four legs, two heads and, weirdest of all, three eyes. Other stuffed animals peered out from dark corners of the room – a surprised-looking fox, a dishevelled owl.

'It's creepy, isn't it?' Ruth had said when they'd arrived.

Kat laughed. 'It's kitsch, darling. I thought you'd love it. The owner's an aging burlesque dancer – with an eye for a pretty boy, I think.' She'd looked towards the barman, who had looked straight back at them. Well, at

Ruth, really. His hair was unruly and there was a glint of silver at his ear, like a pirate. He'd seemed distracted when Kat ordered their food, kept glancing over to where Ruth was huddled in the corner.

'That guy we bump into sometimes,' Ruth says suddenly. 'Richard?'

'Yeah?'

'You like him, don't you?'

Kat looks down at her food. 'I suppose I do.'

'Why are you weird about it?'

'What do you mean?'

'Well, you talk about everything else so openly. Why are you so weird about him?'

'I'm not weird,' Kat says pertly, adding, 'I think he likes you.'

Ruth blinks. 'He doesn't know me.'

'Well, sometimes . . .' Kat doesn't know how to end the sentence, so she starts again. 'Does that matter?'

Thinking of Richard makes her feel guilty. The last time they'd chatted he'd brought up the subject of Ruth and George again. 'It's not just sour grapes,' he said with a short laugh. 'Honestly, Kat, he's bad news.' He looked for a moment as if he were going to say more, but in the end he just said: 'He hurts people.'

Kat weighs up the moment. 'Be careful, Ruth. I know what it feels like now: you feel all sexy and liberated,' she says. 'The endorphins are flowing. You feel amazing.'

'Shh.' Ruth looks embarrassed. The barman glances over again.

'But it's usually followed by a crash. Especially with someone like George.' Kat lights a cigarette. 'It's the un-Holy Trinity: he's got a reputation. He's not in love with you. And sooner or later he's going to get bored.'

'Ouch.' Ruth shifts in her seat. The leg of her chair scrapes across the floor. She takes a cigarette, lights it and inhales angrily. They sit in silence for a while. 'Honestly, I know it's not the love match of the century, but I can cope with it.'

'OK.' Kat stubs her cigarette out. She smiles. 'I'll buy you a drink and we can talk about the sex again.'

At the bar, Kat finds herself peering back at the pheasant to see if she can find the seams, but the lighting in the pub is too dim and the taxidermist has done too good a job. She feels uneasy about Ruth and George, that she hasn't done enough to pass on Richard's warning, but then Kat had been in similar situations lots of times and, like Ruth, she had never seen things for what they were until it was too late. What could one do?

The barman is polishing a glass, which he puts down for a second to serve her. Kat's about to give her order, when he leans in over the bar, rather close to Kat's face, and says in a low voice: 'Why is your friend ignoring me?'

Kat follows his gaze and turns back to Ruth, who is fishing around in her handbag for something. She is sometimes surprised by her friend's effect on men. Ruth is looking scruffy today, anyway, a bit tired. Maybe it's her red hair: she is sitting in a pool of light under a window and the sun catches in it in a spectacular fashion.

Kat laughs uneasily. 'I don't think she is.' It was an odd way to approach a girl, if that's what he was doing.

'So, she hasn't said anything about me?' he persists.

'No,' says Kat shortly. 'No, I'm afraid, she hasn't.' She

sizes him up – good-looking, dark curly hair – still, there was something she didn't like about him, which struck a false note. He's wearing an earring in his left ear, but his voice is well-spoken, as if he's trying to be something he's not. A trust-fund student pretending to be a pirate.

'I've been thinking about her. Hoping she'd come back in . . .'

Kat sighs. 'She hasn't been in here before.' Why won't he just take her bloody order?

He laughs and picks up a glass. 'How would you know? Do you do everything together?'

Kat feels wrong-footed. She looks back at her friend. Maybe Ruth *has* been here before.

His voice becomes a whisper. 'She was here last week on her own, looking for a pick-up. We spent the evening together.' He is polishing the glass very slowly. 'Doing it all night,' he adds unnecessarily. 'And now nothing. No reaction at all. It's like we've never met.'

Kat looks back at Ruth again. Strange that she hadn't said anything. 'Right,' she says vaguely, not sure what to make of it. She doesn't feel like a drink so much any more. She'd been wrong about this pub: maybe it wasn't nice, after all. Maybe there *was* something sinister about it.

'She might have been dicked around before, but we're not all the same,' he says as she walks away. 'Some of us have feelings.'

Ruth is looking at her by the time Kat reaches the table. 'What was all that about?'

'He thought he knew you.' Kat puts her cigarettes into her handbag and slings it over her arm. 'Let's get a drink somewhere else.'

Ruth looks at him and laughs. 'I've never seen him before.'

Kat glances back at the barman as they leave the pub. 'That's what I said.'

Alice

March 2016

Everything seems to have mellowed while Alice was doing what she now thinks of as her house arrest. Now her first trimester has passed, she has returned to work to find colleagues in shirtsleeves, crocuses pushing up in the window boxes outside her office. She's feeling a lot better: not entirely herself, but stronger nevertheless and happy to be around people again.

Her client, Elizabeth Gregory, is clearly feeling better, too. Her bitterness has mellowed. She's been growing out her bob, letting her grey hair wave to her shoulders. Her clothes are different, as well. Today she's wearing a long, flowing skirt and a loose blazer. There's no sign of her Eighties power suits, or the tight fury around her mouth Alice had spotted before.

'You know what I find strange,' Elizabeth says now. 'I never once saw him on the loo.'

'You wanted to see your husband on the loo?' Alice asks, struggling to keep a straight face. She knows Elizabeth well enough to tease her.

The older woman shakes her head, smiling. 'It's not about that. It's about intimacy. I lived with him for thirty-nine years and we never did that in front of each other. I don't even know how many people he's slept with.'

'Well, lots of partners don't know that information about each other,' says Alice. She has absolutely no idea if that's true or not, but she doesn't have a clue how many women George has slept with. She dreads to think. 'Relationships are different.'

Since her separation from her husband, George's former colleague, Elizabeth had got in touch with an old flame through Facebook. She looks happy for it, happier than Alice had ever seen her. Her husband's relationship with his researcher, meanwhile, had fizzled out and he was desperate to win his wife back, but the balance of power had changed. Elizabeth was determined not to return.

'It's what I'm gaining I need to focus on,' she tells Alice. 'I want passion. I want intimacy. It's my turn for that.'

'Nevertheless,' Alice smiles politely, 'I think it might be worth being discreet about it at the moment – what with the press interest.'

She's concerned that Elizabeth's new relationship is distracting her from the bigger picture. It's an enormous thing to lose a partner: the one close witness to most of your adult life. George is no picnic, but it's hard to imagine life without him. She had read recently about the effect of losing a long-term partner being like a loss of self because it *was*, actually, in a way, a loss of yourself. We store memories in other people: that's why she can't change a plug and George doesn't know anyone's birthday. Even Teddy's.

It was a sleepy Sunday in her first year when Alice had first seen him. She and Christie were sitting on the lawn outside the bar enjoying a gin and tonic on an unseasonably warm March afternoon that had brought everyone out of their rooms into the quad. A lank-haired second year strummed the chords from 'Sweet Child o' Mine' by an open window. Alice was finding it hard to concentrate on her book.

There was a roar from inside the bar and a crowd of third years spilt out. They were an eye-catching group; Alice had seen some of them before and they looked particularly good in the soft afternoon light. The best-looking of them, lean and angular, led the way to the centre of the quad, holding a yard of ale in his hands like an ostensorium. The group gathered, quasi-solemnly, around one in particular. His face was tanned dark, his hair brown and wavy, combed back off his face, which had a sleepy, aquiline quality. The good-looking one, holding the yard, presented it to his friend, almost formally.

'Cheers, chaps!' he grinned.

And they started to shout: 'Drink, drink, drink!'

'Who's that guy?' Alice asked.

'The hot one?' asked Christie. 'That's Dan Vaughan.'

'No, the shorter one with the yard of ale.'

'George Bell.' Christie hesitated. 'He's got a bit of a rep,' she said eventually. 'Don't sleep with him. Take it from me.'

'What – have you?'

Christie shook her head. 'No, I quite fancy his friend – Teddy Shelton?'

Alice glanced at a large boy, with darting eyes, on the edge of the group. 'Him?'

'Yes, there's something about him.' Christie smiled slyly. 'And his family owns a castle in Scotland, but, you know, it's not really about that . . .'

'Christie!' Alice flicked a bit of grass at her friend. 'You're awful.'

'I don't know what you're talking about,' Christie said primly and she went back to her book.

It hadn't been long after that that George and Alice got together. She had made him wait three weeks. Probably the longest George had had to wait for anything. It had been worth it in the end. They had spent a whole weekend holed up in his room, drinking champagne and listening to Pink Floyd.

She sighs now at the memory and returns to her client. 'The toilet thing is neither here nor there,' she says apologetically. 'But if you're sure you'd like to proceed with the divorce, we can go ahead.'

'I have never been so sure of anything,' says Elizabeth, her eyes shining. 'I wouldn't exchange how I feel now for all the security in the world.'

George hadn't always been respectful in bed in those early days. Once, when a gang of them had gathered in his room for the after-party, he tried it on while the others were still there lolling around smoking weed. 'No,' Alice murmured when he started tugging down her pants as they were huddled under the covers snogging. And then, more loudly, in a voice that sounded like a schoolteacher: 'I said *no*.'

She had gathered her things and marched back to her room, hearing Dan laugh as she left, saying: 'Well, she's not like the others.'

Who were the others? Alice used to feel haunted by George's others. They only had a couple of terms together in St Anthony's before he graduated and moved down to London, and there had been a lot of toing and froing in the years before she joined him in the city, a lot of breaking up and getting back together. Shagging around on George's part, tears on Alice's. She'd slept with a couple of other people too, but no one got her in bed like George did. She never found it as exciting with anyone else.

'Marriage is an exchange, isn't it?' her client says now. 'Not like prostitution,' she laughs. 'I don't mean that. But, in terms of, "You give me this, I give you that." I traded excitement for safety. Now, I don't want to feel safe any more. I want to feel something else.'

Alice nods. It had been the other way round for her: George had made her feel alive, vital. Alice had had a lifetime of feeling safe before meeting George. Her upbringing had been secure, risk-averse. With him, she had known things would always be interesting. She knew from the beginning that he would make something of his life, that they wouldn't live quietly. She wasn't stupid – she always knew there were skeletons, too. More than once, some girl or other had tried to take her aside to warn her off George. But she'd got used to batting away such admonitions.

'It's fear that keeps people together so long, you see.' The woman taps the desk with a manicured fingernail. 'And I'm not afraid any more.'

Alice wonders if she agrees with this, after her client has gone. She returns to her desk after showing her out to discover an Amazon parcel waiting for her and a note from the office manager. 'We just cleared out the post cupboard and found this hidden at the back.' For a moment, she can't remember what she had bought, but, as she rips the package open, she gets a thrill from seeing Richard Wiseman's face in black and white looking up from the back cover. It's his book – she'd forgotten she'd ordered it when she was ill.

Her hands are shaking as she flicks through the pages to find what she is looking for, but she needn't have worried, the bright red hair makes it easy to find. There she is, at the heart of the book, looking straight at the camera or what must have been the man behind it. It's a direct gaze, slightly challenging. It must have been taken on a cliff walk in St Anthony's – it's a spot Alice recognises, a bench overlooking the sea. Ruth's hair is gleaming in the sunlight. Her face is pale. It's hard to know, from her expression, what was about to pass between the photographer and her: it could be a kiss or, just as easily, an argument.

Sometimes Alice has to get up in the middle of the night to check things – an email she's sent, a document she's working on – having convinced herself, after hours of tossing and turning, that she's got a detail wrong. More often than not, however, she hasn't. It's the mind playing tricks. That's the feeling she has as she looks at the picture:

that she had been wrong to doubt herself, that her instinct was right. But it's better even than that, much better. This is the woman she saw. She is absolutely convinced of it. 'I was right,' she says aloud.

'What?' says her colleague on the next desk, only sounding half interested.

'I was right about something,' says Alice. She doesn't care if she sounds mad, she just doesn't care. 'Something important.'

Naomi

In the office, Tim is sorting through the post. We still get plenty, but not as much as when I first started working for the charity just after uni. These days we keep in touch with relatives of the missing more through email and social media. I began on a volunteer basis during my holidays. It made me feel useful, sifting through the letters, following leads that came in. But, deep down, I knew the reason why I was here: it was because if anything came in about her body, I would be the first to hear.

It's unlikely, of course. I still have to tell myself that. Unlikely but not impossible. The coroner told us that a body lost near an estuary might never be recovered. And the fact that the dress she was swimming in was so torn when it washed up was a very bad sign.

The early days were terrible. It started with Richard arriving at our cottage, knocking on the door, waking me from a strange alcohol-infused sleep.

'Naomi,' he said, looking tired, sheepish. None of us slept much the night of the ball. 'Is Ruth in?'

It was pouring with rain, so I let him in quickly. 'I thought she was with you.'

'No,' he said. And I could immediately tell that something had gone badly wrong between them.

'Oh,' I said. 'I'm pretty sure she's not here. I put my head round the door when I came in this morning and then went straight to bed.'

Did the panic begin then? I don't think so. Life still felt normal as we checked her room, where the bed was made, her jeans still hanging over a chair as if waiting for her to come back.

He hung around in the kitchen for a bit. I could see he was agitated, that they'd had another fight, but he wouldn't tell me anything and I had my own concerns that day. We were friendly then, but I didn't know him as well as I do now.

He left after a while to finish packing, telling me to send Ruth his way when she came home, and I thought about going to bed again for a bit, so I wasn't frightened. Not in the way I was when the policeman arrived an hour or so after Richard – just a local guy, holding her red shoes in one hand, her handbag in the other.

'Is Ruth Walker in?' he asked.

'No,' I said for the second time that day. 'Where did you find those?'

'A member of the public found them on the beach,' he said.

I looked at the red shoes he was carrying and I felt a kind of fear I had only experienced once before, when our father died. A fear that felt like a trapdoor giving way beneath my feet.

'When did you last see her?' he asked.

When you lose someone like this – when they go without warning – you examine all the signs over and over. You look at what she carried, what she wore, who she spoke to, what she said. You look for significance in every little clue. We tell ourselves we will know the truth when we see it; that because we love someone so much we will know in our gut whether they are dead or alive, but the truth is, we don't know. We don't know at all.

For me, there is solace in work: the routine of it, the satisfaction of a job done – black ink on yellow paper, Post-it notes. Ruth would laugh at me, but it helps – that feeling of satisfaction at piecing together other people's lives still gives me some sense of purpose. And I know what the relatives are going through. A few of us here do. Everything has changed in the years since I've worked for the charity. Social media has done wonders for looking for people. One of the first things people tend to do when a relative or friend goes missing now is set up a Facebook page or create a tweet that asks everyone to retweet it. As one of the youngest here, I got roped into that side of things, even though social media sometimes unsettles me: for every genuinely helpful person out there, there's a lunatic at their computer, trying to mislead you. And social media has made it easier for word of false sightings to spread. Something that has become a particular bugbear of mine.

Ruth's case is very different from most. Often, we have even less to go on – the people we're looking for have left one day for school or work or, as the cliché goes, popped out for cigarettes never to return. With Ruth, sudden as it was, everything pointed to her drowning. When I started volunteering here, my mother asked: 'Are you sure you want to do that sort of work?' She knew what I was doing: watching, waiting, hoping.

There was no social media fifteen years ago – no online campaigns with catchy slogans and hashtags. Everyone's more media-savvy these days – if it had happened now we might have come up with a symbol for the search: red shoes, perhaps. A few years back, after the Canoe Man turned up alive, Richard, spurred on by fresh hope, suggested dedicating a Facebook page to Ruth – somewhere people could post sightings – and I considered it for a bit, but decided in the end that I couldn't do it to my mum. People can always find you, if they need to, if they have something important to say.

I switch on the computer and go to the kitchen to make myself a peppermint tea. The course I went on advised starting the day with some positive news on our Facebook page and there is more than you would think: 99 per cent of all missing cases are solved within a year. I log on and look first at responses we have received overnight. I answer a few questions and post something cheery about one of our fundraisers.

'You've got a parcel here,' says Tim and he tosses a package in my direction. It is large, but soft, and weighs almost nothing at all. For a moment, I am frightened by the softness and think perhaps I have been sent some form of hate mail: a dead rat, roadkill, by an unbalanced someone who doesn't want to be found. It has been taped down particularly thoroughly, so I get up to borrow a pair of scissors.

On the way I bump into Sue, who is back from holiday and makes a big fuss about how much my bump has grown in the three weeks since she's been away. It seems incredible that I'm sixteen weeks in. I'm lucky – apart from some queasiness early on, I've felt pretty well. I have friends who have been terribly sick, who could sniff out everything from chewing gum in a back pocket to what sort of hand soap their husbands have used that day with a dreadful clarity. Some have turned against the most innocuous flavours – peppermint, camomile.

I don't say this to Sue now but, despite myself, ever since my encounter in the supermarket at the beginning of the year, I have started thinking of the baby as a boy. I imagine a redheaded toddler playing on the beach in Wales. I think of how I will never let him out of my sight, never let him swim alone.

It's later that I remember the package, which I've left absent-mindedly on the scanner. It has been secured very tightly, with layers of brown tape. I cut off the end and I smell something unbearably sweet and familiar. Coconut oil.

Things continue in the office as if nothing has happened. Tim and Sue are talking about the weekend. Sue laughs. The phone goes; Tim picks it up. Outside, the pub next door is receiving its Monday delivery; the beer barrels crash against the concrete.

And there is Nunny.

Ruth's childhood toy looks up at me with his goggly glass eyes: orange marbles with large dark irises now worn at the surface, clouded over as if by cataracts. His once-pink coat has faded to grey with large patches worn away completely.

She was never without him as a child: in every photograph – by the sea, on a pony, posing on a tractor – there he is next to her. She carried him everywhere in an obsessive sort of way, carefully stowed away in a green bag, with a selection of other items: a yellow spoon, a box of Sun-Maid raisins . . . Our mum had to confiscate the green bag to wash it and Ruth screamed and screamed. After that none of it smelled the same, she said. She gave up on the green bag, but she kept Nunny.

Our grandmother had to knit clothes for him to stop him from falling apart. Ruth left him once on a train, but he found his way back to her. That was the way it was: as if they couldn't be separated.

It doesn't feel real. I take a pinch of skin on the back of my right hand with my left fingers, let the nails grip it until it feels tender with pain. If I were asleep, that would have woken me.

Who, *who* would send me Nunny in the post?

I pick up the phone. I misdial the first time because my brain is fog.

'Hello, darling. You at work?' My mother always asks that. Her voice is bright and sharp. She speaks loudly over the murmur of the radio.

'Did you send me Nunny in the post?' Framed as an accusatory question, it sounds ridiculous.

'What?' I hear her turn the radio off, give me her attention.

'Did you send me Nunny in the post?'

She is quiet.

'Ruth's Nunny,' I say to be more specific.

'Nunny? Ruth's Nunny?'

'Yes.'

'In the post?'

'Yes.'

'Whyever would I do that?'

'Somebody has. Somebody sent him.'

'Somebody sent him?'

'Yes.'

'In the post?' she asks again, as if arranging the facts in her head.

'Yes.'

'Where to?'

'To work.'

'Why would they do that?'

'I don't know. To hurt me?'

But I can't think of anyone who would want to hurt me, who would wish me harm in that way. The thing is: I'm not sure the same could be said of Ruth. Not that she had enemies exactly. Enmities, perhaps. Particularly in the weeks before she went when she seemed jittery all the time, restless and angry. I think of Ruth's friend Kat shrieking at her, that awful scene with Richard when the porters had to get involved, of a sombrero toppling at a party as Ruth punched the person wearing it.

We are quiet for a moment.

'When did you last see him?' I ask. For some reason, Nunny had always been a 'him'.

'I can't remember.' My mother flusters more easily these

days; her memory isn't what it was. 'I can't remember,' she says again. 'Maybe he got lost in the move.'

Our mother still owns the land where the hotel stands and rents the hotel to a couple from Cardiff, but she has moved to a cottage inland. After Ruth's death she found managing the hotel too much – that and looking out at all that water.

'The last time I remember seeing him he was on her bed in her old room at home,' she says eventually. She is quiet for a moment, perhaps thinking, like me, that that memory could have come from any time. 'Did she take him to St Anthony's with her? Might Richard have had him?'

'I can't recall seeing him in St Anthony's. And no, I don't think so.' I shake my head. 'It doesn't sound like the sort of thing Richard would do.'

'I can't think who else might remember anything.' She sighs. 'What about that Kat girl?' Our mother had never liked Kat.

'I can drop her a line, but I don't think they were very friendly by the end.'

Kat had come to Ruth's memorial, though – tottering around on those ridiculous heels, her make-up sliding down her face.

'Oh yes, of course.' My mother's voice sounds small. I wonder if I should have said anything, should have called Carla instead. Then she asks: 'What about the postcode?'

'The postcode?'

'On the parcel,' she says breathlessly. 'The postmark, I mean. Where was he sent from?'

I pick up the parcel. My name and address have been scrawled in capital letters. I look for the postmark. My thoughts are so scrambled that it takes a moment for the penny to drop.

'Well?' my mother asks impatiently.

'St Anthony's,' I say.

It still feels like something from a dream. I hold Nunny up to my face and breathe him in. She's still there, very faint, under the scent of coconut.

Kat

There is more than one Ruth, Kat realises, in the way there is more than one of all of us. Ruth the shy Welsh virgin. Ruth the drama queen. Ruth the nymphomaniac. Ruth her now very drunk friend, flush-cheeked, glass of wine in hand, talking about her favourite subject: George.

'This is how addiction works,' she tells Kat solemnly. 'I used to see it all the time in the hotel bar. There would be these guys who would turn up as soon as we opened for lunch. They'd have their own stools, they would nod their order to the barman, without having to say it aloud, and they would just sit there until their money ran out. Or the bar closed. Or they just couldn't keep themselves upright any more.

'There is a moment,' she holds up a finger as if giving a soliloquy on stage, 'when something stops being a source

105

of pleasure and becomes a source of pain. It is so precise, so exact, it could be plotted on a graph.'

Kat doubts somehow that the specifics of love, or lust-gone-bad, really, would work on a graph, but she suspects it would be best not to argue. She and Ruth are drinking their way through a box of wine like the kind their parents bought in the Eighties. They start getting ready for the evening early, at around five, though outside, of course, it is already inky black. There's a festive atmosphere in college with all the end-of-term exams and papers completed. Gangs of girls in those awful sexy Santa outfits strut arm in arm across the quad, their heels clacking, earrings occasionally flashing like Christmas decorations. Kat shudders. She's never been a girl comfortable in a gang, more of a lone wolf, she smiles, or at least she had been before she met Ruth.

The wine is horrible. The acidity hits the back of her throat and causes her stomach to churn, but it helps Ruth with her jitters. Things have started going wrong between Ruth and George in the way Kat always knew they would. It started subtly, gradually. An argument. A missed date. At parties now Ruth looks across the room at George more than he glances back and the way he looks at her is different, too: still cheeky, still knowing, but more cursory, almost polite – as if it would be rude not to ogle a bit, though the ogling has become almost perfunctory.

'Is there anything more irresistible,' asks Ruth, 'than someone who no longer wants you?'

Kat shakes her head. Ruth has a point there. 'No,' she says. 'There's nothing like it.'

She had thought Richard wanted her that first night.

'I keep waiting for something to happen and it doesn't,' he'd said. And she'd smiled and said, 'Maybe it will.' And he'd smiled back. And that had been it, she'd thought: everything starting.

'That's how they get you,' says Ruth. 'They chase you, they *make* you like them – and we, silly girls, are so flattered, so excited that an actual living, breathing man could want us that we fall for it. And then they move on.'

After their most recent fight, a matter of hours, really, Ruth had caught sight of George from her window walking through the quad with a girl. It was no one she knew, no one from college as far as she could tell. George had thrown his arm lightly around the girl, laughing as if he hadn't a care in the world.

And she'd seen him with a fresh pair of eyes. 'A portly Sloane, as puffed up and pleased with himself as Mr Toad,' she'd told Kat. Since then, the subject of George seemed to have become the source of a fluttery, low-level anxiety. 'Not the good kind – the kind you have before an exam you know you're going to fuck up.'

The best thing to do now would be to walk away, to get an early night, to leave it alone. So instead, of course, she is standing in Kat's room, half-cut, painting her lips with Kat's reddest lipstick and planning battle tactics.

It has become, and Kat recognises it, less about George, more about winning. She looks at her friend closely.

Ruth takes a breath as if she's about to start saying something, then stops herself.

'Are you sure you're going to be all right tonight?' asks Kat. 'Do you want me to come with you? It's the last night of term – I don't like the idea of you being at this party on your own when things are so weird with George.'

Ruth shakes her head. 'No, it will be fine. You go on your course thing.'

Kat had plans to go for supper with the other people in college doing English – largely, though she hasn't told Ruth this bit, because there's a strong chance that Richard will be there too.

She watches as Ruth applies more red lipstick then smudges it off on cigarette after cigarette, then reapplies it again.

'When I used to showjump, I would always know the days when my luck had gone bad,' her friend says suddenly.

'You used to showjump?' Kat smiles. 'You're full of surprises.'

Ruth ignores this, blots her lips on a piece of tissue. 'Anyway, maybe I'd snap at my mum over breakfast – she was always trying to make me eat before these things and I never felt like it – or maybe my pony's plaits would come undone in the horsebox.'

Kat suppresses a snigger at the phrase 'pony's plaits', but again Ruth ignores her.

'Or maybe there would be something in the air that the animals would pick up on. You know how they do that? They would skit across the yard at imaginary spooks. Or maybe they weren't imaginary . . . Anyway, deep down, I would know – though I would do my best to conquer the feeling – that there was no point driving to the competition, because it wouldn't go well. It wouldn't go well at all.'

She lights another cigarette.

'Please don't go,' says Kat.

'What?'

'Tonight. Don't go. Or let me come with you.'

Ruth shakes her head. 'It won't be as bad as falling off a horse,' she laughs.

An hour or so later, when only the dregs of the box of wine remain and the atmosphere in college is reaching fever pitch, Ruth says, 'Perhaps you could come with me, just to his room.'

'Are you sure that's a good idea?' asks Kat, sure that it isn't. She stands up to close the window, blocking out, at least partially, the caterwauling of someone singing along to Mariah Carey's 'All I Want For Christmas Is You'.

'If we speak before the party, that might be a better idea than discussing things when we're there,' says Ruth. 'Maybe I should just end it before he does.'

As they start climbing the stairs to George's room, Ruth practises the sort of thing she'll say. 'How about something along the lines of: "We're both adults. Let's call it a day. I wish you well."'

'Not that last bit,' says Kat firmly. 'Don't overdo it; keep it low-key.'

'Aye aye.' Ruth salutes drunkenly and knocks.

Kat, who has had less of the box of wine than Ruth, eyes the closed door with misgiving.

A girl answers, wearing a vest top and tiny shorts.

'George isn't in,' she says in a singsong voice. She is cherubic, doll-like: porcelain skin, white-blonde candyfloss hair. She wanders back into the room and perches on the edge of the bed, picking up a satin dressing gown that is crumpled on the floor and draping it around her shoulders. She looks young, years younger than Kat and Ruth, but her breasts, pushed up in a Wonderbra underneath her vest, are like peaches.

'Where's George?' asks Ruth.

'Who the hell are you?' adds Kat.

The nymph begins to powder her nose with infuriating nonchalance. 'I'm George's sister.'

Ruth is gripping the door handle tightly. 'George doesn't have a sister.'

'I can assure you he does.' There's a twitch at the corner of the girl's lips, as if she is enjoying her lie. 'Who are you again?'

'I'm Ruth Walker.' It is a bad moment for one of Ruth's heels to give way – she is leaning on the door too heavily and she staggers for a couple of steps into the room.

'OK, Ruth Walker.' The girl smirks as she closes her compact with a snap. It is a gesture that belongs to someone much older: the knowingness of the smile, the finality of the closing. 'I'll tell him you dropped by.'

'It's bullshit, isn't it?' says Ruth as they make their way down the stairs.

'Complete bullshit,' agrees Kat, lighting a cigarette for her friend.

They go to regroup under a huge oak in the middle of the quad.

'I'll show her – I'll get him back right in front of her.' She snorts. 'His sister.'

Kat sighs. She knows she should say something but she

110

doesn't know how to start. The truth is it doesn't matter what Ruth wears now or what she does or says. She could saunter over to George tonight and whisper something sexy in his ear, suggest something outrageous, and he might come with her, or he might not, but Ruth has lost the upper hand and that's a very hard thing to get back. Kat knows, too, that she should probably be with Ruth tonight, but she thinks again of Richard and how, with Ruth out of the way, they might finally have a chance.

'I say this with love,' she says eventually, 'but I think maybe you should go to bed.'

'You don't think I can get him back?' Ruth blinks. 'You think he's too good for me?'

Kat sighs. It's too infuriating. 'I think the opposite, my darling. But I do think you're tired and emotional and have had the best part of a box of wine.'

'Fine,' says Ruth sharply.

'Fine what?'

'Fine, I'll be a good girl.' She grinds her cigarette out with her heel. 'I'll go to bed.'

As Kat hugs Ruth goodbye, she wonders again if she should stay with her friend. And yet she doesn't, not even when she sees Ruth walking determinedly in the direction of the music pumping from the next quad, clearly with no intention of going to bed at all. So it serves her right that the evening is a complete washout. It's one of those nights when you know, as soon as you get there and the only seat left is among the dullest people in an inaccessible corner of the table, the sort of evening it's going to be.

Fragments of conversation about the girl in the year

111

above who's shagging one of their tutors keep drifting down from her friend, Jenny, who's at the fun end of the table, as Kat tries to focus on what the guy opposite is saying about one of their set texts. And all the time, she keeps one eye on the door, waiting for Richard to walk through it. But he never does.

Walking back to college, she wonders how Ruth's evening has gone. The wind is wild, whipping up their dresses, causing their hair to lash against their faces.

'What a dry evening,' she sighs, trying to smooth her dress down.

'I know,' laughs Jenny. 'You got stuck with that boring lot at the other end.'

'I thought you said Richard Wiseman was coming.'

'I said he *might*,' Jenny laughs. 'You've got it bad.'

'Yes,' says Kat. She doesn't feel like joking about it. Not tonight. She should have stayed with Ruth. 'You fancy finding out what everyone's up to?'

She squints across the quad to see where the afterparty might be. There's a noise, some shouting, coming from the other side.

'What's that?' Jenny shakes her foot where the wind has wrapped a dark piece of cloth around her leg.

The shouts get louder as they get closer to a small cluster of people gathering. Someone's throwing something from one of the upstairs windows. Pieces of dark fabric flutter down like birds.

'You're friends with Ruth Walker, aren't you?' someone says as Kat reaches the group.

Something about the accusatory way he asks makes Kat hesitate. 'Yes, I guess,' she says after a moment.

'Looks like she's totally lost it.' He looks above them to the top floor. 'She's cutting up all of George's clothes.'

If she squints, Kat can make out Ruth's long red hair hanging down from the window of George's room. She is shouting something, though Kat can't quite make out the words. Ruth has scissors in her hand and a pair of George's trousers; the process of cutting them up looks oddly laborious, almost comical. Kat catches the word 'prick' and, despite the wind, the trousers make a rather heavy landing moments later sans crotch. Fragments of shirts and jumpers follow next.

Kat looks down at the ground, where the slivers of material start to gather at the students' feet. She picks up a piece of cricket jumper and resists the temptation to giggle. The pieces of material keep falling, occasionally picked up by the wind and tossed around, landing softly like blossom.

There's a shout behind them. The sound of running footsteps.

'Someone's called the porters,' says Jenny.

The cluster of students begins to shift, disperse.

'Ruth!' Kat feels as if she is waking from a strange dream. 'Get out of there.' Her words get swallowed up by the wind.

It somehow feels important, imperative, that Ruth isn't found in George's room. She reaches the staircase before the porter, kicks off her heels and starts to make her way, for the second time that day, to George's room at the top of the building, her calves burning.

When she gets there, lungs tight, still panting, she pushes the door open and switches on the light. The room is in

113

complete disarray, the contents of George's expensive wardrobe strewn everywhere, over the bed and the floor: ties, suits, cashmere sweaters, blazers. Kat even spies, and she is surprised that it's survived the massacre, a satin dressing gown. But Ruth herself has disappeared.

Naomi

How to put it? When I try to access my first memory without her, there isn't one. There isn't memory without Ruth. She was the one person to whom I could say: 'You know that ballet teacher?' And she would know whom I meant, or 'Remember that boy on holiday in Crete, with the burnt skin?' And a web of memories, too, would link to that: how she liked him but couldn't have him because she was with someone else at the time; how he liked her too, *really* liked her, but, pragmatically, went for the girl in the blue bikini instead because she was available. And we never knew her name, so years later I could still say, 'Remember the girl in the blue bikini?' And she would share all the memories that went with the image of her: that strange night out with the boy with the burnt skin and his sister, who was a little unhinged and had tried to seduce the taxi driver on the way back from the club by telling him she was really good in bed, and how he, in perfect English, replied, 'Self-praise is no praise,' and we both laughed.

When we got back to the hotel that night the unhinged sister ordered rounds and rounds of ham and cheese sandwiches, but we didn't eat them because we were teenagers and we weren't eating much back then.

And that's just one memory out of thousands . . . Ruby the hamster, who ran away and died roasted to the side of the oven, though our mother never told us until years later, or Midas and Scipio, our childhood dogs, or the old woman who scared us at the Llewelyns' farm, where we went to stay when our father was ill. Every shared experience – not just the good ones – every teenage humiliation, every crush . . . we share genes, we share memories, how can I be a whole person without you?

I take Nunny to Tim. He's just finishing a phone call as I get to his office, which is small and messy like him, with its door propped open for most of the day unless he's speaking to relatives, in which case he pushes it to, turns the radio off, gives them his full attention.

'What's this?' he says smiling as I walk in with Nunny and place him carefully on the desk.

'It was Ruth's,' I say. And he stops smiling. 'It arrived in the post this morning.'

He picks Nunny up. 'Who sent it?'

I realise my legs feel strange, unsteady. I pull up a seat. 'I really don't know.'

'Naomi.' He reaches out to touch my hand.

'I know.' I swallow, let the wave of emotion pass. 'He was her favourite childhood toy,' I say. 'You can probably see from how battered he looks.'

'Where was it sent from?' he asks, quietly businesslike. He takes the package from me.

'St Anthony's.' I show him the postmark.

'Could someone at the university have found him in a cupboard or something?' Tim asks. 'Sent him to you?'

He is good at this – plausible, rational solutions, bringing things back from the land of ghosts and ghouls.

'There wasn't a note,' I say.

He takes control, gets on the phone to the college, and I stay in the room as he is put through from the porters to housekeeping and then finally, through his insistence, to the Dean's secretary. He works hard to keep me involved, repeating phrases for my benefit, but the long and short of it is that no one knows anything about it.

'What about your mother?' he checks when he's off the phone.

'No, she's as shocked as I am. And neither of us can remember the last time we saw him.'

He shakes his head. 'He must have been somewhere safe and dry all these years – he's not mouldy or damp.'

'He still smells of her,' I say. 'Of coconut oil.'

'Naomi,' he says warningly. 'It's probably not that.'

He's not an unkind man, Tim, just wary of the peaks and troughs of hope and despair, has learned only to work from the evidence in front of him.

I swallow. 'Could someone have imprisoned her?' I ask, knowing he can't possibly answer that question.

I think of a recent case: a woman escaping from her captor after being locked away for decades – the sort of story that fills you with horror and hope all at the same time.

'Naomi,' he says again. 'It could just as easily be trolls.' A catchall word these days for those who feed off the misery of others, like creatures in a dark fairy tale.

'I know,' I say. 'Should we tell the police?'

'Probably,' he says. 'But I'm not going to make you, if you can't face it yet.' He turns to a notebook. 'Let's make a list of everyone that you know who could have sent him. Friends. That ex-boyfriend of hers. And you can sit in here and make the calls in private while I get us some coffee.'

'Thank you,' I say, clutching Nunny to my chest as I get up. 'It's really very kind, but I think I'd rather do it from home tonight.'

Richard sounds shocked at the sound of my voice. I forget sometimes how much I sound like Ruth. My voice is lower, quieter, but the cadence is the same. I had wondered for a moment whether it was too late to call – just before ten – but then I remembered that he was a night owl himself, not averse to making a late-night call back when we were in touch more regularly, his voice urgent with coffee and nicotine.

I picture him at his desk – a mess the last time I saw it, covered in papers, photographs, a sticky tumbler with just a finger of whisky left in it. He once told me sheepishly that a former girlfriend had called his research on Ruth his Ex-Files. He said, back then, 'I didn't tell her that I never really thought of Ruth as an ex – that she was somehow too present for that. It probably wouldn't have helped matters.'

We had to stop seeing Richard a few years ago. It was

awful. I wrote the letter at the kitchen table, as my mother lay upstairs, woozy from the medication, explaining that we loved him, that we would always remember him fondly, but that seeing him was too upsetting – his conspiracy theories, his conviction that she was still alive. It never seemed to end – there would always be one more thing, one more sighting that convinced him, and then his conviction would drag us along with him like a maleficent current. The thing is about hope – you have to manage it. Otherwise it takes over, like water. It might keep you afloat for a while, but eventually it'll rush away like the tide, leaving you stranded. We couldn't live like that. It got too hard.

After the shock, the sudden intake of breath, Richard is off, garbling apologies, as if I have called to bollock him for another article about Ruth, or related to Ruth. Something that used to happen a lot.

'I'm so sorry again,' he says. 'It was the arrogance of youth. No, it wasn't that. It's just I *wanted* it so much not to be true. I'm so sorry. So sorry again,' he says tripping over his words. He pauses for a moment, unsure, perhaps, if I'm still there.

The line crackles. I can hear the shallowness of his breath.

'Richard, something has happened,' I begin. 'No, not that. Something else. Do you remember Nunny?'

Alice

'The thing I find strange,' Alice says to Christie over what is meant to be a celebratory lunch, 'is that he lied about her. It's not as though it matters now.' She pauses over her chicken salad. There is a lot she wants to discuss with Christie, but she doesn't want to come across as too obsessed – perhaps she will start with this simple point and work her way to the weird thing. 'The lie matters, I mean,' she elaborates. 'Not what he did before I came along.'

'Maybe she hurt him. Maybe he hurt her.' Christie shrugs. 'Maybe he just can't remember. It was all so hellishly long ago.'

'Have you ever forgotten shagging someone?' Alice smiles. 'I bet you haven't . . .'

'No,' Christie starts. 'But I'm not . . .'

'But you're not George,' Alice finishes sourly.

Christie's too polite to say it, but it's what they're both thinking. Alice looks down at her plate. She doesn't want an atmosphere, not today.

'When did people change?' asks Christie abruptly.

They are seated very close to the next table. It bothers Alice. The couple next to them are eating in silence. He glances at his phone, scrolling down the screen every few minutes. The woman, in a white cashmere turtleneck, picks at her *moules marinière*, listening. This lunch at their favourite pub is meant to be a celebration of Alice's pregnancy now she is feeling better.

She puts her hand on her belly and smiles to herself. A girl. Just what she had wanted. George, predictably, had been more thrown by the news. 'But I don't understand women,' he laughed. 'You're all bonkers.' Alice smiled and said, 'You might understand this one.' And he replied, 'No, she'll probably mystify me most of all.'

Distracted, she returns her attention to Christie. 'What do you mean?' she asks.

'There was a time at St Anthony's when everything felt so optimistic. People would leave notes and things in my pigeonhole and occasionally cookies – you know, those warm ones you could buy on the high street . . .'

'I think that happened *once*, Christie . . .' Alice smiles.

'Then, at some point, not long before the boys left, it stopped – invitations to parties, all of it. And people stopped looking me in the eye – except you, of course, and George and Teddy – they were different with me.'

No, thinks Alice. It hadn't been that bad. It hadn't been that sudden, had it?

'Maybe it was the Tory thing?' she says instead. 'No one really liked Tories then.'

'Does anyone now?' Christie puts her wine glass on the table too hard. 'Did anyone ever?'

'Christie!' Alice giggles. But she was right, in a way. Something indefinable had cooled. That's how she thought of it. At first, there had been cocktail parties and drinking societies – a big gang of friends. And at some point, the others had drifted away. Leaving what, after all these years, felt like a rather claustrophobic core. 'Do you think about Dan much?' she asks.

'Sometimes,' Christie says carefully. 'He was unknowable, wasn't he?'

'Aren't we all?' Alice smiles.

'Yes. Maybe,' Christie snorts. 'Teddy isn't.'

Alice glances back at the woman next to them picking at her mussels. She thinks of Teddy's sweaty hands on her knees.

'I know he fancies you, Al,' teases Christie. 'I can just tell,' she says smoothly, not giving Alice the chance to say anything. 'Well, I don't have to sometimes. He'll just say.'

'He'll say, "I fancy Alice?"' She tries to keep her voice light.

'Something like that,' Christie agrees. She takes a gulp of wine. Motherhood has made her a speedy, efficient drinker. 'Did you fancy Dan?'

Alice shakes her head. 'He was beautiful, though, wasn't he?' She tries to think of Dan's face, but it's hard to picture it precisely. His features shift. Tall, dark hair, green eyes, high cheekbones. She can't remember anything concrete. His long legs stretched out in his faded Levis. The way he looked around a room, only giving you half his attention. 'I don't miss him,' she adds coolly. She would never say that in front of George.

122

'Does George ever talk about him?' Christie asks.

'Never.' Alice shakes her head. She takes a sip of water, then says quickly, without giving herself time to think about it, 'Something strange happened.'

'Something else strange?' says Christie.

'Yes,' says Alice, not knowing quite where to start. 'Something else strange.'

'OK.' Christie waits for her to continue.

'You'll think I sound mad.' Alice glances to her left, where the woman on the next table has paused too, her fork in mid-air, waiting to hear what Alice has to say. 'But there's a photo collage on George's desk – you made it for his thirtieth.'

Christie takes a sip of wine.

'I was looking at it when I was dusting a while back,' Alice explains, then smiles slyly. 'Not dusting exactly.'

'Yes, yes,' Christie grins. 'Checking what he's been watching on his laptop? I had to show Teddy how to clear his history recently. Honestly, it's embarrassing – we share a computer . . .'

'No,' says Alice. 'Not that. Sometimes, I just go in and look for . . .'

'Clues?' Christie laughs.

Alice glances crossly to the woman on the next table, who hastily makes a show of mopping up her sauce with a bit of bread.

'Something like that. Something to do with what he gets up to – or got up to – when I'm not around . . .'

'Darling, *honestly*.' Christie rolls her eyes. 'It's good to have a few secrets in a marriage.'

Alice waves her hand impatiently. 'Anyway, after I saw

the girl and before George said anything about their fling, I just had a premonition that he knew her, you know? And anyway, there's this photo on his desk from our university days, from the memorial ball . . .' She knows this is where it gets ridiculous.

'And?' Christie prompts.

'I thought I saw a girl with red hair in the corner of the pic.'

'Oh, Al, that could have been anyone.'

'And . . .' Alice pushes on. 'I told George: that I thought I'd seen her in the photo, but the next time I looked at it, the red hair had gone. It had been cropped out.'

There is silence. Christie puts her fork down.

'That seems a bit strange,' she says carefully as if, in truth, it is Alice who seems a bit strange.

Alice feels flushed. Now she's said the words out loud to another person, they sound ridiculous.

'Maybe I imagined it the first time.' She begins to back-pedal. 'Could I have done? I have been dreaming weirdly since I got pregnant.'

'Yes,' Christie nods enthusiastically. 'Yes, it's probably something like that. My dreams were always completely bonkers when I was expecting. And I've had those lucid dreams before, you know, when they are so realistic and you are in the very room, just doing things slightly differently. That would be it . . . you dreamed of dusting – or snooping – and you saw the picture in your dream.'

'Otherwise, what am I saying?' Alice laughs uncomfortably. 'That I imagined the girl in the photo? Or that George or someone else'—though, Alice thinks, who else could it be?—'has cropped her out?'

'It's a bit *1984*, darling,' Christie agrees. 'Rewriting history.'

'Yes, it is mad,' Alice agrees. 'Forget I said anything. I'm just being daft. Seeing that girl at the beginning of the year just brought things back – it's made me start thinking about the past in a way that's not healthy.'

'We all do that sometimes,' says Christie. 'Things that might have been.'

'Look, I know Dan was a big part of our lives back then . . .' Alice pauses. 'I know I shouldn't say this, but I don't know if he was a good influence.' She remembers seeing an ex of Dan's weeping in the post room – the girl wouldn't tell her why but she had been inconsolable. 'There was always something weird about the way he treated women, though I wouldn't have been able to say that at the time.' There had been other things: off-colour jokes, a couple of end-of-the-night scenes with his girlfriends – not that Dan would ever have called them *girlfriends*. Birds, maybe. Pulls.

'I guess the way all of them treated women was a bit . . .' Christie trails off. 'But they got better, didn't they? We trained them well.'

Alice nods. This lunch was meant to be a celebration of the future, after all, not the past.

'Well, now George is going to be a father to a girl himself,' she says brightly. 'Let's see how he likes it when the boys are after her.'

'Absolutely,' laughs Christie. 'The chickens are coming home to roost.'

Kat

'Ruth, you've got a twin,' says Dave, a flamboyant third year, who models himself on Noël Coward.

They are sitting in the corner of the college bar, huddled up in hats and scarves. St Anthony's in February is freezing. The damp creeps off the water, seeps into your bones. The sea is granite-hued, the wind so strong it makes Kat's eyes water.

Dave takes a drag of his cigarette with a gleeful flourish. 'I saw her in Annie's café the other day – well, I say *saw*, I pinched her bottom.'

'Obviously,' says Kat, catching Ruth's eye and smiling. She has the flickering sense of déjà vu, as if Dave has told this story before, which he does have a tendency to do.

'From behind, she looked exactly like you – she was even wearing that stripy cowl-neck dress you have . . .'

Ruth looks at Dave suspiciously. 'How do you know what a cowl neck is?'

'Darling, I'm sorry if I disappoint you by living up to the stereotypes but, really, I knew about cowl necks when you were a babe in arms . . .' Dave loved his jaded third-year routine. 'So, anyway, I gave her posterior a little squeeze in greeting and she spun around and was inches away from slapping me. Thing is, I must have looked so terrified that she knew I'd made a mistake and just laughed instead.'

Ruth smiles. 'You wally.' She opens her crisp packet carefully, tearing the sides and flattening it out to share with the others. She's changed since last term. There's something quieter, more cautious about her. She's started dressing differently too, in clothes too big for her, as if to make herself seem smaller. 'Now did she *really* look like me, or did she just have red hair?'

'She looked a *lot* like you,' Dave says, surveying Ruth's face. 'Not as pretty, of course.' He takes another puff. 'Maybe she's your doppelgänger.'

'Don't be ridiculous,' Kat laughs as she takes a crisp. 'No one could match our Ruthie.'

Ruth rolls her eyes, tries not to look pleased.

The sharpness of the salt and vinegar stings Kat's lips. It comes back to her now.

'There was a guy from before,' she says. 'A barman. He was convinced he was shagging you. I thought it was a bit weird at the time.'

'What do you mean?' Ruth frowns.

'At that awful pub, the Two Pheasants. Maybe it was her – your doppelgänger.'

127

'I don't remember that.' Ruth picks up another crisp.

'It was way back – at the beginning of last term,' Kat sighs. 'Back then I had no idea you were intent upon devoting your entire carnal life to George Bell.'

Ruth pulls a face and throws the crisp at her. As if they've summoned him up, George and his entourage appear in the bar for lunch. They enter as if to a drum roll, as if half expecting applause, wearing the same long, dark coats like a uniform.

'Here they come, the princes of darkness,' Ruth sighs to Kat.

'Ignore them,' Kat mouths and pointedly looks away, out of the bar at the dripping quad outside.

The smell of George's aftershave catches at the back of Kat's throat. She glances at Ruth, but her friend's face is hard to read. Ruth had got into serious trouble for cutting up George's clothes last term. She'd had to pay to replace them, to see a therapist about anger management. 'It's excruciating,' she'd told Kat. 'I have to hit things with a baseball bat. I wouldn't mind, actually, but you can't do it properly in front of someone.'

'Are you scared of your temper?' Kat asked, imagining herself as a psychiatrist in rimmed glasses for a moment.

'No,' said Ruth. 'Yes. Maybe.'

George seems to have forgotten about – or discounted – the incident completely. As he strolls in, he bows in their direction. 'Ladies!' he says theatrically, including Dave in his greeting.

Dan, as ever, is just behind George. There's a cluster of others traipsing in too: bulky Teddy, Fit Felix, baby-faced Jerry, a skinny girl, Laura, who wears very short skirts and likes to perch on the boys' laps whenever she can.

'Why do they always go around in such a large group?' Kat mutters. 'It's pathetic.'

Dave smiles impishly. 'You need me to tell you that?'

Kat sighs. 'I know you think it's a homoerotic thing – but, honestly, not everyone's gay.'

'Don't worry – I know *you're* not gay, darling. You've got all the qualities of a straight girl.'

'You make that sound like a bad thing.'

Dave smirks into his drink in reply.

'Nothing touches him,' Kat addresses Ruth. 'It's as if nothing happened between you.'

'It *was* nothing,' Ruth says, running a finger around the rim of her glass. 'I'm nothing to him, he's nothing to me.'

Ruth hadn't shown much interest in anyone else and, as well as dressing differently, she'd started working harder, drinking less, shuffling off to the library at strange times with armfuls of books.

At weekends she was less interested in parties and would drag Kat, usually moaning about a hangover, for windswept walks along the beach. She shared that in common with Richard, with whom Kat had been spending more time, too. She'd started visiting him in his room, usually on the pretence of borrowing a book or an album, and found him restless, pacing, picking things up and putting them down again. Sometimes he'd say, 'Let's go for a walk,' and they'd go out, walking and walking, following the curves of the coastline, sometimes stopping on the way for pints of cider and cheese sandwiches. Kat couldn't decide if there was any interest on his part, though he'd never flirt, rarely touch her.

'This happens to me when things change,' he said once. 'The restlessness.'

'Is there something new in the air?' she asked.

He smiled. A lovely smile. And pointed at the sky, which was overcast, '*Viene la tormenta*. It's my favourite bit in *The Terminator*.'

Kat had wondered if love were like a storm and decided it wasn't. Not in this case. They had watched Richard's video of *The Terminator* together later that afternoon curled up on his bed, sharing a blanket like an old couple. And Kat had huddled in close, her legs drawn up to her chest, feeling the space between them crackle. But it hadn't happened. Kat smiles at the memory. It hadn't happened *yet*. Being in his bed, that was a start.

Now, as Richard wanders into the bar, book in hand, her heart tightens. His short dark hair always looks as though it has never seen a comb and his face is shadowed with stubble, but it is Richard's assurance she likes the best. The sense he is comfortable in his own skin, even when he is restless, fidgeting, that he knows who he is. Kat glances over at Ruth and she is looking, too. As is Dave, who has the biggest crush on Richard.

'Hi,' Dave calls across the bar.

'Hi,' says Richard brusquely.

'Moody. I like it,' Dave whispers.

'I like it too,' says Kat. 'Come and join us,' she shouts to Richard.

He looks as though he might say no, but when he's

been served, Richard comes over with his coffee. He looks at Ruth.

'Hello.'

'Hello,' she says.

She's a terrible blusher, thinks Kat irritably, watching Ruth flush at the neck.

'Are you feeling better?'

Ruth nods. She looks distracted.

Kat takes off her hat and shakes out her hair. 'Better than when?' Richard's presence changes the dynamic between them. 'Is it too early for a drink?'

'That depends on the drink,' says Dave. 'A Bloody Mary would be completely acceptable.'

'Or champagne?' says Kat.

'Steady on,' Ruth smiles. 'Kat's modelling herself on Dorothy Parker,' she tells Richard.

'Very sensible,' says Richard, glancing pointedly at George, who has started talking loudly about oral sex. 'She had some insightful things to say about money.'

'And homosexuality,' says Dave laconically.

'And love,' adds Kat.

She can feel Richard's proximity in her arms, a sort of fizzing. She puts her hand on the table near his. Her fingernails are red and chipped. She's encouraged by the fact he doesn't move his hand away.

Ruth stands up suddenly. She looks wired. Maybe it's too much caffeine.

'She died alone, Dorothy Parker,' she says. 'No one even came to claim her ashes. So, you know, all of her cleverness didn't save her in the end.'

The way Richard is looking at Ruth, Kat can't bear it.

Her laugh comes out like a bark. 'No one says it saves you, darling.'

'Stay for a drink,' Richard says.

Ruth shakes her head. 'Next time.'

She is quick to leave, grabbing her coat, making for the door. She looks as if she's about to weep. No one does a dramatic exit like Ruth.

When Kat gets to Ruth's room, Ruth takes her time answering the door. It's a haze of smoke with the music, Nina Simone, on far too loud.

'What's up?' Kat says, sinking into a beanbag without taking her coat off.

Ruth sits down primly at her desk, though Kat can tell from the way the books are neatly closed and piled up she hasn't been studying.

'What do you mean?'

'Why are you being weird?'

'I'm not.'

'You are,' laughs Kat.

Ruth gets to her feet and switches off the music.

'I'm not,' she says again, looking out of the window.

'You definitely are,' says Kat.

'There's a gardener weeding the quad,' says Ruth.

'What?'

'You hardly ever see that, do you? Anyone doing the weeding, but it explains why the lawn looks so perfect the whole time. It's like a painting.'

'What?' says Kat again.

'He's so still, he's barely moving at all. Like a picture.'

Kat twitches. She's reminded of the way her

132

mother tells a story. There must be a point in there somewhere.

'A painting before it comes crashing off the wall,' says Ruth. 'Before the movement starts.'

There's a fine line, Kat thinks, between brilliance and craziness. She thinks of the way Ruth dances: that's definitely somewhere in between.

'*Viene la tormenta*,' says Ruth.

Kat, who had thought for a moment she might leave, sits very still. As if it would make a difference either way.

'It means . . .' says Ruth.

'I know what it means,' says Kat quietly. 'The storm is coming.'

'The thing is . . .' Ruth says, as if making a formal announcement, and Kat realises that she doesn't want Ruth to go on, that she knows what the thing is, or at least what sort of thing it is, and that nothing she does or says will be able to stop the thing developing. 'The thing is,' Ruth starts again, 'I gave Richard a blow job.'

'What?' says Kat, though, to be fair, Ruth's statement is not a nuanced one.

'I can't explain it,' Ruth says. 'I was really angry.'

'You were *angry*?' says Kat.

'I just felt like it. In the moment.'

Kat lights a cigarette, puffing out the smoke in angry little blasts. 'In the moment?' she says, wishing she could stop echoing Ruth. She tries not to think about Ruth kneeling in front of Richard, of his hands in her hair.

'You can't just go round doing what you want to do in the moment.'

'*You* do,' Ruth counters. 'You always do.'

133

Kat opens her mouth to argue the point but finds she is laughing instead.

'And what is there but to do what you want in the moment?' continues Ruth crossly.

'Fuck, I do, don't I?' agrees Kat. 'What a fucking hypocrite.' She gets up to hug Ruth. The embrace is fierce and brief. She breaks away and looks at her friend. 'I'm just *jealous*.' She's in show mode, her Dorothy Parker side taking over. 'Did he have a nice cock?'

'Kat!' Ruth blushes. 'You're awful.'

'Oh, don't go all prudish on me.' Kat sinks back on the beanbag. 'How did it happen?'

'It was the night I cut up George's clothes.' Ruth starts to move as she talks – finding an ashtray, lighting a cigarette. 'I bumped into Richard at the party and he told me that that girl George was with wasn't his sister and I lost it. I went to George's room . . . Richard came with me. He just sort of followed me there. And well, you know the rest.'

'Richard was with you?' Kat thinks for a moment the catch in her voice has betrayed her. 'You did it together?'

'No.' Ruth shakes her head vehemently. 'No, he wanted to stop me.'

'He didn't do a very good job of that,' Kat says more sharply than she means.

'No, he couldn't stop me and then afterwards we hid in his room, which is on the same staircase as George's, just beneath it. And the adrenaline, I think . . .'

And Kat can tell she has returned to that night, to the way perhaps they leaned together against the door, the feel of Richard's heart hammering against her ribcage, the smell of each other and how the moment changed, as moments do, from one thing to another.

'You like him, don't you?' Kat says.

Her face aches from the tension of pretending this is OK. She remembers running up the stairs to George's room to warn Ruth, how she couldn't find her anywhere. And all that time they had been just a floor below, doing that. She thinks she might be sick.

Ruth comes to sit next to Kat. 'I know *you* do, I know you like him.'

Kat wants to keep pretending, to keep putting on a show, but she finds she can't in this moment. She rests her head on her friend's shoulder. There is an inevitability to how it will all play out, as if the three of them are hurtling downhill towards something.

'I won't do anything if you don't want me to,' says Ruth.

'Don't say that, Ruthie.' Kat shakes her head. 'Please don't say that.'

Naomi

You can't help who you fall in love with. I think of that after my conversation with Richard. That's what Ruth used to say. I didn't believe it until it happened to me. Years later I would watch Natalie Portman in *Closer* telling Jude Law that there was always a moment where you chose to give in to something, or to resist it. But when it happened to me I was young, and not as wise as Natalie Portman's character, and I fell in love with someone just by looking at their back, if that's possible.

I had been in Roberto's, a family-run café in the town where I went to school. I was waiting for my friend Jess, who was always late.

Roberto's was run by an Italian family who had moved to Wales in the Fifties. It was a small place but popular, with brown paper tablecloths and old wine bottles with waxy candles pushed into them. Roberto's grandson, Andrea, whom Jess fancied like mad, began to light the candles. It was late April and the day's light was softening.

The shadows on the walls lengthened and the atmosphere inside the café-bar shifted to the intimacy of evening. Families with small children packed up for home; a couple of single drinkers gathered at the small bar by the door, where there were a few stools, Italian-style, for those who wanted to eat or drink there rather than at a table on their own.

Jess and I would always bag a table in the furthest corner of the room, where we people-watched together. And while I had been reading and waiting – we were studying *Wuthering Heights* at the time – the owner of this peculiarly lovely back had come in and perched on a stool at the bar, reading as well – I couldn't see what, or I would have undoubtedly noted it down – and smoking. Wearing a deep red jumper, with a scarf knotted at the neck, he had a shock of dark hair. His neck was lovely. Tanned. Hairless. The line of it was elegant and clean. I remember wishing I had a pencil with me, a sketchbook, so I could capture it on paper.

At the time, Ruth had just got together with Richard. I hadn't met him myself yet, but something in Ruth's tone had changed. When we spoke on the phone, she would sound distracted, starting halfway through stories that I hadn't heard before, as if forgetting who I was, that she wasn't telling the story to him. She didn't talk about Richard in that searching way girls often do, trying to decipher him. A part of her had withdrawn from me – simply wasn't mine any more.

The Back looked like it was waiting for someone too, focusing on the door whenever it swung open. The bar began to fill up. I sipped my wine. I didn't drink much back then: I had spent too much time behind the bar at the hotel, listening to the circuitous conversations of the very drunk, watching them stumble and trip over their words.

'You don't like losing control, do you?' Jess had once said to me at a sixth-form disco. She had been dancing wildly, her hair a mess and her cheeks pink. I hadn't known what to say: it wasn't that I didn't like losing control, more that I didn't know how. Losing control was what Ruth did. She threw things and stamped her feet, flung her arms around the ponies and dogs, declared she loved or hated people. 'They're just emotions,' I said to her once as we walked along the beach. 'They pass.' 'Sure,' she said, looking at the frothy white horses charge into the bay; she threw a stick into them, which got sucked in, disappeared. But I could tell she didn't believe me. Not for a moment. To Ruth, emotions were everything.

Andrea brought a couple of diners over to a table near where I was sitting. Once he had seated them and given them their menus, I asked him the time. Beaming at me, he looked at his watch with a flourish. He was nice, Andrea, though he was too old for Jess. Greying slightly at the temples and a little bit where his stubble started to come through, he was tall with messy hair and had a way of looking at your face too long. Jess used to blush like crazy around him.

He nodded at the empty seat where Jess usually sat. 'Where is your friend?'

'I don't know.' I straightened my fork. 'She's late.'

'It's ten past eight.'

'She's very late.' I frowned. 'Has she called?'

138

Those were the days before we all had mobiles.

'I don't think so. I can check at the bar for you.'

'No, it's fine – I'll ask. I'm a bit worried about her.'

I picked up my handbag and coat. I decided, if there were no message at the bar from Jess, I would leave. I didn't want just to sit around worrying.

There was a gap at the bar right next to the owner of the back. I slid into it, my face burning. Suddenly, now I could actually look at the face, I found I couldn't bring myself to do so. I didn't want to ruin it. Before, however many qualities I had liked in a boy, there had always been something missing: eyes too far apart, or the wrong-shaped nose, or too much body hair. I could feel his gaze on my profile. I turned at last and looked at the face. And I thought: there it is. As if I had been waiting for this face all my life. But it was the face of a woman.

It felt like opening a door to a room I didn't know, wasn't expecting. 'I'm sorry,' I almost said. 'I've made a mistake.' The woman was looking at me, but she didn't seem flustered. She said, 'Hello.' Her voice was low. It had a twang, an accent. I could tell she was a Spanish speaker. I was aware of the fact I was sweating.

'Hi,' I said. But the word was over quickly – it sounded shorter, more abrupt than I'd meant it to.

Roberto came over to serve me and was looking at me expectantly. I couldn't remember why I was there for a moment.

'I'm waiting for a friend who hasn't turned up. Has anyone left a message for me?'

Roberto shook his head. 'I don't think so. I'll check.'

'Excuse me?' The woman put a hand on my arm.

I tightened at the contact.

'Sorry.' The woman smiled. 'I didn't mean to make you jump.'

I knew I was coming across as a lunatic. I felt so exposed, as if the woman could read my mind.

She asked: 'I was wondering. I mean – if you're waiting for someone, you're not Olivia, are you?'

'No, I'm not.' That much I knew.

The woman explained: 'I'm waiting for someone I don't know. So I thought I'd check.' She paused for a moment, said quietly, conspiratorially: 'A blind date.'

Words rushed into my head, but I managed to keep my mouth closed, so they didn't spill out onto the bar, ruining this moment where I had been mistaken for someone quite different, for an adult. *I'm seventeen. I'm a schoolgirl. A blind date between women? Are you mad?* But in the end I just said, 'No, that's not me.'

'Well,' the woman smiled. 'Can I buy you a drink anyway? While we're waiting. I'm sure Olivia wouldn't mind. If she ever shows up . . .' Her smile transformed her lovely face into something remarkable. She had her hand on my bare arm again and I looked down at it – her long fingers, her olive skin. She knew what she was doing. She was in complete control.

I thought at the time that everyone could see, everyone could tell what had passed between us. I paused before replying, heard the words in my head first. I would say: 'That would be nice.' And I would drink a glass of wine with this stranger, because there was no harm in two women having a drink together, was there? It was what I had planned to do with Jess, after all . . .

But the words never made it out because, without warning, there was the sound of the door and there was Jess, red-faced and weighed down by shopping bags. There was a story about a sale at Miss Selfridge, a delayed train and a lost wallet that turned up eventually, but I couldn't really hear any of it – couldn't focus on the meaning of the words – until Jess asked: 'The usual table, then?'

'No.' I shook my head. 'Let's go somewhere else.' I couldn't look back at the woman or Roberto, no doubt smiling a welcome at Jess. I focused on the door, on escape. 'Somewhere else,' I repeated insistently. I took Jess's elbow and marched her out of the restaurant.

Alice

Pregnancy has made Alice, who has never found sleep easy, especially on a Sunday night, even more wakeful. And now she can't take her sleeping tablets, can't drink, can't do anything. She has started to wake at the coldest moments of the night, when the heating has clicked off and the pipes and radiators gurgle and groan. George, who is used to his parents' big, cold house in Oxfordshire, which rattles and creaks through the night, can sleep through anything.

They had stayed in a haunted hotel in St Anthony's once as a dare. Alice had woken at four o'clock in the morning freezing and with the sense that someone was standing right outside their bedroom door. When she woke him, George had just laughed and said: 'Don't be ridiculous, darling.' That was back when dead people seemed like a distant, faraway thing. Not something that could actually happen to anyone you knew.

Something she'd read in Richard's book had made her

start thinking of Dan – a fact about him that she'd forgotten: he had been the last to see Ruth alive. She had wandered into George's study earlier that evening for a read while he was out watching the rugby. Richard had quoted a report: 'Missing St Anthony's student Ruth Walker was last seen swimming after the memorial ball by fellow student Dan Vaughan. "I can't be sure," he said. "But the girl swimming looked like Ruth because of her red hair. I know she loved to swim. It must have been around five in the morning, before the rain began."'

Alice had never felt comfortable around Dan. She remembers a night out in St Anthony's with him when George had been at a student union meeting. Dan had been hammered that evening, but Alice had still been new enough to her role as George's girlfriend to make an effort with his friends, even the ones she didn't much like. Dan had drunk so much that he'd needed a lie-down on a sofa. He'd rested his head on Alice's knee as she stroked his sweaty forehead.

'We need to find you a nice girlfriend,' she said.

'You don't need to find me a *nice* one,' he laughed. 'A nasty one would do just fine.' And he resettled himself with his hands under his head, his knuckles digging into Alice's crotch. Not an accident, she thought then, and thinks again now.

She hadn't heard George come in from the pub, but he'd sauntered into his study to find Alice still sitting at his desk. Caught off-guard, she went on the attack.

'Did Dan ever talk to you about seeing Ruth Walker swimming?'

'What do you mean?' George never liked talking about Dan.

143

'Isn't it strange?' Alice said, closing the book and putting it face down on the desk. 'That he was the last one to see Ruth.'

A vague memory came back to her – which she can't place – of Dan knocking on George's door early one morning, of urgent whispers out in the corridor. When would that have been? She picked up the photo frame to give it a wipe.

'Not really, darling.' George took the frame from her, without looking at it, and put it back on the desk. He curled an arm around her waist. 'Someone had to be the last to see her.' He rubbed her bottom through her dress. 'Are you wearing knickers, Mrs Bell?'

Alice smelled the pub on him – beer and firewood. George loved having sex in unusual places. Once, at university, he'd fucked her on his balcony overlooking the quad in the dead of night. Alice had enjoyed that: she had never felt more alive. And it was more romantic than some of his assignations – balconies were one thing, but she was *not* going to do it in the toilet with him, another of his favourites. And not one with which he was unfamiliar, she suspected, though she tried not to think about that. He lifted up her dress and pulled down her pants.

'What about the baby?' she whispered.

'I'll be gentle,' he said. 'I won't even tickle its head.'

As she came, as her grip on things slid away from her, Alice's hand shot forwards, knocking the book on the floor.

George got to it before she could, glanced at the book before he handed it over. 'What's this?' he asked, holding it out.

144

Alice blushed, straightened her dress. 'I think it's fairly self-explanatory.'

'But why?' George asked coldly.

'I was trying to find out more,' Alice said, taking it from him. 'About Ruth.'

George pulled his trousers up, zipped up his flies. 'Why don't you talk to me, Al? Instead of snooping around. Reading Richard Wiseman, of all people.'

'I tried,' Alice said crossly, sitting down at his desk, looking at the photo frame. 'Did you change that photo, by the way?' she countered.

'What photo?'

'The one of you and Dan. Did you cut off the red hair?'

George looked puzzled. 'One of the photos had slipped, so I rearranged the collage.' He was quiet for a moment. 'Yes, I might have moved the one of me and Dan.'

And he sighed in such a sad, heavy way that Alice felt guilty for a moment, remembered how things had been in the days after Dan's death, how ashen-faced and silent George had been. They'd been so young for such a loss. Dan and George were barely out of St Anthony's, just beginning their lives in the real world. After the news, George had retreated into himself. Alice would try to put her arms around him, but he'd gone to a place she couldn't reach. A place she wasn't invited.

George crouched down by the desk. 'Al,' he said softly. 'I'm worried about you. Cutting off red hair in photos? What are you talking about?' He paused. 'You're not yourself.'

'Talk to me,' said Alice. 'Help me to work out what has been going on.'

145

'What do you want to know?'

'Richard Wiseman thinks Ruth might still be alive. Do you think that's possible?'

He rubbed his nose. 'It's possible but not very likely. Ruth was a strong swimmer, but the sea can take anyone.'

He knows that about her, thought Alice. He knew Ruth far better than he let on.

'Why do you think Richard is so convinced?' she pressed.

'Well,' George sighed, hesitant.

'Please, just tell me what you're thinking.'

'He was infatuated with Ruth. That's all I know.'

'What do you mean by that?'

George took a couple of steps towards the fireplace, turning his back on Alice to look into it. 'They had a terrible row. Not long before she went missing. Almost everyone in college saw it.'

Alice swallowed. 'What are you saying, George?'

George turned back to her, holding up his hands, unaccountable. 'I'm just saying he was obsessed.'

'Were you jealous?' she asked spitefully.

'What?'

'I have to ask – or I'm always going to wonder: were you jealous of Richard Wiseman? Did he steal Ruth from you?'

'Steal her?' George laughed nastily. His face curled up into an expression she didn't recognise. 'I could have had her back any time I wanted.'

What have I done? Alice thinks now, looking over at George as he sleeps, as if up until that moment she has been standing by and watching someone else live her life; as if she has, through no fault of her own, woken in the middle of the night lying next to a man she doesn't love.

She has been stupid. No, not stupid, wilfully blind. She remembers a time after he had left college, moved on to the next stage of his life, when she visited him in London. They'd gone out for a meal and drunk heaps, falling on each other as soon as they came through the door. And yet, up in his room, George started tearing the sheets off the bed to change them before they got in. It was most unlike him.

'Gosh, don't worry about those now,' she had said, unzipping her boots. But he had insisted.

A fox shrieks in a neighbouring garden. She guesses now, of course, that he had slept with some other girl in those sheets and he didn't want Alice smelling her on them. Was it guilt over girls that caused his occasional emotional outbursts? Once in the months after he left St Anthony's, not long after Dan's death, he came in late, particularly paralytic. He sat on the edge of their bed and began to cry. 'I have done bad things. Dreadful things, Alice.' He cupped her face tightly as she sat up to comfort him. 'Things I can't undo.'

The next day, it was as if it hadn't happened. 'Oh, don't worry about that, darling,' he said breezily. 'Booze blues.'

Naomi

I sometimes get the sense that the same things happen over and over again: that everything is a variation of something that has happened before and that life works like water, in currents, with things tugged away from us and other things returned. That's the way I think of Nunny as I take him home to show him to my mum.

Our dogs, as children, were Midas the golden Labrador and Scipio the springer spaniel. There was a better reason for Scipio's name than the alliteration, though I can't remember what it was. I think someone suggested it in the hotel bar. It could have been Dai the Poet, for all I remember, trying, as always, to prove how clever he was.

Ruth loved Midas, but she loved him in a sensible way. It was Scipio who won her raw, all-consuming, never-want-to-let-you-out-of-my-sight love. For years, I kept a picture on my wall of her hugging Scipio. Her face is all but concealed in his fur. It looks almost as though she is inhaling him. That kind of love reminds us we are alive more than other types. But, of course, there is a higher price to pay.

Scipio was a bad influence on Midas. They'd go missing for hours, scrounging picnic scraps from holidaymakers on the beach or chasing rabbits in the neighbouring fields. Sometimes they'd turn up after a few hours, smelling bad. At others, we'd have to go and look for them, with our mum or dad driving slowly through the lanes, while Ruth and I hung out of the window bellowing the dogs' names.

And then one time, they went missing for a whole day. After school, we went driving around the lanes as usual, shouting and shouting until our throats hurt. When we woke the next morning, Midas was waiting outside the hotel, looking guilty, but there was no sign of Scipio. In the days that followed, Ruth learned a rhyme – a sort of prayer, really – from a Catholic friend of hers: 'St Anthony, St Anthony, bring what I've lost back to me.' She recited it over and over in the car as we drove up and down the lanes looking for her dog. But he never came back.

I think of this as Carla and I make our way through the Pembrokeshire lanes towards my mother's cottage. Carla was the first woman I took home to Wales. When I told my mum about her, she just sighed and said: 'I always thought it would be Ruth who'd do that sort of thing,' as if I had moved in with a woman to make some sort of point. But then she met Carla – and Carla, being Carla, won her round.

The second time I saw the woman from Roberto's was in school prayers. The sun was streaming through the stained-glass windows. And there she was: dark eyes, high cheekbones, a scarf sweeping her messy dark hair up into a sort of turban. It was a strong face. It had a ferocity to it.

'Who's that?' I hissed into Jess's hair.

'The new Spanish language assistant,' Jess whispered back. 'She was being given the grand tour yesterday.' She glanced at me. I probably looked like death. 'Are you OK?'

I nodded and looked down at my hymnbook. The chaplain ran through the day's notices. 'And a warm welcome to our new Spanish language assistant, Miss Wick, who joins us from Argentina for the summer term.'

'That's her,' Jess told me unnecessarily.

Spanish. That was bad for me. I did Spanish A level, which would mean one-on-one conversation sessions with the language assistant. I almost missed my first one, almost pretended to be ill that morning – something I'd never normally do – after spending the night tossing and turning. But Spanish meant too much to me. And the feelings weren't all bad. My body felt different, shaken by fairground sensations of walking on tightropes, or the teetering imbalance you feel at the top of a rollercoaster. In the end, I persuaded myself it was like sitting out a fever. That I would just have to sweat it out and one day I would wake and the sickness would be over. And I couldn't avoid language class forever.

Miss Wick, on the other hand, hadn't looked flustered, not really. Slightly embarrassed, perhaps, but not shaken by the magnitude of it all in the way I was. I was both relieved and disappointed. Had it meant so little that she could sit and joke about it?

'You are a schoolgirl – a student?' she'd corrected herself. 'I thought you were older.' And that had been that. She had switched to Spanish and told me a bit about herself: she was Argentinian, but she had lived in the UK for some time. She'd studied fine art at Goldsmiths and worked in galleries in London in the years since, though she was hoping to do a master's soon. Did I have a favourite artist?

I nodded and tried to find the right words. As I talked I looked at her face. It was not quite as I remembered it. Had I idealised her? In the event our conversation was easy, and it was easy enough to mask how I was feeling, but as I looked at Miss Wick's face and told her why I loved Frieda Kahlo, I realised I hadn't idealised her, not at all.

'Do you ever think about Polly?' I ask Carla. Polly was her first love, her sixth-form girlfriend.

'Hardly ever.' Carla glances over at me, smiling. 'Are you thinking of Miss Wick again?'

'Only fleetingly,' I smile back.

'Well, it's different for you.' She puts a hand on my leg. 'She broke your heart.'

My mother is at the kitchen sink as we pull up at the cottage, the window a bright rectangle against the dusk outside. She glances up as we arrive and waves at us, looking older than I remember.

As she comes outside to greet us, a tea towel is still thrown over her arm.

'There he is,' she says, holding out her arms for Nunny.

I pass him to her and she looks down at his impassive face.

'What does it mean?' she says quietly. 'Who can have sent him?'

I don't know how to answer this.

'Richard's looking into it,' I say. 'I sent him a photocopy of the handwriting on the package – one of his friends is an expert.'

'Does he have a sample of hers?'

'Yes,' I say. 'A letter.'

'It's weird, isn't it?' She looks from me to Carla and back.

'It *is* weird,' I agree. 'It's beyond weird.'

I'm not sleeping well: the dream is back. Ruth running through the streets in St Anthony's, my voice echoing back at me as I call for her. Once, instead of the shoes, I came across Nunny in the dream, lying on his back, looking up at the sky with his blank marble eyes. I've found myself getting out of bed in the night to check Nunny is still there, or sending strange emails to other relatives of the missing – just a select few I've come to know over the years – to say: has anything like this ever happened to you?

'Could it be her?' my mum whispers. 'Dare we hope?'

Dare we hope? 'I don't know.' That's the simplest answer. I don't know.

She brings him to her face. 'He still smells of her.'

'Yes,' I say, 'though that might fade.'

My mother, who has lost more people than most, knows that the shirts and jumpers, the cuddly toys and dressing gowns, even the pillows, where a human's scent is strongest, all lose the scent of the person eventually, come to smell like dust and mothballs and everything else in the house. She cradles Nunny like a baby, like a lost child. It will be better, I tell myself, when ours comes along.

*　　*　　*

152

We never saw Scipio again. Our father found his body, eventually, in a field miles away from the hotel and buried him there so that we wouldn't see. A farmer had shot him for chasing sheep and not even called to let us know. Ruth seemed to sense it before she heard the words. She screamed and screamed, and fought and lashed out at our father, who had spent the last hour burying her dog, the mud still smeared on his cords.

The weekend after Scipio had died we went for a walk together through the autumnal fields. Ruth said mournfully, 'Scipio would have loved this,' and she started to cry, but our dad gripped her hand very tight and said: 'Look over there, look at the sheep. He would have been chasing after them; we would have been chasing after him.'

I wonder now if he was saying: it was inevitable.

That terrible pain of losing Scipio – I sometimes think it was a kind of training for the greater one that was to come. The person who taught us about the inevitability of loss – did he have any notion of the fact he might be coaching us for his own?

Was it inevitable, too, that our father – so alive and unstuffy, thrumming his fingers on the table, laughing loud, teaching us how to wink, and ride horses, and do equations – was it inevitable, from the beginning, that his heart would give in so early, that he would burn out so much sooner than everybody else? Lesser men, stuffier men, men who wore normal shoes and drove normal cars, who didn't always push for something more. All the men in the world who would still be alive when the one we loved the most had gone.

Kat

March 2000

It had been Luke who had first suggested going to the Peak District for Kat's birthday, she recalls now. She hadn't been keen – suspecting it was just an excuse to get her away for a dirty weekend. A good friend of Richard's, Luke was soft on Kat. Why did life always work out that way? He was nice – kind and funny with a decent dollop of cynicism. Kat liked his freckles, his green eyes, and the way he always laughed at her jokes. But he wasn't Richard.

So she hadn't been that fussed, but then Ruth had seemed interested – and, not long after, so had Richard, funnily enough, and now the four of them are on a road trip in Luke's old banger, while he tries to inspire some enthusiasm for the whole venture.

'Come on, Kitty,' says Luke, who has persuaded them all it would be a good idea to have a look at Chatsworth before getting on with the more important business of getting drunk. 'You love Nancy Mitford's books. Don't you think she's a sort of British Dorothy Parker?'

'Chatsworth wasn't hers,' Ruth interrupts. 'It belongs to that other one – Debo.'

'There were actually six Mitford sisters in total,' Luke points out a touch smugly.

'I know that,' Ruth says, rolling her eyes. 'Everyone knows that.'

'Who's your favourite, then?' challenges Luke.

'Jessica, of course,' Ruth fires back. 'She was the commie.'

'You're a regular red, Ruth,' he laughs.

'She was the only one with decent politics,' continues Ruth, marking the points off her fingers. '*And* she was a writer – though she doesn't get as much credit for it as Nancy.'

Ruth's mood is bright and brittle today. Currently, she veers from a sort of mania to being sulky and withdrawn. She and Richard remind Kat of those Alpine weather houses – when one of them is up, the other's down. She can't tell what's going on.

'Plus,' Ruth adds dramatically, 'she risked everything for love.'

'Of her cousin,' says Kat. '*Very* sexy.' It's stuffy today. She winds down the smeary window for some air.

'Who's your favourite?' asks Luke.

Kat closes her eyes, enjoys the sensation of the breeze on her face. 'Unity,' she says, smirking.

Richard emits a snort from the back. It's practically the first noise he's made all journey. He and Ruth are sitting as far away from each other as they possibly can, and Richard has spent most of the journey looking out of the window in sullen silence. This is not quite the trip Kat had envisaged for her birthday. She'd hoped to be in the back with Richard, or at least with Ruth. As it was, she and Luke are sitting in the front like parents, with Ruth talking too much, too brightly, and Richard not at all.

He had come to see her recently and chatted for ages about films and music like he used to and then, as he was leaving, he said in a voice that was clearly trying to be neutral, unsuspicious: 'You still see much of Ruth?'

'Of course,' Kat said.

He was standing in her room in his scruffy duffle coat, with his hair messy, his face sad. He said: 'She ever mention me?'

And Kat had thought of saying, 'She told me she'd given you a blow job. She said it was a mistake.' But instead, she screwed up her nose as if she were actually thinking about it, feigning nonchalance in the same way he was. Only more convincingly. 'No, not really.'

It was true, in a sense: she and Ruth didn't talk about him much and when they did, Ruth adopted her shiny voice, as cold and bright as marbles. As if nothing could touch her.

'Did Dorothy Parker ever visit Chatsworth?' she asks Kat. No one in the car – apart from Richard – seems willing to allow a moment's quiet to fall.

'I don't think so,' Kat says, though in truth she has no idea. 'I can't imagine it would have been her scene. All those toffs. She would have been too sassy for them.'

'Like you,' says Luke loyally.

156

'Maybe I'm thinking of Charleston?' Ruth persists.

Kat shrugs. 'I'm not sure. She must have known someone from Bloomsbury.'

'They lived in squares and loved in triangles,' Luke says portentously. But his words are met with silence by the rest of the car.

Kat looks out at the landscape and notices how crags have started to loom threateningly above them. She wonders if the trip is a mistake.

It's a sunny day. Ruth springs from the car as soon as they get there and bounds towards the house enthusing about the Painted Hall and Sculpture Gallery. Richard heads for the café in the stables, muttering about finding a cup of coffee, while Kat and Luke are left trailing behind Ruth as she moves briskly, chatting to the guides, stopping suddenly at a piece of furniture or a painting – and then darting off. Inside, the house is cooler, but the incremental effect of gaudy gold paintings, luxury, privilege makes Kat feel strange, almost jet-lagged.

'For a commie, Ruth's pretty keen on this world,' she jokes weakly as they pause for a moment in a guest bedroom, where it's quieter, more discreet.

Luke nods. 'She's a bit . . .' he starts.

'What?' says Kat, unsure if she's going to like what comes next.

'Her head is turned easily,' he says.

Kat nods, though she has never quite thought of Ruth that way before.

'If someone likes her, she responds so quickly.' He smiles. 'She's not like you in that way.'

'What do you mean?' Kat stops, hears Ruth's voice in the next room. She looks at Luke's kind, open face.

'I don't think you're so easily flattered,' he continues. 'Superficially, maybe, but I think there's more substance to you than that. I think once you fall in love, that's it.'

Luke is so close Kat can smell the washing powder on his shirt. It's crisp and clean like pine forests. She doesn't tend to give nice boys a chance, but something has shifted momentarily between them, like the change of a channel. It's as if no one has noticed her before. Not like this. Not even Richard.

Ruth bounds back into the room, breaking the spell. 'I'm going to the maze!' she exclaims.

'Go for it,' Kat smiles. She turns back to Luke. 'Do you fancy climbing the Hundred Steps?'

He glances at her, changes tack. 'What's going on between them?'

Kat is silent. She doesn't want to say it.

'He likes her,' Luke says. 'She likes him. I don't know why they just don't get on with it. Give us all a bit of peace.'

Kat looks at him. Could he really be that oblivious? 'I'm not sure she *does* like him,' she says instead.

It's more of a climb than she expected up the Hundred Steps. As they pass a lone monkey puzzle tree they turn to look back at the maze and make out the figure of Ruth scampering through it, though who her performance is for Kat can't work out. Until she spots Richard in the centre, waiting. As Ruth approaches, they rush at each other like Apache dancers in a move that, from a distance, looks almost violent.

'Well, look at that,' laughs Luke.

Ruth and Richard are kissing and kissing, wrapped around each other, completely oblivious to the small children in the vicinity.

The sight hurts Kat so much it's hard to find the words for it. It's like something wild opening its wings inside her. 'Oh God,' she says.

'I know,' says Luke. 'They're going to get us all thrown out.'

'Let's carry on walking,' says Kat, turning and continuing up the steps. 'I'd like to see the Cascade.' Her face hurts from not showing her emotion, from keeping it neutral.

The afternoon gets even worse.

'I think about you all the time,' says Luke abruptly when they stop to look at the Cascade from the top of the hill. He pulls her around to face him. 'I want to kiss you.'

Kat slides her hands under his jacket and can feel his skin, warm through his shirt. She keeps her head tucked under his chin, so his mouth can't find hers. 'I can't.'

'You can.'

'I can't,' Kat swallows, thinks she might try the truth. 'I'm in love with someone else.'

Luke stiffens. 'Richard?' He pulls away.

'I didn't say that,' she says quietly.

'You didn't have to. Fuck.' He takes a step away. 'I can't believe it's happening again.'

'Again?'

'There was a girl before – in our first year. I was so into her. And he took her off me. Just because he could.'

159

'Believe me, I know a bit about that.' The light spray of water is cool against Kat's back.

'Must have stung a bit to see him with Ruth.'

She nods, checking the pocket of her coat for cigarettes.

'Richard put that other girl off in the end, anyway,' says Luke. 'He's jealous. Obsessive.'

'He doesn't seem it,' says Kat coolly.

Luke snorts. 'Ask Caroline. She won't go near him.'

When they meet back at the car at four as planned, Richard isn't there. Ruth's eyes are swollen, her face pink and prickled.

'We had a tiff,' she says to the others.

'A lovers' tiff?' asks Luke.

Ruth ignores him. 'He says he'll join us at the pub later,' she tells Kat.

Kat frowns. No matter what sort of mood Richard is in, it won't be the same with just three of them. 'I don't want to go without him,' she says.

'For fuck's sake, let's just go.' Ruth climbs in the back and slams the door, glowering out of the window.

'He's a big boy,' says Luke. 'And the pub's not far. I think you and I deserve a stiff drink.'

The evening, as Kat suspected, is a complete write-off. There is absolutely no sign of Richard, Luke is sulking and Ruth doesn't eat or say a thing. Kat orders way too much wine on her father's credit card, as part of his annual guilt splurge on her birthday, and finds herself wondering if she can join a rather Sloaney stag party taking place in the far corner of the bar, which looks, at least, distractingly fun.

'Ruth,' she says eventually, putting her cutlery down. 'This is ridiculous. You should go. Go and find Richard.'

Ruth looks away. 'I don't know what you mean.'

'You *do* know what I mean.' Kat tries to laugh but it feels as if she has glass in her throat. 'Everyone knows what I mean. The landlady knows what I mean. Fuck, even Luke knows what I mean.' She sighs. 'Go and find Richard. That can be my birthday present.'

Ruth, to be fair, looks distraught. 'I didn't want to, I didn't mean to,' she says.

Kat takes a large slurp of wine. She doesn't want to talk about it, doesn't want to be part of it at all. She needs this star-crossed lovers act to play out elsewhere. 'Darling, do fuck off and find him. Honestly, the pair of you are unbearable.'

Ruth gets up and makes her way over to Kat. She presses a kiss on the top of Kat's head. Kat can feel the wetness of her tears.

'I love him. I'm sorry. I didn't mean to.' She spins on her heels and makes for the door.

The table is silent for a moment except for the sound of Luke filling up Kat's glass.

'I love him. I'm sorry. I didn't mean to. Isn't that the plot of *Brief Encounter*?' he asks.

'It's the plot of every film ever made,' sighs Kat. She can't bear to be alone with Luke, not now. 'Hey,' she shouts over to the stag party. 'We have spare wine going. Come on,' she says to Luke. 'Let's see if they'll let us join in.'

The evening passes in a blur. Outside, it starts to rain.

'They're out in that,' Kat murmurs to Luke.

'Fuck them,' he says.

161

And she loves him for a moment for not saying, 'Love will keep them warm.' Or anything shit like that. So she lets him kiss her, lets him lead her up to bed to the snug little room over the bar, with beams and an uneven floor. But Kat's heart isn't in it and, because Luke's decent, he stops and they lie and look at the ceiling, the way the light changes as the night progresses. Eventually, Luke falls asleep and Kat is left alone, lying awake, seeing in her twentieth birthday listening to the rain.

The next morning, Kat and Luke find Ruth and Richard huddled by the fire in the bar with cups of coffee. Their hair is damp, but whether that's from being out all night or freshly washed this morning, she can't tell and she doesn't ask. Even after a night without sleep, Ruth glows. She hides her euphoria better than Richard, who is gripping Ruth's hand and looking at her moonily. And a part of Kat can see now that this was always perfect and inevitable. And another part, which is in control today, wants to die.

'Well,' she says. 'That was quite the night. Did you lovebirds get any sleep?'

Richard grins. 'No.'

At the same time, Ruth says, 'A little.'

Kat doesn't feel like being fun today. 'I didn't sleep much either,' she says shortly. 'Shall we get some breakfast?'

Luke is the only one who eats a hearty meal. Kat can't touch hers, and Richard and Ruth push food around their plates, stealing sly glances at each other.

'Whose turn is it to drive?' asks Luke as they finish.

'Actually, I'm getting the train back,' Kat says, surprising herself for a moment.

Honestly, she thinks to herself, making her way back up the uneven staircase to her room. It's my fucking birthday. And there are limits.

Naomi

I felt like a fish out of water at the school disco – I always did, particularly without Ruth by my side. She'd always gone before me – to Pony Club Camp, to school and, finally, to university. There had always been someone waiting for me, one person in a room I knew would be on my side. It meant I rarely had to start new things alone and I felt her absence in sixth form more than I'd anticipated. And particularly at social events like this – while the younger girls bopped around in Indian skirts or artfully ripped jeans, we prefects had to perform our duties in uniform. It was as awkward as hell. The whole thing was huddles of girls and boys in separate corners, not really mingling. That would come later, right at the end of the night. And my job – mine and the other prefects' – was to keep an eye out for drinking, smoking, and what our teachers called 'excessive contact'.

There had been a long, excruciating discussion about how much contact was allowed. Kissing was OK, for instance; hands under tops were not. Oral sex was a serious no-no. I found the best approach, on the whole, was to stay in the sports hall – there weren't many students stupid enough to attempt a blow job there.

A gaggle of girls brushed past me. Fourth years. They were the worst: hormones stirring and nowhere to go with them. By the fifth and sixth form the girls were given more freedom, but in the fourth year all the fourteen-year-olds would relieve their frustration through bullying and petty politics.

Heading the gang was Lizzie Clark, a pointy-faced girl with a nasty streak. 'Suck!' she stage-whispered to the others, glancing back to check I'd heard. I looked away for a moment, pressing my lips tightly together.

How did girls like Lizzie, with her attitude and tiny skirts, get to be so sophisticated so young? She looked like a weird little girl-woman, with her spindly legs, hollow cheeks and smudgily applied eyeliner. But it wasn't just that it was embarrassing to be bullied by a much younger girl: it was something else, too, something akin to jealousy. Because Lizzie wasn't afraid of sex, I guess. And I still was.

The girls following Lizzie closed ranks around her as she sashayed over to the best-looking boy in the building and I asked myself: what would Ruth do? Ruth never thought things through, but perhaps sometimes that was the best way. I marched over to her and put a hand on her shoulder.

'Lizzie?'

'Yeah?' Lizzie didn't even bother to turn round; she was just staring at the older boy.

165

'Could you do something for me?'

'Depends.' She still didn't bother to look at me.

Out of the corner of my eye, I could see a teacher watching us. I put my mouth against her ear. It smelled of stale smoke and expensive perfume.

'Try not to be such an utter bitch.'

Lizzie pulled away, too surprised to say anything back. And I marched away out of the main hall and into the foyer, my face burning, my heart hammering in my ribcage. It felt amazing. I walked smack into Miss Wick.

'Naomi.' She raised an eyebrow, looking amused. She always looked amused around me. Strange to think she was only seven years older. 'I've been asked to do a round of the games field.' She added in a whisper: 'To catch smokers and heavy petters. Do you fancy joining me?'

I had been very careful about controlling my thoughts about Miss Wick. Whenever I felt a thought meandering in that direction, remembering something she had said, or the way she occasionally looked at me, I would firmly drive it into a dead end and park it. Miss Wick was a woman and a teacher. Sort of a teacher. Not quite a teacher. But similar.

And this was just one of those unsettling experiences that around 40 per cent of women – I had been doing some reading – went through. Any day, I hoped, I would fall in love with a boy and life would be straightforward again.

We walked in silence at first. Miss Wick was taller than me and she took longer strides. When we got away from the sports hall, she took out a pouch of tobacco and began to roll a cigarette.

I cleared my throat. 'We probably shouldn't.'

And Miss Wick laughed and put a hand on my arm. 'Don't worry, Naomi. I have a plan.' She kept walking in her loping gait. She stopped for a moment, at the periphery of the pool of light cast by the sports hall, to concentrate on rolling.

We walked on in silence, away from the lights. At the very edge of the sports field, a line of trees separated the games pitches from a wire fence that kept the space, and the schoolgirls, enclosed. On the eastern side, by the railway track, the fence was particularly high. Behind the trees was a patch where some of the wilder girls went to smoke dope and make out. I remember wondering if Miss Wick knew that. But whether or not she did, that was where we ended up. And, on any other occasion, with any other person, it might have seemed just like a patch of grass by a railway track, but that night with the trees rustling above us, and the music in the distance, it felt as if we'd slipped through to a better version of the world: sharper, brighter.

She took off her jacket and threw it on the ground. And we sat and chatted as she smoked. I've always liked the smell of fresh smoke, the phosphorous fizz of the match – it reminds me of home and the hotel bar at the end of the evening, when everyone sits around talking and whoever is behind the bar starts topping up people's drinks without charging, where all the usual rules are suspended for a short time.

I told her about my fight with Lizzie.

'Nasty age, eh?' She wrinkled her nose. 'They don't know who they are.'

'No,' I said and smiled, looking down to her jacket, where her hand was very close to mine. 'At what age *do* you know?' I asked.

Miss Wick laughed. It was a warm cackle. 'God knows.'

'But you're . . .' I adopted a self-conscious tone. 'A teacher.'

Miss Wick glanced at me. 'Not exactly.'

And the way she looked at me made my heart thunder in my chest. And then we lay back staring at the sky, and she put her arms around me and our breathing settled into the same rhythm. For a while it felt companionable, safe. And then, at some stage, my breathing changed, became swifter, shallower, and it didn't feel as safe any more. When we finally kissed, she let me come to her, she let me make the choice. She didn't rush me, like the boys who'd tried to kiss me before. She knew how to take her time.

The thrum of the music reverberated from the sports hall – just a few pricks of light in the distance. When we broke from kissing, we were holding each other so close that she could feel the pulse of my heart leaping in my chest like a jackrabbit. And she laughed, but not nastily, as if she was happy with the effect she had on me. She kissed me again, more passionately the second time, and my body started to swim beneath her.

The squeal of a train made us jump. We stopped for a second. We could hear the rumble and screech of it in the distance, but we didn't think what it meant. We weren't thinking at all. It's like when the sand slips from under your feet as you get pulled too far out to sea; the ground slopes away from you and you are suddenly kicking out, trying to pull yourself back, out of the current. But the best thing to do about a riptide is to let it take you, because it will take you anyway.

And then two things happened. The train roared into view, illuminating our little strip of land like a searchlight. And faces – strangers' faces – zoomed past blankly. So many faces, even at this time of night – adults and children, couples and old people – every so often seeming to look straight at us as they peered out into the black.

It used to haunt me: could they see anything in the patch of grass just outside their window? Could they see us sprawled out on the grass just yards away from them? Or could they make out, as I could – just a stone's throw away – Lizzie Clark pushed up against a tree kissing the boy from the sports hall?

Lizzie Clark, with her kohl-smudged eyes wide open in the dark, breaking away from her embrace as the train thundered past. In that moment, knowing she could be seen. Knowing, too, what she was seeing.

Alice

'I always satisfied her – in the bedroom, if you know what I mean?' Her client's eyes move from Alice to her junior solicitor, who is making notes on Alice's right. She can hear the younger woman, an ardent feminist with the looks of Brigitte Bardot, shift in her chair, can feel disapproval radiate from her like heat.

'We know what you mean, Mr Peterson,' she says coolly.

He rests a hand on his paunch, looks past Alice out of the window behind her. 'She says I was controlling.' He laughs. 'I never heard her complain when it came to spending my money.'

There is a spluttering to Alice's right. The client frowns. 'Have I said something funny?'

Alice takes control. 'How long have you been living apart?' she asks smoothly, making a mental note to talk to her junior colleague. Once in a while, one's feminist principles had to be left at the door. Or, as someone had once advised her, 'It's about them, not about you.'

She thinks about her morning now as she reaches home, as she drops her briefcase in the hall. It's always more difficult working for someone you don't like. This particular client is trying to protect his assets from a woman he had prevented from working for seventeen years. His wife going back to her career, after bringing up two children, had precipitated the breakdown of the relationship – not another man, as far as she could tell. Not that Alice would blame her. He makes her skin crawl: the way he dyes his thinning hair, the way he speaks in innuendo-laden jibes, his gaze sliding over her legs.

Their hallway smells, as it always does after Mrs T's visits, of old-fashioned polish, which she applies by hand, inch by inch over the floor. Mrs T, who has worked for her mother-in-law since George was a boy, cleans their house twice a week. Her nickname was given to her by an infant George while Thatcher was in power. Her regular visits strike Alice as a little profligate for the two of them, though she's good at ironing George's shirts, not a task Alice has ever taken to and one for which she is particularly grateful at the moment.

Even after all these years, she is still not entirely comfortable with someone working for her at home. She always tidies up for the cleaner and avoids being in the house when the older woman is working. She doesn't like to see her on her hands and knees smoothing the wax on to the wooden floorboards. George never has such qualms and somehow, unfairly Alice feels, Mrs T much prefers him to her.

That was George. He could tease, or flirt with, almost

any woman he came across. Almost. 'Got some shirts for you, Mrs T,' he would say, depositing a huge armful by her ironing board, and she would smile and say: 'That will keep me out of trouble.'

But when Alice politely, ever so politely, asks her to handwash one of her dresses, or to clean their bathroom that week, she always says: 'No problem, Mrs Bell,' in a manner that suggests somehow it is.

Alice has always found managing people difficult. It's something she has had to learn at work, but somehow she can't quite apply the lessons she has learned to her own home – a key point being you can't get too caught up in whether people like you or not. It matters to her that Mrs T doesn't and the more she tries, the cooler the older woman's manner seems to become.

She's home early today after a doctor's appointment and she can't tell if Mrs T has left or not. Alice always knows when George is at home. Not just for the lights glaring from every room or Radio 4 drifting up from the kitchen, but also for the presence of him, the solidity of George. Conversely, he can crash around the house for ages before coming across her in the bedroom or kitchen. 'Hello, darling, I didn't know you were here.' As if her presence were somehow an insubstantial thing.

Mrs T has neatly stacked the post on the hall table, which Alice had regarded with dread when George was still an MP. Most of it went to his constituency office, but the odd nutter would have made that extra special effort to find his personal details.

She picks up the post and wanders through to the living room. Although she wants, more than anything, to make a cup of tea and take it up to bed, she isn't keen for Mrs T to witness this kind of indolence. She drops the post on the coffee table in the centre of the room and lies down on the sofa without turning any of the lights on, blindsided by an unexpected wave of fatigue.

She had finished Richard's book now but she hadn't learned much more about Ruth. He had moved on to other cases, coming briefly back to Ruth in his conclusion, but nothing more than that. There had been no response from Naomi on Facebook and none of her other searches on social media had yielded anything. The case was cooling, as they said on TV.

Christie hadn't been much help. Her energy altered whenever Alice brought it up. She couldn't put her finger on how Christie changed exactly, but she could just feel her friend's focus drift away. Instead, Alice found herself confiding in a friend at work, who had listened carefully to the whole story and eventually said, 'Something similar happened to me. I saw a girl I'd known at school, who had died years before, at Euston. On an escalator.'

'And?' Alice asked, leaning forwards in her seat, relieved to be able to talk about it like this.

'I remembered later she had an identical twin.' Her friend laughed. 'So there was a perfectly reasonable explanation.'

Alice leaned back, disappointed. 'Ruth had a sister, but she wasn't a twin.'

'I'm just saying: there's usually a rational answer,' her friend said kindly. 'It's like those mad people filming poltergeists. It's always the cat.'

Alice smiled faintly. 'That's my equivalent.'

'There will be a logical explanation. You just don't know it yet.'

She just didn't know it yet. She looks down at the post on the table. The one at the top of the pile is addressed to George Bell, MP. Alice finds she still isn't used to the idea of George not being an MP. The day before he resigned, before he read the letter in the House of Commons, there had been a sort of summit meeting at their home: a couple of people from his team, who kept themselves diplomatically out of the way in the kitchen or the study when matters got more personal, and Christie and Teddy, who didn't.

'People don't like me,' George had said from his favourite armchair, looking into the fire.

'They love you,' Christie responded quickly before Alice had had a chance to say anything.

'They love to hate me,' George guffawed.

'They *do* love you.' Alice went to George then, crouched down by his chair, thinking of St Anthony's, of how people flocked to his room, followed him around, repeated his jokes.

'Not everyone,' he said darkly. 'Some of them loathe me.'

The room went silent, thinking, no doubt, of the woman on telly. Her wild hair tied in pigtails. Her red face scrunched up in disgust.

He had made a bad joke. A bad joke at a bad time. A time when the party needed modernising, humanising. 'You are too pretty to do this job.' A throwaway comment. The kind George's father might have made all the time. She wasn't even working on his team – the twenty-something

174

girl in pigtails – but on the team of a colleague. Who knew that one throwaway comment could go so far? There had been uproar – column after column in the papers, women waiting outside his constituency surgery wearing 'Too Pretty to Work' T-shirts, a hashtag on Twitter.

'Did you touch her?' Alice asked that night, not wanting to say it in front of Christie and Teddy but not having much choice. The girl's anger had seemed out of all proportion.

'No,' he shouted. 'I meant it as a bloody compliment.'

'She *is* pretty,' Christie said tartly.

Alice wished Christie and Teddy would go. 'What were you thinking?' she asked quietly.

'I just said what I thought,' George said.

'But you can't,' Alice said. 'You can't – that's the problem.'

In television, his colleagues didn't seem to mind so much. There had been the odd off joke, but compared with presenters punching people, George seemed pretty tame.

The worst of it all had been the girls – the twenty-somethings, millennials – they looked so furious, so disgusted, so strong. What must it be like to walk around feeling so certain of yourself? The girl with the pigtails cornered Alice once in the ladies' loo of a restaurant – she'd obviously tracked her down. 'You're married to him?' she spat.

Alice wanted to ask, 'Why? Why, really, are you so very angry? Is there more? More to the story?'

But Christie, who'd been with Alice, had put her arm around her and said, 'Do you know what my friend does for a living? She defends victims of domestic violence in

175

divorce suits against their beastly husbands. So don't come here lecturing us about women's fucking rights.' And that had shut her up.

Mrs T comes bustling in, interrupting Alice's train of thought. 'Sorry, Mrs Bell,' she says, not sounding particularly sorry. 'I didn't know you were here, sitting in the dark.' The tone is a touch accusatory.

Alice sits up. 'Yes, I'm sorry. Not feeling so good.'

'I see you've got the post there,' the older woman says in the same defiant tone. 'Another one of those postcards arrived.' She bustles out of the room. 'I'll be going then,' she calls back to Alice and leaves with the front door swinging loudly shut behind her.

Alice reaches out and picks up the pile of letters to look at them more closely – a few bills, a thank-you note from a friend and then the postcard. It's sepia in tone, out of focus. Alice has to squint to make out what it is: Cathedral Square in St Anthony's. It's dusty and yellowing, like something that has been lying in someone's desk drawer for years.

She turns it over. It is addressed to George. The writing is in block capitals: 'St Anthony, St Anthony, give what I've lost back to me.'

That's all. It's not been signed, nor is it a hand she recognises. Alice reads it twice. She remembers someone repeating the rhyme to her at a party. She doesn't recall who or why. Stories would circulate about the town among the students. In a place that had lost so much to the sea, there were bound to be rumours, ghost stories. There often were in coastal towns.

Alice fishes her mobile out of her handbag and calls George. He answers the phone a touch breathlessly, as if caught out at something. She says, without introduction, 'St Anthony, St Anthony, give what I've lost back to me.'

There is a pause, then, 'What on earth are you talking about?'

'A postcard arrived for you from St Anthony's,' she says.

'Oh?' says George.

'The thing is,' says Alice, looking down at the postcard in her hand. 'Mrs T said "another one".'

'Darling, I really don't know what you're going on about,' he says impatiently. Behind him, in the background, she can hear other voices, the noises of people going busily about their work. She won't let him make her feel foolish. Not this time.

'*Another* one implies it isn't the first, doesn't it?' she says. 'That someone has been sending you cryptic postcards from St Anthony's for a while.'

'Just a minute,' says George as someone interrupts him.

Alice recognises the voice of one his producers, a no-nonsense blonde in her late twenties.

'I've got to go,' he says wearily as he returns to the call. 'Try to get some rest.'

The following week, Alice waits to catch Mrs T before going to work on the pretence of asking her about the washing detergent they are using, something her skin has started reacting to.

As she's leaving, she asks as carelessly as she can: 'You know those postcards George has been receiving?'

The other woman's face is a blank, an unfurrowed brow beneath tight grey curls.

'What's that, Mrs Bell?'

'The other day,' Alice persists. 'A postcard arrived for George and you said, "Another one of those cards".'

'Did I, dear?' Mrs T says in a more kindly tone than she normally adopts for Alice. 'I don't remember.'

'Yes, you did,' says Alice, trying not to let her irritation show. 'You definitely did. Have you seen other cards like it?'

Mrs T blinks. Her blue eyes are watery as she concentrates. She looks, in this moment, smaller, more fragile than she usually does, bustling through the house. She says at last: 'I think he used to get some strange cards before – from his constituents and things.'

That's not what Alice means and Mrs T knows it.

'Specifically, like this?' Alice holds up the postcard as if it's a piece of evidence in court. 'From St Anthony's?'

Mrs T's face shifts. She looks away from Alice. 'No, I don't think so,' she says eventually. 'I don't think I've ever seen anything like that before.'

Naomi

After the incident by the train tracks, there had been no need for me to pretend to be ill to avoid Miss Wick. A nasty flu started as a twinge in my throat and developed quickly into a hacking cough, aching limbs, headaches, a temperature and vivid hallucinations. I had almost a fortnight off school, sleeping fitfully through the days, dreaming feverishly of Miss Wick, of trains rattling by in the night, of Lizzie Clark's kohl-rimmed eyes always watching me.

I didn't eat for days. My mother brought in food on a tray, all my favourite treats; she pressed damp towels against my forehead and asked, 'What's the matter, darling?' when I cried, which I did a lot, but I couldn't find the words to say: 'I love a woman, I am gay; everything you thought about me, I'm not.'

Eventually, I regained some strength and dragged myself for walks along the clifftops. I knew I would have to go back to school.

On my last night at home, my mother, after a couple of strong gin and tonics in the hotel bar, took my hand and said: 'It's OK, you know, to rebel a bit.'

'Against what?' I smiled.

'I worry that you're pushing yourself too hard – with work, with all your prefect duties. Ruth, at your age, had been hauled up three times for smoking.'

'You want me to be caught smoking?'

'No, darling. I just don't want you to feel you have to be perfect or something.' She took a sip of her drink. 'Do you have a boyfriend?'

'Why does everyone keep asking me that?' I said tetchily. I got up to look for dirty glasses.

'You used to be interested in boys – there was that one with freckles who used to hang around . . .' my mother continued when I returned to the table. She didn't quite look me in the eye. Maybe she was thinking, like me, that that had been a long time ago.

'Until Ruth saw him off . . .' I laughed.

'Well, yes . . .'

It was quiet that night – just a handful of regulars. I felt my mum's eyes on my back as I scurried around emptying ashtrays and wiping tables. At last, I gave up and returned to her, perching next to her.

'Actually, Mum, I have started seeing someone.' That, at least, was true.

'Oh, darling, I'm so pleased.' Our mother is small but her grip has a steely strength to it. 'And are you in love?'

I thought then of Miss Wick, of how I had sat up all night after it happened, shaking with shame. With

180

excitement. 'I don't know – I've certainly never felt like this before.' And that had been true as well.

Of all the things I had been expecting from Miss Wick, concern hadn't been top of the list.

'Naomi.' She stood up as I came through the door for our one-to-one session. 'How are you?'

'Much better.' I always felt very British around her. Buttoned tight. 'How are you?'

Miss Wick waved the query away. She came round the other side of the desk and took my hand. 'I've been so worried about you.'

Without warning, my eyes filled with tears. I looked past Miss Wick to the view outside, the sunlit quadrangle with a single horse chestnut in the centre of the immaculate lawn. The view, the tree, looked as it always did, but everything had changed for me. I wondered, if I thought about it enough, if I could move the tree just through sheer willpower. There is so much I want, I thought. Eventually, I said: 'I'm frightened.'

'This is the first time for you, isn't it?' she said. Her hand was warm. 'Are you sure about it?'

I stopped looking at the tree. I looked at Miss Wick's face. Her high cheekbones, the turban wrapped around her head, her lovely hands. 'Yes,' I said.

Alice

After Mrs T leaves, Alice descends to the kitchen and spends a long time turning the postcard over in her hands. She still can't let it go. Who would send such a card? And why would they send it now? There's something so personal about this picture, this view of Cathedral Square, the anchor there from one of the ships that had gone down in the bay. St Anthony was the patron saint of lost things, but he was also the one you prayed to when you wanted to get something back.

What did Alice want back? She could hardly bear to list it all. She thinks of how, on her wedding day, she'd woken early in the house she'd grown up in in Leamington Spa, how her mother had come to lie next to her in bed before they got up and they'd shared a few quiet minutes before the busy day started. She longs for that sort of tenderness and hope in her life again. Perhaps it'll return with the arrival of her own daughter.

She thinks of the way she used to laugh with Christie

and how it feels as if she hasn't, not properly, for a really long time. She thinks of how she used to believe that her work would change the world, or change something. Anything. She thinks of how it might feel not to wake up exhausted, her skin dry and creased, her hair requiring constant attention, and a new part of her body – her eyelashes, her eyebrows, her ever-growing belly – always needing attending to. She thinks of George when she first met him. The smell of him, the click of his leather shoes as he approached, the way his eyes would meet hers across a crowded room and he'd grin.

He'd badgered her for weeks to sleep with him. It wasn't that she didn't want to, but Christie's advice not to do it straight away rang in her ears. And she'd enjoyed the early days of their relationship – the cocktails and the dressing up – and was worried about what there would be on the other side. She hadn't asked too much around college about him, but she didn't need to. People smirked when they saw George and her hand in hand. Girls she used to be friendly with drifted away from her at parties.

'They're jealous,' Christie reassured her. But Alice wasn't sure if that was it.

There had been weeks of George coming back to her room and their sharing a bit of flirtatious chat over a cup of tea or a glass of wine, which would inevitably end up with them on the bed wrapped around each other, with George's hand creeping inside her dress and Alice batting it away.

'Alice, you're killing me,' he'd said on the day they'd finally done it, when she'd batted his hand away for what felt like the thousandth time. 'Why are you being like this?'

Alice had thought of Dan's cold eyes on her, the chuckling of George's friends, the weird reaction of other girls in college. She couldn't say the words aloud – 'I don't trust you' – so she tried a different tack, asking: 'If we sleep together, will you talk about it with everyone?'

He laughed. 'Are we at school?'

'I don't know,' Alice said, sitting up crossly, straightening her dress. 'Are we?'

'Look,' he took her hand. 'What happens between us is just between us. I promise.'

Alice ran a hand through her hair. She was a bit hungover that day, a little out of sorts. 'I'm sorry,' she frowned. 'I should probably be getting on with some work.'

'No,' George laughed, getting to his feet. 'It's the last week of term. You absolutely should not be getting on with work. You should be coming out for cocktails and a lavish lunch with me. Come on.' He pulled her to her feet. 'Get your coat.'

The hot hit of vodka in her belly had soothed her. They'd gone to a cocktail bar in town, where the soft lighting and mellow music had helped to ease the fluttering in her belly temporarily.

It was quiet in the bar, with just one other couple snuggled up together in the corner. Alice recognised the girl – Nicky Crisp, a second year from college who she'd bumped into once or twice at parties in college. She was one of the girls who had been a bit strange when Alice got together with George. Right now, she seemed to be

184

on a date with a huge guy, who had the distinctive build of a rugby player.

'So, am I going to see you over the Easter holidays?' George asked once they'd ordered.

'I don't know, are you?' Alice replied coquettishly.

He reached across the table and took her hand. 'I'd like that. You could stay with me in our townhouse. I'd show you Big Ben.'

Alice smirked. 'Is that what you're calling it?'

George chuckled. 'You look so sweet and innocent, but you're just as naughty as the next girl.'

The next girl. Alice tried not to think about the phrase as he pulled her towards him for a kiss, tried to shake off the feeling of unease when, after they broke away, she noticed Nicky and the guy she was with looking over at them.

The return of alcohol to her bloodstream after the boozy night before made her face flush hot. She nipped to the bathroom and splashed cold water on her cheeks, stood for a minute or so looking at herself in the mirror. Her day, once again, had been derailed by George's plans – she'd been meaning to get on with some work and here she was half-cut before three in the afternoon. Maybe it was the alcohol but she felt unsettled, slightly paranoid. She decided to tell George, when she returned to the table, that she needed to get back to college. But as she made her way back to him, she saw he'd ordered a fresh round of drinks.

'Cheers!' he said, raising his glass to her. 'To us!'

Alice smiled. Perhaps she'd stay for just one more, she told herself. They could get back to college after this.

'I mean it, about Easter,' George said. 'I'd really love to see you over the holidays.'

He was really making an effort, she thought, leaning forwards to kiss him.

Suddenly, though, George pulled sharply away. Nicky's date had appeared by their table. Up close, he was huge, towering over them.

'George Bell,' the man said sharply, but he doesn't smile.

A strange expression crossed George's face. 'Yes?' For the first time since Alice had been with him he'd looked unsure of himself.

'Will you step outside with me?' asked the man.

'What's this about?' asked George. 'We're in the middle of something.'

'Sure,' agreed the man-mountain. 'We can sort it out here.' And he seemed to think about it for a second before punching George hard in the face, sending him splayed onto the ground.

On the way down, George kicked up under the table and sent their drinks skidding across the floor.

Alice shrieked and leapt to her feet. The barman, drying a glass, shouted something, but the guy dashed for the door, with Nicky close behind him clutching her bag and coat. Alice crouched down next to George. He blinked a couple of times, moved a hand protectively to his nose, which was bloody and swollen, then sat up cautiously.

'George. Fuck. Who the fuck was that?' she asked as she helped him up, setting his chair upright and looking helplessly at their spilt drinks all over the floor.

'That a friend of yours?' demanded the barman, who

passed him a handful of napkins from the bar. 'I don't want that kind of shit in here.'

George shook his head. 'Not a friend,' he muttered in a muffled voice through the tissue paper.

The barman started to clear up around them, pointedly moving their chairs away so he could mop the floor.

'Should we go?' asked Alice. 'We need to clean up your face.'

Clutching the napkins to his face, George nodded grimly, got out his wallet and left a crisp fifty on the table.

'I'll go and get your change,' said the barman grumpily.

'No,' insisted George. 'Keep it.'

'So sorry,' said Alice to the barman, clutching her bag and coat on the way out.

Outside, in the afternoon light, she felt embarrassed. 'Let me look at your nose,' she said. 'Do you think you need to go to A & E?'

'God, no,' laughed George, sounding a bit more like himself. 'It's just a bloody nose. Now, where can we get our next drink?'

'Did you see the size of him?' Alice shook her head. 'Can I just clean it up first?'

'You don't want to be seen with me like this.'

'Yup,' she agreed. 'It wouldn't do at all.'

'I think this is just a ploy to get me back to your room again,' he teased.

On the way there, they picked up some ice from the college bar.

'What've you been up to, George?' asked the barman. 'At it again.'

It was another phrase that turned over in Alice's head

as she cleaned George's face in her room, putting some ice in a flannel and holding it against his nose.

'George,' she said at last. 'Who was he? What was all that about?'

He shrugged. 'I dated Nicky for a bit. She was fun, but she wasn't right for me. Maybe she's still pissed off.'

'That's why her date came to smack you around?'

Alice was quiet for a moment. It just didn't add up. She looked at George's swollen face, his bloody shirt, his polished leather shoes. What was she doing? Could she believe anything he said?

'George,' she said quietly. 'I don't know if this is working.'

Someone turned up the music in the college bar and the sounds of Santana drifted over.

She felt for a moment that the scales had fallen from her eyes: this was wrong, all wrong for her. The idea of not being with him was sad, yes, but the thought of it actually made her breathe a sigh of relief: no more trying so hard, no more decoding everything he said or did, no more trying to decipher the truth.

To her horror, George began to cry. It was one of the very few times she ever saw him do that.

'No, Alice. Don't do this,' he said. 'I like you. I like you in a way I never liked the others.'

'Why?' she said. She comes to sit next to him on the bed.

'You know exactly who you are.' He takes her hand. 'You don't try to please me.'

I do, she thought. I do that all the time.

'I see you,' George said. 'You think I don't, but I see you for who you are – so strong and determined and bloody-minded. You are the type of woman I want to marry one day. Not the party girls – not the Nicky Crisps.'

Alice softened. To be seen, she thinks now, remembering the moment: isn't that what we all want?

'Look,' he said, opening his arms. 'We've been rolling around for weeks and I've waited, haven't I? I've been respectful, I haven't pushed you to do anything, I haven't nagged.'

'You have nagged a bit,' smiled Alice.

He was right, though. After all that time, his interest hadn't waned. He'd been more steadfast and kinder than his college reputation seemed to suggest. She stood up and kissed him gently on the mouth. Maybe, she thought, it was time they did this, after all. Maybe that would make everything clearer, without the question of it hanging over them. She kissed him again, resting her hands on his shoulders.

'Don't worry,' she said as she helped to peel off his bloody shirt. 'I promise I'll be gentle with you.'

They had sex three times that evening – hastily at first and then more gently the second time. The third, George woke Alice in the night, kissing her face, saying, 'I can't believe I'm getting to do this with you.'

The next day, they slept late and at lunch George went out to buy champagne and snacks and returned with them to bed.

'Some girls,' he said into her hair after the fifth or six time they'd done it, as she was drifting back into a boozy sleep, 'wake up with regrets. They try to rewrite history. But you're not like them. You're different.'

Kat

May 2000

George's hand catches on Kat's hip as he brushes past her. 'You're looking sexy tonight,' he says, waving to greet Dan on the other side of the room.

'Thanks, George.' Kat runs a hand through her hair. 'You don't scrub up too badly yourself.' She watches him make his way through the crowded room to Dan.

There's something sexy about men touching your hips like that, Kat muses; it's the right distance from the crucial zone. Close enough to be provocative, far enough to leave something to the imagination. Recently, she's noticed George noticing her, catching her eye across the room at parties. Nothing major – George flirts with a lot of people – but it's as if Kat has come into his radar.

More than once tonight, she looks up and sees Dan and him, handsome in black tie, looking in her direction. It becomes like a joke: she looks up, they're watching her, they look away, smiling, almost bashful, as if caught doing something wrong.

Kat takes another glass of champagne from a passing silver tray. She loves the chance to put on a cocktail dress and tonight's event in the senior common room is a particularly glossy affair. Students more accustomed to Dr Martens and lumberjack shirts have gathered beneath chandeliers, beneath the snooty college deans of old, looking down their noses from oil paintings. Some students seem uncomfortable in black tie, tugging at their necks where the shirt collars dig in or, in the case of the girls, hiding their bodies under baggy cardigans, but Kat loves dressing up, putting on a different persona, teasing her hair into a Fifties do, even painting on a beauty spot. It can be a relief to pretend to be someone else.

Tonight, she is glad of the distraction. It has been a difficult day. She is still finding it hard, after the Easter holidays, to cope with the reality of Ruth and Richard being together. She finds herself thinking of Richard every morning when she wakes up: how he will never be hers now. Worse, on top of that ache, there's the thought of Richard and Ruth waking at the same sort of time. Limbs curled around each other in Ruth's tiny single bed. Isn't the morning the best part of the day when you're in love? When you remember who you're with and their face appears crumpled but smiling, their hair all messy, and then one of you might roll towards the other . . .

Kat runs a hand over her eyes. She has tried so hard to shake off the sadness; Kat is not good at feeling sad, sitting with it. Her head has ached all day, her limbs felt heavy. She even tried to go for a run along the beach, and for a few moments she lost herself in the sound of the sea and her trainers slapping against the wet sand. And then she remembered those times with Richard, walking along the clifftops, and how sometimes – often – in her head he would kiss her: the sensation of him doing this was something she'd imagined so many times it was almost familiar. And beneath the thoughts of Richard, a more painful idea tugged at her: that, despite her red lipstick and her engraved cigarette cases and clever quips, she was small and pathetic and hungry in a way that would always frighten men, always make them leave.

She stopped running – body doubled over, her panting breath echoing back to her from the sand like a sob – and made her way to college via the newsagents to buy some cigarettes. Two packs of twenty because she had the feeling it was going to be one of those days. She had smoked the first pack by four, in between bouts in the library where the words danced in front of her eyes without going in.

Would it hurt Ruth at all if she slept with George? Kat thinks as she takes another glass of champagne, eyeing him across the room; though, truth be told, she is more interested in Dan. With his dark hair, he's a similar type physically to Richard – though he is less scruffy, more at home in black tie, and his face doesn't have Richard's kindness. That could be exciting, though. Now, which one should she pick?

After the disastrous run, the failed trip to the library, Kat thought she'd face her demons – it couldn't be so bad close up: it was only Ruth, only Richard. She'd changed – clothes always mattered to Kat – into a virginal white shirt dress and gone over to Ruth's room to chat, but her plan, once she'd got to the door, was interrupted by the unmistakable noises of sex. The rhythmic banging of furniture and panting breath made her turn away, but not before a moment or two of wallowing in the exquisite agony of it, like a paper cut across her heart.

Later, Ruth, flush-cheeked, dressed in old jeans and a jumper, came to find her. She asked if Kat wanted to go for a drink, trying to 'keep things normal', as they both kept repeating, to show 'nothing had changed'. Kat had kept her earlier visit to herself, but she dismissed Ruth with frosty politeness.

A couple of boys from her course had come over to chat as she sips her champagne trying to catch Dan's eye again, but Kat isn't really interested in what they're saying. One of them has asked her out for a drink several times but she keeps fobbing him off. He's too young-looking, too keen. She and Ruth had both taken a year off between school and university – and Kat found you usually could tell who'd done that. There was something fresh and newly hatched about the ones who hadn't. During her gap year, Kat had gone to Paris to stay with her father, but not long after she arrived he explained he had to move on again. A new opportunity had come up in Brazil, though Kat suspected this particular opportunity came in the shape of a leggy new bit on the side.

She stayed in his flat until the lease ran out a couple of months later, sporadically attending a language school and picking up men. That had been her sexual awakening, really. She had lost her virginity years before at school, but living with her mum in the flat in London there had never quite been the opportunities that there were in

Paris. And she was a sucker for those dark eyes and the sort of diffidence mixed with assurance Frenchmen had. Not like this young one chatting to her now.

She pats him dismissively on the shoulder. 'Let's see,' she says in reply to his question about a drink. 'I've got a ton of work on,' she adds languidly and moves off, making her way to Dan: she has her eye on her prey tonight.

As they file into the dining room for supper, she picks a hair off his jacket. 'Blonde,' she says, holding it up to the light.

He shrugs. 'Not one of mine.'

'You like blondes, do you?' Kat touches her hair, fair at the moment.

'I like lots of different things,' he grins as they file in.

'I'll remember that,' laughs Kat.

She takes a seat at the dining table next to Dan, opposite George. The room is candlelit, the crystal glasses catching the light, reflecting it.

'You're looking good tonight,' murmurs Dan as he takes his chair. His breath is hot on her neck.

'Don't I always look good?' Kat isn't going to make it too easy. She's going to make him work for her.

He toys with a fork. 'Just particularly edible tonight.'

'Maybe later I'll let you eat me.' Which is bold, even for her.

'Promises, promises,' he laughs, filling up her wine glass.

Someone starts playing the penny game, where every time someone drops a coin into your drink you have to down it. George and Dan gang up on Kat, working together to distract her and slip the coin into her glass.

And she, glad of the excuse, gulps the wine down. It's only after getting up for the loo halfway through the meal that time starts to expand and contract. One moment she is sitting on the loo seat talking drunkenly about Richard to some girl she's never spoken to before. Then she's noticing her cheeks flushed in the bathroom mirror, trying to put on make-up to cover them. Then there's a pudding in front of her, which she can't face eating – a pavlova with the raspberries dyeing the cream pink. Someone says, 'Don't you want that?' and takes it from her. Then one of the tutors is making a speech and Dan is stroking her thigh under the table, pushing her dress up inch by inch.

Then they're in one of her favourite late-night drinking spots, a Moroccan-themed nightclub, but she can't remember how they got there. They're sitting huddled together, a small group of them. There's just one other girl and she's with her boyfriend, so Kat is getting a lot of attention, just how she likes it. George keeps buying bottles of champagne, filling up their glasses, being particularly attentive to her. And she's up on her feet dancing to the jazz band on her own, moving her hips to the music. Feeling the men's eyes on her, she knows she is desired and invincible.

She's never felt accepted by this crew before and she realises maybe Ruth was the problem all along: Ruth was holding her back.

'Ruth Walker is a bitch, isn't she?' she says to George at one stage.

He makes a crazy sign, twirling a finger around his ear. 'Nutty as a fruitcake.'

And then George follows her to the loo and tries to kiss her, but she doesn't want to kiss him, she realises. She's made her decision: she's going to bed with Dan, though she doesn't tell George this. And George says: does she want to do a line of coke? So they do that instead.

When George goes to buy the next round, the other girl – Kat can't remember her name – leans over and says, 'Be careful tonight.'

Kat rolls her eyes. 'What do you mean?'

'You just seem like you've had a lot to drink.' The girl shrugs. 'And George and Dan can be trouble.'

Kat lights a cigarette. 'Maybe I like trouble.'

She can't recall how the conversation develops from this into a quarrel, but the next thing she knows she has called the girl a 'boring bitch' and she can't remember why. The girl is huffily asking her boyfriend if they can leave, and they gather coats and bags and bustle out of the club.

'Don't worry, she *is* a boring bitch,' says Dan. 'And now we have two bottles of champagne between the three of us.'

'Three is the magic number,' says George.

Kat thinks of fairy tales – three sisters, three bears, three wishes. She thinks of what her wish would be and then swallows the thought away. Anyone making wishes in fairy tales is always fucked anyway – *just like anyone using someone to block out the pain of someone else*, says a voice in her head, but she pushes that away, too.

They take turns going to the loo to do lines, forging different alliances – sometimes it's George and Dan, sometimes George and Kat. When she has her turn with Dan,

196

she says, 'Do you want to do the blow off my neck?' She lifts her hair up, lets it fall down her shoulder, exposing her pale skin to him.

'Better not waste it,' he laughs and turns to cut the lines on the cistern.

'Want me to blow anything?' She stands behind him, puts a hand on his hip as he leans over, feeling powerful for a moment. She lets her hand wander over his crotch, feels the twitch of his dick beneath it, interested.

He stops what he's doing.

'You're a naughty girl, aren't you?'

'You like that?'

He spins around suddenly, pushing her against the cubicle wall. Her head knocks against it and a few strands of her hair get caught under his hands, pulling at her scalp sharply. And he's kissing her neck and throat roughly, with his stubble scraping against her skin. Kat moans but it's too rough, too quick. He pushes down the front of her dress and the material gives sharply.

'Whoa,' she says. 'Careful with my mum's Chanel.'

He stops for a moment – the polite Etonian returns. 'Oh dear, yes, I seem to have *completely* forgotten my manners.'

Kat is relieved to be back on familiar territory. 'Handsome and ruthless, that's how I like my men,' she says, adapting Dorothy Parker for the occasion.

'Shall we do those lines?' Dan asks, leaving Kat to adjust herself.

'Good idea.' She runs a hand over her cheek, down her neck, where her skin feels hot and prickly. 'And, Dan,' she adds, 'I wasn't saying no, you know?'

He chuckles. 'Oh, I do know that.'

'Did you kids have fun?' laughs George. 'You were gone ages – I was getting rather jealous.'

'A lady doesn't kiss and tell,' says Kat, helping herself to a fresh glass of champagne.

'So, I'll be hearing about it in full detail later,' says George, catching Dan's eye instead of Kat's, shutting her out of the joke.

Time keeps changing, expanding and contracting again, so that some moments seem to last for days and others vanish completely. Kat can't remember leaving the club, but they're walking through the streets, the three of them, with George and Dan's arms around her. Kat is trying to work out how she can get George to leave them alone, but it's late now, or early, and her limbs aren't quite doing what she wants them to – more than once a heel gives way and she feels her legs buckle beneath her, and the boys lift her up, saying 'oop-la' like well-meaning uncles.

As they reach college, Dan takes her by the hand and leads her to his room. 'My place?' he calls back to George without waiting for an answer.

Kat notices how strange she feels, how light-headed. 'I might go back to mine,' she says, hoping Dan will take the hint and come with her, want to be alone with her without George. The buzz, the excitement of earlier, has faded; she wants to curl up in bed with someone and be held.

'No, no,' he grabs her arm. 'I need you to come back to mine, so I can ravish you.'

'And I need to watch,' George laughs.

Kat wishes he would go.

In Dan's room, Kat collapses into an old armchair as Dan pours her a glass of port. She takes a few sips and puts the glass on the floor. It makes her feel sleepy. The boys are in the corner of the room, murmuring between themselves, as she drifts off.

She wakes quite suddenly, with the pair of them looking down at her on the chair. Her mouth is gummed up with the sweetness of the port and she has the beginnings of a terrible hangover.

'Are we going to do this?' Dan says softly.

Kat blinks, rubs her eyes. 'Do what?'

'Ravish you.' George is holding something in his hand, a white silk scarf.

Kat sits up. 'What, both of you?'

Dan laughs nastily. 'What did you think was going to happen?'

'Both?' Kat says again. She is desperately thirsty and the port has made her feel rather peculiar, nauseous, heavy-limbed. She looks for her shoes.

'We thought it would be fun.' George twists the scarf in his hands. 'We thought you'd be the sort of girl who was up for it.'

Kat snags on this thought. She says: 'I don't want to.'

'Come on, Kat, you've been flirting with us both all night. Getting off with us both.'

'Not George,' she says, trying to stand. 'I didn't get off with George.'

'You don't remember?' George laughs. 'Look, it's been a good night. Let's make it even better.'

'I don't want to,' Kat says again. She notices her heart

has started to pound. She is trying to put her shoes on but her hands are shaking. Maybe she doesn't need them. 'Can't we talk about it first?' Her voice sounds high, shrill.

Dan has moved over to the door. He turns the key in the lock, puts the chain on. He picks up a camera from the bookshelf and starts fiddling with it.

'No more talking,' George says lazily as he comes over to where she's sitting. 'It's too late for talking.' He crouches down and takes her shoes off, almost tenderly. 'We can't force you,' he says, climbing on to her, kissing her neck roughly. 'You can stop it if you want.'

The phrase strikes Kat as something a lawyer might say. The weight of George presses down on her; the smell of him is hot and wet; he puts his hand up her dress; she says, *please*. She doesn't know if she says it in her head or out loud. She wants to explain that she is a person: not just a girl, but a person – who has parents, a mother – but she doesn't know how to, she doesn't have enough time.

'Do you mind if I go first?' George says over his shoulder to Dan.

'Nah, I'll watch for now.' Dan is still by the door, like a sentinel. 'There's no rush. We've got plenty of time.'

'We're not making you do this,' says George. And then, 'You'll like it, you'll see.'

Kat closes her eyes. She read somewhere it didn't hurt so much if you try to relax. It's strange, she thinks, that George is so heavy: she had always thought he was plump when, in fact, it was pure muscle.

Naomi

I sometimes get the sense that the same things happen over and over again: that everything is a variation of something that has happened before; that things go missing all the time and there is no way of knowing where they go. Not things. People.

We got into a routine, Miss Wick and I. She'd lend me the keys to her flat, and I'd go there and wait for her. The first time, I was pretty jumpy. I had to try all the keys on the keyring to open the front door of the building – a huge Regency house in a sleepy street not far from school. An older woman whom I passed in the hallway seemed to clock me as I entered the building. I wondered for a moment if she might be a teacher. Miss Wick and I always had to be vigilant.

I had to go through the same palaver with the keys again when I got to Miss Wick's flat. When I finally turned the unfamiliar lock, the heavy door swung shut loudly behind me. I leaned against it for a moment and got used to being there: the cool darkness of the hallway, the tick of a clock coming from the next room, the faint smell of eucalyptus. A strange thought occurred to me: that I could bolt, leave before Miss Wick arrived, and say, when she next saw me, that it had all been a huge mistake – a misunderstanding. I didn't, of course. I never really had a choice when it came to Miss Wick.

In the living room, a couple of the sash windows were open and the net curtains twitched in the breeze. Miss Wick had told me to help myself to a drink from the tray in the corner. I picked up a bottle of red wine that had been opened. Malbec, of course. I examined the other bottles – tried to decipher their meaning. Did Miss Wick drink vermouth or was it something she'd inherited with the flat? Or drank with another girlfriend? I thought back to our first meeting: Miss Wick had been waiting for a blind date. Had anything ever happened with that woman? I glared at the bottle in my hands, when someone wrapped their arms around my waist, said, in a familiar voice, 'You should have some if you want.'

'You made me jump.' My heart was racing. She never seemed to give me any warning. There was never any time to prepare myself, to protect myself. My skin was covered with a light sheen of sweat already. Maybe I *did* need a drink. 'Are you going to have something?' My words tripped each other up. 'I mean, I wasn't – I don't know – but if you're going to have something?'

Miss Wick smiled. 'I don't want a drink right now.' She took my hand and led me towards the bedroom. 'There's something else I want to do first.'

* * *

Afterwards, it was quiet. Words swam in and out of my head in shoals, but none of them felt right. My body was different: tingling and trembling. I thought: so this is what all the fuss is about. It took a while for the horses' hooves in my chest to still.

Miss Wick, Joaquina, didn't look perturbed. I never got used to calling her by her first name. She hunted around for her cigarette papers gloriously naked, wandering past the open windows.

'Your surname doesn't sound Argentinian,' I said at last.

'It's not.' She blew out a plume of smoke, came to join me on the bed, perching on the end with the ashtray in her lap. 'I made it up.'

Her proximity made me want to touch her again. She reached out and trailed a finger along my arm, making me smile.

'I mean, it's my real name,' she continued. 'I changed it. It's just not my family name.'

I didn't know what to say. Why would someone change their name?

'You don't have to tell me about it,' I said too quickly. 'I mean, I've read a bit about Argentina. Terrible things. And you barely know me. So . . .' I stopped to draw breath.

'Dear Naomi.' Miss Wick ground out her cigarette and put the ashtray on the floor. 'I am getting to know some parts of you very well.' She pulled the sheet back and looked at me. 'How long have I got you for?'

Alice

April 2016

Since the arrival of the postcard from St Anthony's, Alice has convinced herself there are more of them. She's increasingly bothered by the locks in the house, by the drawers and boxes she can't access. They have gained a significance, a power they never had in the past, and she has put aside today to look into them. On the pretext of baby shopping, she has booked the day off. Mrs T isn't in and George is filming in Glastonbury, so she has the run of the place to herself.

George's reaction to the postcard had been completely enraging. 'It's just a nutter,' he'd laughed over breakfast the day after it arrived. 'You should be used to them by now.' He tore off a piece of croissant and popped it in his mouth.

'A nutter from St Anthony's?' Alice said. 'That's a very specific kind of nutter. Possibly one we know.'

'Darling, no one we know has been to St Anthony's for years. And any idiot with access to Wikipedia can see I studied there.' He rubbed her arm. 'Please don't let it upset you. Honestly, it's nothing. If you saw half the mail I got back in the day . . .'

'What sort of things?' Alice stirred a spoonful of sugar into her tea.

'All sorts of nastiness.'

'That's too vague,' Alice said. 'I want specifics.'

'Death threats,' said George steadily. 'Some even said they'd harm you.'

Alice swallowed. 'I can imagine the sort of thing.' She took a sip of her drink. 'You never said anything.'

'I wanted to protect you,' George said, reaching over the kitchen table to touch her hand. 'I wanted you to feel safe.'

Alice looked past him into the garden, where a magpie hopped across the lawn. 'But maybe I wasn't,' she said.

It's never bothered her quite so much before. She has her own secrets, after all: a carved wooden box under the bed – ironically, a gift from George on their fifth wedding anniversary. It contains several of her old journals – she's kept them as long as she can remember – and a batch of love letters from an ex-boyfriend who got in touch before she married George to say that he still loved her, that he thought she was making a mistake.

But George has stacks and stacks of locked boxes in the spare room – most of which, she imagines, are papers relating to his work. They never held any interest for her in her life before, but more recently she's started to wonder what else might be in them: other postcards, perhaps.

Letters from all of those nutters, or other things – maybe a memento of Ruth, a photo of them together, a lock of red hair. No, she stops herself, that's ridiculous.

The drawers that bug her most are the ones in his study. It is there, she has convinced herself, that George keeps his darkest secrets. There that she is most likely to find what she is looking for.

She starts by hunting for the keys. She checks in the key cupboard in the kitchen, though they are not there, of course; she looks everywhere in the study, in all the little pots and vases on the shelves, which would make the perfect hiding place for a tiny key or two. Then she checks the drawer in the table in the hallway and all the drawers in George's bedside table, all the trinket pots in their bedroom and all his pockets.

She goes back downstairs and takes a closer look at the locks on the desk. She thinks for a moment of calling a locksmith. Perhaps she could persuade someone that her husband had locked something vital – car keys, an inhaler – in one of the drawers. She imagines for a moment how that conversation might go, the amused tone of the man – it was bound to be a man – at the other end of the phone, possibly going along with the charade or, worse, saying politely but firmly, 'I'm sorry, madam, but that goes against our policy.'

No, the better way round would be to break in herself and ask an expert to fix it, if needs be. That way no one else would be culpable. She goes to the kitchen to get out George's toolkit from under the sink. Coming back upstairs from the kitchen, she catches herself in the hallway mirror briefly. She hasn't showered yet today, or done her hair, and she sees herself for a moment in her pyjamas, with her dressing gown open, her bump visible, her hair on end and a toolkit in her hand about to break into her husband's desk. It doesn't look good.

She perches for a moment on a chair in the hall. She could stop: she could put the toolkit back, she could go out for the day, for lunch or a film or some genuine baby shopping. But it's the thought of the child inside her that makes her get up again. A friend of hers had re-evaluated her life before she got married, looked at her past and taken stock, cleared out her wardrobe, written to exes, built a bonfire, released the ghosts. Alice had never done that, but she needs to do it now and if George won't tell her, she'll work it out for herself. She needs to know what he's hiding.

Alice tries to remember how they did it at school, when they would play at unpicking locks. A friend of hers could open other girls' desks with a couple of paperclips, although Alice never quite got the knack of it.

In George's study, she closes the shutters at the front of the house and puts on the lights. She fishes out her phone from her dressing gown pocket and Googles 'How to pick a desk lock'. YouTube has more tutorials on the subject than she could ever have imagined and she takes her time watching several, making notes as she goes, until she finds one exactly like George's desk, which she watches twice. It's more interesting than she's expecting: the pins in the lock need to be pushed to the exact position where they catch – and then you can rotate the whole cylinder, one vlogger explains.

She needs what her YouTube teachers call a rake and a tensioner – two paperclips would do it, with one curled into a little hook. The tensioner applies pressure in the direction the lock is supposed to go, while the rake scrapes along the pins to move them to the right position.

Alice takes a couple of paperclips from a pot on the desk and has a go. Maybe she won't need the toolkit after all. It proves frustrating work, though, much harder than it looks on the videos. After half an hour, she retreats to the kitchen for a break before returning with a cup of tea and renewed vigour. She thinks she might need a stronger tensioner and she picks a fine screwdriver from the toolkit to do the job. It slips into the lock OK and she applies pressure in the way she thinks the lock will go, but she miscalculates so that, instead, the screwdriver slips out of the lock and heads south, forming a deep scratch in the dark wood.

Fuck. Alice leaps up in frustration, knocking her tea all over George's desk. Just as she does, the doorbell rings.

She stands for a moment in the room, hoping that whoever it is will go away. 'Alice!' She hears Christie's voice. 'It's me.' There's a rapping at the window.

Alice curses quietly and puts the screwdriver down. She shuts the door of the study and goes to the front door, her heart pounding.

Outside, in the bright sunshine, Christie is standing, perfectly coiffured, lipstick on, ready, Alice realises with dread, for some sort of outing.

'Now, a little bird told me you were going baby shopping today,' Christie says cheerfully, diplomatically ignoring Alice's dishevelled appearance. 'And I couldn't have you doing that without buying at least one special present for my future goddaughter.'

Alice blinks. 'Christie, I don't know . . .'

Christie holds up a manicured hand. 'I insist, Al. I won't take no for an answer. I know *all* the places to go. Now, why don't you go and shower,' she says, glancing at Alice's hair. 'I'll just make myself a coffee and do *The Telegraph* crossword.'

And Alice finds herself stepping out of Christie's way, letting her friend into the house, when it's the very last thing she wants.

She herds Christie down to the kitchen, keen for her to get as far away as possible from the study. She grabs a tea towel and says: 'You know where everything is,' waving vaguely at the kettle.

Alice scurries back to the study, her mouth dry, her heart pounding, but she's too late, the tea has drenched George's desk, including the photo collage, which has toppled over into the sea of hot liquid and been completely ruined, with a tidemark spreading through the pictures. Dashing up to the airing cupboard to get more towels, Alice does her best at wiping down the desk and the carpet around it, but it's very unlikely it will recover. She blinks away tears, goes to get the dehumidifier from the hall cupboard.

At the sound of her hauling the bloody thing across the hallway, Christie pops up from the kitchen. 'What's going on? I thought you were getting ready.'

'I was.' Alice stops for a moment. She swallows. On top of everything else, she is going to weep. 'I had an accident.' Her voice cracks a little. 'In George's study.'

'Well, let me clear that up while you get ready.'

'No,' Alice says with such fierceness it makes Christie

recoil. 'It's my mess. I should clear it up.' She starts to cry in earnest.

'Darling,' says Christie. 'What's this really about?'

'George,' Alice says between sobs and she tells her friend about the postcard.

Christie, as always, knows what to do. She puts on the dehumidifier, opens the windows, calls an antiques expert about how to treat the drenched wood and packs the photo collage so she can remake another ('I'm sure we have them all on our computer.') And, then, as if it's the easiest thing in the world, she calls George to ask him where the keys are.

'We've had an accident,' she tells him smoothly. 'A spillage on your desk. No, she's not feeling very well. We need to limit the damage. Ha ha, yes, "bossy Christie", as usual. Where are the keys to the drawers? We need to check nothing's leaked through. OK, thanks.'

She puts the phone down. 'It's here,' she says brightly, emptying out the paperclips from the pot on the desk and pulling out a small silver key from the tangled mass. It's the same one for all of them.'

Alice smiles weakly. The way Christie handled George! She feels light-headed and strange – half grateful, half furious.

She takes the key from her friend and opens the top drawer. There's some personalised writing paper she'd bought George for their first wedding anniversary, a pack of stamps, an unused appointments diary. In the next two drawers there's more of the same – an accounts book, an old school yearbook, an unframed team photo, a white-tie scarf and an old camera she hadn't seen for years. She can't rifle through with quite the relish she would on her own, but, as far as she can see, there's nothing here of interest, only sentimental bits and bobs from school and university – no postcards, no mystery letters, and nothing to do with Ruth Walker.

Naomi

Afterwards, with Miss Wick, I always felt braver. Maybe because I felt empty, emptied of everything, including my nerves. On our last afternoon together, I asked her with my head on her chest, my cheek sticky with cooling sweat, 'When did you first know you were gay?'

'I've always known. What about you?'

I looked at her then – her strong eyebrows, the line of her jaw – until it became too much. 'The first time I saw you.'

A different sort of person might have looked pleased at this, but Miss Wick just said: 'Yes, I think it can be like that.'

I rolled onto my back. It was getting late, the lampshade casting a longer shadow across the ceiling. 'Have you ever done something like this before?'

She got up to roll a cigarette. 'You know I haven't.'

I said to the ceiling, 'I wish I could stay.'

'You must eat before you go,' said Miss Wick. 'I'll heat up that risotto.'

'No.' I began to get up. Better not to prolong the goodbye. I've always hated Sunday nights. 'I should go.' I knew soon I would be walking along the street in the velvety darkness of the evening, thinking about her, and it wouldn't be so bad.

'Naomi, you must.' Miss Wick marched to the kitchen and started clattering around with pans.

When I went to say goodbye, Miss Wick was standing over the oven stirring the risotto with one hand and reading Lorca's *Poet in New York* with the other. 'It's almost ready,' she said.

My words came out in a rush. 'I love you.'

She put down the book, still holding the wooden spoon. She kissed me. 'You need to eat.'

I shook my head. 'I need to go.'

We both acted as if I hadn't said the words at all.

Back at the hotel, my mum was out and the smell of spaghetti bolognese lingered in the corridors. It was stuffy. Some of the guests propped open their doors to let the air in and chords of music drifted up from the bar. As soon as I got back to my room, I missed Miss Wick. I nipped down to the hall to call her. I imagined the burr of Miss Wick's phone from where it sat in the corner by the drinks table. You could hear it wherever you were in the flat. I started to count the rings: ten, twelve, but she didn't pick up.

I tried to study for an hour or two before bed, but the words wouldn't sink in. At eleven, I crept back to the phone. I let the phone ring for longer this time – seventeen, eighteen, nineteen rings. In the end, I put the receiver down for a moment and tried again. I imagined Miss Wick suddenly returning, fiddling with the keys in the door, coming through to the living room after doing some late-night shopping with a bottle of red wine or perhaps just carrying her liquorice cigarette papers. I glanced down the corridor; my mum still wasn't back. I tried the number again, waited for it to connect, but the sound that greeted me was the long, ugly tone of a phone that had been taken off the hook.

Kat

Kat's moods have got darker in the months since it happened – she struggles with being on her own, so that on weekends in the autumn term it wasn't unusual to wake, as she does today, unsure of where she is for a few seconds. Not in her room in college, that much is certain.

She runs through the usual mental checklist. Today her head was OK-ish, manageable – there was usually a headache of some sort and some level of dehydration. Sometimes, too, like today, her lips would feel bruised; her legs would ache, and she'd wonder if she'd have the strength to get out of bed and walk away. She'd look over at the snoring bloke next to her and feel like crying before the day had really begun.

She pieces together the evening before: the union bar, pints of cider and a crowd from the engineering faculty. He'd been among them, this guy – shaggy haircut, tattoos, leather jacket. There'd been a drinking game and lots of shots of something blue. When they'd got up to dance, they used it as an excuse to touch, pushing up against each other on the busy floor. Later, she'd given him a hand job as they waited for the bus to come. Nice.

Occasionally, Kat is pleasantly surprised by her choice from the night before, though that seems to happen less and less these days. Her standards have slipped. She's always known on first meeting a man – instinctively, within a matter of seconds – yes or no. It was that clear: like the needle of a compass.

These days she's lost touch with that gut instinct. She makes allowances: sure, his eyes might slide over her breasts within minutes of meeting her, or he might be making a play for two or three other girls in the bar at the same time, but the more she drank, the less that mattered and the more urgent it would feel for her to go home with *someone*, for her not to go back to her room alone.

Hopefully, just for a bit, in the middle of the excitement, she would lose herself. She would feel like someone else. It didn't always work. Sometimes she would float out of her body, as she had for a moment last night, and see herself as she was – not Dorothy Parker or Mae West but a sad, drunk girl giving a hand job at a bus stop to a guy she didn't even like.

She squints around the room, careful not to move too much; she doesn't want him to wake up. It seems a bit grubby in the light of morning. The floor is strewn with clothes, there's a Metallica poster on the wall and the smell of something rotten coming from the bin. She assesses the situation: her dress scrunched up on the floor, her coat flung across his chair, where they'd done it as soon as they came in. Her handbag is over there too – she'll grab it on the way out.

She gets up quickly and quietly, smoothing down her dress as she puts it on and throwing the fake fur coat over her shoulders. You just had to brazen out the Walk of Shame, which was easy enough when you could feel the booze still pumping in your veins. What was his name? Joshua? Jacob? Something biblical. He stirs, turning his head away from her. Maybe he was faking sleep. She's done that before herself. No matter. She's out of here.

Outside, it's a dazzling November morning – frosty and crisp. The clean air sends her into a paroxysm of coughing. The street is quiet as Kat's heels click along. She wishes she had her sunglasses. It's too far to walk, or at least too far in these shoes.

Waiting for the bus, Kat smokes her last cigarette. She thought she'd run out last night but there's a bashed one at the bottom of her handbag. One for luck. The tobacco has squashed together, making for a stronger hit. She coughs again but can feel her body – her neurons, endorphins – perking up with the fizz of nicotine.

The bus is crammed. A thin film of perspiration prickles the back of her neck – it is too bright, too hot through the glass. There's the sting of last night's alcohol in her sweat. She would take her coat off, but then she's practically wearing a negligee underneath. She catches a man, a short, stocky man in his fifties, gazing at her. He stares at her, really stares, and says something in a low, guttural voice to his companion, an older man, who turns towards her and nods approvingly. And whereas before she might have been pleased, flattered, by such attention, these days her reactions take her by surprise.

Her chest tightens. A thought hits her: if they should try to touch her, she will kill them. The rage is sudden and unquenchable. And though Kat knows, in truth, that it isn't aimed at these men but at someone else entirely, the reaction makes her shake. She reaches out to push the red button, so she can get off at the next stop.

In the high street, she stops to pick up some cigarettes, a Diet Coke and a large bottle of water. On a whim, she grabs the Sundays – a broadsheet and something tacky. She'll go and see Ruth and read the weekend gossip with her. She doesn't want to be on her own this morning. She can never sleep the morning after. Sober and alone, she doesn't know what to do with herself. Her thoughts have become too much for her, too much even to sit with. And though Ruth has snatched Richard from under her nose and though it hurts so much that Kat can't even look at them when they're together, Ruth is the nearest thing she has to a friend. So Kat is hoping that if she pretends really hard that it's all OK, somehow it will be, but it isn't, really. It isn't OK at all.

Afterwards, after they had done what they had done to her, she had started to cry, but the tears didn't have any fight to them, they just seeped out. They started to get dressed quickly then, guiltily, and George just said, 'You could have stopped us.' As if it had all been down to her.

'You've done this before?' she asked Dan before she left, sitting up to take a cigarette off him.

'Done what?'

'You know. Together.'

He shrugged, pulled a cigarette out for himself. 'The girls are always up for it.'

'I doubt that.'

'They never say no, so . . .' He lit his cigarette.

'What are you going to do with the photographs?' she asked. 'Please can I have them?' Not that she ever wanted to see them – just to destroy them, to erase them off the face of the earth.

'No,' Dan grinned. He liked her begging. 'They're for our private collection.'

She's only spoken about it once, to a guy – the first after them. She met him at a party over the summer holidays. They snuck out to a caravan in the garden where they talked and kissed. He was so gentle, so sweet: didn't try anything more. Lying on her back, she said into the darkness, just to find out what it would sound like: 'I was raped, I think. There were two of them. And they hurt me a bit – but, more, they humiliated me and now I can't see myself the same way I did before.' He stroked her hair and talked to her about a friend to whom something similar had happened. But in the morning she woke up in the caravan alone, with the heat of their breath condensed on the windows.

The summer break had helped, though. The time away from Ruth and Richard had given her some breathing space. She hadn't told Ruth about George and Dan. There had been times when she was pissed when she nearly had, but she couldn't quite go through with it. She couldn't bear to, really, because she knew it would change the way

Ruth would look at her and she wouldn't be able to change it back. It didn't help that Ruth was so happy. That she was *blooming* in her relationship with Richard.

They'd returned, after the summer holidays, as one of those quasi-married college couples, so that the new intake of freshers would never have guessed that Ruth might once have been the sort of person to shag George Bell in a pub loo or on a pool table – or to have slashed his clothes and hurled them from his balcony for that matter. It was as if this sane, sanitised version of Ruth had always existed, brushing her teeth, washing her face, and curling up each night next to Richard in his college room and spending weekends in the cottage she rented on Top Cliff with her sister, Naomi.

That was another change. Now Naomi had started at St Anthony's, Ruth was never alone. When Kat goes to see Ruth, Naomi's often – too often – there. Maybe sitting on the bed chatting, or curled up on the beanbag just reading. And though they are kind, polite, though they are careful to explain every story, Kat still has the feeling of being just what she is: a guest at somebody else's house.

She hesitates for a moment before turning up the drive to the cottage. Kat doesn't feel like sharing Ruth at the moment. They were so different, Naomi and Ruth – Ruth was like quicksilver and Naomi, so calm, so still, like a millpond. Maybe she should leave it, try for some sleep, after all, but the thought of her lonely room – its slightly disapproving air as she returns, not for the first time, to the debris of her preparations from the night before – is enough to steel her on.

The front door to the cottage is unlocked, as usual.

220

Ruth never locks doors – that's what growing up in the middle of nowhere does for you. Kat clunks up the stairs to Ruth's room in her heels. She's looking forward to telling Ruth about the guy – Josh or Jacob or whatever his name is. Giggling about it with her. But she can hear laughter billowing from Ruth's room before she reaches it and it's too late to turn back.

They are still at it when the door opens. Ruth is bent double, clutching her belly; Naomi is standing in the middle of the room rocking with laughter. They are both covered in mud.

'Kat!' Ruth exclaims in between chuckles. 'We've been gardening.'

'Oh,' Kat smiles dryly. 'Why don't you pay someone to do that?'

They had so much space here, the pair of them – the garden behind the house. An incredible sea view from this bedroom. It's a shame the place is so run-down.

Naomi smiles. 'That wouldn't be half as fun.'

Kat thinks for a moment that she might cry. Ruth and Naomi look so healthy: well-slept, clear-skinned. Kat is suddenly aware of her panda eyes, her shagged-out hair – not to mention her tiny dress and fake fur. What was that phrase her mother used to say? All fur coat and no knickers. Well, fuck her mother. And fuck them.

Ruth smiles. 'You've got the papers,' she says evenly. 'Let's have a look.'

'I'll come back,' Kat says. 'I need to shower really. I probably stink.'

Neither of them correct her. She is tired to her bones. Maybe she'll have a nip of something when she gets back to her room in college – that might take the edge off the morning-after paranoia. And maybe a sleeping tablet, too. A lovely sleeping tablet.

'You two look very wholesome,' she adds pointedly. 'Rosy-cheeked.'

'We had a chilled one last night,' says Naomi. 'Just some supper at Annie's café and we watched a couple of films here.'

'How rock 'n' roll,' Kat says crisply.

She just wants to talk to Ruth on her own, why can't Naomi get that? She lets the bedroom door slam behind her on her way out.

Ruth is saying something to Naomi as Kat makes her way downstairs – something apologetic. Ever since taking Richard from under Kat's nose, Ruth has been so pathetically grateful that Kat is still talking to her that she'll do almost anything. In her fury, Kat takes the last step too fast and one of her heels gives way. She is airbound, falling forwards, arms outstretched. The sudden pain of her bare legs against the stone slabs makes her gasp.

'Kat.' Ruth is there. She picks up Kat's coat, which has come off her shoulders. 'Are you all right?'

'Fine.' She's grazed her knees like a child in the playground. She tries to scramble up without Ruth's help. The heel has broken clean off her right shoe. 'Just a bit of a shock.' She dusts down her dress. 'Those stairs are a fucking liability, by the way.'

'Are you sure you're OK?' Ruth keeps her hand on Kat's arm. 'You seem a bit . . .' She pauses. 'I don't know – a bit snappish.'

'I'm tired.' Her knees are stinging. She'd better go and

clean them. 'Hungover. I wanted you to myself . . . to go over all the sordid details from last night.'

'I thought so.' Ruth hugs Kat. 'God, you smell like a brewery,' she laughs.

'You used to, too.' Kat can hear the petulance in her tone. 'You used to come out drinking with me and pull boys, and just be more . . .'

'More what?' Ruth's mouth tightens.

'Fun,' says Kat. 'You used to be more fun. Until Naomi came along.'

'Until Naomi came along?' Ruth repeats. A cloud passes across her face.

'She's just a bit . . .' Kat pauses. 'Square,' she settles on. She still sounds like a schoolgirl. 'A bit lesbian,' she adds quietly. Which makes it worse.

'She's my sister,' Ruth hisses, throwing Kat's coat back at her. The force of it makes Kat stumble back a step. 'She'll always come first.' Ruth turns to go back up, but stops for a moment to add: 'You always act like you know everything. When actually you don't know anything at all.'

Kat is silent for a moment. She's never been on the receiving end of Ruth's temper before.

'About people,' Ruth continues. 'About the important things.'

Kat's own rage, which has been simmering on and off all morning, boils over. Ruth doesn't know. She doesn't fucking know anything. And if she had been a friend, a proper friend, she would never have stolen Richard from her. Because what had come from that? Nothing but a whole lot of fucking trouble.

'Well, maybe it was your innate wisdom that Richard fell in love with,' she spits. 'It certainly wasn't your sense of fun.'

'Kat!' Ruth calls after her as she marches out of the house. Which is hard to do with a broken heel.

Kat won't look back. She won't look back at her.

'Why do you have to make everything about that?'

Kat turns: Ruth looks small, rather forlorn. Afterwards, much later, she would remember Ruth like this – alone at the doorway of that funny little house on Top Cliff. Kat could go back, *should* go back and make nice, but she just doesn't want to.

'Because everything *is* about that, Ruth,' she says instead. 'And if you don't know that, *you're* the one who doesn't know anything.'

Naomi

When Ruth returned from St Anthony's at the end of her first year, she came straight up to my room, where the curtains were drawn and I was dozing in the middle of the afternoon like an old person. My mother must have said something.

She climbed into bed next to me. 'It's just an exam.'

Lying on my back, I looked up at the ceiling. The black cat that had come in with Ruth pounced on the bed and padded up to me. 'I choked – I couldn't write.' I ran my hand along the cat's spine. 'It was so hot. Unbearable. I really fucked it. I don't think I'll get into Cambridge now.'

'Well,' she smiled. 'You'll just have to come to St Anthony's with me.' She squeezed my hand. 'What's going on?' Outside, a child shrieked in the garden. 'Mummy thinks it's a boy.'

I sighed. 'I fell in love.'

It sounded melodramatic, ridiculous. The kind of thing

Ruth herself might say. She plucked at the tassels of a rug on my bed, but she was still listening. I could tell.

'And he broke up with you?'

I was silent for a moment. They were playing Bob Marley in the kitchen. Damien's tuneless voice could be heard singing along to 'No Woman, No Cry'. He loved to sing as he cooked. Ruth giggled but I found I couldn't smile.

'She,' I said at last. 'She left.'

Ruth didn't seem surprised. She took my hand. 'Who was she?'

And I told her.

Everything had gone off the tracks after that phone call. Or the absence of a phone call. My thoughts seemed to go off kilter. I tried to revise that night, but I found it very hard to concentrate, finally switching off my lamp at around two in the morning. Usually, to relax last thing at night, to reward myself for a day well spent, I allowed myself to luxuriate in unrestrained thinking of Miss Wick, replaying bits from the last time we had been together. Sometimes it was just a conversation, a compliment, a smile; at others it was more physical: Miss Wick's bare arms or something we had done in bed together earlier. Sometimes my hand wandered between my legs, but that wasn't the primary objective. It was a sort of daydreaming to send me to sleep. But that night every time I thought of Miss Wick I couldn't escape the memory of the ugly sound of the phone off its hook.

During prayers, I looked up to the teachers' gallery several times, but Miss Wick wasn't there. A lapsed

Catholic, sometimes she would skip the service, but after the night before, I had been hoping for something to keep me going – a private look, a secret smile.

I spent the day distracted. I wandered from revision sessions to Miss Wick's room and back again. But she wasn't answering her door. At break, I tried again, but the corridor filled up around me. I couldn't just hang around outside a teacher's room all day.

In the prefects' common room, which was just opposite, I made myself a cup of tea and found Jess in a buoyant mood, full of her first date with Andrea: what he wore, what he said, the way he smiled, how he put his hand on her lower back as he guided her out of the restaurant. 'Much more intimate than a touch on the shoulder – a hand on the shoulder just says "friend", doesn't it? But the lower back is different.'

I nodded but my mind was racing. The way I felt – it was like when you lose a dog. I thought of Scipio. It's as if you split in two: the part of you that knows that any second the beloved pet will trot into sight, tail wagging, as if to say, why are you so worried? And the other part, which is more powerful, more seductive than the first. Which whispers into your ear: you've seen her for the last time, the very last time, and you didn't even realise . . .

When Jess stopped to catch her breath, I asked, as casually as I could, 'You haven't seen Miss Wick today, have you? I wanted to talk to her about something . . .'

Jess frowned. 'Are you OK? You look a bit pale.' She took my hand and gave it a squeeze, and I thought that this small act of kindness might just send me over the edge.

'I am. I'm just feeling a bit ropy.' I swallowed a mouthful of tea, but it was too hot, scalded the back of my throat. 'You haven't seen her then?'

'Miss Wick? No.' Jess shook her head. She paused for a moment and said: 'You can just say it, you know.'

'Say what?' I looked at her face. Her large blue eyes; her unwrinkled brow. Did she have any idea? I thought of all the small lies I had told her and some of the bigger ones, too.

'Whatever you want, whatever's bugging you.'

'I would like to talk,' I said quickly, just as the bell went for lessons to start again. 'Maybe tonight?'

Jess smiled an easy smile and the prefects' common room emptied quickly. I felt a temporary sense of relief, but it didn't take long for the tightness in my chest to return.

By Wednesday, with still no sign of Miss Wick, I started to hear rumours – that she was ill, that she had left in the night – but there were no announcements. We hadn't heard anything official. That night I went to her flat, but there was no answer and no lights on. And I stood there watching the window from the street until it got dark.

The next day, I broke down in Jess's arms and told her everything after school.

'Oh, Naomi,' she said as we sat in my room surrounded by tear-drenched tissues. 'What a pickle.'

I hadn't eaten or slept properly for days and I knew that I was unravelling just weeks away from our exams starting. It was like pulling at a loose thread on a jumper and finding out what kept it together simply wasn't as strong as you thought. At night I slept in a kimono of

Miss Wick's I had borrowed, which still smelled slightly of eucalyptus. In spite of everything, I found myself going back to her room at lunch break.

'I know I'm being silly,' I told Ruth. 'But I kept hoping that there might be a crack I might slip through: a crack into an alternate universe where Miss Wick hadn't disappeared.'

Ruth didn't laugh. She didn't even smile. She said: 'I used to hope that about Daddy.'

I didn't tell her about the last time I checked, at the end of lunch on a Friday. School was quiet at lunchtime, with girls sitting outside in the sun, or quietly revising. There was a soporific atmosphere at that time just before the lessons started again, as if the building itself was postprandial and sleepy.

I thought I was alone in the corridor, but the sound of a sniff made me look up and I realised I was being watched. Lizzie Clark was leaning against a locker, with her school skirt hitched up short, as always. How could she make even a sniff sound like a sneer?

'Didn't you hear?' she said.

I kept very still. I didn't want to speak to Lizzie. I never said anything, anything at all to anyone, about what happened that night. But it was there still. Like a burning shame. Feigning indifference, I said as casually as I could: 'She's off sick.'

'That's not what I heard.' She looked at my face as if reading me for a reaction. 'I heard she's been sacked for . . . well, you'd know.' She stuck up her index and middle finger and waggled her tongue between the two.

I held on tightly to the door handle. My cheeks were

burning. When I felt strong enough, I made my way across the corridor to the prefects' common room. My shirt already felt damp from the sweat.

I said carefully: 'I have no idea what you mean.'

Kat

The exam had been a disaster. An unadulterated fuck-up. Kat had written reams and reams – she never had a problem coming up with something. But it was style over substance and if she knew that, the markers definitely would. She'd picked up her revision notes from where she'd left them outside the exam room, knowing she'd have to retake and wishing, not for the first time, that she could lose herself in work. But that would involve staying still, sitting with herself, and that was something she had found hard to do over the last year.

St Anthony's, as the summer term draws to a close, feels like a carnival, with the students who have just finished exams wearing garlands or smeared with flour and eggs. The drunkest stagger around, heads lolling, hands held by friends.

Everyone in the crowded beer garden is talking too

loudly, including Kat herself, who shrieks when she finally spots Ruth and Richard, 'There they are! Love's young dream! Busy shagging, were you?'

There were no two ways about it: they had forgotten about her. She could tell by the way they were creeping in. Well, she could tell by the way they simply weren't there when she'd finished her exams. She had come out of the building feeling drained from three hours of concentration, still holding her pen and her notes in her ink-stained hand, and scanned the crowd for Richard's face. It had reminded her of how you arrive at an airport and always look out into the crowd – past the drivers holding badly written signs – and hope, even when there's no reason to, that there's someone there for you.

There hardly ever is, of course. Kat's father in particular had a habit of promising he'd be there and failing to turn up, so the feeling was familiar but none-theless deeply unwelcome. And then Luke had pushed through the crowd with a garland for her and arranged it proudly in her hair. Why did nothing ever work out the way you wanted?

Students are packed into the small terraced space, crammed next to each other at picnic tables or standing in cliques, bellowing at friends inches away. The King's Head boasts about its beer garden, but in truth it's a concrete yard, enclosed by buildings on three sides, with the river on the fourth. Kat and Luke sit opposite each other at the end of a wooden picnic table. The pair of them watch Richard and Ruth as they approach.

Luke's mouth is a thin, cross line. 'What happened to you?'

'We went to the river after meeting Richard.' Ruth glances at Richard, who finished his finals at lunchtime. 'A whole gang of us,' she adds. 'I guess we thought you were with us.'

'Nope.' Luke shrugs. 'I suppose someone had to remember to go and meet madam at five.' He drains the last of his beer from the glass.

'Kat.' Ruth puts a hand on her arm. 'I'm really sorry.'

'No problem, no problem.' Kat waves dismissively. 'I'm sure you had more important people – I mean, things – to do.' She's not going to make it easy for them. Actually, she might make it easy for Richard. 'Hello, darling,' she says, getting up to kiss him and only just missing his mouth. Ruth can put that in her pipe and smoke it. 'You smell delicious.'

'I like the hair,' Ruth says, still trying.

Kat has dyed it since Ruth last saw her. It's a gothic black, a shade that leeches the colour from her skin, but it matches her mood somehow.

'Darling, for such a drama queen you're a terrible liar.' Kat returns to her seat. 'Or are you?' She lights a cigarette. 'I can never decide.'

'I thought we were meant to be celebrating,' says Richard. 'What are we drinking?'

'Shots!' Kat says, getting to her feet again. 'Let's have shots!'

'Great idea!' someone calls from the next table.

'Tequila,' says Kat. 'No: sambuca. No: tequila.'

'Not for me – it makes me fight,' Ruth interrupts, bringing Richard's focus back to her.

'Well, something special for you, my love.' When

Richard kisses her before heading to the bar, Ruth closes her eyes as if to block Kat out.

'How was the exam?' Ruth asks when he's gone.

'Awful.' Kat looks down at the pile of revision notes on the table. 'Absolutely bloody awful. I'll be lucky if they let me stay.'

Ruth sighs. 'I'm sure it wasn't that bad.'

Kat glares at her. 'What would you know about it?' She inhales her cigarette angrily.

They sit there in silence. Ruth lights a cigarette of her own.

'I know a bit about it,' Ruth says eventually. 'You know about my sister.'

Naomi had had some sort of meltdown during her A levels and fucked them up. It was all because of a love affair with a teacher. Kat smirks. She hadn't found it funny before, but now, several pints in and furious with Ruth, it struck her as amusing that buttoned-up Naomi had been at it with a teacher.

'Your sister's problems aren't the same as mine though, are they?' Kat interrupts. She feels that warning flicker like the dart of a snake in the grass before the words spill out – barbed words that would hurt the listener. 'Naomi was shagging a teacher during her A levels,' she tells Luke with a smirk. 'A female teacher.'

'Huh,' says Luke diplomatically, clearly keen not to get involved.

'I know.' Kat pulls at a thread on her sleeve, refusing to meet Ruth's eye. 'It caused quite the stir.'

'It didn't, actually. It's a secret. As well you fucking know.' Ruth's voice comes out low with just the thinnest crack in it. 'Why would you say it like that, like it's just another joke?' She gets up suddenly and heads for the bar.

Kat looks into her drink. It's oddly deflating being so horrible to someone.

'I know, I know,' she says, feeling disapproval emanate from Luke. 'I went too far.'

'Go and tell her you're sorry,' he sighs. 'Otherwise today's going to be a washout.'

Inside, the barmen are working quickly, keeping their eyes down on the beer pumps to avoid the rolled notes waved to catch their attention, the bray of the students. Kat spots Ruth and Richard at the other side of the bar, which curves in a horseshoe around the room. They have a couple of shots in front of them. Kat thinks she'll push through the crowd to join them, but they are already knocking back the drinks quite happily, as if they've forgotten her. And then they kiss. A long, lingering smooch. They're always at it, thinks Kat angrily, watching them hand in hand disappear through the crowd to the back of the pub for a hasty fuck in the toilet, no doubt.

Kat hasn't cried for months, but suddenly she knows she's going to. She feels the hot rush of it arrive at the back of her throat, prickling at her eyes. But not here, not in front of everybody.

Outside the cubicle, Kat can hear someone say: 'She's been in there for ages. It's a bit selfish – there are only three cubicles.' There's a loud passive-aggressive sigh.

She looks down at the damp wad of loo roll in her

hand. Perhaps the girl's right, perhaps it was time to vacate the area.

'I know you, don't I?'

'I don't think so.' It's Ruth's voice.

'Yes,' the other girl says insistently. 'We got drunk together in the Two Pheasants. We were playing poker with a group of geography guys – you won all our money.'

'No,' says Ruth again. 'That wasn't me.'

'If you say so,' says the girl in a tone that suggests she doesn't, for one moment, believe Ruth.

There's rap on the door of Kat's cubicle.

'Come on – there's a queue out here.'

Kat dabs her eyes a final time, flushes the wad of paper away. 'Can you wait just a fucking second?'

'Kat?' asks Ruth tentatively through the door.

'What the fuck do *you* want?' Kat snaps, aware of the ridiculousness of communicating like this.

'Are you all right?'

'Yeah, brilliant. Fucking brilliant.'

'Do you want to talk?'

Kat opens the door. She catches sight of herself in the mirror beyond Ruth. She looks shocking. Her eyes are swollen; her eyeliner has stained trails down her face.

'Why would I want to talk to *you*?'

Ruth speaks quietly. 'Kat, whatever I've done, I'm sorry.'

'Don't be sorry. Just act like a proper person.' Kat's voice rises in pitch. A girl at the sink washing her hands slows down to watch the show. 'You forget to meet me and then you drink my drinks and just go for a *bonk* . . .'

236

She sighs, world-weary. 'I imagine that's why you disappeared to the toilet together.'

Ruth's face is burning. She looks down at her feet. 'You don't seem to want us here anyway.'

Kat moves to the sink. Her rage softens, appeased by the drama. She begins to wash her face. When she's finished, she says: 'What I want is for it all to go back to normal.'

Ruth exhales. 'Me too. I want that too. Please. Can we just spend some time? I'll ask the boys to go away.'

The shadows are lengthening across the grass as Kat and Ruth meander their way back to college through the park. Luke and Richard have taken a different route, via a curry house and on to the college bar.

The clusters of students are thinning out in the park – packing up picnics or pulling on jumpers. The drunkest lie starfished on the grass looking up at the sky.

'Do you ever feel nostalgia for the present?' Ruth asks as she and Kat cross over Park Bridge back into town.

Kat shakes her head. 'How do you mean?'

'Do you ever feel a sort of longing for things that haven't passed yet?' Ruth stops to pick up a red carnation that a finalist has left on the wall of the bridge. 'Sometimes I feel that everything to come . . . that none of it will be as good as this.'

Kat smiles sadly. 'That's because you're in love.'

'Maybe.' Ruth stops to look upriver at the cathedral. 'Yes, but it's not just that – we're young and we don't have any responsibilities. We don't need to work right now. Or make money. Or pay a mortgage. We can do whatever we want, whenever we want. It'll never be as good as this.'

Kat looks at the flower in Ruth's hand; the edges of its petals are beginning to brown. 'But this is shit,' she says. 'Everyone's terrified of failing. Of the future. Why do you think we need to get so bloody drunk the whole time?'

Ruth leans over the wall of the bridge. 'I'm not scared,' she shouts into the roar of the water.

Kat comes to stand next to her, elbow to elbow.

'Don't bridges always make you feel strange?' Ruth laughs.

'How do you mean?'

'It's a sort of excitement,' Ruth says. 'They unbalance me. I start to wonder how it might feel to climb up on the wall. To throw something precious over the side.'

There's an intimacy to standing so close, facing in the same direction like this. Like driving or walking side by side, it's as if you could say anything to each other because you don't have to look at each other's faces. Kat thinks for a moment she might say it. She might say, 'Something bad happened to me last year.' Maybe that's how she'll start . . .

'Why don't you throw your notes in?' says Ruth.

'What?' The moment passes.

'Your revision notes – why don't you throw them in?'

Kat blinks. 'Really? What if I need to resit?'

'Then you'll make new notes. Go on – it'll be liberating.'

Kat looks down at the clutch of papers in her hand, scrawled and scribbled with words. She imagines the feeling of it – throwing away not just the rotten exam, but all of it: the unsaid words and the silence of the exam room and the please-turn-over-your-paper and the pressure of this place and the poison between them. And what George and Dan did to her: their hands on her body. The photographs that exist out there somewhere. The pain of it all. The humiliation. What if she could throw that away? She smiles at the prospect.

'You like throwing stuff from high places, don't you, Ruth Walker?'

'Have you got your eye on anyone?' Ruth asks her later. They have drunk the first bottle of champagne Kat's dad had sent and were well into the second. Ruth lies on the floor of Kat's room, smoking.

They've spent a pleasant couple of hours talking and laughing at Kat's conquests as they used to. It is almost like the old days. Almost.

Kat is standing, looking at the mirror above her sink, pinning up her hair and rearranging it again. 'No.' Spitting the grips out, she continues looking at the mirror rather than at Ruth. 'I still can't imagine liking anyone else as much as I liked Richard.'

Ruth catches her eye in the reflection and Kat looks away. 'But I'm sure I will,' she adds.

'Kat,' Ruth says. 'I'm really sorry. I know I hurt you. A lot.'

She stops what she's doing for a moment – her hair half up, half down. 'I'd like to say I wouldn't have done that to you.' Kat shakes her head. 'But I would have done.'

'I feel like a thief,' says Ruth quietly. 'I keep thinking bad things will happen.'

'Don't be silly, darling.' Kat laughs sharply, reaches out

for her mug of champagne; she thinks of Dan's hand over her mouth, of not being able to breathe. 'Bad things have *already* happened. Bad things happen all the time.'

By four, tired from dancing around the room, Kat has put on something mellower. She wanted to get stoned but they don't have anything to smoke. All night she has thought she will tell Ruth. But she doesn't know how to start the story. After this cigarette, she keeps thinking. After the next one. And now she is lying on her bed chain-smoking and occasionally singing along to the records Ruth is playing. Finally, finally, she begins to doze off. It feels as if she hasn't slept in weeks.

She feels Ruth take the still-burning cigarette from her, is aware of her turning off Kat's bedside light and creeping for the door. As it creaks open, Kat whispers into the darkness, just to try it: 'Something happened.' If Ruth doesn't hear, it won't matter.

Ruth pauses at the door. There is a silence and Kat can't tell if she heard or not.

'Kat, did you say something?' she whispers.

Kat pauses. It sounds a bit pathetic the second time round. 'Something happened,' she says again. 'With Dan and George.'

Ruth comes back into the room, closes the door quietly.

Kat lights a candle next to her bed. The flicker casts Ruth's face in light and shade, so that Kat can't read her expression. She finds she doesn't know how to proceed, so says, almost conversationally, 'George is strong, isn't he? He looks podgy in his clothes but . . .' She finds she doesn't know how to finish. His chest pressing down on her, Dan watching. 'It wasn't rape,' she says quickly. 'If that's what you're thinking. It wasn't that.'

'What wasn't?' Ruth hesitates, infuriatingly slow. 'I don't understand: did George and Dan rape you?'

'After it happened,' Kat continues, ignoring the question, 'everything changed. I felt different. People – men – in college, they looked at me differently, as if they knew.'

How terrible she'd looked the next morning, almost grey, and she had to wear long sleeves to hide how bruised she had been, the marks scrawled up her arms. Ruth hadn't noticed a thing. Too busy falling into bed with Richard at the time. A flare of fury flashes through her and then it's gone, almost as quickly as it arrived.

'It's my fault, really, because I put it all out there. So it's not surprising . . .'

Ruth climbs onto Kat's bed with her.

Kat can't look at her face. 'It just feels as if things can never be the same. I can't go back to how I was.' She reaches out for the ashtray by her bed. 'I got the impression they'd done it before,' she says. 'With other girls. It's like a game. They take pictures.' She glances up at Ruth. 'Did Dan ever have a go with you?' She picks up her lighter and cigarettes. 'He's strong too, not weighty like George. Sort of sinewy.'

'No.' Ruth shakes her head. 'Though there are times I don't remember. Black-outs.' She looks confused.

'The thing is,' Kat says, 'I would have done it anyway – with Dan – so I don't understand why . . .' Another sentence she can't finish.

Ruth is silent. Kat wishes she would say something.

'I just didn't know how to make them . . . They said I could have made it stop.'

241

Ruth won't stop looking at her. She says quietly. 'Of course they did.' The room is slowing down around them. 'We need to do something,' Ruth says. She clenches a ball of Kat's duvet tightly in her fist.

Kat looks at her wearily. Sometimes she feels so much older than Ruth. It feels like years, not months, between them.

'There's nothing we can do.' She lights the cigarette. 'It's done.' She inhales, though it's the last thing her throat needs after the amount she's smoked today. 'I don't think it was actually rape,' she concludes, though she's unsure as she hears the words come out.

Ruth looks sad. 'You keep saying that,' she says.

Alice

When Naomi opens the door she looks older than Alice remembers, of course she does, but not so very different. Even with her hair scraped off her face and not a scrap of make-up, she still has cheekbones most women would kill for and a natural kind of beauty that Alice, with her manicures and bob, would never attain. Naomi is wearing a sort of smock, with smears of paint down the front, a pencil in her hair.

'Naomi?' Alice says. 'I emailed you at work, remember?' Her words are coming out too quickly, betraying her nerves. 'To say I might be dropping by? We were at St Anthony's together?' Why is she making everything sound like a question?

Naomi smiles warily. 'Yes, I remember. Alice.' She says the name as if trying it out for the first time. 'You did law, didn't you? You married . . .' She lets the words tail off, pulls the pencil out of her hair, winds the bun up tightly and pushes it back in.

'Yes,' says Alice. 'I need to talk to you about something, like I said.'

'O-kay,' Naomi elongates the vowels in a mock solemn tone and pulls the door open for Alice.

It is a sweet little place, smaller than Alice and George's home: stripped wooden floorboards, with threadbare rugs thrown over them, and plant pots gathering dust on the windowsills. In a shaft of sunlight that pools on the sofa, a Jack Russell lies sunbathing, stretched out, sphinx-like.

'Sit down.' Naomi gestures at a spot on the sofa. 'I'll put the kettle on.'

Alice perches and offers a hand to the dog, who licks it and promptly rolls on his back.

She calls through to Naomi. 'Have you got decaf?'

'Yes,' Naomi replies. 'I was going to make some for myself, so I'll just make a pot.'

Alice halfheartedly strokes the dog's belly. 'Nice place,' she calls through once again. 'You live here with your boyfriend?'

'Girlfriend,' Naomi calls back. Her head pops out from the kitchen and she says by way of explanation: 'Carla.'

'Oh,' says Alice and finds herself smiling rather rigidly back. She hadn't known Naomi was gay. 'You been together long?'

'Forever. Since just after uni.' The head disappears again and Alice is left sitting in the unfamiliar room.

There aren't an enormous number of photographs: a few of Naomi with another dark-haired woman – Carla, she imagines – another of a couple on their wedding day. A small woman with large dark eyes standing next to a handsome man with auburn hair, who looks confidently out at the camera, into the future. Confetti has settled on their hair. Who would wear brown on their wedding day? Alice wonders.

'The Seventies, eh?' Naomi comes through carrying a tray with a cafetière, two mugs and a couple of flapjacks. 'I don't know what my mum was thinking. Her bridesmaids were in orange . . . I hope the milk's all right,' she says, peering into the jug. 'Carla likes to buy organic and it's a bit lumpy.'

As Naomi stands up over the coffee table, fussing over pouring and stirring, Alice glances at her bump. 'How far on are you?'

Naomi smiles shyly. 'Twenty-two weeks. How about you?'

'Eighteen,' says Alice.

'Do you know what you're having?' says Naomi.

'A girl,' grins Alice. The thought still makes her beam. 'What about you?'

'We're waiting to find out,' says Naomi. 'But I have a feeling it's a boy.'

As they compare hospital experiences and morning sickness, Alice has a growing sense of unease. Maybe it was a bad call to come here in person. Glancing up, she sees a photograph she'd missed before on the bookcase of two little girls – one dark-haired, one red – sitting next to each other on the low branch of a tree. She swallows hard. She'll have her coffee first. Then she'll make her case.

Their talk turns to work and Alice finds herself turning out certain phrases, such as, 'Well, it's a type of law that actually means something.' Not that that's always true, of course. Sometimes her work feels emotionally satisfying, but she's not always the hero. Sometimes, she'll be working for the lousy husband, or wife. The wrongdoer. As George might say, it's all about how you tell a story. As George might say, you go where the money is.

He had taken his damaged desk pretty well when he came back from filming in Glastonbury. That was one thing you could say about George: he didn't sweat the small stuff. Alice didn't know whether or not he'd noticed the scratch where she'd tried to pick the lock. She hadn't asked. In fact, Alice wondered if he'd spoken to Christie, if they might have had some kind of powwow about her. George is being gentler, more attentive than usual. He keeps asking how she's feeling and suggesting spa breaks. It's all most unlike him. In truth, it makes her feel even guiltier about being at Naomi's, but she has promised herself that this will be her last stand, her last attempt to find out more about Ruth. If nothing comes of it, she will leave it be. She will return to her husband and she will have her baby. She won't look back.

She needs to gather herself. It's important that Naomi thinks she's rational, logical, normal. But then she catches Naomi looking at her and smiling, and she finds she has to ask her to repeat her question.

'So, tell me: what's the secret situation that brought you here?' She is smiling, but she looks wary.

Alice thinks of bottling it, of making some nonsense up and getting out of here. She plays for time. 'I don't know how to say this.'

'OK.' Naomi looks curious.

'I think . . .' The heat rushes to her face as she realises she's going to say it. 'I think I saw your sister.'

Naomi's face changes from being open and friendly to something quite different. There is a long silence.

'Oh,' she says eventually.

'I know.' Alice doesn't know what else to say. 'I know,' she says again.

Naomi looks at her for a long time. She has beautiful eyes, Alice notices, almost too large for her face – like a cartoon character. Her grandmother had been Spanish; she remembers, suddenly, chatting to Naomi about it in a crowded college bar.

The silence is interminable. The dog jumps off the sofa, sits at Naomi's feet and whimpers for attention. She lowers a distracted hand to him and doesn't take her eyes off Alice.

'You're not the first,' she says eventually. 'She's been spotted before.'

'Spotted?'

She waves her hand. 'In Thailand. London. Once in Leeds. We got excited about that one. Someone called the house another time, pretending to be her. Actually said, "Hello, it's me, Ruth." Can you believe that? That people would do such a thing?'

Alice can hear the house breathe around them, the whir of the washing machine from the kitchen. She sees herself for a moment, as if floating above the scene, and it's not a flattering view: here she is, obsessed with a dead stranger. Visiting the home of a bereaved relative, for what? Her own preening purpose. And yet this is it: her only shot.

She takes a deep breath. 'Look, I know how this sounds. I know it sounds crazy and I know, well, I don't know actually, but I can only begin to imagine what it must be like for you to have lost your sister. I just . . . she was unusual-looking, wasn't she? With that hair. It didn't seem the kind of mistake one could make, with hair like that.'

Naomi exhales. 'The hair,' she says sadly. She looks at the photograph on the bookcase. 'People went wild for it, you know.' She gives Alice a look. 'Some of them got obsessed. It's worse when missing people are beautiful. Well, worse and better. They want to print their photographs in the papers, of course, but then that also attracts the weirdos.'

'No, it's not just the hair,' Alice says quickly. 'The girl – the woman – I saw looked exactly like Ruth did. *Exactly*. And she was a very striking girl – someone I remember quite clearly from college . . . I always admired her, how she looked. I saw her – this girl – on a train coming down from Edinburgh. And I knew . . . knew about your sister, knew that she had . . .'

There's another silence. How can she explain it?

'She ran away,' Alice adds quickly. 'That's the thing: she disappeared after I spotted her. Why would she run if she had nothing to hide?'

Naomi looks tired. 'There are all kinds of reasons,' she says more kindly. 'Maybe you frightened her.'

Alice thinks of George. This is what he has said all the way along. She fishes her card – crisp, white, embossed – from her handbag and puts it down on the coffee table before getting up to leave.

'I'd better go,' she says, her face hot with shame. 'But if you ever want anything, just to talk. Or anything. Here are my details.'

Naomi picks up the card and asks as she looks at it, 'Did you do it?'

'What?' Alice blinks.

'Did you send me Nunny?'

'What do you mean? What's Nunny?'

'My sister's rabbit – toy rabbit – someone sent him to me in the post. Was it you?'

'God, no.' Alice blinks. 'That's a pretty weird thing to happen.'

'It is,' agrees Naomi, getting to her feet.

'I didn't know her that well at college,' adds Alice. 'I didn't even know she had a favourite toy. Someone sent us something, though,' she says, remembering. 'A postcard saying, "St Anthony, St Anthony, give what I've lost back to me".'

All the colour drains from Naomi's face. 'What did you say?' she asks quietly.

'St Anthony, St Anthony, give what I've lost back to me,' says Alice again.

Naomi looks at her. 'Where did you hear that?'

'It was on the postcard, like I said,' Alice explains. 'A postcard to George.'

At the mention of George's name, Naomi frowns. Whatever opened, briefly, is closed again.

'Well, that might explain it. It was probably one of his cronies. I guess lots of people in St Anthony's knew that rhyme.'

Alice doesn't like the way she says 'cronies' in such a disparaging way.

'It's "bring", anyway,' says Naomi as she shows Alice to the door.

'I'm sorry?' says Alice.

'In the rhyme, it usually goes, "St Anthony, St Anthony, *bring* what I've lost back to me." The person who wrote it didn't know it very well. It can't have . . .' She stops.

'Look,' says Alice as she does up her jacket. 'I know this has been weird, but please do call me. If you want to talk. About anything.'

'We call them spotters,' Naomi says, opening the door for Alice to leave. 'The ones who say they've seen her,' she continues quietly. 'We tried to give them a harmless name, a funny name, but it's not funny really. There are far more of you than you imagine.' She sighs. 'The first time we were so excited, my mother and I, waiting for something to happen, waiting for her to come home. Do you know what that's like?' she asks. 'How it works? How every time this happens, you think: this might be the time. This might be her.' She opens the front door to let Alice out. 'Fifteen years. And it never is.'

Kat

On the day that Richard would break up with Ruth, Kat is surprised by a visit. Richard never comes to see her on his own any more. Never. And yet here he is.

'Do you fancy a coffee?' he smiles. 'I thought I would treat myself. I'm free for such luxuries now, after all.'

Kat glances back at her room to check it looks all right. Too late, really, but it's fine: quite tidy, the windows are open, letting in the cut-grass smell of outside.

'Yeah, why not?' She runs a hand through her hair. 'Is everything all right?'

'Ruth is sleeping in.' He shrugs. 'You know what she's like about mornings. In fact, I think she's getting worse.'

Kat laughs, grabs a cardigan. Ruth hates mornings.

'You guys must have had fun last night,' he says as Kat sits on her bed to put her shoes on. 'She staggered in at an ungodly hour.'

251

'We didn't.' Kat pauses, unsure how to explain. She plays for time as they leave her room and she locks the door. It's easier to say it to the back of Richard's head as she follows him down the stairs. 'We didn't go out together,' she says as lightly as she can. 'We had a fight. We went our separate ways.'

'Oh.' Richard glances back at her. 'I hadn't realised.'

'It's no big deal, really,' Kat says, hoping he won't ask more. 'Not a big fight.'

'Never go to sleep on an argument – stay up and fight,' says Richard. 'Who said that?'

'I can't remember.'

'No, me neither. It makes me think of Ruth, though.'

'Yes,' says Kat, glancing at her feet.

It had been quite a bad argument, actually. They had fought about George and Dan. In the weeks since Kat had told her about that night, Ruth had become obsessed with them. 'They just shouldn't be allowed to get away with it,' she kept saying. 'What are we going to do, catch them at it?' Kat would say dryly. 'Maybe,' Ruth would nod. 'Something like that.' Kat couldn't work out why it mattered to her quite so much.

In the post room, Mr Thompson, Kat's favourite porter, is sorting through the morning's mail. He seems absorbed in his task, initially ignoring the pair of them as they greet him.

'Did that girlfriend of yours get home all right?' he says instead to Richard.

'Just about,' he laughs.

'I came on at eight,' Mr Thompson says, slapping the mail down in piles on the table. 'The night porter had a busy one, apparently. All sorts of shenanigans.'

'Oh dear,' says Richard. He sounds uncertain how to respond. 'Students, huh?'

'At least I wasn't involved this time,' says Kat, making light of it. 'It's usually me getting her in trouble, isn't it? Remember the time you had to tell us off for singing Abba?'

'I'm not surprised,' Richard shudders. 'What terrible taste.'

'Still.' Mr Thompson peers at Richard over his half-moon glasses. 'Have a word with her. It's not fair.'

'What did he mean?' Richard muses as they walk through town. 'Whatever has Ruth done? She can be belligerent enough, but it's not like her to be rude to the porters.'

'Don't worry.' Kat links her arm in his. She feels him stiffen just slightly at the contact. 'She probably just made a bit of a racket coming in – and not everyone has finished their exams yet.'

'Yes.' Richard pats her hand. 'That's probably it.' He pulls his arm away, but not unkindly.

Although it's still early, Kat can feel the warmth of the sun on her face as they sit outside La Bottega with their coffees and papers. Briefly, ever so briefly, stealing a look at Richard as he leafs through the pages, she allows herself the fantasy that this is her life.

'This is all one needs, isn't it?' he says. 'Sunshine and a coffee. Something to read.'

'Yes,' says Kat. The happiness is like something fragile fluttering in her hands. She can almost feel its heartbeat.

'Finals are a kind of madness, aren't they?' says Richard. 'The quotes I was trying to learn actually began to invade my dreams. I think I even dreamed in iambic pentameter once.'

'That's ridiculous.' Kat smiles, takes a sip of cappuccino.

It was a strange time of term. Some students had finished their exams and others hadn't. For those who had, normal drinking laws seem to have been suspended. The challenge was to think of new ways to do it. To make it acceptable early in the day, they'd go to the market to buy strawberries for Pimm's or mint for mojitos.

As they sat in the college gardens, or on the riverbank, the girls would be showered and fresh in their summer dresses, and the drinks would contain exotic fruit and ice. But when the fruit and ice had run out, they would descend upon the pub. There would always be someone finishing exams that day. And they'd move on to pints of beer and cider. And things would start to unravel.

Ruth's rages had made more regular outings in the last few weeks. Sometimes it would be funny – the time she poured a pint over the college rugby team for some perceived sexist slight; at other times, it would be more worrying. She'd punched a man in the toilet queue for threatening her and he – a massive meat-pack of a guy – had to be held back from returning the compliment. Her anger was most directly focused on George's gang, of course.

Ruth had started carrying a notepad around with her, questioning girls in college. Kat didn't like it: she didn't want people to know what had happened to her, for starters. Not that Ruth had told anyone; Kat had made her promise that much. The new problem has become how to jettison Ruth's Miss Marple act.

And there was something else, something she couldn't

quite get across to Ruth: the sense that somehow she shared the responsibility for what happened with George and Dan. That somehow it had been her fault. 'It's hard to explain,' she said more than once.

Ruth squeezed her hand tightly. 'Of *course* you feel like that. It's perfectly normal. But I'm not just doing it for you. I blacked out once or twice while I was with George – they could have done something similar to me. Or other girls. First years.'

Kat wondered if Ruth was thinking of Naomi.

Since sharing the secret with her friend, something had eased with Kat, though. She was calmer, sleeping better, for having shared the story. After their fight yesterday, the old Kat would have gone out, got obliterated and slept with someone unsavoury, whereas this Kat had stayed in, despite exams being behind her, cracking on with some reading and starting to pack for the end of term. So, for the first time in ages, Kat is experiencing glimmers of light, which, if she is truly honest with herself, also has something to do with the fact that Richard and Ruth don't seem to be that happy at the moment.

She takes another sip of her coffee, tears the corner off her almond croissant. 'Are you guys OK?' she asks as nonchalantly as she can, careful not to make eye contact.

There is a long silence and Kat half-expects him to deny it, to say of course things are fine, but he says eventually, 'I don't know. Something's changed. She seems angry all the time and I don't know why.'

'Maybe it's the thought of you leaving.' She pauses. 'We'll miss you next year.'

'No, it's not that,' Richard says simply. 'She's on a mission, but I don't really understand what it is.'

It would be so easy to explain, but Kat knows there is no way of doing it without revealing what had happened to her. And she can't. Not to Richard.

'The night we got together . . .'

'My birthday weekend,' Kat says, letting it slip out.

'Yes.' Richard leaves a modest pause. 'Ruth said: "These violent delights have violent ends."'

'What did you say?'

'Can we do it again? Something prosaic like that.'

Kat laughs. 'And you the English student. Just trying to get your end away.'

'It was always more than that,' he says, suddenly serious.

Kat puts a hand across her belly, where she feels a twist of pain. He knows she likes him. Why does he say things like that? She sighs. The spell has broken.

'I could never just be friends with Ruth,' Richard says, apropos of nothing.

It's always been Ruth for him. What was she thinking? Even her few moments of fantasy have been ruined.

'It's a bit much sometimes – your infatuation,' Kat says spitefully.

'It's not an infatuation,' Richard says. 'It's love.'

As they sit silently for a moment, Jerry and Rob, a couple of third years, pass by. On their approach, Jerry says something to Rob that Kat doesn't catch, and the boys glance over at Richard and Kat.

Jerry is still smirking at whatever he's said as he calls over, 'All right, mate?'

Richard smiles. 'Yeah, living the dream.'

'Are you OK?' says Rob. He slows as he gets to their table, casting a shadow over it.

'Yes, fine.' Richard keeps smiling but Rob remains there for a few seconds too long. He blinks a couple of times, then says, 'I heard you'd broken up with Ruth.'

Richard laughs – less a laugh, more an inhalation, a gasp. 'Then you heard wrong.' He shrugs. 'College gossip, eh?'

Kat resists the urge to reach out and touch his hand.

'Oh, right. Wrong end of the stick,' Rob smiles. He's a nice guy. Not like that little slimeball Jerry. 'Well, enjoy your croissants.'

They move on but something unsaid hangs in the air. Kat thinks she hears Jerry say, 'He obviously hasn't heard . . .'

Richard shivers. The sun has gone in. 'What was all that about?'

'Just one of those weird college nights.' Kat shrugs. 'Someone's got the wrong end of the stick, like Rob said.'

Something had woken her early that morning. A shout in the quad. She hadn't thought anything of it at the time. Mini-dramas play out all the time in college. She doesn't know why she thinks of it now. Did she hear Ruth's voice out there? She thinks of saying something but decides against it. It was probably nothing.

Alice

She must stick out like a sore thumb among all the fresh-faced millennials with their notepads and second-hand coats. Alice runs a tired hand through her hair, wondering if Richard would recognise her from college. She is waiting in a packed room at his newspaper's headquarters at the end of a talk. His paper put on public lectures and discussions regularly, but it had been fortuitous that one of his had come up at the right time, while George was away in Spain, making a one-off show about expats and the referendum. She is still feeling cross with George.

She had come back from Naomi's house feeling contrite, prepared to wipe the slate clean, to let go of what she has started to think of as her investigation, but she returned home that night to find George and Christie chatting over gin and tonics in the living room.

'This is a nice surprise,' she'd said, kissing Christie.

But it wasn't nice for long. Her friend, as usual, got straight to the point.

'Darling,' she said in hushed tones. 'We're worried about you.'

'Why?'

Alice walked to the fireplace. The pair of them must have been in touch to arrange this. It strikes her as odd.

'Sightings of dead people . . .' George began, self-appointed chair of the committee, as always. 'Doctored photographs. Mysterious postcards. Locked drawers.'

'I thought you were on my side,' Alice said to Christie. 'Whatever happened to girl code?' She sounded like a teenager.

'Darling,' said Christie again. 'We're just worried that you've become a bit . . .'

'Obsessed,' supplied George. 'With the past. With St Anthony's. With—'

'Ruth?' Alice said crossly. 'Why don't you just say it? Just because you're feeling guilty that you lied . . .'

'It's not that.'

'What is it?'

'It's Dan.' The timbre of his voice changed.

'It's just a coincidence,' Alice sighed. 'That he went so shortly afterwards.'

'Died,' George said sharply. 'Dan died. He didn't *go*; he didn't *disappear*, like one of your mysteries.' He took a large gulp of gin. 'It was bad enough that my best friend died of a drug overdose. In Goa, of all places. I've had a hard enough time getting the press to forget my past, without my own wife raking through things. And now you're trying to pair up with Ruth's sister . . .'

'Pair up?' snapped Alice. 'Don't be ridiculous. And how did you know I saw her? Who told you?'

Christie sighed. 'I mentioned it to him. I was worried.'

'Honestly,' snapped Alice. 'I can't trust either of you . . .'

George stood up and walked over to her. He placed his hands lightly on her shoulders. 'Alice, Alice, listen to yourself. You are making it sound like there's some sort of conspiracy.'

'Why are you trying to obfuscate?' Alice asked, pleased with the word. 'You too, Christie. What are you afraid of?'

George shook his head sadly. 'Darling, you're pregnant. This happens sometimes, apparently. I read an article about it in the *New Scientist*. Some women have hallucinations.'

'It was bugs with me,' Christie said. 'Huge spiders – I used to see them climbing up the walls.'

'Why didn't you mention you were so concerned before?' Alice snapped at Christie, shaking George's hands off her shoulders. 'If you were worried, you could have said something to me, rather than just running to George.'

Christie shrugged helplessly. 'I didn't know what to do.'

'I'm not going mad,' Alice said steadily before leaving them to their gins. 'It's not just in my head. Something's going on.'

She scowls as she recalls the evening; she's feeling fragile at the moment and rather alone. George's mobile reception in Spain is sporadic, so they can't talk much; she's upset Naomi; and Christie – well, goodness knows what would get back to George. They were clearly discussing her on a regular basis.

Alice still isn't sleeping well. She keeps getting up in the middle of the night and lying there, hyper-alert, listening intently to see if a noise outside had woken her.

Sometimes she has to get out of bed to check the front door is locked. At other times, she'll lie awake, as if on the lookout, until just before dawn, when her body sinks into relieved sleep with the onset of daylight.

The scrape of a chair against the floor brings her attention back to the room. At last, the final few students seem to be filing away from Richard. Alice stands up to approach him, but he turns away as she gets closer, starts to gather up his notes. She notices the streaks of grey in his dark hair as she taps him on the shoulder to get his attention.

'I don't know if you remember me?' She smiles through her nerves.

'You look familiar.' Richard pulls an apologetic face. He's still handsome, Alice notices. 'But I'm terrible with names, I'm afraid.'

Alice glances down at his book in her arms. Perhaps he thinks she's going to ask him to sign it.

'The chapter about people who've gone missing near water . . .' she begins. But she hesitates and tries again. 'I think I saw Ruth,' she says quietly.

Richard stops what he is doing. Someone bustles past, tidying chairs away.

'I was at St Anthony's, a couple of years below you,' she continues. 'I remember Ruth. I thought I saw her on the train from Edinburgh.' This is all coming out too baldly, too rushed. 'I went to speak to Naomi about it.'

At the mention of her name, Richard's face softens. He sits down, gesturing for Alice to do the same.

'What did Naomi say?'

'She said . . .' Alice hesitates. 'That it's happened

before. That people think they've seen Ruth in various places.' She looks down at her hands. 'I didn't want to upset her.'

'Her poor family.' Richard shakes his head. 'It's been hellish for them. And it doesn't seem to stop. There's always something else.' He rubs his forehead. 'Ruth used to say there was someone who looked like her in St Anthony's,' he adds.

'I hadn't heard that.'

'No, her best friend always said it was bollocks,' Richard says. 'I never knew what to make of it. Ruth could be a bit theatrical.' He smiles but he looks sad. 'When did you see this person?' he asks.

'In January.' The relief is palpable: that someone is taking her seriously. 'I thought you might be interested, because of your book.'

'Did Naomi tell you about Nunny?' Richard asks.

Alice nods. She is aware that she is making her meeting with Naomi seem more fruitful and friendly than it actually was.

'It's weird, isn't it?' says Richard. 'I'm helping them look into that – using a couple of my contacts to try to find out more. One of them is a handwriting expert. He's comparing the writing on the parcel with a sample of Ruth's.'

Alice thinks of the postcard in her handbag. She wants to show it to him, but not here.

'There's more,' she says. 'I don't know if you have time for a drink?'

'Absolutely,' Richard nods. 'There's somewhere just around the corner.'

262

They walk companionably along Farringdon Road to the pub. It's a pleasant spring evening, with couples on dates wandering on their way to supper, small clusters of smokers outside bars with their end-of-day drinks. Alice already feels more cheerful.

'I don't know about you,' she says. 'But for me it's nice to talk to someone about all this.'

'Tell me about it!' Richard laughs darkly. 'I never married, you know. Funnily enough, women don't like you being obsessed with a missing ex.'

'You say "missing", don't you?' says Alice. 'Other people say "dead".'

'It's a personal decision,' Richard says, pushing open the door of a tiny pub on the street corner. 'I understand why her family have made the decisions they've made. I don't suppose you're drinking alcohol,' he says, heading for the bar.

'Elderflower,' Alice calls after him. 'Or fizzy water.'

She has the brief, and deeply inappropriate, feeling of being on a date.

When Richard is back at the table with their drinks, Alice plunges in again: 'Do you remember Dan Vaughan? You mentioned him in your book. He was the last person to see Ruth alive.'

'Yes, I knew Dan,' Richard says curtly. 'What sort of person he was.'

Alice tries a different tack. 'Did he have a thing for Ruth?'

Richard frowns. 'What do you mean?' The tone of his voice has changed. The friendliness is eking away.

Alice hesitates. She doesn't want to risk losing what

might be her only ally. 'It's nothing,' she says quickly. 'Just a hunch.'

'A hunch based on nasty rumours?' Richard takes a swift gulp of his beer.

Alice shakes her head. 'No, it was just an idea. And I saw some red hair in a photo of him and George.'

'George?' Richard's voice wavers.

Alice hesitates, wishing she hadn't said anything. George's name sometimes had that effect. She knew he hadn't been friends with Richard, but what had George said? That Richard couldn't stand him?

'Yes,' she says. 'My husband – George Bell.'

'You didn't say that,' Richard says angrily, getting up.

'You didn't ask.' Alice gets up too, flustered. 'We didn't exactly do introductions.'

'No,' says Richard. 'You just came to find me to say you'd seen the ghost of my dead girlfriend, with precisely no explanation of who you are.'

'Missing,' says Alice lamely. 'Not dead.'

'Do you know how hard this is?' Richard hisses.

He is pale with fury. Alice glances around them to see if anyone else has noticed. She feels glad for a moment that they're in a public place.

'Do you know how hard it will *always* be?' Richard continues. 'I'm trying to move on. I stopped writing about it. It even stopped being the first thing I thought about every single day when I woke up. Do you know what that's like?'

'I do a bit,' says Alice. 'Not in the same way, of course,' she adds hurriedly. 'But I can't sleep, I can't concentrate at work. I feel terrible – all the time. I have a baby on

264

the way – and my husband actually thinks I'm going mad.'

Richard snorts. 'Well, I wouldn't worry about what *he* thinks.'

'Look,' says Alice. 'I saw her – I really saw her. And . . .' Her hands are shaking as she fishes the postcard out of her handbag and smacks it down on the table. 'It's a postcard. To George. From St Anthony's. It was a rhyme Ruth used to say.'

Richard glances down. He gets out a pair of reading glasses and sits again to look at the postcard.

'She did say that,' he says quietly.

'Is it the same writing?' Alice asks. 'As the package?'

Richard picks it up. 'I can't tell. I could ask my friend to check.'

Alice nods. 'Maybe.' She hesitates. 'No, on second thoughts, let me keep it for another couple of days.'

'Do you need to talk to George?' Richard sneers.

'I'll get back to you about it.' Alice decides she's had enough. 'Can I find you at the office?'

'I'm sure you'll manage. You seem to be good at finding people. It's creepy.'

'You can talk about creepy,' Alice snaps, putting her coat on angrily. 'Writing a book about your ex-girlfriend.'

'Ask your husband what *he* thinks happened to Ruth,' Richard says softly. 'He and Dan ruined everything that was good between us. I blame them – I blame them for her mental state the night she went.'

'But he won't tell me anything,' Alice says fiercely. 'No one will tell me a fucking thing.'

265

Kat

Kat's second visitor the day of the break-up is Nicky Crisp. 'I come bearing news.' She is at Kat's door, holding a paper bag full of biscuits.

'OK,' says Kat. 'Well, you know what they say: I won't stand for gossip, I like to sit down for it.' She puts the kettle on.

Everyone knew Nicky Crisp – one of college's party people. She was good fun – perceptive, too. She'd spotted the bruises Dan had left on Kat's arms and said: 'I had marks like that after sleeping with Dan Vaughan.' And something about Kat's reaction must have given her away, because Nicky said, 'Oh, I see. That makes two of us. Like a club.'

'More than two, I suspect,' Kat said.

'Quite,' Nicky agreed. 'Well, I wouldn't go back for more.'

And they hadn't said much more than that, but somehow it had made Kat feel less alone.

266

Kat liked Nicky: she was tough and no-nonsense. She didn't put on airs and graces, but she didn't seem to be intimidated by the Etonian crowd, either. She was herself – steely and bright. She didn't try to downplay her strong Glaswegian accent – Kat envied her that; she'd always felt the need to perform, for almost everyone, but particularly for people with backgrounds like George's. She started acting as if she were in an F. Scott Fitzgerald novel.

'It's about our mutual . . . well, it's about Dan Vaughan,' Nicky says once she's settled with a cup of tea in her hand. 'I wasn't there but I was in the Snowman's room early this morning doing a few lines of Colombia's best – so anyway, I didn't see it . . .'

'See what?' Kat blows on her tea – talking about Dan makes her feel unsettled, even with Nicky.

'I thought you might be pleased to hear,' Nicky continues, 'that he's in massive shit. Got called to the dean's office this morning . . .'

'They can't do much now, can they?' Kat shrugs. 'He's done his finals.'

'Well, he's still waiting for his tutor to write a reference for Goldman Sachs, apparently . . .'

Kat puts her drink down for a moment. 'What happened?'

'Mary – you know, the junior organ scholar – went to practise this morning and found Dan shagging a girl in the chapel. Trousers round his ankles.' Nicky chuckles. 'Gave her the fright of her life.'

Kat smirks. 'That's embarrassing.'

'Mary's only seventeen . . . went running to the porters about it.'

'Well, he's a prick,' Kat says. 'It's about time he got his comeuppance.'

'Quite,' Nicky snorts. 'Nasty piece of work.'

Kat picks her drink up and begins to sip it again. She's about to change the subject, ask Nicky what she's up to over the summer, but Nicky is leaning forwards in her chair. She looks concerned.

'I don't like to gossip,' she adds. 'Well, I do, but I thought you'd know. Or maybe you don't?'

She's not making much sense. 'What?' says Kat.

Nicky looks uncomfortable. 'The girl in the chapel? They're saying it was your friend, Ruth.'

'That's daft.' Kat swallows. 'Ruth wouldn't. She's with Richard.'

Nicky nods. 'That's what I thought. It's weird, though, she asked me the other day about Dan.'

'What?'

'If we'd slept together. I thought you might have said something.'

'No, I didn't.'

'I don't know.' Nicky crosses her legs and then uncrosses them. 'I'm not scared of that lot. Not exactly.'

'But what?'

'If they think she's started rumours about them. They might do the same about her. Stir things up.' She sighs. 'It's so easy for them, isn't it?'

'What is?' says Kat.

Nicky shrugs. 'Everything.'

After she leaves, Kat lights a cigarette and thinks. A part of her feels like she should dash over to Ruth and tell her what is being said about her, so she can defend herself. Another part is cautioning something else: Ruth hasn't come to confide in her, after all. And there was another thing, too. Something she hadn't mentioned to Richard or Nicky. Ruth had developed an obsession with Dan, hounding him to admit what he'd done to Kat and possibly to Ruth too, on one of the occasions when she was out of it.

A couple of weeks ago, Kat had spotted them sitting together at a Mexican-themed party in one of the large rooms in front quad. Kat hadn't been in the mood for the party, so she hadn't arrived with Ruth, but at the last minute she had thought: what the hell? And come out to join her friend. She couldn't see Ruth for ages. She always looked out for her hair in a room and it was covered that night with a Mexican headscarf. When she finally spotted her, she saw she was sitting with Dan on a sagging sofa, not looking at Dan but into the fireplace. Dan was talking with his mouth very near to Ruth's ear, his arm dropped loosely over her shoulders. They were sitting so closely that Kat had wondered for a moment if something was going on.

Ruth's dress had ridden up, exposing her thighs, pale, lean and tightly crossed. But she didn't seem to notice. She didn't seem to be in the room at all. She looked odd, haunted, though Dan seemed to be enjoying himself, teasing her, perhaps. Suddenly, he cupped her face in his hands and kissed her, full on the mouth.

The kiss didn't last for long – a moment perhaps – before Ruth sprang away from Dan, leapt to her feet and marched towards George. Standing behind a first year in hot pants on the Twister mat, George looked up as Ruth approached. 'I'm going to expose you,' Ruth shouted. 'I'm going to let the world know what you lot are like.' And she punched him straight on the torso. Amid shrieks from the other players, George and the sombrero on his head toppled down on the mat, and Ruth moved on again, pushing her way, white-faced, to the door. When Kat asked her later what Dan had said, Ruth was brusque. 'It was nothing. An insult. A threat, really.'

'What do you mean?'

'He said he hadn't had sex with me yet but that he would one day.'

'Charming,' said Kat.

'Well, that's Dan,' said Ruth. 'He just wanted to creep me out.'

So there had been a kiss, but a strange one. Kat sits in her armchair for a long time, mulling it over. Would Ruth ever shag Dan after all that? She didn't think so, but some girls were strange. Gluttons for punishment. Kat knew more about that than most.

She doesn't know how long she has been sitting there, but a scream interrupts her reverie. And she knows immediately, instinctively, that it is Ruth. She goes to her window, where she sees Ruth in her long white dress, shrieking at Richard. He is glowering at her, with Luke standing by with a hand on his arm as if to restrain him. The sounds Ruth's making are ungodly. People stop – not in a crowd, but individuals at different points in the quad – and stare like statues, as Kat is now. She is watching them again, as she always seems to be; as she watched Richard looking at Ruth for the very first time; as she watched them kiss at Chatsworth. It seems to be her role.

And then, Kat notices, Dan has joined the bystanders

in the quad and Ruth is flying at him, with nails and teeth, and the porters bolt from the porters' lodge and carry her away with Naomi following, holding Ruth's red shoes. Kat sits in the darkness and waits. She starts to count. When she reaches fifty-three, there is a loud rap at the door. It's Richard.

His hands shake as he lights a cigarette. 'It was bad,' he says darkly. 'She went wild.' He perches on her bed. 'Everyone says it was her with Dan: her hair, her legs, the dress she was wearing, for God's sake – the one she was wearing last night.'

'So what happened?'

'She says it wasn't. That there is a girl who looks exactly like her. And she kept saying, "Just ask Kat." Because I guess she thought you'd be a witness.'

'A witness?' Kat tries not to laugh. 'It's not a murder.'

But she gets up, starts to wander around the room to avoid his gaze. *Why is your friend ignoring me?* That's what he'd said, the barman in the Two Pheasants who'd thought he'd known Ruth. Had she imagined that? Kat frowns. Or had Ruth lied? And there had been another instance, though Kat can't remember what, of someone mentioning a lookalike, but does Richard need to know that, if she can barely remember herself?

'Is it true? Could it have been someone who looked like her?' Richard's tone is incredulous.

Still avoiding eye contact, Kat picks up from the shelf a paperweight she inherited from her grandmother, the seedhead of a dandelion preserved intact under the glass. She feels the weight of it in her hand and decides upon a compromise.

271

'No one looks like Ruth,' she smiles. 'She's one of a kind.' She places the paperweight carefully back on the shelf. 'And she hates Dan,' she continues. 'You know that.'

'Does she?' He hesitates. 'She *says* she does.' Richard hunts around for somewhere to tap the ash from his cigarette. 'That first time we were together – she just went down on me like that. She didn't know me at all . . .'

Kat passes him an ashtray. 'What are you trying to say, Rich?' Her voice is cool. They're all the same, men, in the end.

'I don't know.' He shakes himself. 'I don't know. Maybe I should talk to her. She probably went back to the cottage . . .'

'Look, why not leave it for today?' Kat goes over to sit next to him. 'I think you both need to calm down a bit. We could go for a quick drink?'

Richard shakes his head. 'I am not going to the college bar. Absolutely not.'

'Fair enough,' Kat agrees. 'Maybe somewhere in town?'

He pauses. 'Yeah, all right then.' He rests his head on her shoulder for a moment. 'Thanks, Kat.'

She feels suddenly, ridiculously, a surge of excitement. She tries to rein in her smile. She says, 'I'll buy.'

Back in her room, sitting together on her bed, Kat realises that, though she is quite drunk, Richard's alcohol consumption has taken him to another plane.

'Maybe we need to write it all down,' he is suggesting. 'Who said what. Have you got a pen and paper?'

Kat doesn't want to make notes about the evening before. It seems a bit mad. Nevertheless, she passes a notebook and a pen to Richard, who starts to scratch away at the pad.

'Bugger.'

'What?'

'Turns out I can't write any more.'

Kat peers at the pad on his lap. 'It's your . . .' She can't remember the words – something to do with an engine. 'Your motor functions. They're fucked.'

They'd started on pints. And then there had been whisky and, at one stage, long, refreshing drinks with vodka in them, and Richard had gone on and on about Ruth. And yet there had been a moment, as they'd stumbled out of the heat of the bar, when he had reached for her hand and walked down the street holding it. St Anthony's had looked different for a short while and Kat had allowed herself a few moments of giddying happiness.

'I'll try.' Kat takes the notepad off him, but she struggles remembering the order of things. 'We met at 7 p.m.' It's very difficult to control the pen. She holds it tightly, tries forming the shapes of the letters, but the words look nothing like her writing, nothing like words at all. She begins to giggle. 'I can't write, either.'

Richard looks at the pad and begins to laugh. 'What a pair of twats.' And he kisses Kat quite suddenly, quite roughly. The force of the kiss unbalances her. Then, as quickly as he started, he pulls away. 'Sorry. I'm so sorry.' He slumps back on the bed. 'Fuck.'

Kat feels a hot rush of joy. This must have been what it felt like to be Ruth all that time. The rush is followed by a wave of incredible calm. She says quietly, 'Don't be sorry.' She stands in front of him and takes her top off.

'Kat,' he says. 'I don't think this is a good idea . . .'

'Richard.' Kat smiles beatifically, Zen-like. 'This is the best idea.'

She removes her bra and stands looking at him. She climbs on his lap and puts her cool mouth over his inebriated one.

Naomi

Perhaps it wasn't fair to have called Alice a spotter. I know something about spotting myself. I, too, have spied the outline of Ruth in crowds, by the sea, at a station. I have felt that heart-stopping certainty as I shove past people to get to her, or make Carla drive back down a street, as I retrace my steps, or tap strangers on the shoulder. Usually, almost always, she is moving away. It's the back of her head, her profile. I dream of that, too. I know what it's about – it's a longing for certainty. In my darkest times, I wonder if it might be easier if she had died a more normal way, which is to say: left us a body to mourn over.

The baby shop is warm and brightly lit and strangely busy for a Tuesday afternoon, though I suppose mothers with infants are less tied to working hours. Carla paces around picking things up and waving them at me with a questioning face. I smile back and gesture: whatever you think. We haven't been very organised about this – we should have a list – but it's fun to see Carla so happy, bounding down the aisles. She's ten years older than me – she's been waiting ten years longer. We were fortunate, really, that I conceived so early – just on the second round of IUI. I'm not used to thinking of myself as lucky.

Since Nunny appeared, I don't feel myself. I find it hard to focus, find myself gazing into space as I am now at the shelves where beige bears, dogs and a strange preponderance of giraffes stare blankly back. They remind me of Nunny, who actually started his life as bright pink but ended up beige like the toys I'm looking at now, worn out from too much love.

Ruth isn't the only ghost from my past I've glimpsed in unexpected places, though strangely I never conjured up our father. Maybe that's the difference between those we have buried and those we haven't. Perhaps, the unburied must haunt us. When I lost people before Ruth, we put them to rest. Even my grandfather, who disappeared into water too, washed up days later. Even he is buried now in the earth, which is solid and definite. Not like water.

Occasionally, over the years, we've allowed ourselves a flicker of hope, my mother and I. After a couple of glasses of wine, when Carla's not there, one of us will say 'Maybe,' and it will last for a second or two. But that's all, usually. We indulged a little more when Nunny turned up, of course. Just because the idea is preferable: that she might be out there, living as a poet on a Scottish island – the Shetlands, perhaps, or the Outer Hebrides. Or that she's joined a travelling theatre group in America, like Gypsy Rose Lee, zigzagging her way across that vast continent. Or living as a gaucho in Argentina, that's my favourite – that she's out there, working with horses. She'd like that: bantering with the cowboys, her freckles coming out in the sun, her arms turning pale gold.

It's not just our dead who haunt us. After Miss Wick disappeared from school, I started to see her too, to look twice at tall dark-haired women, anyone wearing a scarf in their hair. Once, on a tube, as my train stopped at a station, I glanced up from my book to see her standing there. She was carrying a bag, looking askance at something further along the platform.

It was particularly bad in my first year at St Anthony's, the year after our break-up. Working on an essay as I sat in the gallery of the library, I thought I spied her through the gaps in the carved wood of the balcony, thought I caught the low cadence of her voice, asking the librarian something. When I bounded down the stairs to take a closer look, the woman had gone and I persuaded myself I'd been imagining things. But for a long time it felt as if I might turn a corner to find Miss Wick there. And then, when it did happen, she still took me by surprise.

I don't recognise the ring of my own phone at first. It's new and I'm still finding my way around it. The ring, which Carla chose, is a cheery Latin tune. I fish around in my bag as its chirpy tones get louder and see it's my mother calling. I think for a moment of leaving it, but then decide to explain where I am, to suggest we speak later.

'Darling?' Her voice is higher than usual. 'Where are you?'

'We're shopping.'

'So you're with someone? You're with Carla?' She sounds wired and I know immediately that it's bad.

'What's wrong?'

'Are you sitting down?'

'Of course not.'

But something in her tone of voice makes me want to sit down. I look for chairs and see a couple in the corner near the changing rooms. My legs feel weak as I walk towards them. There's a tired-looking man perched on one, running a hand across his stubble as if he's only just realised he hasn't shaved. He shifts his bags from the other chair, so I can sit.

The crackle of the line fills my ears, as Carla turns towards me and realises that something is wrong, as I wait for my mother to say it.

'They've found something – haven't they?'

'They say human remains,' says my mother. Such a small impersonal phrase. 'A female skeleton. They found her close to the cottage in St Anthony's, in the woods nearby.'

'But she was swimming,' I say. 'She was in the water, she wasn't . . .'

But I find I don't know which words come next. 'She wasn't buried' – is that what I'm trying to say? 'She wasn't murdered.' And it's not until now – despite my longing for resolution, my years of wanting an answer, any sort of answer – that I realise I never have been, never will be ready for this: the certainty that Ruth isn't with us any more. That I will never see her again.

Alice

Alice knows she looks a fright in her bright pink dressing gown with her facemask slathered on. She doesn't care, she just doesn't care any more. She used to dress up for George, buy clothes with him in mind. She would think about him admiring her in them, or out of them, what lingerie she might wear underneath. The thing is: none of it mattered. None of it. She used to think if she did enough, if she was *enough* in some way, then he would let her in. But perhaps it had never been down to her.

He is due back from Spain tonight. Alice waits at the kitchen table, arranging her evidence: Richard's book, the postcard from St Anthony's and, in place of Nunny, a piece of paper simply saying 'Nunny'. If she were a detective in a police drama, she would have pinned these to the wall of the room by this stage in an unhinged manner. But Alice isn't unhinged. She is in the dark, but she isn't unhinged.

These are the facts: she saw Ruth on the train. Ruth, or someone who knew something, had sent Nunny to

279

Naomi as a message, but what? To say, I'm safe? Or something else? And if it were Ruth – why not just come back? Why send a toy rabbit in her place? Then there were the postcards. Ruth, or the person acting for Ruth, had sent the message not to Naomi, who might have understood it, but to George. 'Give what I've lost back to me.' *Give*, not bring. It sounds like an order. Or a threat. And the question was: what had George taken?

Alice tidies her pieces of evidence back into a box and places it under the kitchen table. She will have a stronger case with George if she builds up to showing him the box after they've talked. It will seem less mad. She gets up to make herself a camomile tea. She's still not sleeping well. She's been dwelling on the conversation with Richard – the violence of his reaction to George's name, and the way he linked George and Dan to Ruth's disappearance. With Christie away on a yoga retreat, Alice had ended up calling her mum, desperate for someone to talk to. She always thought twice about telling her parents about her marital problems. Not because her mum would say, 'I told you so.' Not that. But she might think it.

She didn't go into the details, just said that she thought George was keeping something from her. And her mother said: 'Talk to him.' So that's what Alice was going to do. Her resolve stiffens as George wanders into the kitchen, tanned and laden down with bags.

'Darling.' He opens his arms. 'What a sight for sore eyes. What the fuck is that on your face?'

Alice doesn't move from her seat. 'Why does Richard Wiseman hate you?'

280

George puts down his bags, rubs his forehead wearily. 'You've heard then, I take it?'

Alice frowns. 'Heard what?'

'That they've found her.' George makes his way to the fridge and pours himself a large glass of white wine.

'Found who?' asks Alice, wrong-footed.

'Ruth, of course.' George comes to sit opposite her at the table. 'The subject of your investigation.'

Alice feels her heart beat a little faster. 'What are you talking about?' This is classic George, she thinks. Always the first to know.

George smiles calmly. 'What are *you* talking about? I imagined it has put your detecting into overdrive.'

'What have they found?' asks Alice urgently.

'Human remains,' says George. 'In St Anthony's. It looks as if Ruth has been there all along. Poor old thing.' He swings back on his chair. 'Case closed.'

He almost looks pleased, thinks Alice. 'Do they know for sure it's Ruth?' She thinks of Naomi: what must she be going through right now?

'You didn't know?' crows George. 'I imagined your new friends Naomi and Richard would have kept you abreast.'

'They're not my friends – don't be ridiculous.' Alice gets up to put the kettle on. 'I did see Richard, though.'

'Ha! I knew it,' says George triumphantly.

He looks so brown and well, thinks Alice resentfully, while she has been here suffering sleepless nights.

'He *really* doesn't like you,' she says pointedly.

'No, he wouldn't,' George responds lightly.

'Why not?' Alice stands by the kettle as it begins to whistle.

281

'Well,' George says. 'We're very different.'

'It's more than that.'

'He was jealous, darling. A lot of people were – and I'd been with his girlfriend before him.' He chuckles. 'Sloppy seconds.'

Alice blinks. She feels anger flare through her body. Ruth has been found dead, possibly killed, and this is his reaction. She flings her almost empty cup against the wall, where it bounces off the Cath Kidston noticeboard and shatters on the slate floor.

'You're not a teenager any more,' she says. 'That kind of thing, from a middle-aged man, is . . .' She pauses; she can't think of a word that quite cuts it.

They both stand for a second looking at the broken fragments.

'It's repellent,' she says softly.

George is quiet for a moment, then says, 'I'll get the dustpan and brush.'

He takes his time clearing up, is careful, methodical. First, he sweeps; then he gets a damp cloth and wipes the tiles carefully.

'Darling,' he says. 'Please sit down. Put your feet up.'

Alice swallows back tears. She doesn't want to cry. Not tonight. She takes a large slurp of his wine. It's strangely soothing watching George on his hands and knees clearing up after her. She takes his advice and sits down at the table. She hasn't even got to her evidence box yet.

'Ruth and Dan had a bit of a thing,' he says as he wipes up the fragments. 'That's another reason why Wiseman can't stand me.'

'A thing?' asks Alice.

'Well, yes, they were bonking.'

'Are you sure?'

George chuckles. 'Well, I wasn't in the room myself . . .'

'Might Dan have hurt her?' She pauses. 'Killed her, I mean.'

'Don't be silly,' says George. 'You *knew* Dan.'

Alice doesn't know how to respond: she didn't, she thinks, not really. They'd only been at St Anthony's together for a couple of terms, after all.

'What about Richard?' George suggests. 'He was the one who was angry with her.'

'No,' says Alice, unconvinced. 'He's spent his entire career trying to find her.'

'And what a great cover that would be,' George says, wrapping up the fragments of the cup in newspaper. 'A double bluff. It's certainly got you convinced.'

Alice puts her hand on her bump, decides not to rise to the jibe. 'Was there someone who looked like her? Did you ever hear that?' she asks.

George turns away from her to get some Sellotape from the Welsh dresser, tapes up the newspaper carefully and throws the package in the bin.

'No,' he says shortly. 'Only from her when Richard dumped her. The thing you've got to understand about Ruth was . . .' He stops himself.

'What?' says Alice. 'Just say it.'

'Well,' says George with some venom. 'She was a little slut.'

Alice blanches at the word, opens her mouth to say something, to object, but before she has a chance, George comes to sit opposite her at the table with a serious look on his face.

'Look,' he says and for a moment he sounds solemn. 'I love you very much and we have a fresh start, a fresh person on the way.' He pauses. 'Please can we put this stuff behind us? They've found a body. It's over. Please.'

He takes her hand and she is reminded of his proposal on a beach in Jamaica.

She blinks. 'Is it definitely her?'

'My sources say it is.' George smiles. 'And you know how good my sources are.' He swallows, says more seriously again, 'Alice, you're the only good, the only pure thing in my life. You are certainly the only person I have loved in this way. I honestly cannot imagine what my life would be without you. It started with you, really; everything before was just bullshit. Please, Alice, please promise me you'll stop: stop investigating, stop visiting people. Just let it go.'

Is it possible, after all this, that Ruth is really dead? That Alice didn't – couldn't – have seen her, after all? She is silent – it's always difficult to accept: that one has been so wrong about something.

'I'd better go and wash my face,' she says in the end.

Upstairs, she perches on the edge of the bath for a few minutes searching for the news on her phone. It seems George is right: they have found human remains in St Anthony's. A skeleton buried near Ruth's old house. A third party must have been involved. Her poor family. She thinks back to the face on the train and finds she can't picture it properly this time. Is there something wrong with her mind? She takes time washing her face, feeling the cold water against her skin. What an idiot she has been. And how frustrating – *beyond* frustrating – that George has been right all along. She feels a little weak.

When she returns to the kitchen, Alice realises how hungry she is.

'Shall we have something to eat?' she asks. 'I haven't prepared anything but we could order in.'

'No.' George starts to rifle through the bags he'd walked in with. 'I bought some goodies.'

He gets out some ham and cheese, and a tin of delicious olives, while Alice makes a salad. She puts on the radio. There is a chance, she thinks, that life could get back to normal, that all this could be put behind them.

Later, more relaxed, with a full belly, she sits holding hands with George.

'You're very tanned,' she says, looking down at their entwined fingers.

'Am I?' George puts a hand to his face. 'Thanks, darling.'

'But for Spain, I mean, at this time of year,' Alice says.

Her uncle had a house in the Pyrenees. They used to visit occasionally over Christmas and Easter, but she didn't think it would have been warm enough in April for him to be quite so tanned, especially while he was working.

'We popped over to Morocco for a bit.'

'For the show?' Alice wonders why he hasn't mentioned this before. 'What's Morocco got to do with it?'

'No, just for fun. You remember that?'

Alice rolls her eyes, but things are so much better that she lets that one rest. A little sheepishly, she gets out her evidence box. To George's credit, he just smiles patiently.

'I just want to go through a few things with you for the last time, I promise.'

'OK, detective.'

Alice grins despite herself.

'What the fuck's a Nunny?' George picks up the piece of paper with 'Nunny' written on it.

'That's Ruth's toy.' Alice takes it from him. 'It arrived in the post for Naomi.'

'That *is* weird.'

'Isn't it?' Alice gets out the postcard next. 'I showed you this before.' She passes it over.

George tosses it aside. 'Some psycho.'

Alice holds Richard's book open to show George the photo of Ruth. The girl's face looks back at her. All that sass and poise at nineteen.

'I was so sure I saw her, George,' she says, looking at it for the last time before putting it away. Her gaze returns to the things on the table. What does she have, really? A postcard and the mysterious Nunny. 'I'm sorry,' she says. 'It's been a weird time.' She starts to cry but they are tears of relief. 'I don't know what I've been thinking.'

George opens his arms for a hug and Alice makes her way over to where he's sitting. 'It's just me and my girls against the world,' he says. He wraps his arms around her belly and kisses her bump.

She presses her face into his hair. It reminds her of the old days, of how the physicality of George can make it all seem better. She breathes in the scent of him, but it's not quite right. She recognises the first smell straight away: it's not one she's smelled in their bedroom for a little while. It's the unmistakable scent of sex. But there's another smell there, too. And that's familiar, as well. Cleaner, more refined. It's a woman's perfume, musky but definitely female. It's that rare Paloma Picasso. The one that Christie wears.

Naomi

When human remains are discovered, it turns out there is a strict protocol to how they are dealt with. It also turns out that none of this requires the potential sister of the skeleton. Our family liaison officer arranged for my mum to have a buccal swab, which will be compared with the skeleton's DNA. Now, it is simply a matter of waiting. That doesn't make it easier, of course. I go back to Wales to wait with my mother for a few days. The first night we stay up talking, jumping every time the phone rings as if there could be news so soon.

It doesn't look good. We don't need the experts to tell us that. That a skeleton has been found so close to the house where we used to live. My instinct is to go there. To make the journey to St Anthony's. But at this stage, while the tests are being carried out, there's not much we can do. It might not be her: it might even be a skeleton from another era, as my mother keeps suggesting in a shrill tone.

I howled in the baby shop at the finality of the news.

At the thought that someone had hurt her, that my darkest fears had not been unfounded. I hadn't cried properly for a long time, not like that. Carla held me. Parents and children moved silently away. The urge to be with Ruth was so strong. Even just her bones. To lie down beside them, to put my arms around them.

I've never been to Argentina, but Miss Wick told me once about the Mothers of the Disappeared who would walk circuits around the Plaza de Mayo with their white headscarves on, decades after their loss. That's what it does to people when their loved ones disappear with no trace. *Los desaparecidos.* Later, I thought of how well the word applied to Miss Wick herself.

After the time I thought I saw her in the library at St Anthony's, I bumped into her with Jane. It was the summer term – the end of my first year at university – and I had been seeing Jane for a couple of months. She was a third year with a pale, round face. Jane took over my life at a time when I felt I needed that, needed someone else to make decisions for me, but then it got a bit much – she wanted to do absolutely everything together. I began to fake visits to the library to get away from her, or I'd pop off to the cinema on my own for an afternoon. I caught a matinee performance of *A Matter of Life and Death* in the town's tiny ancient cinema and wept all the way through it, longing for something that I couldn't quite put into words.

I didn't say much to Ruth about it: I knew what she would say. Ruth thought Jane was a control freak. At that time, in the months before she went, she got rather obsessed with control, with the idea of it. She started spending a lot of time with Kat, who would come to the cottage and sit holed up in Ruth's room talking intensely. They'd go quiet when I came in.

'Talking about boys, are you?' I would tease. 'You can do that in front of me . . .'

'Well, we know they're not *quite* your thing,' Kat would say in that affected way she had.

And I suppose she was right.

I met Miss Wick again in an old bookshop just off Cathedral Square. She was ahead of us in the queue, but her hair had changed – it was shorter – so I didn't realise it was her. Jane was a couple of people after her in the queue and for some reason, when she got to the till, she got quite heated about the book she was looking for. Jane had a habit of rubbing everyone up the wrong way, being rude to waiters, people who served her in shops. And during the low-level kerfuffle, I felt the lightest of touches on my waist. 'Naomi, I thought it was you.' The same low voice, the same hands.

I looked at the door, out to the square, but my feet were fixed to the spot. I said: 'Why are you here?' And, because it was the first thing that came to mind, I added: 'You left me.'

'Naomi.' I'd forgotten exactly what her voice was like, how that was always one of my favourite things about her. 'I had to. I was your teacher. Someone had found out.'

I wanted to say: 'You broke my heart.' I wanted to say: 'I never got over you. Because of you I didn't get into Cambridge, I had a sort of breakdown, I ended up here, with an awful girlfriend and a sense of grief that I will probably carry with me forever.' But instead I said: 'Your hair is different.'

Miss Wick put a hand to her head. 'I needed a change.'

'You look like a boy,' I said spitefully.

She didn't seem bothered by this. 'Are you here with someone?'

'Yes.' I looked at the counter, where Jane was shaking her head crossly. 'Are you?'

'No,' she said. 'There hasn't been anyone since you.' She took a step closer to me and I could feel the heat coming off her body, smell the woody scent of eucalyptus.

I wondered what it would feel like to run my fingers through her hair now it was so short and I remembered an afternoon I'd bunked off school – it had been the only time I'd ever done anything like that. It had been warm outside, but we had spent the afternoon in Miss Wick's flat, drinking wine, having sex. And as I stood in the hot little bookshop waiting for Jane, I had a very clear memory of Miss Wick's head between my legs, the feel of her hair under my hands.

She took another step closer.

'You're not my teacher any more.'

'No, I'm not.'

She raised a hand to lift an eyelash off my cheek. Such a tiny thing, but she knew that I would let her, knew I wouldn't fight it, probably knew, too, of the lovely heat that would flush through me at the contact.

And then there was Jane, breaking the spell, saying, 'Hello, I'm Naomi's girlfriend.'

'I'm an old teacher of hers.' Miss Wick smiled. 'Well, not teacher exactly.'

We chatted for a while. She told us she was doing an MA at St Anthony's the following year; that she was in town to sort out her accommodation. I just stood there, blushing to the roots of my hair, saying little as the pair of them talked.

'I might be able to help you. I'm good friends with the housing officer,' said Jane, as if this was something to be particularly proud of. Poor Jane. Not just for that. For all of it. For the way I was in Miss Wick's arms by that very evening.

The sense that I would find her again never left me – on buses, walking through London – it sometimes felt overwhelmingly strong: the feeling that she would be waiting for me, to call me back with the lightest of touches, just like she did then.

Kat

April 2016

The vibration of her mobile against the hard ceramic of the sink makes Kat jump. She climbs out of the bath carefully, picks it up with a damp hand and reads: 'Are we still on for tonight?'

How long has it been since she last saw him? Two years? Or is it three? Kat frowns as she tries to remember. She places the phone back on the sink and returns to the heat of the bath. She'll answer later. He can wait for once.

For years after university, Kat would find herself, at times when she wasn't concentrating properly on being busy, caught unawares by the telephone. Just for a second as she lurched to pick it up, her heart would tighten at the thought it might be Richard. Sometimes, on quiet Sundays, the doorbell had the same effect. Or on seeing an unopened envelope flashing on the screen of her mobile, she would allow herself to think – just for a fraction of a moment – that it might be him. This April afternoon is not one of those times.

The news at the hospital that morning had not been good. It hadn't been good at all. What had been the word they used? Metastatic. It had spread to her bones now, too. She had called the office to say she'd be taking the rest of the day off. Which was rare for her. She'd have to tell them at some stage. There would be so many people to tell. She should write a list. First, of course, there was her mother. Kat closes her eyes. She doesn't feel strong enough for that yet. There would be tears, and endless cigarettes, and wine, no doubt, and a fight. 'They're more likely to get it, aren't they? Women who don't have children?' her mother would say as she had said before and she would pour herself another glass of wine. 'Why didn't you settle down? You never looked after yourself. All those cigarettes, all those men.' And she wouldn't see the irony.

Even today, of all days, Ruth was managing to take the limelight. A skeleton had been found near her old house in St Anthony's after all these years. A sordid ending for her family but, it looked very likely, an ending nevertheless. She and Richard had arranged to meet up to talk about it, perhaps to say a sort of goodbye to Ruth.

Ghastly though it is, it looks likely that Ruth died at someone else's hands. She thinks of the last time she'd seen her friend at the memorial ball. It wasn't a happy memory. Ruth hadn't spotted her at first: she hadn't seen her because she was only looking at Richard, as usual, kissing him passionately before he went on stage with his band.

Kat had wondered if Ruth might return from Wales, where she'd fled after the break-up, for the last night of the year – Richard's final night in college. Kat was dressed in white that night, in an elegant evening dress she'd borrowed from her mother. 'No man can resist a woman in white,' her mum had said when Kat paid her a visit to borrow it. She'd remembered it from photos of her parents in the Eighties, but it had aged well with its simple, clean style and an elegant high neck. 'I'm sure he will fall in love with you,' added her mother, who had, admittedly, only heard part of the story.

'Don't do what I did,' her mum had advised her as they both admired her reflection in the white dress. 'Don't let yourself go.'

But dressed in white, holding two glasses of champagne – one for her, one for Richard, which she'd picked up to give him before he went on stage – Kat felt like a jilted bride.

To be fair, Richard hadn't made any promises. The night he and Ruth broke up, Kat woke a couple of times, frightened to move in case she should disturb him, break the spell. It wasn't the most romantic of scenarios – the room reeked of alcohol and Richard was a fitful sleeper, his skin clammy to the touch as he sweated out the booze – but Kat had an irrepressible sense of wellbeing. Waking at dawn, she was worried he might disappear if she fell back to sleep, so she lay very still, eventually only extracting herself carefully to go to the loo, brush her teeth and put on just a touch of make-up in the bathroom.

She opened a window while she waited for him to wake, considered popping out to get them coffee and croissants. But, no, she decided, she wouldn't leave him.

She sat up guarding him like treasure, trying to look casual for when he woke, but he slept and slept. When he did eventually wake, he looked so crushed as he remembered the night before that she almost wished he were still asleep, keeping the fantasy alive.

He sat up slowly, rubbing his head, muttering, 'Christ, oh Christ.'

'Would you like me to get you coffee?' Kat asked, chastened.

He shook his head, croaked, 'Maybe some water.'

Kat went to get a glass from the kitchen, glad to have this task to do, at least, and that was how the day went, and the days that followed. It wasn't that they were together, exactly – you wouldn't call it that – but he hadn't told her to go away either, to leave him alone. He seemed to like her popping by with a sandwich from the bar or the day's newspaper to distract him. And if largely all they talked about was Ruth, then, Kat told herself, that would change. That would change eventually.

A few days after Ruth had left for Wales, a letter arrived for Richard. It was very long and tear-stained, swearing over and over that she would never be unfaithful to him, that it must have been someone else, the girl who looked like her. She scrawled, more than once, 'Just ask Kat,' underlined lots of times.

'Not that again,' Kat tutted when Richard showed her. Which was another way of avoiding the question about the lookalike, of avoiding lying again.

After the first night, there had been the odd moment when it had seemed like more than a friendship. An occasional lingering look. She held his hand once or twice as he wept, kissed the tears off his face as they hugged, enveloped by the breath and the heat of him, until he stopped her gently.

'Don't you want to?' she asked.

'It's not that,' he said.

No need to ask what it was. That was the only time she cried. 'Please don't say for sure,' she said, becoming the begging woman she never wanted to be, 'that that was our only time. Please just let me hope that it's possible.'

And he hadn't taken that away from her.

'If you were mine,' she said, promising herself this would be the last she would say on the matter, 'I wouldn't look at anyone else. Ever.'

She had taken her kicks where she could, burying her face against his neck or resting it against his chest when they hugged, feeling his heart thumping against her ear.

When Ruth returned to claim him, it was the first time Kat had genuinely given in to hatred. Looking at the back of her friend's head nodding along to Richard's music, she had wondered for a moment what it would feel like to crack the champagne glass across it. The thought gave her a moment of satisfaction at the time, but now the memory of it makes her feel sick with guilt.

When the bathwater has cooled, Kat nudges the hot-water tap on with her big toe and breathes in the steam. Has she ever had a friend quite like Ruth? Kat's not sure that she has. She's always thought of herself as a sociable person. She's never found it difficult picking people up with a smile, a one-liner. There were parties and dates throughout her twenties, though she found, with Ruth gone, that she had to work at keeping her life full. She had transformed, in a way, into one of those try-hard girls at college: everything effortful, all the lists, the rushing around. There had been no time for lying in bed, smoking joints, quoting Dorothy Parker to each other and perhaps, because of the lack of time invested in her friendships, none of them had really endured.

As for men, it had begun to feel that every encounter was a permutation of one that had gone before. There had been lots of Richards: men who resembled him in one way or another. Maybe it would be the messy hair, or the dark eyes, or the certain way they would hold a guitar, or look up from a book. But the patterns of the relationships – they were similar, too. A fair few of the men had been infatuated at first – there would be nights of sleeplessness and endless shagging, and the sense of chasing moments that blotted out the past. Moments when she would think: this is it; this can mean a fresh start.

But then one day he – the paler version of Richard, whichever one it was – would wake and get dressed a bit too quickly. Or they would be at lunch and she would notice him give a particularly winning smile to the pretty waitress, and she would know that that magic thing that kept them together would be on the wane. It was so wispy, so insubstantial, this thing that if you tried to pin it down, you would make it vanish all the quicker. And no toss of your hair or artful smile could ever make you seem the same way to him. Because it had gone and you weren't new any more.

A ridiculous part of her still feels excited at the thought of seeing him again: a glimmer of blind hope against years and years of experience. It feels hot and bright, the hopefulness, and it makes her want to cry, because she knows she will never quell it; that it will always be disappointed. But perhaps she needs the distraction today of all days. She sighs and gets up again, knowing already how she will answer: 'Yes, of course. Coach and Horses at six?' She didn't add any kisses.

She puts the phone back and returns to the bath, sinking her head slowly into the water. Her hair is shorter, much thinner than it was, but she enjoys the feeling, as she leans back, of it splaying out, clouding the water with conditioner. Mildew is eating its way across the ceiling. The bathroom needs work. The window frame is bruised with mould and condensation drips down the tiles. She thinks that now she won't have to do it. Dying is a pretty extreme way to get out of DIY, says a stupid, chirpy voice in her head. But she doesn't smile.

Shivering as she gets out of the bath, Kat stands for a moment in front of the mirror, appraising her body. She's still getting used to the mastectomy scar on her chest, still taken aback by it when she catches sight of it like this. She's never had much fat to spare and now her pale skin is pulled taut over her ribcage. Her eyes look changed, dimmed.

She puts her dressing gown on, knots a towel around her head and pads through to her bedroom. She dresses carefully: nice lingerie – not that he would see it – a navy wool dress and lipstick. She takes great care with her make-up.

It's still too early to leave, so she wanders to the living room and sinks into the sofa. Her cat makes his way over to her from his basket. He climbs on her lap, pushing his knotty head into her hand.

There are no photographs on the walls. It had never seemed quite the time to do it. Kat thinks: I'm not sure that I would recommend it though, living. It all comes down to a series of choices and at the time you don't even know you are making them, or that they will stay with you forever, that you can never go back to the time before you made them.

The cat is purring very loudly now and rubbing his ginger fur against her wool dress. Kat gets up and removes the fur with a clothes brush. She thinks there might be time for a drink before she leaves. She still hasn't cried.

She had known before she saw him, before she had even washed the hair mask out, that it would be him to whom she told the news. A condensed version of her telling him, and his comforting her and ending up, well, ending up back at her flat, in bed, flashes through her head on the tube but, pleasant though it is, this line of thought, too, needs to be extinguished.

It's still early evening, not yet dark, but Piccadilly is buzzing with tourists, commuters, theatregoers and large groups of European students. The journey has made her feel particularly nauseous and she takes a deep gulp of air as she comes out of the station. She stops for a second on a crowded pavement looking up at the advertisements and neon lights. The Eros statue, the theatre billboards, the pigeons, a small group of street dancers performing to a scratchy track. All this – the tourist crowds who bottleneck as they pour out from underground, the shrill whistles of the rickshaw drivers, that Tennessee Williams play that has run forever that she still hasn't seen, which there probably won't be time to see – all this will still be here when she has gone.

For a second she pauses and looks at him, waiting by the bar, as she goes in. It's a line from *The Age of Innocence* she thinks of: 'Each time you happen to me all over again.' He looks up with a careful smile. Kat joins him, kissing him brusquely on the cheek. He still smells like Richard.

'You've cut your hair,' he says.

'Yes.' Kat touches her neck self-consciously. She wants a drink before she tells him anything. 'Have you ordered yet?'

'Not yet.' Richard shakes his head, starts intensely: 'You know something of hers arrived in the post for Naomi?'

Kat doesn't know why, but the urge to laugh bubbles up inside her. She shouldn't have had that drink before she left. The young woman behind the bar, with ample breasts straining under her T-shirt, glances up at her.

'I'm looking into it,' Richard is saying. 'Doing some research. Did Naomi call you about it, too?'

'She emailed.' Kat wishes he could have waited until they were sitting down. She catches the barmaid's eye: 'G and T,' she mouths, then adds to Richard, 'I couldn't help. I couldn't remember anything about her teddy.'

Richard orders his drink as well – just half a pint, Kat notices with disappointment – and they make their way to a small table in the corner. He takes a gulp of his London Pride and puts it down again.

'Someone came to see me: George Bell's wife.'

Kat feels the muscles in her legs involuntarily tighten at the mention of George's name. 'Why?'

Richard picks up a beer mat on the table and then puts it down. He won't quite look at Kat. 'She thought she saw Ruth.' He glances up. 'On a train coming from Scotland.'

There's the urge to laugh again. Stronger now. What's the matter with her? 'That's ridiculous.' She goes for a reassuring smile instead. Over the years this would happen. Something would happen to make Richard think of Ruth – specifically that Ruth was alive; that she hadn't drowned that night – and he would want to meet and discuss it with her after everybody else had lost patience with him.

'That's what I said to her: that it sounded insane.' Richard looks a little more relaxed. 'Actually, because of the Bell connection, I guess I was a bit ruder than that. Anyway, that was before I heard the news from St Anthony's.' He is quiet for a moment. 'I can't bear the thought that someone hurt her,' he says softly.

Kat takes a sip of her gin. She wonders how to start telling him her own news. Maybe she'll have a cigarette first and tell him with the second drink. She doesn't want to talk about Ruth all night. Not tonight. In the first years after she'd gone, Richard and Kat would meet up at irregular intervals, ostensibly for comfort or to remember Ruth, but really for increasingly bitter postmortems.

Kat chews the inside of her cheek. It had been messy. They had both almost always drunk too much. There had almost always been a fight. Once or twice it had ended up in bed. Those years had been among the worst of her life. Her coke habit had got a bit out of control. 'I am broken,' she would tell strangers in bars over a round, or a line off the toilet seat. 'Life has broken me.' And they would laugh as if she were joking or – no better – compete with their own stories of brokenness.

At its lowest ebb it had looked as though she might lose her job, but her features editor took her out for lunch and told it to her straight: fearless and catty ('scuse the pun), she was a good journalist. But the coke would have to stop. And the sleeping with her interview subjects. It made things messy. And Kat listened and she found not God but work. And it saved her.

She takes a gulp of her gin.

'It was weird, though: she was so convinced she'd seen Ruth.' Richard is looking at her expectantly.

'For fuck's sake, Richard.' Kat puts down the glass a bit too hard. 'Let it go. Let it all go.' She sighs, says more kindly: 'She's gone. She has been gone for fifteen years. They even have a skeleton now. I know it's unbearable, but it's looking very likely that she was killed by some sicko.' A memory springs up, unbidden, of Dan's mouth on Ruth's. Her friend thumping George at that party. She swallows. No good would come of encouraging Richard's conspiracy theories. 'It's over,' she says definitively.

He shakes his head. 'I know, I know.' He looks away from her out of the window. 'Does it sound sick to say: I'd like to see the skeleton, once they know for sure it's her?'

Kat shakes her head. 'I'm sure, if they can, Naomi and her mum will let you.'

She puts her hand on his and gives it a squeeze, then places hers on the table. It is close enough that she can,

302

just about, feel the tiny hairs on his hand brushing against hers. She thinks: I would rather this proximity than heaving, panting sex with anyone else in the world. She thinks: I would give up a lifetime of tidiness and security and stability for an afternoon in a grubby pub with dim lighting and the sensation of your hand close to mine. She thinks: but I have. I have sacrificed all those things for crumbs such as these.

'Have you given up?' she asks eventually.

'What?' He is still distracted.

'Smoking. Have you given up smoking?'

'Aren't you bothered by this, Kat?' he says, moving his hand away from hers. 'You don't seem remotely shaken. They've found what could be Ruth's body and at the exact same time someone arrives *convinced* she's seen Ruth. And what about Nunny?'

Kat sighs. She thinks of the scene she has been rehearsing in her head. It had not gone like this.

Richard drains his drink and looks, for a second, as though he might leave.

Well, fuck him. Fuck them both. The rage, years old, is in her throat now.

'I bet it was someone else she saw on the train,' she says quickly, too quickly. 'Can you remember that girl who looked like her? I bet it was her. It kept happening.'

Why is he looking at her like that? The colour is draining from his cheeks. Everything feels as though it is slowing down. The background noise seems to fade away. It is so slow, so quiet she can almost hear the synapses in her memory straining to make the connection. And then they do.

'What kept happening?' Richard is still looking at her.

She thinks she's going to be sick. 'I've lost my thread,' she says quietly.

'What kept happening?'

Kat looks out of the window. It's getting dark. They won't have that cigarette now, huddled around a lighter. He will leave. Leave the pub. And she won't see him again. She could say it now. Say: I'm dying. Say: I love you. I have always loved you. And now I'm dying. But instead she looks him in the eye and says: 'They kept on getting confused. People who didn't know Ruth very well would mistake her for this girl. And vice versa.'

He blinks. 'A doppelgänger.'

'Yes, I know. It's ridiculous. That word. Isn't it? It's not quite what I meant . . .'

She has never felt frightened of Richard before, but there is something about the way he is staring at her. His eyes look flinty, hard, like one of her mother's boyfriends used to, before he said or did something terrible.

Richard puts a hand over hers and gives it a squeeze. He doesn't know his strength. There's the searing pain of her knuckles crushing together.

'Richard, fuck!' She pulls her hand away. But he is still looking at her, not at all apologetic. It was a lie she'd always stuck to, her one last betrayal of Ruth: *No one looks like Ruth*, she'd said. *She's one of a kind*.

He gets up to go. 'I think that is exactly what you meant.'

Naomi

Sometimes I miss alcohol. I was never a particularly heavy drinker – never sought the sort of oblivion Ruth did – but there are certainly moments when I could just do with a quick nip of something to level out the nerves. I settle to make the call from Carla's home office. The space is tidy, impersonal, with none of our usual clutter – just a box of tissues on the coffee table at the centre of the room, a small bookcase with her psychotherapy textbooks.

It's a Saturday, but Carla's working at the centre for the day and, while she doesn't *disapprove* exactly of my contacting Alice, she is calling me more often from work at the moment, has started asking, 'Have you meditated today?' or 'Do you want me to book you an appointment with Jill?' How do I explain? I don't want to speak to Jill, one of Carla's colleagues at the centre. I want to speak to Alice. Everything has changed.

As always, the news came when we least expected it, while I was chatting to my mum's gardener at the cottage, admiring the vegetable patch. Suddenly, my mother was running across the lawn, a hand raised to interrupt us. Our family liaison officer had been on the phone.

'It's not her.'

It's not her. I still say the words over and over to myself now as I did when I first found out.

I don't know what to make of this development, but I do know that something in me has changed since I found out; something in me has woken up.

I half-dial the number three or four times before finally making my fingers complete it. I want to speak to her at home, not at the gym or wandering around the shops. I want an old-fashioned conversation where we are both in our houses and able to think straight. As the call connects, there's a moment's silence in which I think of hanging up, then the phone begins to ring. I imagine it in an old-fashioned hallway in their Notting Hill house, on a console table perhaps, a polished floor, heels clicking across it.

'Hello?'

A man's voice. His. I didn't really know him at St Anthony's – by the time I started he and Ruth had long broken up – though I knew who he was, of course. Everybody did: president of the union, leader of the pack. I never understood what Ruth, who didn't like any sort of club, saw in him. She tried to explain once, when she was very drunk, but all I could understand of what she was saying was that she liked the way he smelled.

My voice sounds thinner than I would like as I ask: 'Can I speak to Alice, please?'

'Who is this?'

I remember the way he speaks: plummily, a hint of humour, like he's enjoying a private joke with himself.

'Naomi Walker.' I can't help myself. 'Ruth Walker's sister.'

The warmth vanishes from his voice. 'Right.'

He approached me once at a party, in my first year. I was standing on my own, waiting for Ruth, and he appeared next to me out of nowhere. 'We've been rating the freshers,' he said, nodding back to his group of friends on the other side of the room. 'And I thought you'd like to know you're the only ten in the room.'

'Ten?' I didn't understand.

'The only ten out of ten. The best-looking girl here.'

I didn't know what to say – that it was immaterial how he rated me? That I wasn't interested in men anyway? I felt fragile back then, as if I were wrapped in cotton wool. After Miss Wick it was a long time before I felt things properly again. I forgot how to interact with the world in a normal sort of way.

At the other end of the phone, there's a muffled sound of conversation. Then Alice, sounding worried, says, 'Naomi? I'm so glad you called.'

A door slams and I can hear her breath slightly ragged. I find myself wondering if Alice was at the same party, if George approached her next, if he marked her out of ten, too. I never knew how to handle men's advances back then. Anyway, in the event, Ruth came along and said: 'This is my sister, George. Fuck off.' And that was that.

'They found human remains – a skeleton in St Anthony's – you may have heard.' My words come out in a rush.

307

'But it's not her. I mean – they've done tests and it's not. I thought you'd like to know.'

She is quiet for a moment. 'How are you feeling?'

The question takes me by surprise. 'Strange,' I say. 'Confused.'

Jacques trots into the room, squeaks to be let on to my lap. I lean back, making room for him, and he jumps on. The heat of his body is a comfort.

'I spoke to Richard last night,' I say carefully.

'Yes?' Alice sounds flat, restrained. Perhaps she's worried George is listening in.

'He said you went to see him.'

'That was a mistake,' she says quietly. 'He was very angry.' She sighs. 'I'm sorry: I seem to have upset you both – that wasn't my intention. I can't let things go. George would say it's one of my shortcomings . . .' A brittle laugh. 'But it can help with my job.'

'I don't know,' I say. 'Maybe I wasn't fair to you. Things have been weird for me, too. With the skeleton being found . . . and Nunny arriving. It feels like something's being unearthed.' I can hear the blare of a siren at her end. I wait for it to stop. 'It would be nice to speak to someone. Maybe we could talk some more? If you're interested.'

'Yes, yes, I am,' she says quickly. She pauses. 'Tuesday, maybe. I've got a client meeting near you. I could come along afterwards.'

I think for a moment. Carla's at the centre on Tuesday evenings. That would work well for me.

'Yes, that sounds good.'

Alice is silent for a couple of seconds and I think she's

going to say goodbye, but she says instead, 'It's a funny word "unearthed".'

'Yes.' I think for a moment of the dreams, of Ruth running as I chase her through the streets of St Anthony's, of her shoes left on the pavement like a clue. I pause. 'It feels as if there's something I don't understand about that night,' I say, stopping short of explaining what I really think, what I really feel: that it's as if Ruth is trying to tell me what happened.

With Alice in my house again, I feel shyer. She looks, in her Chanel suit, fresh from work, as immaculate as she did the last time I saw her. I wonder for a moment if that's how I looked to Miss Wick. She used to say she liked to mess me up. The way my hair would come alive when we made love, the way I'd sweat.

I need to talk about the night Ruth went. It is a night I have revisited so many times, from so many different angles: Ruth's, Richard's, mine. I have even talked about it on autopilot, switching myself off from the content, letting my mouth and hands do the talking, so I don't have to think about it too much: the last time I saw her.

I'm not sure how to begin. So I begin with Jane.

'The night Ruth went missing – you'll remember it – it was the memorial ball,' I start.

The student union had spent an obscene amount of money on the party – with dancers, performers on stilts, comedians, a champagne bar, vintage photography studio, fireworks. But the truth is I can barely remember anything about the evening at all.

'I'd been seeing this girl,' I continue. 'She was only my

second girlfriend.' Jane appears in my mind like a snapshot: her pale, round face. 'My first was a Spanish conversation teacher at school,' I add without meaning to. I try to allow myself a brief ironic smile, to make it all appear like ancient history. 'I know. Disaster.' I feel my breathing change as I talk about her. I look out of the window. The wind tugs keenly at the sheaves of ivy on the fence. 'Actually,' I try to say casually. 'Actually, she broke my heart. Miss Wick. Twice. So . . .' I let the words fizzle out.

'So,' I say with renewed vigour, turning back to Alice. 'I was with Jane – she was older, pretty bossy, and I was a first year then. I think she took advantage a bit.' I focus on not thinking about how, in the eyes of the world, this was precisely what Miss Wick had also done. 'My sister couldn't stand her,' I add, though that point was neither here nor there. 'Ruth was with me that evening – at least we got ready together at the cottage. She and Richard had had this big bust-up and she'd gone back to stay with our mum for a week or so, but she'd come back to St Anthony's on the night of the ball to surprise him.' I swallow. 'To get him back.'

Alice, to her credit, doesn't make a soothing noise from where she's sitting on the sofa, just asks, 'Did you see Ruth much that night?'

'No, not at all.' I hesitate. I'm not sure how to continue, how much to share. The autopilot version of the story doesn't include Miss Wick. It doesn't even really include Jane. 'I was dancing, I was watching Richard's band . . .' That's how I usually put it. I had considered telling the police about Miss Wick, but it was just another confusing

310

detail in an already confusing night – and nothing to do with Ruth, after all.

'Someone from my past turned up. The teacher I told you about? She was at the ball, too. We'd started seeing each other again. I didn't behave very well,' I admit. 'Dropped Jane. Snuck off. Oh Christ,' I blush. 'And then Jane caught us. It seemed so dreadful at the time. Then, later, when what happened happened, none of it seemed to matter, really. I didn't stay at St Anthony's, as you know. I came back home, went to Cardiff instead. I never saw Jane again after that night. Nor Miss Wick, for that matter. I wonder if we ever would have stood a chance in the real world,' I say more to myself than Alice. 'It was a fantasy, really. Still . . .' I sigh. 'It was a pretty potent one.'

'What about Ruth?' asks Alice.

'I told her about Miss Wick,' I smile. 'That she'd come to St Anthony's to be with me. Ruth was thrilled – she was such a romantic and, as I say, she'd never liked Jane. Anyway, after we got ready together she went off to find Richard and was with him for a while – he last saw her at around eleven when his band went on stage. But they had some sort of fallout and Ruth stormed off, spent the evening smoking weed with a friend from her course. Richard was looking for her all night, but he couldn't find her. Then, she left that friend's room at three-ish and wasn't seen again until Dan Vaughan saw her swimming at dawn.'

Alice seems to sit up straighter. 'He was good friends with George.'

'Yes,' I say.

Everyone knew that. They were inseparable those two. Ruth used to call them the princes of darkness. I don't say that to Alice now.

'He was a piece of shit,' she says crisply. 'I never liked him.'

She looks pleased to be able to say the words out loud. I get the feeling it's the first time she's said them.

'Yes,' I say cautiously. 'He wasn't a nice person.'

I don't know how freely I can speak about someone who was such close friends with her husband.

'I'm leaving George, by the way,' she says lightly as if reading my mind. 'He's been fucking my best friend. I think it's what you call the end of the road.'

I don't know what to say.

'Are you sure?' I ask eventually.

'About which bit?' Alice says, brushing dust off her skirt. 'The fucking or the leaving?'

'Both,' I say. 'All of it.'

I think of Alice as she was in St Anthony's. The way she would look at George as if she had just won a prize. I feel sad for that Alice. The young Alice back then. I wish I could go back to her and say something.

'Naomi,' she says firmly, getting to her feet. 'What were Dan and he up to at university? Why did people hate them so much? What did people say?'

I make a polite sort of cough. I'm not sure how to answer.

'Please tell me,' Alice says fiercely. 'No one else will.'

I'm still sitting, looking up at her as she stands above me. She is not a stupid woman, a delicate little flower. She wants to hear the truth. She wants to hear exactly what people said.

'They said they were bastards.' I recite it like a list. I can't look at her as I say the words. 'That they hurt girls, got them really drunk, took advantage of them, sometimes even took photographs.'

Alice folds her arms. There is a look of something close to relief on her face.

'I knew it,' she says.

Kat

Water is one of the few things that help: the sensation of weightlessness, the rhythm of breaststroke, the push and pull of it. The spa is dimly lit, womb-like, with the cedar scent of the sauna, of lemongrass oil and eucalyptus. There was a time when Kat might have laughed at the kind of woman who frequents this sort of place, but she doesn't care what her younger self might think now. What had she known, anyway?

Kat has seen Richard for the last time, she thinks as she dries herself off and makes her way unsteadily to the sauna, her legs tired from the swim. The first of many lasts. Perhaps some had passed without even saying goodbye. The last compliment from a stranger. The last time she'd wake after snowfall, her bedroom strangely bright in the refracted light, the landscape outside otherworldly.

There would be others: the last article she'd write, the last time she'd see her mother; there would be the last time she would wake with the comforting weight of her cat on her belly, the last time her toes would dig into sand, the last time she'd drink champagne, the last time she'd dance around her kitchen to Portishead, her eyes shut, the curtains closed.

Where had she been happiest? At her early days in St Anthony's, in a way, on cliff walks with Richard; dancing around her room and talking about boys with Ruth. Perhaps she should go there one last time and look at the sea. Perhaps she should buy a bottle of the most expensive champagne she could find, drink it on the beach and walk out into the water. Her younger self would have approved of that sort of gesture at least.

'It's Kat, isn't it?'

She recognises the voice. A Glaswegian accent, less strong than it used to be – smoother, deeper. Kat opens her eyes. The sauna is dark but she can make out a small woman with shoulder-length hair leaning towards her.

'Nicky Crisp,' Kat says aloud.

Everyone always used both names for Nicky. She doesn't see much of anyone from college these days. Whenever she spots someone from St Anthony's – at a press junket, perhaps, or in the audience at the theatre – Kat avoids them if she can: looking the other way, darting into the loo. She doesn't know if it's because she feels so different now, or because she feels so much the same. In fact, she had thought that perhaps she'd recognised Nicky the other week, climbing out of the pool, and had swum extra lengths so she wouldn't bump into her.

'I hear you're at *The National* now,' Nicky says.

315

Kat blinks the sweat from her eyes. 'Yes.'

'I like your articles . . .' She pauses. 'Witty – you were always witty – and brave, too.' She looks at Kat intensely.

'Thanks.' Kat never knows what to say when people say her writing is brave. It sounds to her like 'interesting' or 'unusual', as if they mean something else. 'They're not my stories,' she adds. 'I can't really take credit for them.' She had been enjoying her rather self-indulgent daydream; she slightly resents Nicky for interrupting it.

As the door opens and a third woman joins them, the air cools. Kat stands up, wrapping her towel around her tightly. 'It's been nice catching up,' she says politely.

The words sound disingenuous, but what is the point of it now? Her focus is on narrowing things down, whittling them to a fine point, like the sharpened end of a pencil, a tiny pinprick of light at the end of a dark tunnel. Letting go of things, not taking them on.

'I've seen you here before,' says Nicky, ignoring Kat's goodbye. 'A few weeks ago – swimming – but you seemed in the zone, so I didn't like to interrupt.' She gets up herself and follows Kat out of the sauna.

Kat smiles politely. The sweat is cooling rapidly on her skin; she glances towards the changing rooms.

'Anyway, it made me think of something I'd like to ask you.' Nicky's voice sounds as it used to – for a moment, the accent is stronger, more solid. 'Do you have time for a drink?'

Kat thinks of her empty flat, looking at its empty walls. She doesn't want to play catch-up, but she doesn't want to be alone, either. And she could do with a drink.

'Why not?' she says, surprising herself.

In the old coaching inn in Holborn, which Kat didn't know was there until Nicky darted down a narrow alley, she sits in the corner by the window with the warm burr of voices around her, waiting for Nicky to come back from the bar. She thinks of Richard, of how they'd left things in the pub. She had tried to call – or at least she had found his name in the contacts list of her phone and stared at his number. But what was there to say? The cat was out of the bag. What surprises her most of all is the relief of it: how she feels lighter, unburdened. A secret she had been holding onto all these years had lost its power. Perhaps she should tell him the rest of it.

They've had one drink already, during which Nicky largely talked about herself – not that Kat minds. She's surprised by how much she's been enjoying herself: the warmth of wine in her belly, drifting in and out of Nicky's stories. Nicky works in the City, making more money than she knows what to do with, escaping on exotic holidays whenever she can. She's been telling Kat about a recent adventure in Mexico, where she spent a week on an organised trip and ten days exploring the country on her own. She had 'an experience' in a sweat lodge on a beach near Cancún. 'No, not that kind of experience,' she said with a quick smile. 'Spiritual . . . The sweat lodge is shaped like an igloo and they actually seal you in: push a stone across.'

'Intense,' Kat said.

'It is. You sit there for hours in the dark looking at the embers of the fire – talking and sweating. Remembering things. Sometimes just sitting in silence. All that time in the heat – and it weakens your barriers, you know?'

Dying does that too, Kat thought. You suddenly become aware that you could say or do anything. That social barriers don't matter as much as you think they do.

'At the end, you cover yourself with honey and your pores are so open your skin just drinks it up,' Nicky continued. 'And then you jump into the sea in the moonlight. Beautiful . . . Anyway, the point is' – she stabbed the table with a manicured fingernail – 'I had an epiphany.'

'Crikey, I thought I was a lightweight these days.' Kat barely suppressed a giggle. Nicky is on end-of-the-night revelations already.

'Shame grows in the dark,' said Nicky portentously. 'The truth will set you free.'

'Which film is that the tagline for?' Kat laughed. She couldn't remember Nicky being into all that New Age stuff at college, but whatever helped you get through the day.

Nicky smiled. 'It's from the Bible.' And she stood up to get the next round.

Alice

'I knew it,' she says again, almost triumphantly. She thinks of George's camera hidden in a desk drawer, the white-tie scarf neatly arranged next to it. 'I knew they were up to something,' she says more softly.

The moment of triumph is followed by a swift, pulsating nausea. All these years she has been sharing a bed with a person who might have done such things: tied women up, raped them, taken photographs. She has always known George liked skating close to the edge – the buzz and the risk of sex. The bravado of it – even the theatre, the pretence. But this is something else. Things start falling into place. Memories.

Her legs feel strange; she sinks to sit on the floor.

'Nobody would talk to us,' she says to Naomi. 'To Christie and me. People stopped asking us out.' It sounds pathetic out loud. 'It's not the social thing,' she says quickly. 'It's not that I care about invitations, but it's that they all knew. And we didn't.'

All those women whom he had damaged. The women he'd had affairs with since. The furore about the girl he worked with. She realises she has seen only one world when there has always been another one – the real one – out there, running parallel.

'Where's your bathroom?' she asks calmly. She is going to be sick.

Afterwards, Alice feels better. She cleans herself up and comes back to the living room. Naomi has fetched her a glass of water.

'We don't know how much is true,' she says kindly. 'We don't know anything, really.'

'He has a camera,' Alice says. 'From that time, but he never uses it any more.'

'Have you found any negatives? Any pictures?'

'No.' Alice shakes her head. 'He's too clever for that.' She smiles as if at an old joke. 'He hides things too well.'

They are quiet for a moment. Alice remembers her last conversation with George.

'Did you hear about a girl who looked like your sister while we were at St Anthony's?'

'Yes, didn't I mention it?' Naomi says quietly. 'Ruth used to say she had a lookalike.' She pauses, glances down at her feet where her Jack Russell has flopped. 'But I never saw her myself. Apparently, this other woman had a thing with Dan. It caused a terrible fight with Richard because everyone thought it was Ruth.' She shakes her head. 'But I know Ruth wouldn't have slept with Dan – she loathed him – so there must have been some sort of mistake.'

'George doesn't believe there was someone who looked

like her,' Alice says, draining her glass and putting it back on the coffee table. 'That's what he said. But then George says a lot of things.'

Where is she going to sleep tonight? How is she ever going to go home?

'Ruth wanted to prove that she wasn't with Dan.' Naomi nudges her dog's stomach with her foot. 'And Kat never backed Ruth up – which Ruth was furious about – because, well, she liked Richard, you see. It was a sort of open secret, so if Ruth split up with Richard over this Dan thing then all the better for her.' The dog rolls back on his feet, trots into the kitchen. 'But why would George care?' adds Naomi, thinking aloud. 'What would it matter to him?'

George's voice saying, *She was a little slut*, echoes in Alice's head.

'He painted a certain picture of Ruth,' she says carefully. 'That she was promiscuous.'

Naomi rolls her eyes. 'I can imagine.'

'He said she and Dan had a thing – but why was he adamant that there wasn't anyone else involved?' Alice recalls the cropped photograph. 'There was a redhead there, though, with George and his friends on the night of the ball. There was a bit of her in a photograph I found – red hair, the strap of a red dress.'

Naomi looks up. 'A red dress?'

'Yes,' Alice says. 'I'm sure of it, from what I could see.'

'Someone else said something about a red dress.' Naomi frowns. 'But I can't remember who. Ruth would never have worn red. She loved it – her bedroom was covered in red things – but she never wore it. She said it clashed with her hair.' She glances up, trying to recall. 'That was it,' she says. 'The supermarket psychic – a woman I met in January – she said that she thought Ruth was wearing a red dress. I didn't think anything of it at the time, but she was working at the ball. She might have served this other woman.'

Alice feels a flutter of excitement. She wants the whole truth now. She wants to know all of it.

'Do you have a survivors' photo from that night?' She gets to her feet. 'I don't suppose you do? We could look at that. See if we could spot this mystery woman.'

'No, I don't.' Naomi reaches for her phone. 'But a friend of mine does. I know because I used to hate seeing it in her loo when I went over. She's taken it down now. Ruth's not in it, of course, but we might be able to look for other redheads – I'll ask her to send us a photo.' She starts to text.

'Maybe,' Alice suggests, having a thought. 'You could ring Richard, too – ask him what he knows about this lookalike.'

While Naomi is out of the room calling Richard, Alice picks up her own mobile and looks at the screen. She can't phone George; she can't call Christie. She considers again where she might sleep tonight. She has barely spoken to George since he returned from Spain. Or Morocco, as it turned out. She wonders for a moment if anything he ever said was true. If she hadn't actually seen him on television, she might start to doubt that, too. But she hasn't let on that she knew anything about him and Christie. They still didn't know she'd found out, which suits her perfectly. For two relatively bright people, they'd fucked up, really, messing with one of London's best

322

divorce lawyers. Alice puts a hand on her belly. It gives her all the power. Not that she would stay in that house. She would make a fresh start. A new part of town. Maybe a new city altogether.

Naomi comes back in the room. Her face is flushed with excitement.

'There *was* someone who looked like Ruth,' she says. 'Richard is sure of it. Apparently, he met up with Kat recently – and she said that people kept mistaking Ruth for someone else. Someone from town.'

'As opposed to a student?'

'Yes,' says Naomi, pacing. 'A barmaid or something. Kat doesn't know exactly.'

'If she was from town, she might still be there,' considers Alice.

'That's what I was thinking,' says Naomi. 'Isn't it strange that she never came forward? That she looked so like Ruth and yet we never heard.' She looks down at her phone as it buzzes.

As the survivors' photograph is so long, Naomi's friend has taken pictures of it piecemeal. Naomi looks at them with Alice as they come through on her phone. They examine the small jaded faces of the last remaining party-goers looking up from the quad at the photographer in the clock tower. There's no Ruth, no Naomi, as she'd said, but not a single other redhead in the picture, either. No Alice, of course, who had long been in bed. But, strangely, also no George or Dan.

'It's weird,' says Alice, thinking aloud. 'They loved stuff like that – being the last ones standing at a party – and they were definitely still up then.'

'I was with Jane,' grimaces Naomi. 'We had to have a sort of postmortem about me and Miss Wick. She actually locked me in her room – she was crazy.'

'Is Miss Wick in the photo?'

'No,' Naomi smiles. 'She didn't go in for stuff like that – anyway, she was waiting for me back at the cottage. Or that was the plan. She wasn't there when I got back. Maybe she got tired of hanging around.' She gets up as if she's just remembered something. 'I never showed you Nunny, did I?'

She leaves the room for a moment.

'We never took him to the police,' she says, returning with a package in her hand. 'I'm not sure that we will now – I don't know if we could bear for him to be away from us.'

'You should,' says Alice. 'They might be able to track down who sent him.'

Naomi shrugs. 'The results from Richard's handwriting expert were inconclusive. There were similarities to Ruth's handwriting,' she says, looking at the address on the Jiffy bag. 'But it's very hard to tell with block capitals after all these years.'

'Still,' says Alice, reaching to take Nunny from Naomi. 'It might be worth letting forensics have a look. They might be able to pick up on something you've missed.' She touches the marble eye of the old grey rabbit with her fingertip. 'What does he know?'

Naomi passes her the Jiffy bag he came in. 'Look at the postmark.'

'Oh,' Alice says. 'St Anthony's.'

'Do you want to go back?' Naomi asks suddenly.

'I think we should,' she says, sounding excited. 'I think that's why he was sent from there. And we should try to find this lookalike, too. What if she has been lying low on purpose all these years? What if she knows something?'

Kat

Returning with a bottle of Rioja, Nicky pours a large glass for Kat and then for herself. She looks as though she might return to recounting holiday stories, so Kat heads her off by asking: 'What was it you wanted to talk to me about?'

Nicky takes a breath. She looks serious for a moment. 'You know that series you write with anonymous women? When they tell you their secrets?'

'Yes.'

'Would you like to do one with me?' Nicky had never been shy.

'I'm leaving soon,' says Kat. She takes a gulp of wine. Taking her leave. That's what they called it. She was taking her leave of the world. It's funny how letting go of one more thing, saying no, like this, to each assignment, was like letting go of the ropes of a ship, one by one. 'I can ask whoever takes over.'

'I'd like it to be you,' Nicky says. 'Could you try? Could you fit it in before you go?'

'I don't think there will be time,' says Kat. 'And it will depend on your story – whether the editor's interested.' She sighs. She doesn't want to talk shop, she just wants to drink, she wants to let go. 'What do they call the ropes that keep a ship in port?' she asks. 'Is it guy ropes?'

'No, that's tents, I think.' Nicky frowns. 'Lines, maybe.'

The pattern on the seats is a swirling mass that blurs in front of Kat's eyes. Maybe she has drunk too much too quickly – she doesn't have the tolerance for it these days, not with the medication. She feels as if she is in water already, bobbing up and down on the tide. She thinks for a moment that she might tell Nicky that she is dying. That would shut her up. She's done a lot of listening tonight. Nicky and her wonderful life, unimpeded by loneliness or regrets; Nicky and her fabulous stories, her epiphanies. How is she so undamaged? Well, maybe it is Kat's turn to share.

'It will depend on your story,' she says again. 'It'll need to be a good one.'

'How about: I was raped by an MP? A former MP. How about that?' Nicky's gaze is steady. 'I imagine you can guess who it was. It wasn't just Dan, you see, it was George as well. I never made a fuss at the time. I didn't want them to think that I wasn't *fun* – you know how they'd put it – but I hadn't bargained for . . .' She takes a gulp of her wine. 'I think maybe you know . . .' She is looking at Kat.

The way the pattern works: it swirls into a single point.

A pivotal point. For a moment Kat is back there that night, with Dan standing in front of the door, so that she can't leave.

'I guess I wanted to fit in,' Nicky continues calmly, allowing Kat to sit in silence. 'With those middle-class kids.'

Maybe she could have done more to stop them. '"Rape" is such a big word, isn't it?' Kat says at last. 'I always found it difficult to call it that.'

Nicky tsks angrily. 'Why can't we say it?' she says. 'Why do we still want them to like us?'

'It's not that.' Kat shakes her head. She thinks of Nicky boasting about the number of people she'd slept with. She thinks of her own bravado, with her fuck-me shoes and Dorothy Parker quotes. 'Aren't we partly responsible? Didn't we want to be free?'

'We wanted to be free, yes. But we didn't want *that*. You know we didn't want that.' Nicky sighs. 'And they fucking knew it. They weren't thinking about us at all.'

'Maybe they just weren't thinking,' says Kat. 'We were all so young. How were they to know that we would carry it with us for all these years?'

'It is like that, isn't it? You carry it with you.' Nicky looks past Kat at a couple of girls at the bar. They are nineteen, perhaps, or twenty: coltish bodies, glossy hair falling down their shoulders. Their lives stretching ahead of them. 'I think it still goes on at universities. There's a group of feminists in Durham. They look out for each other – we should have done that.'

The thing is: it was hard to stop looking at yourself as they had – as something worthless. It was hard not to let the shame grow in the dark. Might things have been different for her, without it? Without what they'd done. Now Kat will never know. And George would still be alive when she wasn't. He would carry on living his life out in the light.

One of the girls at the bar picks up her phone, smiles at whatever's on the screen and shows it to her friend.

Kat says: 'Do you think there were others?'

Nicky nods. She is quiet, waiting to see what Kat will say next.

Kat feels something that is the opposite of letting go. An anchoring in the present. A cause. She feels the certainty of it in her blood. She puts the wine glass to one side and fishes out her water bottle from her gym bag before gulping the cold liquid down her throat, into her belly. That's better. The sense of purpose gives her a boost. She needs to sober up. She needs to find her notebook.

She says: 'Do you want to find them?'

Alice

On the way to St Anthony's, Alice finds herself looking at everything through two pairs of eyes. It's as if her younger self has slipped into the carriage next to her – and stayed by her side. Her mind drifts back to her last summer in St Anthony's with George. After the memorial ball she'd gone to stay with his family in their London house. He'd insisted and she loved it when he was like that. 'I can't say goodbye to you yet,' he'd said. 'Your family don't need you. Not straight away.'

As usual, she hadn't even considered her own family, so she'd more or less moved into the large townhouse in Notting Hill, not far from where they would eventually live together. They would wake to croissants and political discussions over the papers with his parents, sharing long lunches and boozy evenings with their friends in West London bars, where the girls swapped anxious updates on Ruth Walker's disappearance and the boys drank to forget.

In one of those late-night drinking places they'd ended up with a bunch of people they didn't know very well. It had been a funny sort of evening – one of those baking-hot nights in London when the city feels wired, jittery, like a different sort of place. Everyone was pretty plastered and the conversation had turned to Ruth, as usual.

A guy in the group who'd been quiet all evening – Alice forgets his name, but he was trying to grow a moustache – said, 'The police have been talking to Dan Vaughan, haven't they?'

'Not exactly, old boy,' George said. 'He just saw her swimming is all.'

'Is that right?' said the moustached chap. 'And did you see her swimming, too? I thought you two did everything together.' He chuckled to himself. 'The police will be on the phone to you next. But then your dad's a barrister, isn't he? I imagine that'll help.'

It hadn't bothered Alice much at the time. The guy had been trying to wind George up – people got so jealous of him – but a day or two later, she woke to find George sitting on the bed with a couple of tickets.

He tickled her cheek with the paper. 'Who wants to come with me to Jamaica?'

She sat up. 'George, really?'

'My aunt's a bit lonely out there.' He grinned like it was the most normal thing in the world. 'Come with me. We'll summer in the West Indies.'

'George, no one says the West Indies any more.'

'Come on, Alice. We'll drink rum on the beach and forget all our problems.'

While they were out there Dan, on an escapist holiday

of his own, had died, taken too much coke on a night out. Was that linked in any way to the police questioning? Or the fact that his job offer at Goldman Sachs had been withdrawn? Whenever they talked about it, which was rare, George insisted it was nothing more than a terrible accident.

She and Naomi had become quieter on the train as they passed the wide expanse of estuary entering the town, and Alice had felt the tug of the past as the familiar landscape flew by. She hadn't expected to be so unsettled. With things as they were with George, she had anticipated feeling strange, but she hadn't bargained for a different feeling, a type of excitement: the flutter in her belly at the smell of the sea, the scream of the gulls.

She's been staying in a hotel; she told George that her father had been taken ill, that she would be staying with her family for a week or so to help. She took her mum into her confidence. 'Don't call the house,' she said. Not that George would notice, she thought at the time; he was probably enjoying lots of lovely free time with Christie.

Her mother, to her credit, was very restrained, didn't ask too many questions.

'You are all right?' she checked. 'You and the baby?'

'She's fine,' Alice confirmed.

She always hoped to impress her parents or, more specifically, hoped that George did. She can see now that they never cared about his status in the way she had done herself. She had got everything upside down.

When they get into town, their first stop is the cottage where Naomi and Ruth used to live.

'This is it,' Naomi says when they get there. 'Not so remarkable.'

But that doesn't do it justice, really. It's an unusual place: on its own patch of land away from the others on the street, with a small rectangle of grass between the house and its own steep tumbledown route to the sea. A much larger garden behind it merges, unfenced, with the wooded clifftops.

'The owner bought that neighbouring bit of land recently,' says Naomi, looking over at the woods. 'She was having some landscaping done. That's how they found the skeleton. The police never searched around the cottage at the time – everything was so focused on the beach where her stuff was found.'

Through the trees, Alice can make out the yellow tape of the police investigation.

'Have you heard any more about that?' she asks.

'No.' Naomi follows her gaze. 'They're following leads, but now they know it's not Ruth, they haven't told us any more.' She looks up at the house. 'It looks smarter than it did – and they've added the conservatory, too – it was pretty run-down when we rented it.'

The cottage has new windows and a freshly painted black door.

'Do you want to see inside?' asks Alice.

'Let's try,' Naomi says.

The woman who answers is in her sixties, with a carefully made-up face and one hand still in a rubber glove, covered in bubbles. She frowns at the pair of them.

'We used to live here when we were students,' Alice

begins, though she's not sure why she's included herself. 'Well, my friend did.'

She looks at Naomi – whom she feels should say something at this juncture – but Naomi is peering past the woman at the house.

'We were wondering if we could have a quick look around?' Alice pushes. 'A trip down memory lane.'

'I don't know.' The woman hesitates. 'I'm going out in a minute. There's been a lot of coming and going recently.' She purses her mouth. 'People stomping through the garden, walking their muddy boots through my house.'

'What a nuisance,' Alice agrees, but she doesn't move. 'I'm sorry – we should have rung ahead.' She is not leaving now.

As the woman assesses them both, Alice finds herself working overtime. They had studied at St Anthony's, she explains. Pregnancy has made Naomi nostalgic. The cottage looks so light, so spacious. Was the renovation recent? They really won't take up much of her time.

She's mid-flow, when Naomi interrupts: 'It was my sister.'

They both look at her.

'Who went missing from here, in 2001,' says Naomi. 'You must have heard. We got the call when they found the skeleton.'

'Oh,' says the woman quietly. 'That's a bit different.' Her manner changes, becomes more conciliatory. 'We're new to town – only came here for our retirement a couple of years ago – but we've heard, of course. Especially when the gardener dug up . . .' She doesn't finish. 'Come in.'

The house is immaculate – all cream carpets and

sparkling surfaces – very different from how it used to be, says Naomi as she wanders from room to room. Embarrassingly, she spends the longest time in the master bedroom, which used to be Ruth's, not looking at the room itself but out to sea.

'Ruth loved this view,' she says to me *Alice*. 'We got ready here for the ball the last time I saw her. It was all red,' she smiles. 'She used to collect red pictures and postcards and clippings and pin them to the walls.'

Although the ground floor of the house has been extended, the upstairs just includes two bedrooms, Ruth's old bedroom overlooking the sea and Naomi's old bedroom overlooking the garden, and a small bathroom in between.

'We want to extend up here, too,' says the owner, almost apologetically, standing on the landing, waiting for Naomi. 'It's a bit cramped. And those stairs were a death trap when we moved in. We've changed them already.'

'You've done a beautiful job,' says Naomi politely. 'It's much nicer than when we lived here.'

Just before they leave, she asks if she can go upstairs once more. The owner, looking a little restless now, nods. As Alice waits with her in the hallway, she keeps glancing upstairs at Naomi's tread on the landing.

'I hope you find out one day,' the woman says as they finally leave the house. 'What happened to your sister.'

'Did you ever hear of anyone who looked like her in town?' asks Naomi. 'Someone who worked in a bar maybe. A redhead.'

The woman shakes her head. 'My husband drinks at the King's Head,' she says. 'I could get him to ask there.'

Alice and Naomi gather their thoughts at Annie's café, which had always been a favourite with the students. It's a cosy place, with the same cottage-style decor – patchwork cushions and driftwood mirrors – that it had in their day. Alice orders them peppermint tea and carrot cake, though neither of them feels like eating much.

'Shall we get our list out?' asks Alice.

They've made a list of all the pubs in St Anthony's, reasoning that the woman might still work at one of them. They'd also agreed that the town's pubs would be the best place for gossip. The only trouble was: St Anthony's was bigger than they remembered and there were lots more pubs than they bargained for.

They leave Annie's café and start to work their way through the list, but it proves to be oddly tiring. They've decided between themselves not to mention Ruth – just to ask if there was a redhead their sort of age working at each place, or anyone who fitted that description in town.

The two of them, with their bumps, don't go unnoticed in the pubs in the middle of the day, however. Often, their entrance is greeted by a hush in the conversation as the handful of locals drinking at the bar look up at them with undisguised interest. Often, too, their questions lead to more questions back – 'She's a friend of yours, is she?' 'Ooh, what's she done?' 'No, I think I'd remember a redhead if she's anything like you two'. And so on. Sometimes a name would be mentioned and a Facebook page pulled up and examined, but they were completely wrong – much too old or much too young. It wasn't going well.

'We could mention Ruth?' hisses Alice as they leave the King's Head. 'It might make them pay more attention.'

'We don't want *more* attention,' Naomi snaps back. 'We're getting enough as it is.'

She is looking pale, thinks Alice. She wonders, for a moment, if they're overdoing it.

The road they're on, steep and cobbled like most in St Anthony's, winds down to the sea, which looks almost black today. Alice recalls how the colour of it changes: the way you can tell what kind of day it will be from the look of it.

'Are you OK?' she asks. 'This is too much, isn't it?'

'I don't know what I was thinking.' Naomi shakes her head. 'Coming back. It's hard.'

She is quiet for a few minutes as they walk down the hill from the top of town.

'I thought I would remember something. I thought something would come to me, some detail. Or that we'd find something important.'

'We will,' says Alice, determined.

'The door was open,' Naomi says eventually. 'The morning after the ball. It wasn't locked. When I finally got away from Jane, I thought Miss Wick was waiting for me. But she wasn't there. And neither was Ruth.' She brushes a hair out of her eyes. 'I thought Ruth was with Richard then – I didn't know they'd had another bust-up until he came looking for her the next day. I just went to sleep.' She looks bereft. 'Something so terrible had happened and I just went to sleep.'

Alice takes her arm. 'Maybe you need some sugar. Shall we stop for a break?'

'Her shoes were on the beach. So neatly,' says Naomi. 'It wasn't like her. Red shoes, like Dorothy.'

'You said,' Alice murmurs. Whatever her problems at the moment, this trip was always going to be much harder for Naomi. Maybe something to eat would settle her stomach, she thinks as she passes the small general store on the seafront. 'Shall I get you something?' She nods towards the shop.

'You get something.' Naomi shrugs. 'I'm going to call Carla.'

When she'd been at university, Alice had been on first-name terms with the woman who'd owned the shop, though she couldn't remember her name now. Anyway, the layout is completely different and there's a teenager on the till, who barely looks up from his phone as they enter.

'Where's the fruit?' Alice asks.

He waves a non-committal hand towards the far left corner. The place is bigger than she remembers. At the back, the shop used to stock a strange selection of greetings cards, dusty and unfashionable. Alice had picked one up for Christie's twenty-first, but Christie hadn't really appreciated the joke.

Now, fruit lines the wall on the left, with the cool section for dairy at the back and the booze in the opposite corner. Above the fruit, a large convex mirror reflects the rows of bottles. The selection isn't great. Alice picks up a blackening banana. The door tinkles as someone enters. Alice hears Naomi's tread in the next aisle.

'Do you want a banana?' Alice calls out to Naomi. 'I thought it might help.'

There's a muffled sound in reply.

It's not the best-stocked place. There are gaps in the shelves, where goods have run out and not been replaced. The shelving is flimsy, so that through the gaps you can see flashes of the next aisle. Alice can see now that it's not Naomi.

She had read once that red hair didn't go grey in the same way as other colours; that it faded through various shades of copper and strawberry. She remembers this as she glimpses fading red hair in the opposite aisle. In the convex mirror, she can see it from above, piled messily on top of someone's head.

'I don't think you mean me,' says a voice in the other aisle.

It has a local accent, a Geordie lilt. It sounds friendly.

Alice walks towards the voice as if it's the most normal thing in the world.

'I'm so sorry,' she says. The woman is her age. Red hair, slender. Shockingly familiar. 'I thought you were someone else.'

Naomi

'Come home,' Carla is saying. 'Just call it a day. I'm worried about you.'

I have crossed the road opposite the shop and am looking out to sea. It's almost high tide and there is just the thinnest strip of sand, where seagulls gather in a huddle.

'I thought if I could just stand on that spot where we said goodbye . . .' I start to say, but I can't finish the thought – not even to Carla. That if I returned to that spot, if I stood at the top of the stairs in my old cottage, where I said goodbye to Ruth before she went to the ball . . . That what? If I said a prayer, made a wish, something would happen; something would change; that she would slip between the world in which she had gone and the world in which she hadn't, like some sort of magic trick.

'I wish I were there,' says Carla. 'I should have come. Are you going to be all right?'

'Yes,' I say. 'I don't know,' I say. 'If I had just paid more attention back then; if I had just kept my eyes open, then there's a chance it wouldn't have happened.'

'Naomi, you are not responsible for any of this. That's just how it *feels*,' says Carla. 'That feeling of guilt is just part of it.'

'If only I'd done something different,' I continue. 'If only I hadn't broken up with Jane, gone off with Miss Wick.'

Carla sighs. 'Naomi.'

'I might have got home earlier; I might have caught her there; I might have prevented her from swimming.'

If she'd suggested it, would I have stopped her? Or would I have gone with her? It might have been like when we were children, pulled out to sea together. 'Where you die, I will die, and there will I be buried.' The Book of Ruth. That was where our names came from.

There's the faint tinkle of the shop door and I turn back as Alice comes out. And for a moment I think it has happened: my prayer has worked. My heart swoops and falls.

But I've got it wrong. The woman with Alice isn't Ruth. No. It's just a resemblance. Her features are longer than Ruth's, her eyes slightly closer together.

'I've got to go,' I say to Carla. 'I'll call you back.' And I hang up.

Alice is watching me carefully as they cross the road. She doesn't know how I'm going to react, but I can tell she is pleased, a little pleased with herself, for succeeding on our mission.

'This is Paula,' she says.

Faded copper hair, swept up messily. Loose trousers, a

tie-dye top. A Morrison's bag in her hand. A beautiful face, I'll give her that – not my sister's, but you could see the likeness.

'I used to get mistaken for Ruth,' she says. 'It happened quite a bit.'

Her voice is unexpected. Higher than Ruth's. A local accent.

'You wore a red dress,' I say. 'On the night of the ball.' I turn to Alice. 'Is this who you saw on the train from Edinburgh?'

'No,' says Alice. 'Her hair was brighter.' She says to the woman, 'It wasn't you, was it? You haven't seen me before?'

The woman shakes her head.

'But you were there at the ball?' I persist.

'I was, yes.' The woman shifts her weight from one foot to the other. 'The Hope's just round the corner. Perhaps we could have a drink there.'

The Hope and Anchor smells like the hotel used to when we were children: beer and sea salt. Everyone knows Paula. Alice buys her a drink – a large glass of the house red, which blackens her mouth and teeth as she sips it.

'It used to happen all the time,' she says to me.

'You said that.' I tidy a few peanuts left on the table into a neat pile.

Alice looks at me reproachfully. But I ignore her. To Alice this is just a mystery. Like Agatha Christie. Nothing real. Not her family.

'And then it stopped,' Paula continues.

'When she died,' I say.

'Yes.' Paula looks back at me steadily. 'But I helped it

to stop. I dyed my hair for a while. I couldn't bear it – being mistaken for her.'

A heavyset man in a flat cap comes up to our table.

'All right, Paula,' he says. He looks hopefully at Alice and me. 'Who are your friends?'

'Not now, Jeff,' she says. 'Give us a second.'

He wanders off, thankfully, and returns to the bar to pester the barmaid.

'As I said, I met your sister,' says Paula as she begins to roll a cigarette. She pauses for a moment. There's a burst of laughter from Jeff and a couple of the other drinkers at the bar. 'On the night of the ball,' she explains.

I am sitting too close to the table. It makes me feel fenced in, so I push the chair away. My breathing is shallow.

'Where did you see her?'

'At the house at the top of the hill.'

'On Top Cliff?' Alice says breathlessly. 'The cottage?'

Paula nods. She fiddles with the tobacco, pushing it onto the paper, and it occurs to me that she is more nervous than she has let on.

'Why didn't you tell the police?'

'There were lots of reasons.' She carries on rolling with infuriating exactitude. 'I was married. I didn't want my husband to know I'd been seeing one of the students.'

Alice blinks. We are all silent for a moment.

I say, 'Dan?' I think of the scene in the chapel.

She nods, picks a fleck of tobacco from her lip. 'Let me smoke this,' she says. 'And then I'll tell you everything. It's a long story and it's likely you'll want me to tell the

343

police again afterwards, but let me tell you my way first.' She smiles, looking relieved for a moment. 'You're George's wife, aren't you?' she says to Alice. 'And you're Ruth's sister?' She nods at me. 'I always had a feeling you two might come looking for me.'

Alice

In the pub, someone has put 'Light My Fire' on the jukebox. Paula returns to the table, smelling of fresh smoke. Naomi is in the loo. Paula waits for her to come back before she begins.

'Dan came into the pub where I worked back then,' she starts softly. 'That's how I met him. I thought he looked like a movie star. He was so beautiful, you'd never imagine the filth going on in his head.'

Alice shifts in her seat. She wonders if Dan hurt this woman, too, forced her to do things she didn't want.

'I dream of him sometimes,' says Paula, glancing down at the table. 'In one dream he came back from the dead and asked, "What was so special about you, then?" And I said: "I survive. I forgive myself." You have to forgive yourself, otherwise how can you ever move on?' She pauses briefly. 'He brought out the worst in me,' she continues. 'Have you ever been with someone like that?' She looks at Alice.

'I was married,' Paula continues. 'And Andy was on the road a lot, so for all I know he was screwing around behind my back. But, still, it wasn't right. There were times when we crossed the line, like when Andy was in the pub, and I went and did it with Dan in the toilet. And the church thing, in college. I went to that very same chapel when I was a child.' She sighs, takes a sip of wine. 'When I heard he died, I was shocked. *Really* shocked. But I also felt something else – like relief.'

Alice realises she is barely breathing. She looks over at Naomi, who is sitting like a cat, poised, tense.

Paula continues, 'It was like a dream that night. I was never sure if it happened.'

'What do you mean?' asks Naomi coolly.

'I was really out of it. So for ages I couldn't work it all out – it took me a long time.'

'Tell us,' says Alice as she might to a stressed client. 'Just tell us what you remember.'

Paula shrugs. 'I hadn't been invited to the ball, of course.' She smirks. 'They were having a laugh with the price of the tickets, in my opinion. I looked better back then.' She puts a hand to her fading red hair. 'It was satisfying, just to wander in at the end of my shift – there's no one on the door then – and nick one of the best-looking boys from under the noses of those posh girls.'

'When did you get there?' asks Alice.

Paula wrinkles her nose. 'It must have been around midnight.' She takes a gulp of her wine. 'Dan looked like James Bond,' she smiles. 'Only a bit rough around the edges. I thought I'd never seen anything so sexy in all my life. At first, I didn't speak to him in front of the others.

That wasn't usually part of it. The game we played. I just watched him from a distance, smoking, and sooner or later he wandered away from his friends, made his way to me.'

Dan used to hold his drink pretty well, recalls Alice. Not like some of the boys back then, whose cheeks went all pink and puffy. They'd stumble around, their bow ties undone – so unsubtle, so transparent. When Dan was pissed, there wasn't much change: just the pupils slightly bigger. That's dangerous, though, in its own way.

'This time was different,' Paula continues. 'He introduced me to his friends. We had a few shots – I should have known then.'

'Should have known what?' asks Alice.

She gives Alice a sidelong look. 'They were being too friendly. Dan wouldn't normally make a fuss of me. It wasn't the kind of thing he did – and not just because I was married – he never held my hand or told me I was pretty. It wasn't about that. He didn't even know my surname.'

'You had some shots,' Naomi reminds her, still sitting very straight.

'Yeah.' Paula looks away. 'And we went for a quickie in his room at one point, I remember that much.'

'And then what?' presses Naomi.

Paula blinks. 'The evening sort of scrambled.'

'How do you mean *scrambled*?' asks Alice.

'I was in one place and then I was in another, and I can't remember how I got from A to B. You know how things happen in flashes when you're pissed – there's a flash, like a snapshot, and one minute you're at the bar. And the next you're on the dance floor . . .'

'What do you mean?' says Naomi impatiently.

'I came round in someone else's house,' says Paula. 'Somewhere I'd never been before. I've thought about this over the years,' she continues quietly. 'And the thought of it has got worse, not better. Some things you think over and the crapness sort of wears out, so that something that seemed like the end of the world appears a bit brighter. But not this.' She shakes her head. 'This gets worse every time I think about it.' She takes another gulp of wine. 'I probably would have done it anyway,' she says. 'They didn't need to drug me. They must have done – why else was I so out of it?'

'Where were you?'

'A red room in the cottage.'

Naomi looks pale. 'Ruth's bedroom?' she asks.

'Yes,' says Paula. She pauses for a moment.

'But it was so tidy,' says Naomi, her voice getting higher, more agitated. 'When I got back, it looked so tidy.'

'Someone like George,' says Paula. 'You think he would leave a thing like that undone?' She laughs as if she knows him well.

Alice thinks of his study, the way his books are lined up so neatly. 'George was there?' she says. But she knew – she always knew, deep down – that he was involved somehow.

'It was like *Twin Peaks*,' Paula says. 'The whole night was like that: red velvet curtains, the men in black tie and not being able to understand anything because everyone's speaking a backward language. When I woke up in Ruth's room, Dan was on top of me. I couldn't remember getting there or how it started. I just woke up and we were doing it. It's hard to explain.' She rubs her forehead. 'George was there too, standing there watching, with a camera in his hand. I wanted Dan to stop. But it was like moving through syrup – I couldn't speak properly, couldn't move my limbs. And then it felt for a moment like I was watching myself: that there was another me in the room.'

'What do you mean?' asks Alice.

'I thought at first it was a mirror. That I was watching myself in the mirror. But, you know, my brain wasn't working properly. Why would I be watching myself fully clothed?'

'What are you talking about?' asks Alice more impatiently.

'Ruth was there,' Paula says. 'Ruth was suddenly in the room.'

'What time was it then?' asks Naomi.

She's trying to work it out, thinks Alice, but the story is moving too strangely, too quickly.

'God knows,' says Paula, giving her a withering look. 'But Ruth starts shouting and screaming. She goes for George and he's fighting her off. And Dan is on his feet, putting on clothes.'

'And you?' asks Alice.

She has heard about nights like this before in her work. Nights in which one thing leads to another, events get out of hand and, before you know it, life has changed irreparably.

'I could barely move. I just wrapped a blanket around myself.' Paula shivers at the memory. 'And then Ruth picks up a poker from the fireplace and starts thrashing it around, and the boys are laughing at her. Really laughing. And all the time I was wondering how I might get dressed and get out of there. I was already thinking,' she smiles sadly, 'about the stories I could tell at the pub. They loved hearing how fucking weird the students were. I would have changed it, made it less . . .'

'Rapey,' says Alice coolly.

'Sure,' agrees Paula. 'Yeah, I might not have told them everything, but I was thinking: this'll make a story.' She swallows. 'Mentally, I was already out of there, you know.'

'Did they hurt her?' says Naomi urgently. 'Did they hurt her next?'

'No.' Paula shakes her head. 'That's not how it went.'

'Tell us,' says Naomi. 'Just tell us what happened.'

'One minute I'm trying to pull on my dress while they're all shouting and fighting. And the next minute, there's a terrible smack. The sound of someone falling down the stairs like a sack of potatoes.'

Alice remembers seeing an old lady fall down an escalator at a train station. The way her body collapsed and folded. The way she had been struck then – as bystanders flapped and panicked as they looked for the button to stop the machine, as her limbs flipped over, as her body crumpled like paper – by how fragile humans could be.

'I got there a few moments after the rest of them,' continues Paula. 'At first I thought it was Dan on the floor because of the short dark hair – I couldn't see the face. The body was bent all wrong and it wasn't moving. But then I saw it wasn't Dan, because he couldn't be looking down at himself any more than I'd been looking down at myself earlier.'

Alice wishes that she would get to the point.

'What do you mean?' she snaps.

'It was a woman who had fallen,' says Paula. 'But she was wearing a tux.'

Naomi

A tuxedo, she'd said. A tux. An American word, stolen from the movies. The wearer hadn't been British either, so I don't know why it bothered me. She may well have called it a tux herself. I don't know the word in Spanish, or why I think of that now, or remember that Carla, who'd spent a few months in Argentina in her twenties, had told me stories of beautiful, charming friends, as unreliable as the wind. '*Fantasmas todos*,' someone had told her. And, as the years had gone by, I had put Miss Wick's disappearing, twice, down to that.

Someone cheers at the telly in the corner of the pub. There's the plinkety plink of the quiz machine. The silence at our table hardens. Paula puts a hand to her hair, waiting. It occurs to me how long she must have been waiting like this. For us. But then something shifts, like a lens refocusing, and I understand that another person waiting to be caught, who I haven't seen straight on all this time, is Ruth.

'It was Miss Wick,' I say. 'It's her skeleton that they've found.'

The others are quiet.

I think of the back of Miss Wick's head in the queue; her hair closely cropped; that sense of déjà vu and then wondering, as the years passed, if she had come to St Anthony's at all, if it had been a figment of my traumatised mind.

'George took control that night,' says Paula. 'He knew exactly what to do.'

Alice snorts in derision. 'That sounds like him.'

'It's like he was born for it,' agrees Paula, almost in wonder. 'He told Dan to take me home – I wasn't in a fit state to do anything. And Ruth was wailing, so he made her take something to calm down.' She rolls her eyes as if at a harmless prank. 'Probably similar to what he gave me, just a lighter dose. He said she needed to be quiet, so he could think.' She adds as an afterthought, 'He was gentle with her, though. Tender, almost. Anyway, Dan and I left – we staggered home together – it was still dark – and I collapsed into bed.'

Paula missed the early days of the search, she explains to us, as the pub gets noisier, filling up with evening customers.

'Whatever they put in my drink wiped me out for most of the week. I nearly lost my job. And when I found out that they were looking for Ruth, I was so confused,' she says. 'I was in the newsagent's looking at the papers and I said to the guy in there: "They're looking for the wrong girl – it happened to that other girl. The dark-haired one." But he just said, "What are you on about? Ruth Walker's been missing for days." He said: "It's funny how much she looks like you, Paula."' She pauses, pushes her hair behind her ears. 'I bought some cheap black dye that afternoon,' she says. 'I dyed my hair straight away.'

'When did you let it grow back?' I ask, wondering if she has rehearsed this conversation and if she has told anyone before us.

'Quite recently,' she says. 'It's never been the same as it was, but the truth has to come out eventually, doesn't it?'

'All these years,' I say bitterly. 'All these years and you never said a thing.'

'I didn't know who to talk to,' she says. 'I went to the house once but there were so many people there – your mother, you.' She looks at me. 'Police officers everywhere – and someone came out and said, "Can I help?" I just said no, that I'd made a mistake, and I ran away. I had no idea what to do: Dan had gone by then, like most of the students. I tried to persuade myself that the woman in the tux had recovered and that maybe Ruth's disappearance was pure coincidence.'

'What changed your mind?' asks Alice.

'I started seeing George on television,' says Paula as one of the barmaids passes our table, looking for glasses. 'I worked out who he was – it was easy to track him down. I just wanted to know what happened. He said he didn't know what I was talking about, but I kept at him and eventually he said he had some pretty interesting photos of me from that night, so I might like to keep my mouth shut. He offered me money, too. People like that think everything can be bought.' She looks angry for a moment.

'Did you say anything?' I ask.

She shakes her head. 'You've got to understand –

I didn't know myself, at first, what had happened. And later, when it was clearer, I'd left it too long. But it weighs on you – keeping a secret like that.'

'But Ruth hated George,' I say. 'I can't get the pieces to add up.'

'Ruth was in a terrible state,' says Paula. She gets her tobacco and cigarette papers out again. 'She'd killed someone. And George took control.' She glances at Alice to see how she will react.

'He and Ruth must have buried her,' says Alice softly.

'Yeah,' says Paula. 'It was his idea. Just like it was his idea for Dan to make up some story about how he'd seen Ruth swimming and for Ruth's stuff to be left on the beach. Magicians call it misdirection.' She takes a gulp of wine, begins to roll another cigarette. 'There aren't many things you can choose,' she says. 'We all think we're free, but we're not. I see students come to St Anthony's year after year. They act like they own the place, strutting around Cathedral Square, getting in the way on their bicycles. They're everywhere – in the pubs, rowing on the river, lazing around in the park. And then they move on.

'It's like their lives are carved out for them: private school, posh university, job in London, husband, babies.' She glances at our bumps. 'Nice house. Pearls. The same kitchens. When I worked in the kitchen shop in Morpeth, the mums used to come and look at everything, like they were thinking about it really hard, and then they'd pick precisely the same kitchens, down to the same sink – those heavy ceramic ones that look as if they belong in a farmhouse. They think they're free, like they're making their own decisions, but they aren't at all. Any more than me.'

She looks down at the rolled cigarette in her hand. 'I can understand how it might be tempting – to start all over again, to slip through the system, to run away from it all.'

'From me,' I say quietly. 'She ran from me.'

And I remember how when we were children and she had broken my arm by accident, she had run off into the fields and spent the night in our treehouse, worrying our mother sick. To look at what you have done, that can be the hardest thing. But Paula is right: if we don't forgive ourselves, how do we keep on living?

'She must have been terrified,' says Alice.

'It's true,' says Paula. 'After all that booze, all that weed, and then hurting someone like that.'

'No,' says Alice. 'I mean of facing Naomi.' She turns to me. 'Of telling you what she'd done. How do you begin? How do you start explaining something like that? And George wouldn't have supported her.' She frowns. 'He might have helped her to get away, but it wasn't in his interest for her to come back, to come clean. Even if she had, it's likely *he* would have got away with it somehow. Slippery little fuck. And what would the future have held for Ruth? Prison? Estrangement from her loved ones. Lost years. Trying to build her life again from the beginning.'

We are quiet for a moment. I think of Ruth on a train or a bus. Maybe a boat. Her hair dyed, cropped short, perhaps. An old bag at her feet stuffed with George's cash. Nunny on her lap watching the landscape fly by with his marbled eyes. We never even noticed he was missing.

'That night,' says Paula eventually, fiddling with her

cigarette again. 'It was the worst thing that I ever did – that I was ever involved with. But this – telling you – letting it out is the best thing. And no one will know how hard it is – how hard it is to keep a secret like that, but also how hard it is to let it out.' She sighs. 'That's your story. You'll want me to tell the police again, won't you?'

Alice looks at me.

I'm feeling calm, strangely clear-headed. I nod at her.

'Shall I call them?' says Paula.

Alice gets up. 'I'll do it.'

While she is gone, I say one last time to Paula: 'But Ruth hated George. Loathed him.' I can't get past that, that she would have colluded with him, that she would have done what he suggested.

'She made a deal with the devil.' Paula picks up the cigarette and lights it, ignoring the tutting barmaid as she approaches. The smoke curls up to the ceiling. 'And maybe she didn't want to live in a world where people like him were in control.'

She – the runaway Ruth of my imagination – would have got somewhere eventually. A sprawling metropolis, or a dusty town. As my mother and I sat bolt upright, sleepless, by the phone in the days after her disappearance, she would have pushed the door open to an unfamiliar hotel room or hostel dorm or dingy flat. Did she pick up the phone, wherever she was? Did my number come into her head? Did she think of dialling it?

Kat

'Don't hang up,' Kat says quickly, quietly. She can hear Richard breathing, the chatter of the newsroom behind him. 'I just wanted to say: there was nothing going on between Dan and Ruth. I let you think there might be.'

'I know that now.' Richard's voice would sound calm, measured, to someone who didn't know him well, but Kat, who has also had difficult interviewees, knows it's an acting trick. She imagines him standing up – another trick – to sound more assertive, in control.

'Ruth was trying to get him to confess.' She speaks quickly, still aware she could lose him. 'She'd become obsessed.'

'Confess to what?'

'Date rape,' she says. She perches on the edge of the sofa and looks down at her bony feet, the Rouge Noir varnish on her toes, so trendy in the Nineties, is back in fashion. 'That's what they call it now – you didn't hear the term so much back then.'

'I heard rumours . . .' Richard pauses. 'Can I ring you back from somewhere quieter?'

As Kat waits for him to call, she turns her mobile over in her hands, remembering what she did to Ruth. It's going to be difficult to tell Richard, but she doesn't have anything to lose now. She thinks back to that night, watching Ruth in the marquee, singing along to Richard's songs at the memorial ball. She didn't see Kat as she'd sidled up to Ruth, pressing her cold champagne flute against the other girl's bare shoulder so that she spun around in surprise. Ruth's face, on seeing Kat, had been uncertain. She'd smiled in a worried way, as if working it out: friend or foe?

'You're back,' Kat said.

Ruth struck a pose as if to say: *here I am*. Up close, Ruth smelled of coconut hair oil, as usual, and fresh sweat.

'How was Wales?'

'Awful,' Ruth scowled. 'As you can imagine. I left messages for you. Why didn't you call me?'

'So you're back together?' Kat ignored the question.

Ruth nodded, glanced towards the stage. 'Well, we've still got a lot to talk about, but yeah.'

'How was the make-up sex?' Kat asked. 'Pretty hot, I imagine.'

Ruth frowned, looks back to the stage. 'Shut up, Kat.'

'Was it?' Kat persisted, feeling a lump in her throat.

In that moment, she had remembered her own night with Richard, the way she'd woken early the next day with her heart brimming. She pictured, for a moment, a pair of scissors in her hand, severing all ties with Ruth, like cutting through a ribbon at an opening ceremony.

'Was it really good?' she asked again. She was committed to her course. 'I imagine it *is* really, really good with someone you love that much. Especially when he's as hot as Richard.'

Ruth took a step away from her as if she were a tramp at a railway station. Which suited Kat perfectly: she hadn't wanted to be too close for the last bit – certainly not within swinging distance. She drained the dregs of champagne from her glass. On stage, Richard was in the middle of dedicating a song to his 'beautiful girlfriend'. Kat leaned in to stage-whisper: 'I don't have to imagine any more. I had a go myself while you were away.'

The ring of the mobile in her hand makes her jump. Kat blinks and steels herself. 'There are two things I've got to tell you,' she begins.

'OK.' He sighs. 'I have something to tell you, too.'

'Brace yourself. It's bad.' Kat stands up. Richard's not the only one who knows the tricks. She walks to the window.

'I'm braced.' She can hear him smiling.

Kat swallows. Outside, her cat is sitting on the patio, looking up at her purposefully.

'It's really bad. You might never forgive me.' She can feel the emotion in her throat. 'I have always loved you.' She has said the words casually, lightly to him before. But not like this. 'I have always loved you in a way I haven't loved anybody else in the world.' This isn't what she meant to say. It's all coming out wrong. 'And now I don't have time.' She can feel the tears start. 'None of it has gone how it should.'

360

'Kat,' he says softly.

'I lied,' she says. 'There aren't two things to tell you. There are three things. Countless things. I love you. I'm dying. And . . .' This is the hardest one. The real kicker. 'I told Ruth.'

'Kat,' Richard says again. 'What do you mean you're dying?'

She is crying fully now. Horrible snotty sobs. Thank God he can't see her.

'Just cancer,' she says. Which sounds ridiculous.

'Oh, God,' he says quietly.

'I told Ruth,' she says again. 'That we had been together. The night she went.'

Richard is quiet for a very long time. 'I know,' he says at last. 'She left me a note.'

'What did it say?'

'Just that I was a bastard and I wasn't to try to get her back.'

Kat wipes her face and begins to laugh. 'Well, you haven't obeyed that order.'

'I gave it to the police. Not that it swayed them. I think they were convinced she had drowned once the dress turned up.'

'But it wasn't in your book.' Which Kat had admittedly only skim-read. Too much love, too much Ruth.

'It didn't make me look good,' he says sheepishly. 'But it convinced me she was out there. Out there, but not with me: to punish me.'

Kat moves to the kitchen and puts the kettle on. 'That would be a hell of a long game just to make a point.' She is weak with relief. All this time. Thinking that Richard would hate her. And he knew. All along. They had been locked in the secret together. 'Weren't you mad with me?'

'Yes, I was. That's why I couldn't talk to you for months. But look, it was true. I did it. I slept with you. You told the truth.'

'What did you have to tell me?'

Richard is quiet again.

Kat stands by the kettle, waiting.

'I had a weird experience with George,' he says at last. 'At a party, in our first year. He offered me a girl he'd just shagged.'

'Offered you?'

'I'd passed out on his floor. She was completely out of it, too. When I woke up, he'd just finished having sex with her. He said: "Do you want a go?" Something like that.'

'Something like that?' Kat repeats. She catches her face, drained of colour, reflected in her oven. A thought bubbles. *He could have warned you. He could have said something.* 'Did Ruth know?'

'No,' Richard sighs. 'I didn't want her to think . . .'

'You didn't want her to think you'd been part of it?' Kat finishes.

'Yes.'

Kat sighs. She says eventually: 'Something similar happened to me. With two of them. Him and Dan. I wasn't prepared.'

The shame had grown in the dark, but now just saying the words out loud, bringing the matter into the light, made it shrink slightly.

362

'Oh,' Richard says quietly.

'Ruth never told you?'

'No.'

'I asked her not to.'

'Well, she could keep a secret.'

'Yes,' says Kat. 'She could.' She goes to her desk, picks up the pad where she's started making notes. 'I thought there might be a story here for *The National*. About what they did to me. To lots of girls.'

Richard is so quiet that Kat wonders if he's still there.

'Let me help you,' he says at last.

Naomi

On the long train journey back to London, I remember how, when our father died, Ruth knew before I did. Our mother picked her up from secondary school, told her first. As for me, my grandmother drove me home from primary school, strangely silent in the car, braking too suddenly, giving elliptical answers to my questions. Ruth couldn't be there when I was told. She couldn't bear it; she'd gone off to the Llewelyns' stable, to bury her face in her pony's mane, no doubt. She needn't have worried – I didn't scream like she did but was sick, quietly, efficiently. Would it have been easier with my sister in the room? Perhaps.

A coward. I never thought of her as that. I always believed she was so fearless, that I was the timid one. But then there are different kinds of bravery.

They buried Miss Wick like a dog. So swiftly, so

unceremoniously. What does it take to do such a thing? How do you live with yourself afterwards?

We'd found a bathroom in college, a secret place to go, hidden away from Jane. We'd locked the door and she'd made me come on the bathroom floor as the music thrummed below. It was a humid night and that little square room at the top of the building trapped the heat. Afterwards, we opened the skylight and lay out on the cool tiles watching the gulls circling above us, made plans for the following year when she would be in town permanently. We watched as they let 350 silver helium balloons into the air, one for each year of college, how they drifted away towards the sea. We stood side by side on a rickety old chair, watching them becoming smaller and smaller until they were just freckles on the face of the sky.

And that was where Jane found us – she was screeching and screaming, and Miss Wick said, 'Go and talk to her; do this properly.' I told her where we kept the key to the cottage, where she and I had snatched some stolen hours together before, and said I'd meet her back there. We didn't know how unhinged Jane was, didn't guess how she would lock me in her room and waste those precious remaining hours of the night – where, if I had been home, everything might have been different.

Alternately berating and trying to seduce me, she told me how inscrutable I was, how unreadable – trying to get into my head, not knowing that the people who did weren't the ones who stayed and wept but the ones who left without a trace in the middle of the night. It wasn't until she'd fallen asleep that I was able to prise the key from her hand and let myself out, slipping back through the streets to an empty cottage.

Bent all wrong, she said. Miss Wick coming up the stairs, not knowing what was going on, maybe even wanting to help Ruth. And then being hit like that: falling. Like landing after a jump or coming off a horse – so important to soften with the fall, not to brace against it. But Miss Wick, Joaquina, didn't ride, so she wouldn't have known that.

While we were waiting for the police – while Paula was smoking and the barmaid was flapping, and the pub had gone strangely quiet around us – Paula said: 'I found out later how furious Ruth was with those boys. She'd been on to them, you see.' She said urgently, to Alice, ignoring my face perhaps, knowing she didn't have much time left with us: 'Ruth had told George that she was going to reveal everything to you – about what they'd been up to. I think he wanted to take some nasty photos with me in her bedroom to make it look like it was her. To keep her quiet.'

It was as if she didn't notice how silent Alice and I had become. The police arrived then. There was a shift in the pub, a crackle as they entered, but I didn't care. I said to Paula as she got up: 'What do you mean: you found out later? Who told you that? Not George?'

I put my hand on her arm; I wanted to stop her going. 'The postcards, Nunny: they came from St Anthony's. You've been in touch with her, Paula, haven't you? Haven't you? Paula?' I started to shout. 'Paula? Where is Ruth?'

She didn't say a thing. Her face changed, but it wasn't

smug, like she was enjoying the secret, it was more as if she had made some sort of promise.

Alice and I had to speak to the police, too. I gave them Miss Wick's name, for what it was worth: her new name for a new country. I didn't know any of her relations or friends or even where she was living at that time. No one had seemed to miss her or, if they did, to place her in St Anthony's that night. And even I – who loved her hands and her hair and her mouth – even I thought she'd just disappeared again, the way she did. As if she were some sort of phantom, not a living, breathing being, whose neck had been broken, whose body had been buried a matter of feet from where I lived.

Ruth, on the other hand, had been missed and longed for. She had been spotted on trains and in crowds. She had been imagined many times by people who knew her – and even Alice, who didn't: a pale face reflected in dark glass, the swish of red hair disappearing around the corner.

'It was her, wasn't it? On the train,' Alice says at one point on the journey home.

'Maybe it was,' I agree. 'Maybe you were right all along.'

She looks pleased for a moment. 'Poor thing,' she half-smiles. 'She was so startled. Maybe I gave her as big a fright as she gave me.'

'Perhaps.' I look out of the train window and think of Agatha Christie's *4.50 from Paddington*, the way it all begins on a train. With her love of mysteries, would Ruth have remembered that? With her love of drama, might she have staged the whole thing? I wonder if she might have read about Alice's high-profile clients, about the family law conference in Edinburgh, and followed Alice to the station.

It's far-fetched. But not impossible.

I don't share these wilder theories with Alice now. I keep them to myself.

'We're going through the same sort of thing, aren't we?' I say instead when she goes quiet. 'We're both looking at someone we loved with fresh eyes.'

She looks out of the window at the countryside beyond. Rows of windmills, bone white against the sky.

'Perhaps,' she says eventually, 'I always knew, deep down, what those boys were like. I just didn't want to look at it.'

How could Ruth do it? Live another life? Another life without me in it.

Just as we're coming into London, I drift off into a fevered sleep. In my dream I'm back at the hotel, in the kitchen, but the police are there with their yellow jackets and their walkie-talkies, asking us about what happened to the man who went missing from the cliffs all those years ago.

I'm there with Ruth, but for the first time I can see her face: I can see it in such detail. She is standing very close to me and though her skin is as young as it was when she left, she looks sadder than I have ever seen.

'Maybe his wife's dogs didn't run off the cliffs,' she says. She's talking not to the police, but to me. 'Maybe he lost them.' Her eyes fill with tears. She says in a cracked voice, 'Maybe he *hurt* them – by accident, but maybe he did.'

'Why would he hurt the dogs?' I ask.

But she turns away; she can't look at me. Ruth who loved animals: burying chicks, rescuing worms from the dirt, screaming for Scipio, who had been felled by a bullet. Ruth, climbing over the halfway line between us; who would have done anything to defend me; who can remember Dai the Poet and Damien the Chef, and who I mean by the girl in the blue bikini and why public school boys are like avocados. Things nobody else in the world could understand.

'Why would he hurt the dogs?' I say again, but she shakes her head. The realisation is like the falling of snow: silent and clean. The brightness of it hurts my eyes. 'That's why he couldn't come home,' I say at last.

She is leaving again, moving towards the door. I want her to know, even though the police are listening: 'I know you didn't mean to hurt her.'

Infantile words, as if we are children again and all it needs to push the years back is for someone to say sorry, someone to forgive, for us to go back to that moment on the landing, for everything to be different. Yet, there's nothing either of us can say, nothing either of us can do.

'I know you didn't mean it,' I say again and I start to cry.

Ruth stops at the doorway. She turns back to me.

And then I wake up.

Back in London, I get the tube to Ealing Broadway and decide to do the twenty-minute walk home to clear my head. The air smells different, like summer's on its way, and the cafés on Ealing Green are setting up tables outside. There is something hopeful in the air.

I think about what might have happened.

Perhaps she was keeping an eye on me from a distance, watching me on Facebook as Alice did, tracking news of my pregnancy. Perhaps she felt the pull of me, of family, more strongly then than she ever had before. Perhaps after all these years something had changed.

Perhaps she had started to forgive herself.

Perhaps she got in touch with one of the two other people in the world who knew what had happened that night. Perhaps she and Paula started to make plans.

And it could have been that it wasn't just love that made her consider returning – it could have been something else: news of George's career change, for example. It could have been that, of the missives she sent in the post, Nunny represented love and the postcards promised revenge. She'd always enjoyed a bit of drama.

Perhaps she simply wanted to prepare us for her return. Perhaps.

As I approach home, I realise I am a different person from when I left a few days ago. The house is different, too – its expression is hard to read: secretive, knowing. Pushing the front door open, I feel a flutter in my belly. A tickling, as if the baby is blowing bubbles. I think of him then, taking his first lungful of air. I think of her, too: not in the water, as I have always imagined, but walking somewhere on this Earth. Not dead. Alive.

There's the sound of voices at the other end of the house – Carla's and another. I switch on the lamp in the hall and drop my keys into the bronze letter tray.

I call, 'I'm home.' And the voices go quiet. The lamp's light catches on a pair of red shoes in the hallway. They are pointing towards the kitchen, as if they've been put there on purpose. As if they are a sign.

Acknowledgements

Everything changed for me when *The Girl Before You* was picked as runner-up in the Cheltenham First Novel Competition. As my prize I was fortunate enough to win representation by LBA Books – first by Danielle Zigner, who worked closely with me smoothing out the novel's ending, and for whose insight and sensitivity I'll always be thankful, and later by the equally brilliant Louise Lamont. I'm incredibly grateful to both. Thank you, too, to everyone at the Intercontinental Literary Agency and Emily Hayward-Whitlock at the Artists Partnership.

My heartfelt thanks to the team at Avon: to Rachel Faulkner-Willcocks, whose eagle-eyed editing has made it a better book, and to Elke Desanghere and Sabah Khan for their guidance and support.

I would also like to thank Gwen Davies, who worked with me on an earlier draft of the novel, and Emma Bamford and Kim Thompson, my beta readers. My uncle, Richard Gwyn, has been hugely supportive throughout the writing of this book, and many other things besides, and I would also like to thank Siân Humphreys and Lynn Lewis, who read early excerpts.

Thank you to Nicole Alleyne-West, marketing and communications officer at Missing People, Professor Dame Sue Black, Jeanie Cordy-Simpson, Dr Sioned Gwyn, Aimee Parnell, Elen Stritch and Sarah Warwick for helping me with research and answering lots of questions. Needless to say, any mistakes are entirely of my own making.

The kindness and support of the following during the writing of this book meant a great deal to me: Camilla Akers-Douglas, Omer Ali, Nancy Alsop, Zoë Anderson, Di Barough, Micki Biddle, Helena and Hilary Gerrish, Georgina Gordon-Smith, Jonathan Gray, Rhiannon and Rose Gwyn, Daphne Hall, Vivienne Hambly, Steve Handley, Emily Hughes, David and Richard Humphreys, Alexander Larman, Emily and David George Lewis, Carole Mattock, Ruth Meech, Ann Mottram, Tania O'Donnell, Joseph Paxton, Miriam Phillips, Arabella and Alex Preston, Charlotte Rogerson, Marco Rossi, Gerald Schwanzer, Laura Silverman, May Steele, Jo Turner, Jane and Charles Wright and Kerstin Zumstein.

Thank you to the James, Morison and Fonseca families, every single one of you (with a special mention for Emma, who introduced me to St Anthony).

Huge thanks to my writing group for their amazing help: Saneh Arora, Adam Lively and Conrad Stephenson.

Thank you to my dear friend Jenny Wilkinson. I hope she knows why.

This is a story about siblings and I couldn't have written

it without my own – Lucy, Sophie and Mark, thank you for everything. Thank you, too, to Pierluca, Olav, Russell, Leonardo and Nora. And thank you to Carol and Matthew, and Chota, who always ensured I got fresh air and exercise when I most needed it.

I would like to remember three family members who are no longer with us: my father, Russell Rayner, who taught me about the value of persistence, my grandfather, Dr Richard Cenric Humphreys, who passed on his love of books, and my father-in-law, Colin Draper, one of the kindest people I've known.

And thank you, above all, to the two people to whom this book is dedicated: to my mother for her patience, generosity and endless love, and to my Jason, who with this project, as in all things, has been on my side every step of the way. I couldn't have done it without you: I wanted to tell you.